MODERN FAIRYTALE

BOOK ONE IN THE MAIDENS OF FAIRHAVEN TRILOGY

DANA GRICKEN

OLIVERHEBERBOOKS

CHAPTER 1

When the ballroom downstairs glittered with magical light, Esme wished she had run away when she still had the chance.

She watched from her bedroom window upstairs in the castle, hearing the sounds she hated the most—idle chit-chat from boring royals. She knew it was going to be a long night. As she looked in the mirror, she heard a knock on the door.

"No one's home," she called out. "Go away!"

The door opened a moment later and her father—King Tedros—stepped inside the room, his red cape trailing behind him. Several guards in silver knight uniforms waited in the hall-way, following him wherever he went. He looked around at her messy room and nightgown and scowled.

"Esme, you aren't even dressed!" he cried. "The celebrations are starting."

Esme rolled her eyes. "How'd you even get in here? I locked the door behind me."

"I used a lock-melting potion. I'm getting wise to your tricks, daughter," he said, stepping toward her. The golden crown above his dark hair glimmered in the light. "Look, I know you haven't wanted to attend parties since..."

He trailed off, but Esme knew what he meant. She looked back at him and nodded. "You can say it. Since Mother's death."

"Yes, right," he muttered, looking down, "but this will be good for you. You're always locked away inside your room. Now, I want you to get dressed and meet me downstairs."

"But Father, I don't want to go. Please—don't make me!"

"No pouting, Esme. You know I hate it when you throw a tantrum," he muttered. "It will look bad if the only princess of Fairhaven misses out on the anniversary celebration of our kingdom. Just grin and bear it, and before you know it, your torture will be over and you'll be back in your room."

"But—"

"I'll send your Fairy Godmother in to find you something suitable to wear, then I expect to see you mingling downstairs. Understood? Splendid."

Before she could argue again, King Tedros turned on his bootheel, stepping out into the hallway. The guards looked at Esme awkwardly before following him down the stairs. As she mumbled un-princess-like words under her breath, she heard light footsteps approaching.

"Sorry to disturb you," the sweet voice said. "I know how dull you find parties."

Esme couldn't help the smile that spread across her face when she looked back at her Fairy Godmother, Odelia. She had her white hair tied in a bun, a purple gown on, black slippers, and a magic wand in her left hand. A peaceful, calming energy seemed to follow her wherever she went, making Esme feel at ease.

Every family was assigned a fairy godmother, and Esme was thankful she had gotten the best.

"It's all right," Esme said, turning to her. "I feel better now that you're here."

"Your father was upset when he couldn't find you. I told him to leave you be, but you know him—always so stubborn," she said with a pearly-white smile. "Anyhow, are you ready for your transformation?"

Esme grinned, rising to her feet. "Always."

Fairy Godmother Odelia held up her wand, which was glimmering with purple light. She aimed it toward Esme, smiling. "Our fair princess needs a dress—give her something to impress. Abracadabra!"

With a spray of purple dust, a pink, fluffy gown with pockets appeared on her body. Lipstick, eyeshadow, and blush were also applied, along with nail polish and diamond slippers. Esme turned, looking in the mirror.

"So?" Fairy Godmother Odelia asked. "Do you like it?"

"Like it? I love it!" Esme cried, fluffing her pink dress. "Although I hate parties, getting dressed up is pretty fun— especially when you're in charge of the costumes."

Fairy Godmother Odelia giggled, placing the wand in her pocket. "I aim to please. Now, are you ready to head downstairs?"

"I guess I have no choice," Esme said, locking arms with Fairy Godmother Odelia. "Will you stay at the party all night?"

Fairy Godmother Odelia grinned. "It would be my honor. Your mother loved ballroom parties you know. She never missed a chance to meet with the people of her kingdom."

Esme reached toward her dresser, grabbing a picture of her mother. It was a magical picture—one where her mother was waving. It even smelled like her old perfume, and she could feel the warmth of her skin through it.

"That's one thing I didn't inherit from her, I guess."

"I'm very sorry she isn't here anymore, but I know she

wouldn't want you to mope like this," Fairy Godmother Odelia said, pinching Esme's cheeks. She giggled and pushed her away. "There's a smile. Let's have a good time downstairs, okay? That dress is begging to be shown off."

Esme opened the door, walking out into the hallway with her fairy godmother. She glanced over the railing and noticed the hundreds of people mingling downstairs. She sighed, walking down the red, spiral staircase to reach the bottom. It was packed—and much louder—in the ballroom than Esme liked.

"I think you should go see your father first," her Fairy Godmother said, "just so he knows you're here."

Esme nodded, looking through the crowd. "Sounds good—though, there are a lot of people in our way. Ugh."

Fairy Godmother Odelia reached for her magic wand again. "Part this crowd like the Red Sea. Leave space for Esme and me. Abracadabra!"

A red carpet rolled out in front of them, gently pushing the partygoers to each side. It left a direct path for Esme and Fairy Godmother Odelia to walk through. As they did, people murmured and stared at them.

"Seeing you use your magic never gets old," Esme whispered. "But this is the part I hate the most—all the eyes watching me..."

"I can magically put them all in their underwear if it would make you feel calmer, dear."

Esme grimaced. "No, thanks. I'll just grin and bear it as Father says."

Across the ballroom, her father sat on his golden throne. He had guards around him as he spoke to Senator Remus, a blond-haired man in a red suit. The senator had two blonde-haired women with him—his wife, Dr. Breya, in a red gown, and his daughter, Lady Nyssa, in a golden dress. Esme looked down at her gown, suddenly feeling self-conscious.

"...which is why I think we should tell Earth about us," Senator Remus was saying to King Tedros. "You could have another kingdom to rule over—their entire planet!"

King Tedros sighed. "Senator Remus, you've brought this up before. What have I always told you? Earth is not to be touched, and our existence is better kept as a secret. Besides, magic doesn't even work up there. It isn't compatible."

"Ah—not yet, Your Majesty," Senator Remus said with a grin, turning to his wife. "Tell him, darling."

"I've been doing lots of research into magical potions," Dr. Breya began, "and I think I could adapt them to the human world—"

"My answer is still no," King Tedros interrupted. "It's far too dangerous. I don't authorize any research into this, and I demand you drop the subject. When I promoted you to head scientist, Dr. Breya, I only authorized you to make Fairhaven better—not meddle with Earth."

Senator Remus scoffed. "But Your Lordship, think of all the possibilities! Earth is far larger than Fairhaven—"

"Did you not hear me or are you just stubborn?" King Tedros hissed. "I said no, just as I have the million other times you've asked me. Besides, a celebration isn't the time to discuss this."

Senator Remus looked so angry, Esme thought he might burst. "I *have* brought it up in the conference room, but you always dismiss me—"

Lady Nyssa stepped forward, careful not to trip over her gown as she placed a hand on her father's arm. "Father, you heard King Tedros. I think we should respect his wishes. After all, he knows what's best for our kingdom—not us."

"Yes—thank you, Lady Nyssa." King Tedros bowed in her

direction, then turned back to Remus. "Your daughter is always the voice of reason, Senator."

Esme rolled her eyes.

Senator Remus sighed. "Of course, Your Majesty—whatever you say. Come now, darling."

As he and his wife walked away, scowling as they passed Esme and Fairy Godmother Odelia, Lady Nyssa hung around. "King Tedros, I want to apologize for my father. He was never one to follow the rules."

"That's all right. I have a daughter just like that," he mumbled, shaking his head. His eyes widened when he looked over and noticed Esme. "Ah, there you are! I didn't think you'd join us."

"Well, you left me no choice," Esme muttered.

"And you look just wonderful," King Tedros continued, ignoring her comment. "Bravo, Fairy Godmother Odelia."

She blushed. "Oh, you flatter me, Your Highness."

"My fairy godmother made my dress, too," Lady Nyssa said, doing a little twirl. "What do you think, King Tedros?"

He nodded, smiling. "You look wonderful, Lady Nyssa. Like a true princess."

Esme scowled. "I'm going to get some punch. You three can stay here and chat."

She didn't give anyone the chance to respond as she rushed away from the throne, heading toward a table of beverages. The drinks looked purple and Esme wondered what kind of magical concoction was in them. People tried to talk to her, but Esme ignored them and filled up a red cup.

"Too bad it isn't alcoholic," she muttered, raising it to her lips.

As she took a sip, she noticed Senator Remus, his wife, and a dark-haired woman standing between two pillars across the room. She recognized her as Fairy Godmother

Zamira, the witch assigned to Lady Nyssa's family. She had wrinkly skin, sunken eyes, and wore a black gown. They spoke in hushed whispers and looked to be up to no good. Unable to resist her curiosity, Esme pushed through the crowd to listen in.

"...and I knew the fool wouldn't listen to me," Senator Remus whispered. "He never does. I've served by his side for years—made many suggestions that improved Fairhaven—and this is how he repays me?"

"Fear not," Fairy Godmother Zaria said as Senator Remus scowled. "Everything is going according to plan. Isn't that right, Dr. Breya?"

Dr. Breya nodded. "Yes—I just need a little more time."

Fairy Godmother Zamira smiled, showing off her black, crusty teeth. "Excellent. Soon, we will all get what we desire."

As they walked away, Esme hid behind the pillar. They didn't notice her as they returned to mingle with the crowd. Esme stayed silent for a moment, considering their words. What was almost ready? What kind of plan did they have?

"There you are!" a familiar voice cried behind her. "Now I know this party is going to be fun."

Esme spun around, coming face-to-face with her best friend —Lady Alva. She had dark hair, caramel eyes, and was always dressed like a goth princess thanks to her fairy godmother. Her father was General Orion in charge of the king's army, and her mother designed weapons for them. Her parents were both mingling in the crowd and keeping an eye out for trouble.

"Alva!" Esme cried, throwing herself into her friend's arms. "Boy, am I glad to see you."

Alva chuckled, pulling back. "That's what I like to hear. Why aren't you with your father?"

Esme scoffed, looking over her shoulder. Lady Nyssa was still chatting with King Tedros and making him laugh. Fairy

Godmother Odelia stood there, looking awkward. "One word—suck-up. Or is that two words?"

Alva looked over, noticing the two of them together. "She never misses an opportunity to get on his good side, does she? I can't believe I had a crush on her when we were kids."

Esme kept staring at them, nearly crushing the cup in her hand. "You don't know how badly I want my fairy godmother to curse them all..."

Alva laughed, taking the cup out of Esme's hand. "Here—give me that before you hurt yourself. I know what'll cheer you up."

"Are you going to break me out of here?"

She snorted. "Sadly, no—but we *can* go dancing. That should liven up this party."

Esme took her arm. "Well, it beats standing around. All right—let's show them what we're made of."

Esme and Alva pushed their way to the dance floor where a small band was playing in tuxedos. The music was soft and relaxing—not the dancing kind. Esme leaned toward the bassist.

"Think you can play something more upbeat? No offense, but your music's a total snooze fest."

The bassist nodded and changed his music. A few seconds later, as the bass rattled the floor, Alva grinned. "That's more like it! Come on, Esme."

She grabbed her hand, and the two of them started twirling. It didn't take long for the crowd to notice. Some people cheered and joined them while others looked shocked at their antics. King Tedros, Fairy Godmother Odelia, and Lady Nyssa were staring at them, and Esme couldn't figure out if they approved or not.

"Okay, this is way more fun than being in my room!" Esme

called out. "If more of my father's parties were like this, maybe I'd come downstairs more often!"

Alva just laughed, continuing to dance in a manner that her parents wouldn't approve of. A few minutes later, Esme felt a tap on her shoulder. She turned around and noticed it was Duke Cullen, heir to the house of artisans. He had greasy black hair and sharp, pointy ears that reminded Esme of an annoying little elf. He followed her around all the time, desperate to make a good impression, but Esme wanted nothing to do with him.

"Excuse me, Your Highness, but may I have this dance?" he asked, extending a hand.

"No, thank you," Esme said, turning back to Alva. "I'm dancing with my friend."

Duke Cullen placed a hand on her shoulder. "Come on—just one dance. That's all I'm asking."

"And I said no," Esme hissed. "Get off me!"

"Yeah, you heard her," Alva said. "If you don't want to lose that hand, I suggest you move it."

Duke Cullen's face twisted in anger, but he didn't have a chance to respond. Several armed guards walked over, getting in between them. King Tedros trailed behind and looked angry.

"All right—the inappropriate dancing ends here. Band, I demand you play something soft again," King Tedros said, and the band nodded. "Esme, I'm disappointed in you. Again."

Esme shrugged. "You asked me to come downstairs and enjoy the party. I am. Make up your mind, Father."

"You know that isn't what I wanted," he hissed. "You never fail to make a scene, do you?"

"Oh, right—I forgot I have to be prim and proper all the time. I'm sorry I'm not perfect like Lady Nyssa," Esme spat, making everyone stare. "Why don't you make her your daughter instead? It's clear you like her so much better than me."

King Tedros flinched as though he had gotten slapped. "Esme, you know that isn't true. You're my daughter and I love you dearly. It's just, sometimes...you are *very* hard to handle."

Esme scoffed. "I'll stay out of your way, then. Enjoy the party, Father."

He sighed as she stormed away, pushing through the crowd. She grabbed another cup of punch and hid in the back corner. The people murmured before the party started back up again, and soon no one was talking about her anymore.

She noticed her father looked upset as he returned to his throne. Alva got stuck talking to her parents—in what looked like a scolding—and couldn't join her. Esme just sighed, sinking to the floor as she sipped her juice.

"Lousy father. Can never have a good time."

"I thought your little dance was exciting," a familiar voice said behind her.

Esme craned her neck, noticing Lady Nyssa standing there. She scoffed. "Exciting? Didn't know you had that word in your vocabulary."

Lady Nyssa sighed. "Look, I know you think I'm some uptight, royal wannabe—"

"Among other things," Esme muttered, sipping her drink. "Most of which I'd get in trouble if I said out loud."

"Well, it isn't true," Lady Nyssa said, sitting beside her. "In reality, I have thoughts of rebellion just like you. I can just... control myself better. And I think you should try again to make this party more fun."

"You do?" Esme asked, cocking an eyebrow.

Lady Nyssa nodded, gesturing at the cup. "I'm sure you have some ideas. Spiking the punch, for starters."

Esme's eyes widened. "I didn't know you were capable of thinking such devious things."

"Oh, I'm full of surprises," Lady Nyssa said with a grin as

she rose to her feet. "I'm just saying it would be a lot more exciting around here if you did. But if you're too scared to try—"

"I'm not scared," Esme said quickly as she stood up. "I'll do it. I just need to find some alcohol first."

Lady Nyssa reached underneath her gown, pulling out a flask. "Here—I stole this from my father's secret cabinet. He says it helps him with stress."

"I'm learning a lot about you tonight," Esme muttered, taking it from her. She hid it beneath her gown and looked around. "All right—wait here."

As Esme snuck through the crowd, she passed by the thrones. She heard her father speaking to her Fairy Godmother. "...and I just don't know what I'm going to do with her. Esme seems to be getting more and more scandalous by the day!"

"Be patient with her, Tedros," Fairy Godmother Odelia said. "She's been through a lot. She just needs time."

King Tedros sighed, looking down. "All right, but she'd better start showing improvement soon. Fairhaven deserves better..."

"I'll show you *and* your precious Fairhaven," Esme muttered under her breath.

She tiptoed toward the punch bowl, making sure no one was looking. When they were all distracted by the music or boring conversations, she opened the flask and emptied it into the bowl, then used the spoon to swirl it around. She even splashed some on the food.

"Now, we wait," she muttered to herself.

King Tedros rose to his feet, lifting his glass. "Thank you, everyone, for coming to our celebration tonight. I have the privilege of presiding over Fairhaven during its thousand-year anniversary—due, in no small part, to my ancestors' leadership before me—and I hope we have many more celebrations together. I'd also like to raise a toast to my late wife, Queen Marabeth, who I wish was still by my side."

The crowd took a moment of silence, bowing their heads.

"Thank you," King Tedros said, softly. "Please, help yourselves to the punch and food. My Fairy Godmother, Odelia, prepared it with magic herself."

Esme moved out of the way as the people descended on the table of snacks and punch, filling up their plates. She walked around and tried to hide her grin as they sipped and ate. A few seconds later, she noticed some of them beginning to sway.

"Oh, my," one man in a tuxedo said. "I'm feeling a little light-headed..."

"As am I," another woman in a blue gown and shawl said. "I think I might throw up!"

As the party fell into chaos—with some walking around tipsy, other people belching and arguing, and some vomiting up alcohol—Esme laughed and dove beneath the table, unable to remember the last time she'd had so much fun.

CHAPTER 2

When the fists started to fly, Esme wondered if she had taken things too far.

One man tackled another one, sending them both plummeting into a table. The women sitting there—also drunk themselves—staggered out of the way. As the men wrestled back and forth, the women giggled, swarming around them to watch.

"This is the best party ever!" a woman in a white dress proclaimed, then passed out drunk along a row of plates.

Esme winced as more fights broke out. She stayed hidden beneath the table, watching as people stumbled around. She glanced toward her father and noticed the horror on his face.

"What is the meaning of all this?" King Tedros demanded, rising to his feet. "Everyone, stop!"

But his kingdom didn't listen to him, too drunk out of their minds. Esme glanced across the room and noticed Lady Nyssa, Senator Remus, Dr. Breya, and their Fairy Godmother Zamira laughing.

"I think they're intoxicated, Tedros," Fairy Godmother Odelia said, looking around with wide eyes. "I can't believe it..."

"Do something, Odelia!" he cried, his eyes still on the brawling men. "Before someone gets hurt!"

Fairy Godmother Odelia nodded, pulling out her wand. She aimed it toward the fighting men who had knocked over countless tables. "End this brawl. Take away the drunken state of all. Abracadabra!"

But as she flicked her wand, nothing happened. Esme glanced over at Fairy Godmother Zamira and noticed she had her wand out, too, and was mumbling beneath her breath. If she strained to listen, Esme could hear her through the crowd.

"Forget what she said," Fairy Godmother Zamira muttered. "Leave everyone drunken and belligerent instead. Abracadabra!"

The fighting and belching continued. When a food fight started, Fairy Godmother Zamira grinned, stepping back into the shadows. King Tedros and Fairy Godmother Odelia watched in disbelief.

"What happened?" King Tedros asked. "Why didn't your spell work?"

"I don't know," Fairy Godmother Odelia muttered. "I'm sorry, Your Majesty. I can't help you."

King Tedros turned to his guards. "Break the fights up—now! I want everyone sent home and sobered up."

The guards nodded, rushing into the crowd. They used their batons to break apart the men fighting. It took them a few minutes, but they managed to get the crowd calm and stumbling out the doors of the palace. General Orion stayed next to King Tedros to protect him and Fairy Godmother Odelia.

"Now, to slip back upstairs," Esme whispered to herself, crawling out from beneath the table, "and pretend like I didn't have anything to do with this..."

But as soon as Esme tiptoed toward the staircase, she heard

a booming voice stop her. "Esme! I know you had a hand in this."

Esme spun around, noticing her father standing near his throne. The ballroom had turned silent and empty except for them. Alva, her mother, General Orion, and Fairy Godmother Odelia stood near her father, waiting for her answer.

Esme gulped. "How do you know it was me? You have no proof."

"Don't I?" he muttered. "Whenever something goes wrong, you're always involved somehow. I knew you couldn't just do what I asked for one night!"

"Hey, you're the one who made me come to this party!" Esme spat. "I was happy in my room. I tried to tell you that, but you wouldn't listen!"

"Ah, so it's my fault? How typical. You always blame people instead of taking responsibility for your actions," her father muttered, turning to his guards. "Search her gown. If there *is* evidence that she was responsible for this, I want to find it before I decide what to do next."

Before Esme could run up the stairs or get rid of the flask, the guards descended on her. They reached into her pocket and pulled out lipstick and other makeup before they found the flask. One guard rushed back to King Tedros, showing it to him.

"We found this in her gown, Your Majesty," the guard said, sniffing it. "Oh, that smells strong."

King Tedros took it, sniffing it. He made a face of disgust and pulled the flask away. "Yes, you're right—it smells like alcohol. I banned this substance a long time ago. How did you get your hands on it?"

Esme didn't want to be a tattletale, but she had no choice. She pointed across the room toward the shadows where Lady Nyssa, her parents, and Fairy Godmother Zamira stood.

"Lady Nyssa convinced me! She claimed she stole the flask from her father."

Senator Remus scoffed. "I never drank alcohol a day in my life! I wouldn't even know where to find some."

Esme rolled her eyes. "You're a Senator—I'm sure you could get your hands on contraband if you wanted to."

Senator Remus glared at her. "You lie! You take that back before—"

"Everyone, calm down. There's no need for threats—I intend to get to the bottom of this myself," King Tedros said, making Senator Remus hush. "I want to hear from Lady Nyssa. Is it true?"

Esme glanced back at Lady Nyssa, expecting her to confess. But she only shook her head and looked King Tedros right in the eyes. "I most certainly did not, Your Majesty. I'm shocked and hurt the princess would lie about me like this."

Esme's mouth hung open. "What? That's a lie. We were both there when you gave me the flask!"

Lady Nyssa just shrugged. "I don't know what you're talking about, princess. I'm sorry. Perhaps you're a little confused?"

Esme scoffed, looking down. She realized then that it was probably all a set-up. Esme came off looking like a disobedient brat while Lady Nyssa got all the praise. Irritated that she had fallen for it, Esme crossed her arms, scowling.

"It's all right, Lady Nyssa. Thank you for your honesty," King Tedros said, turning to Esme. "It's more than I can say for my own daughter."

Esme fell to her knees, her gown splayed around her. "Father, I swear to you—I'm telling the truth. Lady Nyssa was the one who encouraged me to do this thing!"

"I'd like to believe you, Esme, but you've been dishonest before. And you know the story about the boy who cried dragon. Liars only end up in more trouble. Besides, even if I did believe Lady Nyssa convinced you—"

"Which I didn't," Lady Nyssa added, making Esme glare at her.

"You still did it," King Tedros continued. "She didn't forcibly take your hand and make you spike the punch, did she?"

Esme hesitated. "Well...no, not exactly. But—"

"Then I rest my case. You knew adding alcohol to the punch was wrong, yet you did it anyway. You also knew this celebration was important to me and chose to ruin it," King Tedros said, looking down. "And now you must pay the price."

Esme gulped, rising to her feet. "What kind of price?"

He paused. "I'm not sure yet—I need time to think. But I can't let this go unpunished, Esme. I've been far too lenient with you already."

"Okay, maybe I went too far," Esme said, "but it was just a joke. No one got hurt!"

"No? Those two men brawling had bruises. You got everyone drunk against their will," King Tedros said, his hands on his hips. "What if I had gotten drunk? Or my guards? If someone had tried to assassinate me, they wouldn't have been sober enough to save me!"

"And we wouldn't want that," Senator Remus muttered.

Esme rolled her eyes. "I knew you and the guards wouldn't drink from the punch. You have a private chef."

"And thank goodness for that," her father spat. "You can try to spin this whichever way you like, but it was a reckless, dangerous thing to do."

Esme turned to Alva. "You thought it was funny, right? A harmless prank?"

Alva shifted uncomfortably. "I don't know, Es. I mean, dancing is one thing...but spiking everyone's drink? Seems kind of extreme."

Esme scoffed. "Fine—take his side! What about you, Fairy Godmother Odelia? You've always defended me."

"You're right—I always have, dear," she said, bowing. "But this time, I'm afraid I can't. You took it too far."

Esme couldn't believe it. When had her friends become sticks in the mud? Why couldn't everyone see she meant no harm?

"Go back upstairs to your room, Esme. We both know it's where you belong," her father grumbled. "You'll be locked in there until further notice. In the meantime, the guards and I have a lot to clean up. You should be grateful I'm not making you clean this mess."

Esme glanced around, noticing the splattered food, drinks, and knocked-over tables. She pitied the guards who didn't look too thrilled to have to clean up after her.

"We should get going, Your Majesty," Senator Remus said. "Thank you for the lovely party. Well, it *was* lovely until your daughter ruined it and accused my daughter of something heinous. It's only fortunate we weren't thirsty."

Esme watched Senator Remus, wondering if Lady Nyssa's parents were involved, too. She found it suspicious that they hadn't drunk any punch. And she couldn't forget what they had whispered about earlier.

King Tedros nodded. "I apologize, Senator Remus. Never in a million years would I think your daughter capable of something like this. Rest assured I'll deal with my daughter appropriately. Safe travels home."

"Lady Nyssa's a liar," Esme growled. "I can't prove it yet, but she's not as squeaky-clean as you think. You'll be disappointed when you find out, Father. I just hope it isn't too late by then."

King Tedros sighed. "There you go again, blaming someone else. Just go upstairs, Esme. I can't even bear to look at you right now."

"Wait!" Esme cried, glancing back at Lady Nyssa. "I know how we can settle this. Get Fairy Godmother Odelia to give Lady Nyssa a Truth Spell. Then we'll know for sure!"

Fairy Godmother Odelia nodded. "Esme has a point. I would be open to it."

"I also support it," Alva said.

"Absolutely not!" Senator Remus cried. "I won't have my daughter treated like a common criminal. We both know the Truth Spell has been used only for crooks and thieves!"

Lady Nyssa looked worried until King Tedros shook his head. "Fear not, Senator—I won't put your daughter under that kind of stress. You may leave now."

Esme gawked. "But Father—"

"I told you to head to your room," he snarled. "Don't make me have the guards drag you up there."

As her father turned away, Esme picked up the hem of her gown and approached the staircase. Even Fairy Godmother Odelia and Alva looked disappointed in her as they watched her go. Lady Nyssa, her parents, and Fairy Godmother Zamira passed by Esme on the way to the exit. Esme grabbed Lady Nyssa's arm.

"We both know you're lying," Esme accused. "You set me up on purpose, didn't you?"

"Oh, Esme. You were always *so* easy to play with," Lady Nyssa whispered with a growing smirk. "But I'm afraid I have no idea what you're talking about."

Esme rolled her eyes, turning to Fairy Godmother Zamira. "You can act all innocent now, but I saw you. You deliberately cast a spell to stop my fairy godmother from ending the brawl."

"You're wrong," Fairy Godmother Zamira said. "Perhaps you drank some of the tainted punch, too."

Esme scoffed. "I know what I saw. I heard you before, too. I know you're planning something—and I intend to find out what it is."

"Stay out of things that don't concern you, dearie," Fairy Godmother Zamira warned. "I wouldn't want you to get your pretty little face hurt."

Esme stared her right in her dark eyes. "Is that a threat?"

"Merely a warning," Senator Remus said, his gaze hard. Then he turned to his family and adjusted his tuxedo. "Come, now—we have to get home."

As the four of them left, slamming the door shut behind them, Esme turned and began walking up the staircase. She didn't dare look back as she entered her room and closed the door. As she fell onto her bed, she heard a knock.

"Oh, go away," she grumbled. "I don't want to see anyone right now."

The door opened an inch and Fairy Godmother Odelia poked her head inside. "I'm sorry, Esme, but your father wants me to magically lock you inside. I hope you understand."

"Fine—do whatever you have to," Esme said. "I won't come downstairs again. You have my word on that. Everyone hates me down there."

"We could never hate you." Fairy Godmother Odelia glided across the room to her. "We're just upset with what you did. I'm sorry I couldn't defend you downstairs, but I doubt your father would've listened to me, anyway."

Esme rolled over, facing her. "Do you at least believe me when I say Lady Nyssa set me up?"

Fairy Godmother Odelia sat down on the bed, sighing. "I do. You've done some terrible things before—greasing your father's throne comes to mind—but never once have you accused someone of anything. And with a fairy godmother like hers...I'm not surprised Lady Nyssa was behind it."

Esme sat up in bed. "What do you mean?"

"Well, as you know, fairy godmothers must attend the College of Magic to strengthen our powers before we're given a family. I attended school with Zamira, and let's just say...she was a bad child."

"How so?"

"She gravitated toward the dark arts—forbidden subjects. Fairy godmothers tend to be placed with families they're most like, and Senator Remus has always rubbed me the wrong way."

Esme thought for a moment, nodding. "You know, I overheard her talking with Senator Remus about some plan. I think it has something to do with making magic work on Earth."

Fairy Godmother Odelia's face turned pale. "I certainly hope not. Magic on Earth would be disastrous. I wonder what they're up to."

"Me, too. I think getting me to act out was part of their big plan. I can't believe I fell for it!"

Fairy Godmother Odelia rose to her feet, placing a hand on Esme's arm. "It's all right, Esme. No matter what happens, I shall protect you and your father as best I can—from Zamira, Lady Nyssa, or anyone else."

Esme hugged her. "I know you will."

"Rest now, dear. I don't know what punishment your father has in mind, but you'll need your strength," she said, crossing the room to the door. "I'll see you soon."

Esme jumped to her feet. "Can you tell my father and Alva that I'm sorry? I really didn't mean to hurt anyone."

Fairy Godmother Odelia smiled. "I will. Pleasant dreams, dear."

And then she shut the door, sealing Esme inside with a spray of magical light.

~

Esme had managed to fall asleep, curling up in her pink gown before the yelling downstairs woke her up.

She rose to her feet, walking toward the door. The handle was still locked when she jiggled it. She placed an ear against her door, hearing King Tedros arguing with Alva and Fairy Godmother Odelia.

"...and the punishment is too severe!" Fairy Godmother Odelia cried. "You must rethink this, Tedros!"

"She's right—and Esme could get hurt," Alva added. "Please, Your Majesty—"

"Stop—all of you," she heard King Tedros hiss. "I've made my decision. I'm at wit's end and don't know what else to do. Now, let's go upstairs and tell Esme."

When she heard footsteps, Esme backed away from the door, gulping. What did her father have in store for her? She opened her window and considered jumping, but the ledge was too high.

The door opened behind her a second later. Her father, the guards, Fairy Godmother Odelia, and Senator Remus entered. Alva trailed behind, tears forming in her eyes.

"Look—she already wants to run away," Senator Remus said, turning to King Tedros. "I'm sure she'll agree to the plan."

"What plan?" Esme spat. "And I thought you went home."

"I came back to make a suggestion," Senator Remus said with a smirk. "I'm pleased your father listened this time."

"Yes, well, I *did* appoint you as my senator. Some of your suggestions are good," King Tedros said, turning to Esme. "I know what I'll do with you now. Esme, you are lazy, irresponsible, selfish, and disobedient—easily the most rebellious twenty-four-year-old I know. It isn't the first time you've acted out—and I know it won't be your last."

"Father, you're scaring me," Esme said, her heart pounding.

"Well, you've humiliated me. I'm banishing you to Earth—a

world without magic. The storm drains above us lead to a human city called Toronto. Your fairy godmother will give you a potion that will fool others into thinking you're human."

"You're banishing me?" Esme asked, her eyes wide. "But that's never been done before!"

King Tedros nodded. "You're right—we usually send criminals to prison. But since you're my daughter, I've decided to be merciful."

"A pity," Senator Remus muttered, too low for King Tedros to hear.

"I wouldn't call this merciful!" Esme cried, stepping forward. "I know nothing about Earth. I've lived in Fairhaven my whole life! What am I supposed to do up there?"

"Blend in as best as you can," Senator Remus said. "I'd suggest getting a job."

Esme wrinkled her nose. "A job? Oh, I think I'm going to be sick."

"I know this may seem strange," Fairy Godmother Odelia said with a sigh, "but fear not. You're capable of more than you think, Esme."

"Hang on," she muttered, glancing at her father. "You were just arguing with Senator Remus. You wouldn't let him go to Earth. Why me?"

"This is a different case. I think time among the humans will help you. As for everyone else, they'll be required to stay in Fairhaven."

Senator Remus rolled his eyes.

"Can I...ever come back?" Esme whispered.

"Ah, good question," King Tedros said, pulling out a piece of paper. "You may—but only if you follow the rules I've laid out. Go ahead—read it."

Esme looked down at the paper, watching as the magical

ink wrote itself. It mentioned things like living on her own, volunteering, and helping other people.

"I'm giving you thirty days to complete all those tasks," her father continued, thrusting the note into her hands. "If in a month's time I deem you've become a better person, I'll let you come back."

"You can't be serious, Father! This is absurd—"

"You will leave in the morning, so I suggest you rest and eat," her father continued, turning his back. "You can say goodbye to your friends tomorrow morning. The journey will be difficult, but you need this, Esme."

"I won't forget this, Father," she called out as he walked away. "I won't forget how you abandoned me!"

Her father said nothing as he vanished, the room turning silent.

Senator Remus chuckled. "Good luck, Esme. You'll need it."

Esme sneered. "Oh, I'm sure you're loving this. Getting me out of the way is what you've always wanted, isn't it? What you and Lady Nyssa planned?"

It looked like Senator Remus wanted to say something but then remembered the guards were still there. "Have fun on Earth, Princess. You won't last a week."

As he stormed away, the guards tugged on Alva and Fairy Godmother Odelia's arms. As Esme watched them leave and the door slammed behind them, she sunk to her knees, wondering how she was going to survive in a world she had never seen.

CHAPTER 3

E sme stayed on the floor for the rest of the night, crying into the list her father had given her. Her tears stained the words, but the magical ink would spell them out again. She crinkled the paper up and threw it across the room into the trash can.

"That's what I think of your rules," Esme muttered, sniffling.

The paper magically unfolded itself and cascaded toward her. She sighed, stuffing it into her pocket. She reached for her mother's photograph instead and held it up under the light.

"Oh, Mom. I wish you were still here," she whispered, caressing her mother's face in the picture. She looked regal in her crown and dress. "I wonder what you would've done with me—if you would've sided with Father or not. But then again, maybe I wouldn't have done all these things if you were still alive."

The tap on her window made Esme jump. She looked over, noticing Duke Cullen on the other side of the glass. He smiled at her and gestured for her to unlock the window. She rose to her feet, her hands shaking.

"What are you doing out there?" she called, moving toward the door. "How dare you come up to my bedroom!"

"Please, just let me in," Duke Cullen said through the panes. "I won't hurt you!"

"Father!" Esme called out, turning toward the door. "There's an intruder. Guards?"

But no answer came.

Esme decided to pound on the door. "Can anyone hear me? I said there's an intruder—"

"Nice try, Princess Esme," a guard's voice said from down the hallway. "We know all about your tricks and what you're trying to do. It won't work!"

"No—please!" she cried. "Duke Cullen is outside—"

The guard scoffed. "Duke Cullen left the party hours ago, and no one has gotten into the palace—let alone your room. Now, settle down before I ask your Fairy Godmother to make your room soundproof!"

When the guard's footsteps vanished, Esme scoffed. "So much for them. I'll deal with him myself."

She rushed across the room, banging on the window. Duke Cullen began to sway outside and looked angry. "Hey, what are you doing?"

"Trying to dislodge you," Esme said. "How did you even get up here?"

"Climbing equipment," Duke Cullen said, gesturing at the rope underneath him. "Look, just let me in!"

Esme scoffed. "Why in all of Fairhaven would I do that? I told you already—I don't like you. I'll never want to be with you, so just take the hint and go away!"

Duke Cullen smiled. "I don't think you'll be saying that when you hear my offer."

Esme rolled her eyes, turning her back. "I don't care what

you have to say. Now, on the count of three, I want to turn around and see you gone. One—"

"I know how you can stay in Fairhaven."

Esme blinked and spun toward him. "What are you talking about?"

"Let me in and I'll tell you."

"All right," Esme said, stepping toward the window. "But I *am* still the princess of Fairhaven, you know. Father would have your head if you did anything to me."

As she unlocked the door, he crawled in through the window and scoffed. "I told you before—I'm not here to hurt you. I've come with a proposition."

Esme narrowed her eyes. "What kind of proposition?"

"The kind where you get to stay in Fairhaven," he said, brushing dirt off his peacoat. "Your father respects my family. I come from a long line of artisans—bakers, artists, you name it. We're very well-respected in Fairhaven."

Esme rolled her eyes again. "Uh-huh. Do you have a plan, or did you just come up here to brag?"

Duke Cullen laughed. "Don't you see what I'm getting at, Princess? I could convince your father to keep you in Fairhaven —that he's made a terrible mistake."

"How?"

"Marry me."

Esme's eyes widened. "Why would I ever want to do that?"

"Everyone loves a royal wedding. If your father knew we were getting married, he wouldn't send you to Earth."

"Hang on a second," Esme exclaimed. "How do you even know I'm getting sent to Earth?"

"Senator Remus told everyone already. He's happy you're leaving, you know—a little *too* happy. News spreads fast in a small kingdom like this."

"I guess I shouldn't be surprised—he was the one who

proposed the idea to my father," Esme said. "How are you so sure a royal wedding would keep me here?"

Duke Cullen grinned. "I can be very persuasive, Esme. I'm sure if you accept this ring I had my fairy godmother make for you, everything will turn out. The people will be eager to see us together—and it wouldn't be right to keep a blushing bride away from her dear husband."

When Duke Cullen pulled out the ring, it glimmered in the light. It looked very expensive and bursting with magical energy. As Esme stared at it, she wondered—could she do it? Could she marry a man she didn't even like to keep her place in Fairhaven?

When she looked back up at Duke Cullen, he was still smirking. He thrust the ring at her. "Come on, Princess Esme— you're a smart woman. I'm sure you see what the right decision is."

"But you don't even love me."

He shrugged. "I like you. Maybe one day, I could love you. You might feel the same, too."

Esme scrunched her face in disgust. "No offense, but you're not really my type."

His smirk faded. "Look, I didn't say we had to be madly in love. I only want to help keep you here. You have friends, family, and a life. It wouldn't be right to send you away."

Esme crossed her arms. "Yeah, right. You just want to marry me so you'll become a prince, and then one day when my father dies, you'll become king."

The smile returned to his face. "That would be a nice benefit, of course."

Esme took a step back. "You've only been after me all this time for my crown! Sorry, but I can't marry a man who only likes me for my title. I want to marry for love."

"Love is overrated. You'll never find true love, anyway," he said, stepping closer to her. "Just try the ring on—"

"No!" Esme shouted, slapping it out of his hand. It fell and clanged on the floor. "I don't want your ring—or anything of yours. Just get out of my room before I call the guards."

Duke Cullen snarled, picking up the ring. "You'll regret this, Esme."

She rolled her eyes, shoving him toward the window. "I think I'll be fine—but thanks for your concern."

"Senator Remus was right, you know," he muttered, kicking one leg out the window. "You won't survive a week on Earth. You'll never be able to live without your father, Fairy Godmother, or servants. You're going to meet your death up there."

Esme swallowed the lump in her throat, fearing he was right. She forced herself to hold her head high. "We'll just see about that. You were already wrong about one thing, you know."

He sneered. "Oh, yeah? And what might that be?"

"My parents had true love. They adored each other," Esme said, firmly. "I know I can find that, too. Now, get lost, Cullen— or I'll tell my father you tried to force me into marriage."

When he had cascaded down the rope he had come in on, she slammed the window shut, hoping she was making the right choice.

～

Esme barely slept, tossing and turning all night. When she did manage to close her eyes, she had only nightmares—mostly of Earth. What was it like? What kind of people were these humans? She didn't know—and that worried her the most.

When it became lighter outside, a plate of breakfast magically appeared next to her door. Esme rose to her feet—still in her pink gown—and rushed toward it. She smiled, picking up the fork when she saw the note.

For you, my dear, Fairy Godmother Odelia had written. *I packed it with extra protein to keep you full longer.*

"Thanks, Fairy Godmother Odelia," she said, digging into the griffin eggs. "Always looking out for me."

When she finished eating, she tapped the plate and it magically disappeared downstairs into the kitchen sink. After she heard a knock on the door, she rose to her feet, wiping off crumbs from her gown.

"Come in!" she cried.

A second later, the door opened. A dozen guards flooded the room.

"You must come with us," one of them said. "We've been instructed to take you to the storm drain exit."

Esme scoffed. "I'm not allowed to walk there myself?"

"No offense, Princess Esme, but your father doesn't have much confidence in you these days," another guard said. "Now, come on—he doesn't have all day."

As they grabbed her arms, she squirmed against them. "Wait—please! You can't let King Tedros kick me out. It isn't fair! I'm the princess—and I'll be queen one day. You should be supporting me!"

"But your father is still in charge—and what he says goes. I'm sorry, my lady."

"But what about my luggage?" Esme called out as they dragged her into the hallway. "I haven't packed yet!"

"Your fairy godmother will make all the arrangements," the guard replied, not even looking at her. "If you have any more complaints, take them up with your father. We're just here to enforce the rules—we don't make them."

She scowled as they tugged her down the staircase, taking

her toward the exit doors. She remembered when the guards used to listen to her—but now, they treated her like a criminal. The entire castle looked cleaned up, and Esme didn't see a single trace of the damage she had caused last night. The servants watched and murmured as the guards reached the doors.

"Don't worry—I'll be back!" she called out, feeling around for the paper in her dress pocket. "A month on the surface is nothing."

She felt the guard holding her shiver. "I don't think I'd last up there. I've heard some pretty awful things about Earth."

"Like what?" she asked, opening the door to the palace.

The guard hesitated.

She crossed her arms, gripping the archway. "I'm not leaving until you tell me."

The guard sighed. "Fine. I just heard that humans can be nasty to each other—that they kill, steal, and destroy. I don't know if it's true."

Esme gulped. Just what kind of place was her father sending her to? He either didn't know the truth or thought Esme could handle it. She wasn't sure which was worse. Esme knew a little about Earth through movies and books humans had tossed down the storm drains, but other than that, much was a mystery.

She tried to think of it as an adventure instead of a dangerous mission.

"Uh, I'm sure you'll be fine, Your Majesty," the guard stammered. "Someone will probably take pity on you. Anyway, let's go."

As Esme stepped outside the castle, she realized she didn't get out much. Their kingdom sat beneath a human city and only received light through the holes of the storm drain. It was often dark and humid down in Fairhaven, with castles that connected to each other and a marketplace to buy goods. Frogs ribbited in murky ponds as they passed by.

"Where's my father?" Esme asked. "I demand to see him before I leave!"

The guard nodded. "And you will. He and your friends are waiting by the storm drain. They're right over there."

Esme looked ahead, realizing several people stood next to a ladder that extended to the human city. King Tedros usually kept it up high so people wouldn't be tempted to climb it. Alva, Fairy Godmother Odelia, Senator Remus, and a slew of guards stood next to him. Fairy Godmother Odelia gave Esme a potion to make her seem human inside and out. After drinking it, Esme turned her hands over in wonder as her skin became more tanned, and the telltale magical shimmer she was accustomed to disappeared.

"Ah, there you are," King Tedros said. "Are you ready to leave?"

Esme crossed her arms. "And if I say no?"

King Tedros sighed. "It wouldn't change much, I'm afraid. My decision last night was final."

Senator Remus smirked.

Esme turned to him, sneering. "Here I thought you'd be jealous of me. I get to see Earth while you have to stay down here in the dark."

Senator Remus' smile faded. "I was a fool to suggest using magic on Earth. I see that now."

The more Esme looked at Senator Remus' smug face, the more she doubted that. She knew he was planning something —something big.

Alva threw herself into Esme's arms. "Oh, Esme—I'm so sorry."

Esme hugged her back. "It's all right, Alva. I'll be okay—and back before you know it."

Senator Remus snorted. "Not likely."

As Esme glared at him, Alva leaned in toward her ear. "I'll keep an eye on Senator Remus and Lady Nyssa for you. If they try anything while you're gone, I'll stop them."

"Good. I feel better with you here," Esme whispered, pulling back. She turned to Fairy Godmother Odelia. "Well, I guess this is goodbye for now."

Fairy Godmother Odelia leaned in and kissed her cheek. "I will miss you, dear. Take care of yourself up there. And remember—magic isn't compatible on the surface. No spell will work."

Senator Remus raised an eyebrow at that but stayed silent.

"And that's a good thing. Magic is our birthright and no one else's," King Tedros said. "And don't tell anyone about Fairhaven, you hear me? We're separated for a reason. If we were meant to mingle, we would have already."

Senator Remus rolled his eyes as Fairy Godmother Odelia hugged Esme. "Even if we're not together, I'll always be your fairy godmother, wishing the best for you."

Esme nodded, pulling away. "So, about my things. Am I allowed to take them with me, or do you expect me to go completely alone?"

King Tedros sighed. "Fairy Godmother Odelia, can you get her luggage?"

Fairy Godmother Odelia nodded as she pulled out her wand. "I ask for Esme's things. She has a lot of stuff she wants to bring. Abracadabra!"

Three pink suitcases flung toward her, landing at her feet. Esme unzipped one and looked inside. It had more than a dozen gowns and undergarments, as well as dried food, water bottles, and a picture of her mother.

When she looked back up, Fairy Godmother Odelia winked.

"I think you have everything you need to make it, dear. We're all rooting for you."

Senator Remus chuckled under his breath.

Esme ignored him, turning to her father. "One of the guards mentioned Earth was dangerous. Something about humans fighting each other?"

Her father shifted uncomfortably. "Well...yes. Humans have gone to war from time to time and—"

"War?" Esme asked, scrunching her face in disgust. "And you want me to live among those barbarians?"

"Respecting other cultures is one of the things on your do-list, Esme. You can be very small-minded at times," he muttered. "From what I've heard, humans are capable of good things, too. I think they might surprise you. They look like us, so you won't have trouble blending in."

"What if I get hurt? I'm still a princess, you know. I demand you send guards with me."

Her father shook his head. "That would defeat the purpose of sending you off alone to be independent. Besides, do you really think I'd send you to Earth if I didn't believe you'd make it back?"

Esme blinked. She had no idea her father had that much confidence in her. "Really?"

He nodded. "You can be resourceful when you need to be, Esme. Use that to your advantage—but stay out of trouble up there. If you get arrested, I'm not coming to your aid. Earth has rules, too, so follow them."

Esme shivered. "I'll try my best."

"I plan to send guards to the surface every now and then to check on you, but you'll be alone for the most part," he said, gesturing at the ladder. "Now, whenever you're ready."

Esme was about to start climbing when she turned, hugging him. "Be careful, Father."

He hesitated but hugged her back. "Of what, exactly?"

Her eyes flickered to Senator Remus, thinking of the plan she had overheard. "Just in general."

King Tedros nodded, pulling back. "I will. You, too, Esme. I look forward to seeing the person you've become in the next month."

Esme took a deep breath, reaching for the ladder. "All right, here goes nothing..."

As soon as her feet were both on the ladder, Esme noticed Fairy Godmother Zamira in the distance, casting a spell. Esme felt the ladder pulling her toward the surface at the speed of light. She screamed as she looked up, noticing the cracks of sunlight. A second later, she shot through the storm drain, landing on the ground with a thud.

She panted, reaching for her suitcases as the storm drain locked behind her. "Oh, that hurt."

As she grabbed her suitcases and stood up, she looked around. A bunch of people on the sidewalk—dressed in strange, casual clothing—were staring at her. She realized she was standing on a busy street with honking cars around her, something she had only seen in human television and movies. She looked up and noticed a sign that read DUNDAS STREET.

"Dundas Street?" Esme muttered. "What an odd name—"

As she crossed the street, she felt something slam into her back. It knocked her off her feet and caused her suitcases to roll away. As she fell to the ground, she looked back, realizing one of the cars had crashed into her.

And then the searing pain settled in, making Esme cry out.

A man in the driver's seat stepped out, dressed in a white t-shirt and jeans. He had spilled the coffee in his hands as he looked down at her in concern. If Esme wasn't so hurt, she would've thought he was handsome with his curly blond hair, green eyes, and muscular arms. The dimples on his cheeks turned downward as he frowned at her.

"Oh my God!" the man cried, rushing toward her. "Are you okay?"

"Been better," Esme groaned, trying to stand.

A large crowd of people swarmed her, mumbling about her condition. Even the traffic on the street stopped as people glanced out their windows with looks of concern.

"You came out of nowhere," the man continued, holding her up. "What were you even doing in the middle of the street?"

"I saw her come out of that storm drain," a woman on the street said. "And why is she dressed like that?"

Esme looked around, realizing how much attention she had gotten already. She didn't want to get in trouble—not when she needed to prove herself to her father.

She laughed, trying to forget the ache in her back. "I'm an actress. We're filming a movie here on Dundas Street."

The man glanced around. "I don't see any camera crews here."

She tried to push him away. "Look, I have to get going now. Thanks for your concern, but—"

When Esme staggered, falling to her knees, the man helped her up. "I think we should get you to a hospital."

Esme shook her head, wincing from the pain. She started to feel light-headed and dizzy. "No, it's okay. I'll be fine..."

When she felt her eyes closing, she didn't resist. As the man carried her back to his car, her world fell into darkness.

CHAPTER 4

When Esme woke up again, she expected to see her father, Alva, and Fairy Godmother Odelia. She expected them to embrace her and tell her that sending her to Earth was just a bad dream and that she was home again, safe and sound.

But that didn't happen.

As she looked around, she noticed she was lying in a hospital bed. The room was blinding white with a light overhead that buzzed almost rhythmically. Someone had stripped her out of her old clothes, leaving her in a strange, white gown. Her pink dress, suitcases, tiara, and diamond slippers had gotten tossed over the nearby chair.

When she spotted the familiar checklist poking out of her gown pocket, she slumped back into bed, groaning.

"Hey, you're finally awake."

Esme looked to the left, noticing the same handsome man from Dundas Street who had hit her with his car. He fiddled with his hands nervously in the chair before he stood up and walked toward her. His green eyes peered down at her, and he had an energy that immediately made Esme feel comforted.

"Where am I?" she managed to ask, her voice hoarse.

"Toronto General Hospital. I brought you here myself," he said, frowning. "Don't you remember?"

Esme clutched her head. "Yeah, it's coming back now. Thanks for helping me out."

"Well, I couldn't just leave you lying there on the street. When you passed out, I rushed you to the hospital. They took you away for tests before bringing you back here," he said, sitting back down again. "So, what were you *really* doing coming out of that storm drain?"

"I told you," Esme said, sitting up straight. "I was filming a movie."

The man studied her for a moment. "We both know that's not true. I think your co-stars or director would've come looking for you by now—"

A knock on the door startled them both. A red-headed woman in a white doctor's coat poked her head inside the room. "Sorry to interrupt, but may I come in?"

"Of course, doctor," Esme said, sighing in relief that she didn't have to answer the man's questions for now.

"How is she doing?" the man asked, looking at the doctor.

The doctor looked down at the chart, nodding. "She passed out from the pain, so it's a good thing you brought her in when you did. You may experience some back pain, but we gave you painkillers for that."

"So, I'm healthy?" Esme asked, perking up.

"As a horse," the doctor said with a grin. "It's a good thing, too. It could've been a lot worse."

It was a good thing her people healed quickly Esme realized. Or she might've been even worse off.

"That's a relief," the man said, sighing. "I'm really sorry I hit you with my car. As I said before, you came out of nowhere— too fast for me to hit the brake."

"It's okay," Esme said. "Don't blame yourself."

The man gave her a small smile, making butterflies flutter in her stomach. A man had never made her feel that way before. She looked away, trying not to blush.

"If you're feeling up to it, I'd say you're good to go home," the doctor continued. "All your things are on that chair—including the gown you were brought in with. Were you heading to a party or something?"

Esme shrugged. "Something like that. Well, thank you for healing me, doctor. I'd like to leave as soon as possible."

I've only got a month to prove myself to my father and I have no time to waste, she thought.

The doctor nodded, crossing the room toward the door. "Of course. I'll leave a prescription for a week's worth of painkillers at the local pharmacy, and you can pick them up anytime you'd like."

Esme nodded. "Thank you again, doctor."

As the doctor left the room, the man was still staring at her. "I didn't know your name, so they put Jane Doe in your file. You'll have to give your real name at the front desk."

"I will," Esme said, stretching her back with a grimace. "Oh, that still hurts—even with the painkillers. I've never experienced pain before."

The man's eyes widened. "Never?"

"No. My fairy godmother always used magic to take it away."

He turned silent for a moment. "Your...fairy godmother?"

Esme blushed, remembering how her father wanted her to be discreet. "Uh, yeah. That's what I call my grandmother. She makes the best soup that tastes like magic."

He seemed to buy it, nodding. "Oh, I see. Grandmothers are the best, aren't they?"

Phew, Esme thought. *Dodged a bullet there.*

The man chuckled. "Here I thought you might have a concussion. Fairy godmother...yeah, right."

Esme laughed, nervously. "Yeah. So silly."

"Anyway, if it's all right with you, I'd like to know your name. Doesn't feel right calling you Jane Doe still," he said, walking toward her. "I'm Noah Crawford."

When he held out her hand, she shook it. "Princess Esme Penelope Alexandria of Fairhaven. It's a pleasure to meet you."

He blinked. "You're a princess?"

Esme paused. "Maybe I've said too much. Father wanted me to keep a low profile."

"Hey, it's okay. I won't tell anyone."

Esme shrugged, not seeing the harm in telling him. He seemed like the honest sort. And Esme was desperate for a friend—a confidant on the surface. "Well, you *did* save my life, so I figure you deserve some answers. That's right—I'm a real princess, in the flesh. But if anyone asks, I'm just an actress. I'm supposed to keep my identity a secret for safety reasons."

"I see. Well, it's safe with me," he said, pulling his hand back. "Should I curtsy or something?"

Esme laughed. "No—that's all right. Technically, I don't have any authority on Earth—Toronto. I mean Toronto."

"Oh, that's too bad. Where is this Fairhaven?"

Esme rose to her feet, trying to use the blankets to cover her body. The hospital gown left little to the imagination. "Far, far away. I'm sure you wouldn't have heard about it. They don't teach it in schools."

"Yeah—the name doesn't ring a bell. What are you doing in Toronto if this kingdom of yours is so far away? And alone? Doesn't seem safe to send a princess by herself."

Esme crossed the room to get to her dress. "Yeah, you're right—but this is a different situation. My father...kind of banished me here. He wants me to learn some life skills before I return.”

Noah nodded. “I saw that note in your pocket. Didn’t mean to pry, but I wanted to find out who you are. Contact your family to let them know about the accident. I put it back after I read it. I saw the tiara, too. It mentioned stuff like etiquette and being a better person?”

Esme sighed. “That’s right. I have to change or else I’m not welcomed back.”

His eyes widened. “That seems kind of harsh.”

“If you knew what I’ve done, maybe you wouldn’t think so,” Esme muttered. “Anyway, Senator Remus told me I’d never last a week in Toronto. My first day here, and I get hit by a car! Maybe he was right.”

“Well, I don’t know who this Senator Remus guy is, but he seems like an asshole,” Noah replied, making Esme chuckle. “I live by a simple motto—you gotta do what you gotta do. If you need to do this stuff to get home, I think you’ll find a way.”

Esme smiled. “Thanks, Noah. Now, if you wouldn’t mind, I’d like to change back into my gown.”

He nodded, reaching for the doorhandle. “Of course—I’ll wait for you outside. I brought your suitcases in, by the way. I’m just glad you’re going to be okay.”

After he left the room and closed the door, Esme felt the strange butterflies again. She wondered if she had accidentally drunk another prototype of her fairy godmother’s potions and tried to push it aside. She shimmied out of the uncomfortable hospital gown, throwing her pink dress and diamond slippers back on. It might have not been the same as getting dressed with her fairy godmother at home, but it made her feel closer to her kingdom.

She grabbed her suitcases, rolling them to the door. When she opened it, she found Noah waiting a few steps away, just as he promised. He smiled when he saw her and gestured down the hallway toward the exit.

"Are you ready? I've got my car parked outside."

Esme nodded. "I think so. Just need to check out."

When Esme headed to the reception desk, she only gave her name as Esme Fairhaven to not draw too much attention to herself. She signed the discharge sheet and pushed through the crowd of people to follow Noah outside. Her eyes squinted underneath the bright glare of the sun as they exited through the doors into the parking lot.

"Oh, your city is so bright," she muttered. "I can barely see where I'm going."

"Here," Noah said, reaching into his pocket. "I have some sunglasses you can wear."

"Sunglasses?" she asked, confused. "What do they do?"

"They protect your eyes from the sun's UV rays. You've never heard of them?"

Esme shook her head, taking the sunglasses. "No—my kingdom is very dark. We barely get any sunlight, so there's no need for them. How do I wear these?"

"Like regular glasses," he said, taking them from her hand. He gently set them on her face. "There you go. They look good on you."

Esme smiled. "Thank you, Noah. I didn't expect anyone to be nice to me here. I don't get out much, but from what I've heard, people can be jerks."

He laughed. "Yeah, they can. But helping people is kind of my job. Come on—let's walk to my car where there's shade."

"What do you do for a living?" she asked, following him across the parking lot.

"I work for a humanitarian organization called Human Connection. It's one of the fastest growing companies in the city. We do all sorts of things—charities, fundraisers, auctions

—for homeless shelters, hospitals, and schools. Whatever we can to help the world become a better place. In fact, I was on my way to work when I hit you."

Esme frowned as they reached his familiar sedan. "Oh, I'm sorry. Don't feel obligated to spend time with me or anything."

He shook his head. "It's all right—I already called my boss and told her what happened. Besides, I figured since I put you in that hospital, I should be responsible for you. Is there somewhere I can drive you?"

Esme shifted, awkwardly. "Well...I don't actually have a place to stay yet. I have to start looking for one. When you hit me, I was brand new to Toronto."

"Oh, I see. Well, if you don't find it weird, you can stay with me. I just moved into a new two-bedroom apartment. I have a vacant room after...well, after someone moved out. You can stay there if you'd like—it wouldn't be a problem."

Esme shook her head, reaching into her pocket to pull out the checklist. "That's very kind of you—and I'd say yes—but I don't think I can. My father wants me to live by myself. Something about being more independent."

Noah looked disappointed but shrugged. "No problem—living alone is awesome, too. You've never done that before?"

"No—I lived in a big castle with servants."

Noah's eyes widened. "Well, I think you'll have to lower your standards a bit for Toronto. We don't have any castles out here—just a lot of apartments. No servants, either. Anyway, we should probably go apartment hunting for you."

Esme was too shy to tell Noah she didn't have money yet for that. But she kept quiet, hoping to find a job soon to afford her new life.

When Esme noticed Noah getting into the driver's seat of his vehicle, she walked around and got into the passenger seat. He put his seatbelt on as she struggled with hers.

"I don't understand," she muttered. "What is this odd contraption?"

He laughed. "It's a seatbelt—you put it on so you don't fly out the window if you get into a car accident. Here, let me help you."

Once he clicked it in, his fingers brushing against her, she almost swooned. The butterflies had returned. Not wanting to make him uncomfortable, she just smiled. "You made it look so easy. Thank you."

"It just takes practice," he said, putting the car into drive, "like anything else. So, no sunglasses or seatbelts where you come from. What *do* you have in Fairhaven?"

Magic and fairy godmothers came to mind, but Esme just shrugged. "The usual. I'm more interested in seeing how people in Toronto live."

He nodded, pulling out of the parking lot. "I can show you around a bit. But first, I need coffee. Can't live without it."

"We don't have coffee where I come from. I look forward to trying it."

Noah laughed, stealing a glance at her. "Oh, trust me—it'll be love at first sight. You've gotta make up for all the years you've gone without it."

Esme found the noise and jostling of the car strange at first, but chit-chatting with Noah made her feel much more comfortable. He even turned on the radio and showed her the most popular musicians. The music was different—not at all like the bands from Fairhaven—but Esme liked it. Noah smiled when he saw her tapping her foot to the beat, intrigued. Once they had made it downtown, Noah waded through traffic to take her to a small café with a sign that read TASTY TREATS.

"Here we are," he said, parking his car on the side of the road. "My favorite coffee shop in the whole city. They make the best muffins, too. You coming?"

When she saw him unbuckling his seatbelt, she copied him, stepping out of the car. "Ready—lead the way."

When she followed him into the store, there was a long line of people waiting for their orders. The barista was doing her best to get everyone their drinks and food but looked a little overwhelmed. When people noticed Esme, they started staring.

"Is it just me," Esme whispered, "or is everyone looking at us?"

Noah glanced back at her. "I think it's *you* they're looking at. It's not every day they see someone in a pink Barbie gown."

"Who's Barbie?"

He shook his head, trying not to chuckle. "Never mind. Isn't there anything else in those suitcases of yours that you can wear?"

"No—sorry. In Fairhaven, it's customary to wear gowns and suits, especially when attending ballroom parties."

"Fancy. Sounds like fun."

Esme looked down, sighing. "Not really."

"Next, please!" the barista called out.

Noah stepped forward, pulling out his wallet. "We'd like two Venti lattes with whipped cream and almond milk. Oh, and two blueberry muffins—they're always so fresh here."

The barista smiled, taking his money. "You got it. Please, step off to the side while I get your order."

"Thanks for buying it for me," Esme said, stepping off to the side with Noah. She tried to ignore the stares from the crowd as she waited. "I would've paid, but I don't have any money. My father—King Tedros—always handled our finances."

"I figured you wouldn't have much. We should get you to a clothing store—you'll need something better to fit in. My treat."

Esme smiled. "Thanks. I'd probably be lost without you."

"It's funny how life works, isn't it?" he asked, his eyes sparkling. "How a stranger can suddenly become so important."

Esme blushed as the drinks and muffins came. Noah thanked the barista, then gave half the order to Esme. She followed him to a secluded table in the back where people wouldn't stare anymore.

"I'm really excited to try this coffee," Esme said, sitting down across from him. "What does it taste like?"

"There's only one way to find out—"

Noah's eyes widened as Esme chugged the entire latte, wiping her mouth with the sleeve of her gown. "Wow—that *is* good! Ouch, that's hot."

He chuckled. "Esme, you weren't supposed to drink it all in one sip. Coffee is meant to be savored. Didn't you burn your tongue?"

She looked down, embarrassed. "Yeah, I did. I just thought you were supposed to drink it like that. Oops. Sorry—I didn't know."

"That's all right," he said, handing her a napkin. "I should also warn you that it has caffeine. You might have more energy."

Esme gasped as she wiped her mouth again with the napkin, her tongue still burning from the hot coffee. "Oh, no—Father told me not to take any drugs."

It took everything in Noah not to burst out laughing. "Really, Esme—it's all right. Caffeine isn't a dangerous drug, and it'll wear off. Billions of people around the world drink it. It makes work a little more bearable."

Esme sighed in relief as she bit off a piece of this muffin. "Oh, good—you had me worried for a second. Oh, wow—this muffin is delicious."

Noah smiled. "I told you. And don't worry—it doesn't have caffeine in it."

Esme swallowed it, sighing. "I miss the food back in Fairhaven. The servants knew the way I liked it, too."

"Maybe you can show me those foods one day. You know, if you manage to impress your father enough to go back home."

Esme knew Noah would never be allowed inside Fairhaven—and that her father would punish her for just telling him about it. Everyone knew it was too dangerous, that humans had a reputation for being violent. Giving them magic in their world was just an invitation for trouble.

She faked a smile. "Maybe one day."

Once they had finished eating, Noah carried their wrappers to the garbage and escorted Esme to the door. The people were still staring and murmuring behind her back. When she looked at their peering eyes, she felt bad for the humans and how they had to live without magic.

"I was thinking we should get your meds first, then get some new clothes, then look for an apartment," he said, opening the door for her. "But just to warn you, you'll need first and last month's rent. And renting in Toronto isn't cheap. I can afford to buy you clothes, but I'm not rich enough to loan you rent money."

Esme sighed, stepping outside. She glanced in the direction of her suitcases in Noah's car. "That's okay—I don't expect you to pay my way forward. My father wouldn't want that, either. I'll have to find a way—"

Esme groaned when someone collided with her. She looked back, realizing it was a blonde woman in a pantsuit. She looked like she was in a hurry. Her brown eyes scanned Esme for any injuries, looking apologetic.

"Oh, I'm so sorry! I should've been watching where I was going," the woman said, fixing the purse on her shoulder. "I was just so desperate to get my coffee—"

"Jill?" Noah asked, looking closer at her. "That *is* you, isn't it?"

The woman named Jill looked tense when she noticed him. "Oh, Noah. Nice to see you."

"Yeah," he mumbled, looking sad. "You, too."

Esme didn't know much about humans, but she knew when they were uncomfortable. The air turned silent and awkward.

"How do you two know each other?" Esme asked, confused.

"This is Jillian Burns," Noah said, his shoulders stiffening, "my ex-fiancée."

CHAPTER 5

Esme looked between Noah and Jill, noticing that they both seemed like they had more to say, but couldn't find the right words. Whatever had happened between them looked tense. Finally, Jill sighed.

"I'm so sorry, Noah," she whispered. "I've been meaning to call and explain—"

"Explain what?" Noah asked, a little more hostile now. "It's pretty clear. You love your new fiancé more than me."

Esme frowned. A new fiancé? Just what had happened between them?

Jill shook her head. "No, that's not it at all. It was a really tough choice to make—"

"Oh, that's good to know," Noah muttered. "I was *so* close to being your first choice, but not close enough. Thanks."

Jill stepped forward, placing a hand on Noah's arm. "Don't be like that, Noah. We should talk—just the two of us. It might help to give you closure."

Noah pulled away. "I don't need your closure. I got the message loud and clear, and now, I'm trying to move on."

"Noah, please—"

Footsteps echoed behind them before a tall, dark-haired man appeared. He had the same blue eyes as Noah but didn't have their sparkle. He beeped his BMW a few parking spots over to lock it.

He pecked Jill's cheek, looking between them. "Is everything okay, babe? I finally found a spot. This place is packed."

Jill faked a smile, looking back at him. "Everything's fine, Jerry—thanks for your concern. I just...ran into an old friend."

"Old friend," Noah muttered. "Yeah, right."

The man named Jerry held out his hand. "Nice to meet you —I'm Jerry Horner, Jill's soon-to-be husband. And you?"

"Noah," Noah replied, shaking his hand a little too hard. "Noah Crawford."

"Always nice to meet a friend of Jill's," Jerry said, wincing at their handshake. "That's a strong grip you have there."

Noah released his hand, and Esme noticed how red Jerry's was. Noah shrugged. "Sorry—force of habit."

Jerry laughed. "Hey, no problem. So, I assume you already RSVP'd to the wedding?"

Noah shook his head. "No, I didn't."

Jerry frowned. "Oh—why not? It's going to be a great day. We want all our friends and family there to celebrate with us."

"I think Noah's invitation must've gotten lost in the mail," Jill said, laughing nervously. "It doesn't matter, though—I'm sure Noah has better things to do that day."

Jerry shrugged. "Maybe, maybe not. He doesn't even know the date yet. Do you, Noah?"

Noah gritted his teeth. "Can't say that I do, no."

"It's August second," Jerry said with a smile. "We're having it at that cute little chapel on Merton Street. You know, with the garden out back?"

"Sounds lovely," Noah mumbled.

"If you could come by, that would be amazing," Jerry said,

unable to see the tension in the air. "The wedding ceremony is taking place at ten a.m., then we'll celebrate with brunch afterward. The food and cake are worth coming for alone—trust me. What do you say?"

Jill turned to Noah. "Really, there's no pressure. If you don't think you can handle it..."

Noah's eyes narrowed. "Oh, I can handle it. Can I bring a guest?"

Jerry shrugged. "Sure, why not? The more the merrier."

"Good," Noah replied, grabbing Esme's hand and locking his fingers with hers. She frowned and looked down at them. "Because I'm bringing my girlfriend, Esme Fairhaven."

When Jill looked at Esme again, there was jealousy in her eyes. "Your girlfriend? I see. Well, at least she'll be well-dressed for the wedding."

Esme looked down at her gown, nodding. "Yeah, I do like to dress up."

"Esme and I are getting married soon, too," Noah blurted out. "She's even moving into my apartment. Isn't that great?"

Esme's mouth opened in shock, though she said nothing. Was this how humans found mates on the surface world?

Jill's eyes didn't match the smile she gave. "Yeah...it's wonderful. I'm happy for you two."

Jerry patted Noah's shoulder with a grin. "And hey, maybe we can come to your wedding. Isn't this all so wonderful? We can do couple things now. Like take trips together!"

"Sure," Jill muttered. "Anyway, Jerry, we should get going now. We have to get to work."

Jerry nodded. "Right. Well, if you and your girlfriend ever want to catch up over coffee, just give Jill a call. We'll be taking time off soon so we'll be able to properly sit down and chat. Everything will be better when the hectic wedding is over. Those things take so much work."

"Sounds great," Noah muttered, sarcastically.

Jill tugged on Jerry's hand. "Come on—you know I can't live without my coffee, and the line is getting longer by the minute."

Jerry laughed. "Typical Jill, huh? See you at the wedding!"

As Jerry entered the café with Jill and the door closed behind them, Noah pulled away from Esme's hand and sighed. "Sorry about that. I don't know why I lied."

"I do," Esme said, the butterflies disappearing when their hands dropped. "Jerry was flaunting his perfect relationship with Jill right in your face. You had to do something to prove you weren't bothered by it."

"Oh, good. You understand," Noah said, sighing in relief. "So, you'll play along?"

Esme smiled. "Of course. I guess you're going to their wedding, then?"

"I have no choice now," Noah said, wistfully looking through the window at Jill and Jerry laughing at something. "If I don't show up, Jill will think I chickened out. I have to put on a brave face—as hard as it is."

"What happened between you two?"

Noah looked back at Esme, sighing. "We were in love and planning our wedding. She works for a rival humanitarian organization, and we met at a charity ball. We dated for three years —even moved in together in that place I'm living in now. But eight months ago..."

When Noah trailed off, Esme leaned in. "What happened eight months ago?"

"Sorry—it's just hard it re-live," he mumbled. "Anyway, eight months ago she told me she ran into an old high school boyfriend. Apparently, they were madly in love and dated for four years, but then he moved away for college and they lost touch. I guess they got to talking and realized they still had feelings for each other."

Esme followed Noah as they began walking to his car. "Did she cheat on you?"

"She swore nothing happened between them until she broke it off with me. I'm not sure what to believe," Noah mumbled, reaching for his car doorhandle. "Anyway, she broke up with me and moved out to live with him. He's working for the same charity as she does now. The last I heard they were just dating. I had no idea they were getting married."

"What did you mean before when you said you were so close to being her first choice?"

Noah sighed. "After catching up with Jerry, Jill stayed at a hotel for a week. She told me she had to think it all over—us, Jerry, the future. When she finally came back and told me her decision...it wasn't the name I wanted to hear. Then she took her stuff and left. This was the first time I've seen her since then."

"That's awful," Esme whispered, and Noah nodded. "It seems kind of quick—only eight months. Is that really enough time to decide if you want to be with someone forever?"

Noah shrugged as he got into the passenger seat. "Well, they were together all through middle school and high school. They probably dated longer than me and Jill. And they say you never forget your first love..."

Esme got into the passenger seat, shrugging. "I wouldn't know. I've never been in love before."

Noah started his car engine, looking at her in disbelief. "Never? Not even, like, puppy love?"

Esme shook her head. "No. I mean, I've had a few crushes, sure, but they never worked out. The men were always intimidated by my title—and my father."

Noah laughed. "Yeah, I guess it would be a little nerve-wracking dating a princess. There's always a fear of the king's guards coming after you if you break her heart."

"I guess," Esme mumbled, looking down. "Anyway, there was this duke named Cullen who wanted to marry me. He wouldn't leave me alone, in fact..."

"Oh?" Noah asked, pulling out of the parking lot into traffic. "Do you like him?"

"Of course not! He was rude and desperate. In fact, he tried to bribe me into marrying him by promising he'd get my father to take me back. I had to say no."

"Good for you," Noah said, stealing a glance at her. "I'm proud of you."

Esme felt a warm tingling in her stomach again. "Thanks. Maybe I'll have better luck in Toronto with love—when I'm not too busy trying to do everything on this checklist, that is."

"Yeah, who knows?" Noah asked with a shrug. "Life changes fast. A year ago, I thought I was marrying the love of my life. Now, here she is with another man, and I'm all alone."

Esme placed a hand on his shoulder. "I'm sorry, Noah."

He cleared his throat, and she could tell he was trying to push his emotions away. "Thanks, but I'll be fine. It's all in the past now. I need to move on—for real this time. Maybe get out more and find someone new."

"Well, if you help me with my checklist, maybe I can help you?" Esme asked with a smile.

Noah laughed. "Deal, Princess."

"And one more thing, Noah. What you said before—about being alone? You're not. You lost Jill, but maybe it was for a reason. Where I come from, we believe in fate and magic. You deserve to be with someone who won't hesitate to choose you."

He considered her words for a second. "Thanks, Esme."

Noah drove her to the pharmacy first, waiting in line with Esme to get her the painkillers. The pharmacist explained the medication and the side effects.

"Good thing there's free Canadian healthcare, huh?" Noah asked. "Sadly, it's not free everywhere."

Esme frowned. "Why not? That's awful."

Noah shrugged. "I agree, but I don't make the rules. Is your healthcare free where you come from, too?"

Esme thought of all the magic her fairy godmother had performed. "Yeah, but it's a little different than yours. Anyway, where to next?"

He pointed at her dress. "I told you we needed to get you some new clothes. Your dress is appropriate for a wedding, but everyday wear? Not so much. I don't want you to be a target for people to make fun of."

Esme looked down at it, shrugging. "If you say so. Do you have a marketplace where you can barter and trade for new clothes?"

Noah laughed. "Not since the medieval ages. But there's a cool thrift store a few blocks from here. You can buy all kinds of stuff there. Come on—I'll show you where it is. I may as well pick up a suit for the wedding, too."

Noah led Esme to the car again, opening the door for her. Once they were in, he drove to the thrift store down the street, the neon sign hanging above it that read FINDERS KEEPERS. Noah parked in the busy parking lot, leading Esme inside through the bustling crowd of shoppers.

"Wow," she muttered, looking around the store. It had racks of clothes and the store resembled a giant warehouse. "This reminds me of the markets back home."

"Oh, yeah?" Noah laughed. "It does have a wide selection— second-hand clothes, trinkets, decorations. Some people prefer to shop at big box stores for new stuff, but I think there's a charm to old things."

Esme smiled. "Me, too—and hey, look over there!"

Esme rushed toward a rack of colorful women's pantsuits.

"These are so fancy. Very different from the gowns we wear back home."

Noah checked the price tag. "And affordable, too. The women where I work wear these all the time. Want a couple?"

Esme smiled sweetly. "If you wouldn't mind."

Noah took a pair in different colors. "All right, where to next—"

The next thing he knew, Esme had run off to a different rack, pulling all kinds of clothes she liked. Most of them were brightly colored with pants instead of trains and skirts. Noah just laughed, struggling to hold all of it in his arms.

"Oh, and these shoes, too!" Esme cried, throwing a pair of sandals into Noah's arms.

Noah stumbled, barely able to see over the height of the clothes anymore. "Uh, I think my arms are going to break soon..."

Esme blushed, taking some of the pantsuits from him. "Sorry—let me help. If you couldn't tell, shopping is my favorite sport."

Noah laughed. "Yeah, I figured that. Let me get a cart."

After Noah returned with a cart, he threw all of Esme's clothes inside and sighed in relief that he didn't have to carry them anymore. Esme took some sparkly sneakers off the rack and put them in the cart, pulling Noah's arm to lead him toward a rack of used tuxedos.

"Oh, over here!" she cried. "You'd look great in this blue one with the green handkerchief. It'd match your pretty eyes."

Esme blushed in embarrassment as soon as she said it. *Way to play it cool,* she thought.

Noah nodded, picking the tuxedo hanger off the rack and holding it against his chest. "Hey, I think you're right. I'll still try it on to make sure it looks good."

"Oh, I'm sure anything will look good on you."

Fortunately for Esme, Noah didn't hear that one as he entered the changing booth. She waited patiently a few minutes—wishing she had her fairy godmother's magic to speed things along—before Noah exited, making Esme's jaw drop. He fit perfectly into the tux and looked even more handsome.

"So?" he asked, adjusting the bowtie. "It's too flashy, isn't it?"

"Are you kidding?" Esme asked, looking him up and down. "You look so good, Jill's going to regret leaving you."

Noah beamed. "That's what I was going for. I think I'll take this one. Have you gotten enough clothes?"

Esme glanced at the full cart. "I think so—at least, until I get my own money. Thanks again for taking me out."

Noah shrugged. "No problem. It was fun shopping with you —you find everything so exciting. It's adorable."

Esme giggled as Noah went back into the booth to change into his old clothes. "Well, I've never been to Toronto before. Everything in the city is new to me."

And everything on Earth, she wanted to add.

Noah came out a second later in his old clothes, carrying his tuxedo over his arm. "I'll have to show you some more things so you don't leave empty-handed. Speaking of leaving empty-handed, I should find Jill and Jerry a wedding present."

Esme groaned. "You have those here, too? I remember all the presents my best friend's parents got. Having to sit there and watch them open a thousand gifts wasn't fun."

Noah laughed, aiming the cart toward the home decoration section of the store. "I bet. It's only exciting when you're the one getting the presents."

Esme nodded. "And I hear my parents got even more presents when they were married. Not only was it a wedding, but my mother was coronated as the queen, so it was a huge celebration. I saw the pictures—someone gave them a griffin."

Noah frowned, glancing at her. "A griffin? Like the mythical creature?"

Esme wondered how she was going to explain that slip-up when she noticed a seeing guide dog—a golden retriever—helping a blind man around the store. "Griffin was the name of our pet. It looked similar to that."

Noah noticed the creature she pointed at it, nodding. "Oh—you mean a dog. Cute name."

Esme sighed in relief she had thought of something. "Yeah—he was pretty loyal to Mom, too. He stayed by her side until he died of old age. I don't recommend it as a gift, though—they can be a handful."

Dogs and griffins both, Esme thought.

Noah browsed an aisle of picture frames. "Jill never liked dogs, anyway. But I'm curious...what does your mother think about your father sending you away? Didn't she try to stop him?"

Esme looked down. "She passed away a year ago. We were pretty close—we spent a lot of time together. Sometimes...she was my only escape from everything. A safe place to rest my head. It's just me and my father left now."

Noah turned to her, looking upset. "Oh, Esme—I'm sorry."

"It's okay," she said with a shrug. "You didn't know."

"That must be hard. My parents are both still alive, but I know I'll be devastated when they die—even though my dad and I aren't that close," he mumbled, looking back up at Esme. "That's the part that doesn't make sense, though. His wife died, and he sends away his child next?"

Esme turned away, unable to look at him. "I haven't been the best princess, Noah. I've been disrespectful, bratty, uncivilized—"

"Who hasn't been all those things from time to time?" Noah said, placing a hand on her shoulder. "Look, I don't know what you did or the customs in your kingdom, but he shouldn't have sent you away. I'm sure of it."

Esme held back tears, turning to face him. "Thank you, Noah. Now, if you wouldn't mind—can we talk about something else?"

He nodded. "Of course—like what the hell I'm going to get Jill. I'd really like to put a flaming bag of crap on her doorstep, but I don't think they sell that here."

Esme snorted. "I did that once to a royal family I was in a feud with. Good times."

Noah glanced at her, laughing. "Really? What happened?"

"Oh, they were furious. Father punished me for it, too, by not letting me out of my room for a week. I guess I should've seen my exile coming, really. Maybe I was blind. And ignorant."

When Esme turned silent, looking sad again, Noah wanted to cheer her up. He grabbed an orange vase. "What about this? It's not too expensive, and they won't know it came from the thrift store after I scratch the tag off."

Esme nodded. "I think it's fine. Jill should just be grateful you're getting her something after leaving you."

"Tell me about it," Noah muttered, putting it in the overflowing cart.

Noah took the cart to the front of the store, waiting in line next to Esme. When it was their turn at the cash register, Noah paid on his credit card, dividing his things from Esme's in separate bags.

"Do you need my help carrying it out to the car?" Noah asked as he took his receipt.

Esme shook her head, picking up the bags. "Please—if there's one thing I'm good at, it's carrying new clothes."

Noah laughed as he followed her out the door. "If you say so."

After he helped Esme put the bags in the backseat, she hopped in next to him. "Where to now?"

He smiled as he started the car. "Well, we could start looking for apartments, but I want to show you around Toronto first. Think of it like...a royal tour."

"Sounds exciting," Esme said with a grin, buckling her seatbelt as Noah pulled out of the parking lot.

As they drove along, she stole a glance at Noah, starting to wish the day with him would never end.

CHAPTER 6

Noah pulled into traffic, checking his watch. "It's only eleven-thirty. What do you say we spend the afternoon sightseeing, then check out some apartments?"

Esme smiled. "I'd like that. What do you have in mind?"

Noah pointed up as he waited in traffic at a red light. Esme glanced out the window, noticing a giant tower in the distance. It stretched to the sky with a tall spire. It loomed over the town and looked like it had a small, orb-shaped room attached to the middle of the building.

"What's that?" Esme asked. "We don't have that kind of architecture where I'm from."

"No? That's too bad. That right there is the CN Tower—it's five-hundred meters high, the tallest building in Toronto. It has a spinning 360-restaurant in it where you can look at the city from up high. It's kind of become a national symbol for Canada."

"Cool," Esme said, looking up at it. "I've never been that high before. Is that where you're taking me?"

Noah nodded as the traffic moved again. "If that's okay with you. Are you sure you'll be all right up there?"

"Only one way to find out," Esme said with a smile.

Noah drove past a sign displaying big letters that read CANADA—with swarms of people taking pictures in front of it —before driving toward the CN Tower. Noah paid for parking on the street before stepping out with Esme, leaving their dozens of bags of clothes in the trunk. She followed him through the crowds and entered through the double doors.

"Sorry about the line," Noah said, standing on his tippy-toes to look ahead. "The CN Tower is super popular—both with Canadians and tourists."

"Too bad my Fairy Godmother isn't here to magically fly us to the top..."

Noah looked back, frowning. "What?"

"Nothing," Esme said sweetly. "I'm just excited to see it."

When the line started moving, Noah paid the entrance fee. The guard took it and gestured for them to move along. They stepped into a long room, following it to the end where several elevators waited.

"Here we are," Noah said, holding the elevator door open for Esme. "We're riding it to the top."

As Esme crowded into the elevator with Noah and the other tourists, she looked out the glass window. As the elevator ascended, the view of Toronto became more beautiful. She could see rooftops, the lake, and parks from above as cars and people on the streets became as small as ants.

Esme whistled. "Toronto sure is a beautiful place."

Noah smiled. "And there's a lot to see."

When the elevator dinged, Noah had to gently nudge Esme away from the window to follow him. They stepped into that funny, orb-shaped room she had seen from a distance, and it had more windows and binoculars to look at the city with.

Esme immediately ran toward a set of binoculars, looking out. "Wow—I can see everything up close!"

Noah pointed out a neighborhood through the binoculars, standing behind Esme. "See that row of houses in the distance? That's where I grew up. My mother's a retired professional cleaner, and my dad works as a detective."

"That's awesome," Esme said, glancing back at Noah. She then realized how close they were standing to each other.

Noah nodded. "My dad was really tough on me growing up, though—he was a total perfectionist. I guess it came with his job."

Esme sighed. "Yeah, I know what you mean. My dad can be hard on me, too."

"Of course, you understand—you probably had it worse. Your father's a king, after all. No offense, but I'm kind of glad I'm not a prince. Too many responsibilities, so much pressure…"

Esme laughed. "Yeah, everyone thinks it's glamorous. In truth, it's a lot of hard work and sacrifice. I almost wish I grew up here instead, in a normal place."

"Well, Toronto was a great place to grow up—always lots to do. My friends and I would go to the park every night and play basketball. It's a sport where you toss a ball into a net to try to win."

"Sounds like fun. We have our fair share of sports back home too," Esme said. "My friends and I did all kinds of stuff like that when we were young, too."

"Oh?" Noah asked, raising an eyebrow. "Like what?"

All the things she had done in her youth came back to her— like riding griffins with her mother, watching as her fairy godmother cast bubble spells to play in, and growing magical plants in the garden. She couldn't tell Noah about any of it. It broke her heart just a little bit, wanting them to grow closer. Yet there were so many secrets and things she couldn't say.

Esme blushed. "Oh, you know—regular kid things. My best friend, Alva, and I grew up together. We would run all over my father's castle and play games of hide-and-seek."

It wasn't a total lie—she and Alva *had* made the castle their playhouse, stealing magical potions, disturbing spellcasters, and going into forbidden rooms. What she neglected to mention was that her fairy godmother had caught her and her father had banished her to her room. Sometimes, even the portraits would come alive and keep an eye on them.

Noah smiled. "This best friend of yours...you miss her, don't you?"

Esme nodded, looking down. "I really do. I hope I can do everything on my father's checklist...or I'll never see her again. I almost feel guilty for enjoying Toronto when I have so much to do."

"Come on—don't be so hard on yourself. You *did* get hit by a car, after all. And ever heard the phrase, 'all work and no play?'"

Esme blinked.

"No, I guess you haven't," Noah muttered. "Well, what it means is that you have to enjoy yourself every now and then. Spending a few hours exploring Toronto—a place you've never been before and probably never will see again—isn't a bad thing. In fact, it could help you relax and be more focused."

Esme paused, thinking. "Yeah, you might be right. Thanks, Noah."

He smiled. "Anytime. Now, what do you say we get some lunch? They've got some great food here."

Esme nodded, following him across the room. They waited in line behind a few groups of people who were waiting to be seated by the waiter. As he led one group to a small table that overlooked the city, Esme turned to Noah.

"So, you've been here before?"

Noah sighed. "Yeah—once as a kid with my parents, the

next time with Jill. We celebrated our engagement party here. All our friends and family came and were so excited for us to get married. Now I just feel like an idiot for doing all that."

"I don't think you're an idiot," Esme said as the line ahead of them kept moving. "Jill was the one who ruined everything."

Noah smiled. "And good luck to Jerry. Jill could be a handful sometimes—she always had to have the best."

After the line moved again, they were up next to see the waiter. He wore a black and white tuxedo and nodded at them while reaching for two menus. "Table for two?"

"Yes, please," Noah said. "With a nice view."

"Right this way," the waiter said with a smile, gesturing for them to follow him. "Is this your first time at the CN Tower?"

"Not for me, but for Esme it is," Noah said, gesturing at her. "I'm honored I get to be the one to take her here."

"Oh, you'll enjoy eating in a 360-restaurant," the waiter said to Esme, leading them to a cozy table in the back. "The gentle turning is so relaxing. Regular restaurants just won't compare after this."

Esme nodded, taking a seat across from Noah. "I've never experienced anything like it before. This place is awesome!"

The waiter chuckled, setting their menus down. "Glad to hear it. Are you two celebrating something special? An engagement or anniversary, perhaps?"

Esme blushed. "Oh, we're not..."

"Not dating," Noah added. "We're just friends."

The waiter's jaw dropped. "Oh, my—I'm sorry. You two just make an attractive couple—that's all."

Neither of them said anything. Esme could feel Noah's eyes on her, but she couldn't bear to look at him. She kept her gaze on her diamond slippers and felt her cheeks burning.

"Anyway, forgive me," the waiter said, gesturing at the

menus. "I'll give you a few minutes to decide what you'd like. Take your time."

As the waiter walked away, Esme cleared her throat and looked down at the menu. "So, what's good here? I want to try something different."

Noah smiled. "Oh, the cheese plate is delicious. The wine, too. And I think they still have these little chocolates that were amazing."

"Cheese, chocolate, *and* wine?" Esme asked, closing her menu. "Sign me up."

Noah laughed, waving his arm toward the waiter. "Sir? We'd like to order a cheese plate, a bottle of your fanciest wine, and some little chocolates if you still have those."

The waiter nodded, walking over to retrieve their menus. "Excellent choices. Shouldn't take long."

After the waiter walked away again, Noah was the first one to speak. "Tell me—what's your favorite kind of fish?"

Esme thought about all the sea creatures that came from Fairhaven—and how most of them were magical. She just shrugged, reaching for a glass of water on the table. "You go first."

"Jellyfish. Aren't their colors so beautiful?"

Esme nodded, not knowing what jellyfish were. "Oh, uh— yeah. Why do you ask?"

Noah pointed out the window. "Well, after our lunch, I figured we could stop by Ripley's Aquarium. It *is* across the street, after all."

Esme smiled, glancing at the big sign across the street. "Sounds like fun."

"And don't worry—I won't make you kiss any frogs."

Esme looked back, frowning. "What?"

"You know—kissing frogs to turn them into princes? It's what all the fairytales say happens when a princess kisses one."

"Oh, how strange. I've never done that."

"It's funny—I did the opposite," Noah muttered, playing with the rim of his glass. "I kissed my ex—someone I thought was my princess—and she turned into a frog."

Esme placed a hand on his. "I'm sorry, Noah."

"I know. And I'm sorry I keep harping on it—I'm only dragging us down. Let's just have a good day and forget about her and that father of yours."

Esme smiled. "Deal."

A few minutes later after chit-chatting, the waiter brought their food. Esme's eyes widened at the tasty array of the cheese and chocolate balls. The waiter placed the big plate in front of them, then popped open the wine bottle.

"Here you two are," the waiter said, filling up their glasses. "Enjoy!"

Noah pushed the tasting plate toward Esme. "Here—you have the first bite."

Esme picked up a piece of cheese off the plate, popping it into her mouth. "Wow—so creamy."

Noah picked up his, placing it in his mouth. "It's just as good as I remember. How's the wine?"

Esme winced, remembering the last time she had seen alcohol. Spiking the punch bowl was the reason she had gotten kicked out of Fairhaven.

"What's wrong?" Noah asked, noticing the look on her face.

"I just...haven't had alcohol before. It's actually banned in Fairhaven. Father fears it could make people act foolishly. He's right—it did."

"Oh...well, now that you're not in Fairhaven, the same rules don't apply, right?"

Esme thought for a moment and then smiled. "Yeah—exactly. What my father doesn't know won't hurt him."

"That's the spirit," Noah said with a laugh, picking up his

wine glass. He clinked it with Esme's. "Here's to new beginnings."

Esme nodded, bringing it up to her lips. "May they be even better than we've dreamed."

They both took a sip at the same time, swirling the red liquid around in their mouths to taste all the flavors. They both pulled back and nodded.

"Delicious," they said in unison, then laughed.

"Only one last thing to try—the chocolate balls. Are you ready?" Noah asked.

Esme shook her head. "I had the first bite of cheese. You go ahead this time."

Noah nodded, picking up the chocolate ball off the tooth-pick. Esme watched as he placed it in his mouth and nodded. "Oh, yeah—that's gotta be what heaven's made of. You try."

Esme picked it up next. "You know, that puts my servants' cooking to shame. I could eat a million of these chocolate balls."

Noah laughed. "Same here, but then I probably wouldn't fit into my tux for the wedding. You do have chocolate back home, right?"

Esme nodded, biting into another one. "Oh, of course—but Father demands I watch what I eat. Royals were supposed to be slim and attractive, he always said."

Noah shook his head. "That's awful. I can't imagine living under so much scrutiny."

"There were a lot of difficult parts. But don't feel too sad for me—life in Fairhaven was still happy."

"We have a saying here—there's no place like home."

Esme nodded, wiping her mouth with a napkin. "Exactly. As beautiful as Toronto is, I wasn't born here. But maybe I should try to make it feel like home if I can't get back to Fairhaven..."

Noah rose to his feet, pushing in his chair. "Let's not think like that. I told you—only positivity from here on out. Let's head over to the aquarium."

Esme nodded, pushing in her chair as she followed Noah to the waiter. He paid the bill and tipped. When they walked down the corridor and entered the elevator of windows, he pulled out his cell phone, typing something in.

"What is *that*?" Esme asked, pointing at it.

"Oh, this? It's my iPhone," Noah said with a frown. "You don't have phones where you come from?"

Esme shook her head.

"Then how do you communicate with people across long distances?"

She couldn't tell him it was through a magical singing clam, so she just shrugged. "Fairhaven's a small kingdom. If we want to say something to someone, we just go over and tell them. Sending a letter works, too."

Noah gestured at the window. "Toronto's a big city—lots of people. We need phones. I'm looking up some apartments that are available for a showing later today. What about this one?"

When Noah held up his phone, Esme looked closer, realizing it had a picture of a small living room. The words above it read FOR RENT, ONE BEDROOM. SHOWING AVAILABLE ANYTIME.

"That looks nice," Esme said.

"And cheap, too," Noah added, pulling his phone back to look at it. "I wonder why. Doesn't have any other pictures, though. We can check it out once we're done at the aquarium."

"This is so exciting," Esme said with a smile as the elevator dinged at the bottom level. She stepped off, following Noah through the crowd. "That could be my future apartment."

Noah smiled. "See? I told you things were looking up."

After walking outside and getting into his car, Noah drove them across the street, finding parking outside the aquarium.

Parents with their children, elderly couples, and students on field trips all strolled along next to them.

Noah walked up to the booth, pulling out his wallet. "Two admission tickets, please."

"Here you go," the employee in the booth said, handing them to him. "Enjoy your time at the aquarium."

As Noah and Esme entered the aquarium, it was even more packed inside. Noah reached for her arm and held onto it tightly. "Stay next to me—just so we don't get separated."

"Okay," Esme said, looking down at Noah's arm as she felt something growing for him. "But I'm sure you'd be able to find me. My pink gown sticks out."

Noah snorted. "Good thing you haven't changed yet."

Esme pointed at a tank. "Oh, those creatures look cool. I love their shape."

"They're called seahorses," Noah said, walking toward them. He began reading the plaque on the wall. "It says here that the male seahorses carry the babies instead of the females. They're one of the only species that does that. Who would've thought?"

"And they mate for life," Esme said, reading the other plaque on the wall. "Unlike other fish, they're extremely monogamous and never change partners."

"Jill could learn a thing or two from them," Noah muttered. "Oh, look—those are the jellyfish I was telling you about."

Esme and Noah walked along the tanks, noticing the pink jellyfish swimming around. They looked like babies that were as small as specs of dust. They flitted around in the tank, sticking in small groups.

"Turns out jellyfish aren't really fish at all," Noah muttered, reading their plaque. "Well, I guess I'll have to find a new favorite fish. Maybe a shark. Ever heard of those?"

Esme shook her head as they continued down the corridor. "No, I haven't. Have you ever spent time with one?"

Noah laughed. "Are you kidding? They can be dangerous. They're fierce predators of the ocean with lots of teeth."

Esme shivered. "Oh, that doesn't sound good."

"Then you'd better not look up," Noah said, "because they're swimming over our heads."

But Esme *did* look up, noticing several sharks swimming above them in a tank that had been attached to the roof of the corridor. But instead of fear, she felt awe as she watched them. The water was so clear and blue and the fish looked happy.

"Wow," Esme murmured, her eyes glued to the ceiling. "They're all so amazing. Thanks for missing a day of work to take me here, Noah."

Noah shrugged. "Believe me—going out around town was a lot more exciting than paperwork. I've been working non-stop these past few months, ever since..."

When he trailed off, Esme knew what he meant. "I understand. It's good to get out, isn't it?"

When Noah nodded, Esme felt a pang of sadness. Her father rarely let her out of the castle. Even though it wasn't her home, Toronto was beginning to feel like freedom.

"Aw, look!" a woman ahead of them said, pointing up as she held the hand of her boyfriend. "It looks like those two fish are kissing."

When Esme and Noah looked up, they realized it was true. Two red fish had stopped above them to press their noses together. Noah didn't know exactly what they were doing—sharing food, maybe—but it looked romantic. He couldn't help but feel envious that even fish had someone.

When they both looked back, the couple in front of them was kissing underneath the fish.

"Come on—let's get out of here," Noah whispered, grabbing her arm. "Let's see what else the aquarium has."

For the next hour, they wandered around, peering in at the tanks. Esme saw all kinds of incredible creatures she never knew existed. As they walked toward the exit, throwing out their day passes, Noah pulled her into a photobooth.

"Smile," he persuaded, nudging her to look at the camera.

As it snapped a picture of them, Noah and Esme stepped out. He pulled out the long strip of photos—saving one for himself and one for her.

"For you," he said, handing it to her. "When you get back home, you'll look at it and remember our time together."

She smiled, holding the photos close to her chest. "Thank you, Noah. It's a lovely gift."

Noah nodded, clearing his throat. "You're welcome. Well, I think it's time we get down to business. Ready to check out those apartments?"

"Of course. Lead the way."

As Esme followed him, she thought he was blushing—but couldn't be sure.

CHAPTER 7

As Noah and Esme got into his car, he pulled out his cell phone again, finding the address for the open apartment. As he plugged it into his GPS, Esme noticed a small store across the street that read BEST DEAL PAWNSHOP. It had many baubles and gold trinkets sitting in the window.

"What's that store?" Esme asked, pointing in the distance.

Noah briefly glanced up before looking back at his phone. "Oh, that? It's a pawnshop. You can buy and sell things there—like jewelry."

Esme removed the tiara off her head, looking down at it. "Sounds just like the markets back home. I wonder…"

Noah noticed her fiddling with the tiara. "What do you have in mind?"

"Well, you said it yourself. Apartments aren't cheap. If I like the one we're going to see, I'm going to have to pay for it somehow. There's only one solution."

It took Noah a second to understand what she meant. "You're going to sell your tiara?"

"It should be worth a lot of money, and it's one thing I don't really need—unlike my diamond slippers."

Noah doubted that it would be worth much—it didn't look like a regular tiara he had seen before—but he still nodded. "Okay, I guess that could work. Won't you miss it, though?"

Esme caressed it one last time. "Of course—it was sized perfectly for my head, you know. My own mother gave it to me."

She had a brief flashback of the ceremony as a child—her mother lovingly setting the tiara on her head, smiling down at her. Her father had been too strict and demanding, adjusting the crown for a while, but her mother insisted she looked perfect.

She missed her terribly.

"Wow, I'm sorry," Noah said. "Won't it be hard to give your tiara up since it came from your mom?"

"Very much. But I have no choice. What else did Father expect me to do when he left me here without any money?"

"Yeah, he could've at least given you an allowance," Noah said, starting the ignition. "All right—I'll take you to the pawnshop. Just be careful, though. These pawnshop owners will take all they can from you if you're inexperienced."

"Sounds personal. Did they do that to you?"

He nodded, pulling into traffic. "Yeah—I sold an expensive watch of mine to be able to afford an engagement ring for Jill."

Esme looked up at him. "Oh, I'm sorry. Did you ever get the watch back?"

He shook his head. "No—it was sold when I went back there. Who knows where it is by now? That's why I asked if you'd miss the tiara—you may never be able to find it and buy it back one day."

"That's okay," Esme said as he pulled into the pawnshop parking lot. "Father will just have to make me a new one. If I manage to get home, that is."

Esme got out of the car, following Noah to the door with the bars on it. They opened the front door with the chime of a bell. Several people were in the store—some trying to sell items, others browsing the display cases. A bearded man with a badge that read OWNER was arguing with an elderly man.

"Come on—you have to take it," the elderly man said, thrusting a watch at him. "I really need the money. I need to buy food with it!"

"Not my problem. Like I told you before, that watch is useless," the owner spat. "But that wedding ring on your finger looks like it could be worth something. Is it pure gold?"

The elderly man pulled back, looking angry. "I'd never sell that! My late wife bought me that ring when we were young. We were married for fifty-six years. It's too important to sell."

The owner rolled his eyes. "Hey, I didn't ask for your life story. If you won't sell me that ring, then we have nothing to discuss."

"But—"

"Move it along, old man. Can't you see you're holding up the line?"

The elderly man scowled, thrusting the watch into his pocket. "Go to hell."

He turned around, storming past Esme and Noah. Noah leaned in to whisper in her ear. "I told you—some pawnshop owners are like snakes. If you have nothing they want, they treat you like garbage."

"Pretty rude," Esme said, and Noah nodded in agreement.

When the owner turned and saw Esme, he grinned. "Wow —hello there, pretty lady. Nice gown. Did you just step out of a fairytale book?"

Esme shook her head. "No—these are just my regular clothes. I'm here to sell something."

The owner smirked. "Oh? Why don't we talk privately in my office? We can share some champagne—"

"Watch the way you speak to her," Noah threatened, "or you'll be missing a few teeth by the end of this conversation."

The owner held up his hands. "Hey, no need to get angry! I didn't know she had a boyfriend."

Noah sneered. "You shouldn't be speaking to any woman like that—whether they have a boyfriend or not. Apologize to her."

The owner turned to Esme. "My sincere apologies. I hope I haven't offended you."

"It's all right," Esme said, glancing at Noah. "Anyway, as I was saying, my name is Esme. I saw your pawnshop across the way and decided to come in."

"Well, you made a good decision," he said with a smile. "The name's Marty Best. I'm the owner of this pawnshop, and I'm always on the hunt for valuable things."

"Glad to hear it. Now, I have this tiara to sell—"

"A tiara?" he asked, scoffing. "Get real—nobody owns a real tiara. You're just like that last guy who wanted to sell me his worthless watch."

Esme shook her head, handing it over. "Take a closer look at it. I'm sure you won't be disappointed."

Marty sighed. "Look, I'm a very busy man. I don't have time to waste on a hunk of worthless junk—"

"Just look," Noah said, firmly. "It won't kill you."

Marty rolled his eyes, picking up a pair of glasses. They weren't a regular pair—they looked like a jeweler's loupe, designed to examine objects in great detail. He took the tiara out of Esme's hands, placing it on the counter as he examined the gems set in gold.

He pulled back, his eyes widening. "My God...are those real?"

Esme nodded. "Yes, that's what I was trying to tell you before. It's all authentic. How much would it be worth?"

"Hang on—I'm a bit in shock. I've just never seen this many diamonds before," he said, his eyes as big as saucers. "Let me see..."

He placed the tiara on a small scale, looking at the numbers. Esme and Noah waited to hear the magic number.

He took off his loupe, looking excited. "It's worth more than I have in my register. Wait here—I need to access my safe."

As he went into the backroom, leaving the tiara behind on the desk, Noah turned to her. "I'm shocked, too. I had no idea it could be *that* valuable."

Esme smiled. "We may not have many materials from where I come from, but my father doesn't skimp on tiaras."

Noah smiled. "Smart thinking. Why don't we wander around the store while we wait?"

Esme nodded, grabbing the tiara so nothing would happen to it. She looked through the display cases with the rest of the people in the store. She came across a golden watch, noticing a familiar inscription on it.

"Noah?" she called out. "Can you come here?"

He tore his gaze away from a necklace, walking over to her. "What's up?"

"That watch has your name on it," Esme said, pointing at it. "Look!"

When he looked in through the glass, he gasped. "You're right! Esme, I think that's my old watch I sold. What are the odds we'd find it here?"

"Must be fate," Esme said with a smile. She glanced at the price tag. "It says it's five-hundred dollars."

Noah groaned. "I don't have that much—not after today. Maybe if I'm lucky, it'll still be here by payday."

A woman walked over, glancing at the watch. "Oh, that's very nice. My son's name is Noah. I wonder if he'd like it for his birthday..."

Noah sighed, glancing at Esme. "Or maybe not."

Esme looked at the watch again. "Is the watch *really* special to you?"

Noah nodded. "My grandfather bought it for me—engraved with my name—as a birthday gift. I didn't want to sell it, but I felt like I had to. Jill wanted a fancy ring and I didn't want to disappoint her. It was all for nothing now, though."

Esme was about to respond when she heard the door to the backroom open. Marty returned with a big grin, carrying a giant suitcase. He set it down on the counter as Esme and Noah walked back over. Everyone in the store murmured and stared, wondering what was going on.

"So?" Esme asked. "How much is it worth?"

Marty opened the suitcase, revealing racks of money. "Now that I've taken a proper look at it, I estimate it to be worth fifty thousand dollars."

Noah and Esme said nothing, their eyes wide. The rest of the people in the shop looked shocked, too, as everything turned silent.

"Is it *really* fifty grand?" Noah asked, crossing his arms. "Or is that the lowest you're going so you can sell higher?"

Marty laughed. "I do have to make a profit, you know. Buy low and sell high is my motto. If I can sell this to the right buyer, I'd be set for months. Rest assured, I'm giving you the best deal possible—no need to go to other pawnshops in town."

Esme turned to Noah. "What do you think?"

"Well, fifty-grand *is* a lot of money—especially for someone who doesn't have anything."

"Will it be enough for an apartment?"

Noah laughed. "Are you kidding? You could rent a dozen apartments with this."

"I only need one. Well...do you think I should sell it?"

Noah shook his head. "I can't be the one to make that decision. It's your tiara—your choice."

Esme thought about it for a moment, nodding. "We'll do it."

Marty beamed. "Excellent! Here's your money—and be careful with it. If you get mugged, it's not my problem. I won't be giving you a refund."

As Marty took the tiara into the backroom, Esme sighed. "Goodbye, tiara. Maybe we'll meet again one day."

He popped his head through the doorway. "A pleasure doing business with you. If you ever have anything else to sell, don't hesitate to drop by. You two have quickly become my new favorite customers."

"Wait," Esme said, grabbing the suitcase of money. "I want to make a purchase, too."

Noah frowned. "Of what?"

Esme pointed over her shoulder. "There's a watch over there with the name Noah. It's selling for five-hundred."

"Uh-huh. I'm familiar with it," Marty said, walking back over. "It's been hard to sell since it's engraved. I took it with the hopes that I'd find a buyer with the name Noah."

"You have," Esme said, glancing at Noah. "It was his watch originally before he sold it, and then it ended up here."

Marty looked surprised. "Really?"

Noah nodded. "Yes, it's true. I came back to buy it and it was gone. Must've been being cleaned or something. And while it's nice you want it back for me, Esme, you don't have to—"

Esme ignored him, looking at Marty. "I think you should sell it to me at a discount after giving you the tiara. I'm thinking... three-hundred dollars instead."

Marty considered it, then shook his head. "Three-seventy-five."

Esme looked him dead in the eye. "Three-fifty."

Marty thought for a moment before he grinned. "You know how to haggle, lady—I'll give you that."

Esme shrugged. "We had a marketplace back home. I've had some practice. So, what do you say?"

Marty walked over to the display case, opening it with a key he kept in his pocket. The woman who had looked at it previously seemed jealous they had gotten to it first. Marty locked the display case, walking back over with the watch in his hand.

"Three-fifty it is."

Esme reached into her suitcase, pulling out the correct number of bills. "Here you are."

"And here *you* are," Marty said, handing over the watch. "Now, is there anything else I can do for you?"

Esme shook her head, taking the suitcase and the watch. "Not today. Thanks a bunch."

As Marty dealt with the next customer, Esme turned to Noah. "Here you go—it's all yours now. I can't erase the heartbreak Jill caused you, but having your grandfather's watch back is something I can do."

Noah gawked as he took it from her. "My God, Esme...I don't know what to say. Thank you. Thank you so much."

Esme shrugged. "Please—it was the least I could do after the awesome afternoon adventure you took me on."

Noah put it on his wrist immediately. "Thank you, Esme—I won't let it go to waste. But you walking around with that suitcase of money is making me nervous. I don't want you to get robbed. Do you have a bank account you could put it in?"

"Well, I did back in Fairhaven. It's where all the royal family's money was kept. We had this giant Basilisk that kept watch—"

Noah frowned. "Basilisk? Like...the giant mythological snake?"

Esme blushed. "No, ours was just a regular snake. Anyway, I

don't have a bank account here, and I can't go back to Fairhaven. I don't even have I.D. to get a bank account."

Noah nodded. "Yeah, that would be a problem. You'd need a birth certificate, too. I think I have an idea—let's get to Wal-Mart."

As Noah and Esme left the store, she pulled out the checklist in her pocket. "Well, at least I can check one thing off. 'Make some money'. My father always said having your own money was freedom."

Noah nodded. "He's right. Too many people rely on their spouses or parents for money. If those relationships fall through, they have nowhere else to turn. Makes me sad."

Esme looked across the street, noticing the elderly man was still there. He stared at the pawnshop while twirling the wedding ring on his finger.

"Maybe I can check another thing off my checklist and do a random act of kindness," Esme muttered. "Hurry, Noah—before he leaves."

Noah frowned, following her. "What are you doing now?"

When Esme reached the man, she gestured at the pawn-shop. "You were trying to sell your watch, right?"

The elderly man hesitated before he nodded. "Yeah, that's right—but the stubborn owner wouldn't give me anything for it. I mean, it has to be worth something."

"How much did you want for it?"

"Only a hundred dollars. That's all I need for groceries. I don't want to sell my wife's ring, but it's getting to the point where I have no choice."

Esme reached into her suitcase and pulled out a grand. "Here—take this. It should help a little bit."

"Wow," Noah whispered. "Generous."

"Are you serious?" the old man asked. "You'd...you'd just give it to me? A thousand bucks?"

Esme nodded. "Yes—I don't need your watch. Maybe you can sell it. For now, just take the money and use it wisely."

"Oh, thank you!" the man cried. "You don't know how badly I need this. My name is Edgar Little, by the way."

Esme shook his hand. "Esme Fairhaven. A pleasure."

Edgar grinned. "Thank you, Esme. I'll never forget you."

"If you need help after the money runs out, head to Human Connection Shelter," Noah said, pulling out a business card from his pocket. "I work for them. They help people in need from all walks of life—just like you. I'll personally tell my boss to keep an eye out for you."

The man took the card. "I'll keep that in mind. Thank you—both of you."

After the man walked away, Noah turned to her. "That was a nice thing you did, Esme."

She shrugged, scratching off something else on her checklist. "It was the right thing to do. And look—Father will be pleased I've helped a stranger. In many ways, it's because of you. Because you helped me, a total stranger, I can do the same for someone."

She found herself blushing. In such short time, Noah had already managed to change her life for the better. She thanked her lucky stars he had been the one to hit her with a car and not someone else.

Noah smiled. "Then I'm glad I've had such a positive impact on you. Now, come on—this isn't a great neighborhood, and that suitcase is awfully shiny."

Noah helped Esme to the car, and she tucked her suitcase under her legs. He got into the car after her and drove to their local Wal-Mart. She wandered around the store for a few minutes—never having seen one before—until he took her to a section where they sold safes.

"Ah, here we go," Noah said, picking up a heavy safe. "This

looks big enough to keep your money in. It's fireproof, water-proof, *and* requires a code to get into."

"Sounds like a good purchase. And don't worry—I'll buy it."

Noah laughed. "You could buy this entire aisle—maybe more."

After they bought the safe at the register, Esme left with Noah and got into his car. He turned his attention back to his GPS as the robotic voice inside led the way to the apartment.

"Ready to see your first place?"

Esme nodded. "I am. I'll be living there for a month if I'm lucky. If I'm not...maybe permanently. The tiara helped me now, but one day, I'll run out of things that I can sell."

"Don't worry—I'll help you. Anything I can do. Just name it and I'll be there."

Esme bit her lip to hold back a grin. Her first day in the human world, and she had already found a great person. She didn't think it was possible with everything she had heard about the humans.

Noah kept up with traffic, passing a giant stadium to their right. Esme looked out the window with wide eyes. "Wow, what's that place?"

"Oh, that's Rogers Center. It's where the Toronto Blue Jays play."

Esme turned to him. "Birds play in there?"

Noah laughed, briefly glancing at her surprised face. "No, silly—the Blue Jays are a sports team. They play baseball. It's a ball game between two teams. Takes place in a field with four bases. It's really popular around the world, but especially in Canada."

"Oh, okay—I understand. Sorry for having to explain every-thing to me."

He shook his head. "Esme, you don't need to apologize. I don't expect you to know our culture, just like I don't know anything about yours. I'm more than happy to explain anything you want to know—anytime."

Esme smiled. "I'll keep that in mind. Do you think maybe... the two of us could go to a game?"

He nodded, the watch glistening on his wrist in the sunlight. "Sure, though it might take me some time to get tickets. And if you think that's awesome, I should take you to Canada's Wonderful. It's a giant theme park here in Toronto with tons of rides, splash parks, and more."

Esme's eyes widened. "That sounds amazing. We have to go!"

Noah laughed. "As they say, Rome wasn't built in a day. We have plenty of time to see the sights before you have to go back home."

Esme nodded, leaning back in her seat. She didn't think the human world could be so exciting—especially without magic— but Noah made it sound so incredible. She stole a glance at him, wondering if he could feel their chemistry, too. She couldn't believe how fast she had grown attached to someone in a day.

"Almost there at the apartment," he said, looking at the street numbers. "Are you ready?"

Esme smiled. "With you? Of course."

CHAPTER 8

When the GPS beeped, Noah looked to the left. "Ah, here we are—Greenway Apartments."

Esme looked at the dead flowers out front. "Nothing green about it. My fairy godmother could make those flourish again."

Luckily, Noah didn't hear that last part as he concentrated on pulling into the small parking lot. There was only one space left, so he squeezed in between two trucks. Esme looked at the window and grimaced.

"Wow, that's a tight fit."

Noah turned off the ignition and tried to open the door, but it wouldn't budge. "You're telling me. I think we're going to have to crawl out the windows. Just leave them open for when we get back."

"What about our stuff in the trunk? I wouldn't want anyone to steal it."

Noah laughed. "I'd like to see them try. They'd need to be really flexible."

Noah rolled down the windows, crawling out first. Esme shrugged and copied him, her pink gown getting snagged on the doorhandle. She tugged it free and crawled away from the car.

"Sorry about that," Noah said, helping her to her feet. "There aren't any other spots, and the street is full."

"That's okay," Esme said, wiping off her gown. "But if the parking lot is *this* small, I wonder what the apartment will look like."

"Oh, I'm sure it'll be fine," Noah said, leading her toward the building. "We're supposed to meet the landlord upstairs."

Esme nodded, walking through the door into the lobby. She realized it was just as small as a crowd of people tried to push through to their apartments. When they entered the elevator, they had to cram together with five other people, her face nearly mashed against the door.

Esme noticed the sign on the wall. "Thirty-person maximum? You wouldn't even get ten in here."

Noah nodded, standing sideways next to a tall man so he'd fit. "Yeah, the elevator does seem smaller than average. First the parking lot, now this..."

When the elevator arrived on the fourth floor, Esme and Noah let the crowd out first. When it was their turn, the elevator doors almost shut on them, but Noah pried them open and helped Esme through. They followed the signs on the walls to the open apartment.

"Here we are," Noah said, checking his phone for the number. "Apartment 415. Let's see what it looks like, shall we?"

Esme nodded, knocking on the door. A short, dark-haired woman answered it a moment later. "Oh, hello. Are you here for the open apartment viewing?"

"Yes, please. May we come in?" Esme asked.

The lady moved to the side, letting Noah and Esme enter. "Of course. You're our second viewer of the day."

"The first viewers didn't want it?" Noah asked.

The landlord hesitated. "Uh, no. They said they required something with more...legroom. But I assure you, this is a well-maintained apartment. Utilities come included."

Esme nearly walked into a wall when she entered the apartment. It had a small closet—one that could barely hold two jackets—and opened into a living room. There was only enough space for a single chair. The small kitchen connected to the bathroom, and the terrace was so cramped that Esme couldn't even stand out on it.

"This is a lot smaller than the photos," Noah said, glancing around. "There was only one on your website."

The landlord blushed. "Ah, yes—we don't really like photos. We prefer people to come and see the apartment for themselves."

Esme frowned. "Where's the bedroom?"

"Oh, we got rid of it to build an extra apartment next door. Not to worry—there's plenty of space to put a mattress on the floor. Maybe in the kitchen, next to the stove?"

Noah and Esme said nothing for a moment, waiting for the woman to laugh, but she didn't. She looked dead serious about the whole thing.

"No offense," Esme began, "but this apartment is *really* small."

The landlord shook her head. "Small is such a negative word. We prefer to use the terms cozy and quaint. Will you be living here with your husband?"

Esme blushed. "Oh, we're not married."

It was the second time someone had assumed Esme and Noah were dating. She was beginning to feel as if they saw something she missed. Did they give off the vibes of a couple in love? Noah said nothing, thrusting his hands into his pockets awkwardly.

"Oh, I see," the landlord said, glancing at Noah. "My apologies. But this way, you'll have more space in here. It's the perfect apartment for a single person."

Noah didn't look convinced. "Can we have a moment to discuss it?"

The landlord nodded, walking toward the door. "Of course —take your time. I'll be in the hallway."

Once the lady had left, Noah turned to Esme. "You can't rent this apartment."

"Oh, good—it's not just me," Esme mumbled. "I feared living in a big castle would cloud my judgment."

Noah shook his head, able to touch the ceiling. "No, you're right—no one in their right mind would want to live here. But I guess when you don't have much money, you take what you can find. I think you can get a better place—especially with your kind of cash."

Esme nodded. "All right—I won't take it. Have any other places in mind?"

Noah gestured at his cell phone in his pocket. "Yeah, there were a few I saw. Let's get out of here first. No wonder there was such a lack of photos—they don't want anyone to know this place can't fit a grown adult."

Esme giggled. "Oh, I don't know. Having my shower *and* my bed in my kitchen does seem like it could save time."

Noah laughed. "You can make yourself a grilled cheese while you soak in the tub. Versatile, isn't it?"

As he opened the door, he came face-to-face with the land-lord. They hoped she hadn't heard them gossiping about the small apartment. She looked at them with hopeful eyes, holding out a piece of paper.

"Here—I already took the liberty of printing you a renter's agreement," she said with a smile. "So, can I put you down as a tenant? I'm really eager to get some new renters in here."

Esme shifted uncomfortably. "Actually, I think we're going to keep looking for apartments."

The landlord's face dropped. "But...why? I worked so hard on this apartment, you know. My husband and I were partners, but when he died, I had to take on the remodeling myself. He was always better at these things than me."

The woman looked sad, so Esme placed a hand on her shoulder. "Hey, it's all right—the apartment is beautiful. It's just not the right fit for us, because...because..."

"Because Esme might want to have kids," Noah lied. "And there's just not enough room for a bassinet here."

Esme nodded. "That's right. But I can tell you a put a lot of work in it, and I'm sure someone else will want to lease it."

The woman looked hopeful again. "You really think so?"

Esme smiled. "Yes, so don't give up. Thank you for the tour."

"You're welcome," the woman said, beaming. "I'll keep what you said in mind."

After they walked off down the hallway, Noah turned to her. "That was nice what you did—sparing her feelings like that."

Esme shrugged, pulling out her checklist. "The woman looked like she was about to cry, and I couldn't just stand there and do nothing. Besides, 'make someone feel better' is also on my list. Twice today since I bought back your watch. Check!"

Noah laughed as they got into the elevator, and this time, it was vacant and gave them enough room to stand. He pulled out his cell phone. "Good for you. Now, let me look for another listing..."

When the elevator arrived downstairs, he was still going through his phone. Esme followed him outside. "Remember where we parked?"

Noah snorted. "Yeah—sandwiched between two trucks. And look, I found another apartment. Check out this photo."

When Esme looked at it, her eyes widened. The kitchen was spacious, it had an actual bedroom, and the bathroom could fit more than two people inside. "Oh, I like that. Let's head there next."

Noah nodded, slipping his phone into his pocket as he reached his driver's side window. "Sounds good. Let me get in first—I'll back up so you can get in properly. Boy, I won't miss trying to find parking here..."

After Noah had crawled inside and started the engine, he backed the car up, giving Esme the space to jump inside. Once she was, they waved goodbye to the smaller-than-average apartment, and Esme wasn't sad to see it go.

"Tell me about this castle of yours," Noah said as he drove down the street. "How many rooms does it have?"

"At least a hundred—my own private room included. It has a few secret passages, a hall for banquets, and a sports arena."

Noah whistled. "Sounds like a beautiful place to live. These apartments must seem disappointing to you."

Esme shrugged. "They don't have the same space I'm used to, sure. But to be honest...it's nice looking for my own place. I can do whatever I want there. The best thing is that my father can no longer banish me to my room."

Noah smiled. "See? I told you there was a silver lining to all this. Your life as a princess must've kept you pampered, but there *are* perks to being a free adult. Trust me."

Esme hoped he was right as he drove them to their next location. When they pulled into the parking lot, it had more space than the last one, but Esme's eyes widened when she looked up. The building had vines growing on it that never looked like they got cut, dozens of trash bags out front with flies around it, and dog poop that owners hadn't picked up.

"Well," Noah mumbled, pulling into a spot, "this place doesn't look very clean."

"I don't understand," Esme said, turning to him. "The pictures looked spotless!"

Noah nodded, stepping out. "Yeah, well, after that last apartment, you can't trust the pictures. Maybe the inside will be better?"

Esme scoffed as she followed him inside. "That's what you said last time."

"You got me there," he said, opening the door.

As they stepped into the lobby, Esme immediately plugged her nose. The smells of burnt cooking, cigarettes, and dog poop filled her nostrils. Someone had vomited up nasty, orange stuff on the floor, and the building's cleaners hadn't gotten to it yet.

"Just ignore that," Noah said, leading her to the elevator. "We're heading to floor five."

When they stepped inside, one man was standing there. He smiled at them, showing off a row of crusty teeth. Esme shivered, having flashbacks of Fairy Godmother Zamira.

Once the man got off on his floor and the doors closed, Esme exhaled. "Is there any chance the apartment will smell better?"

Noah was still plugging his nose. "The odds are low, I'd say."

When they arrived on the fifth floor, Esme followed Noah to the door of the apartment for rent. They were about to knock when an elderly man in stained, dirty pajamas answered it. He had a messy beard with flecks of gray.

"You two here for the apartment?" he asked, scratching his armpit.

Esme nodded. "That's right. Is this it?"

"Yeah—come on in," the man said, stepping aside. "You look a little fancy for this place, but I'm sure you'll fit in fine."

The apartment didn't match the photos at all. Everything looked stained, dirty, and old—especially the refrigerator that buzzed and sounded like it was going to explode. Most of the cupboards were falling apart, the wall had holes it in, and Noah spotted asbestos on the ceiling.

"Uh, does the furniture come with the apartment?" Esme asked, glancing into the bedroom. "There's a bed here that hasn't been made."

The man nodded. "What you see is what you get. The old tenants couldn't pay their rent, so I evicted them. If you want it, the bed's all yours—just lay down a towel and it'll be like new."

"When was the last time this place was cleaned?" Noah asked, trying to hide his look of disgust.

The man thought for a moment, counting on his fingers. "Let me see...my daddy was still living here, so probably 1998."

Esme opened the cupboard to check out the space and screamed. "Oh my god!"

Noah rushed over. "What is it?"

Esme pointed at the scattering cockroaches. "I don't know what those things are, but they look disgusting."

Noah turned to the landlord. "How can you let your apartment look—and smell—like this?"

"Hey, it's not my fault!" the landlord cried. "It was clean once. Then I took on too many tenants and couldn't keep up with the cleaning, and...well, the mess and cockroaches sort of happened. But it's still a good place to live—I swear. All utilities are included with free Wi-Fi!"

Noah grabbed Esme's arm. "No offense, but I think we're going to look elsewhere for an apartment. Have a good day."

He tugged Esme out of there, and she ran as fast as she could to keep up with him. "Are you still optimistic I'll find a place?"

Noah pulled out his cell phone when they were in the elevator again, nodding. "I am—and now I'm even more determined. I promise you, there are better places to live in

Toronto. My building for one—it has a fitness center and a pool."

Esme perked up at that. "Oh?"

He frowned. "Sorry, but I already checked the website. There aren't any apartments for rent in my building. Anyway, here's another place that looks good."

When Noah showed her the phone, she looked at the pictures. The apartment was on the top floor with a view of Toronto. Everything looked clean, bright, and spacious.

"It looks nice," Esme began, "but so did the others."

"Well, there's only one way to find out if it's your dream apartment or not," Noah said as the elevator doors dinged. "Come on—this isn't over yet."

After Esme and Noah got into the car, they drove a few blocks down to reach the next apartment. It had private parking, so Noah had to pay to get in. Esme looked up in awe as he parked the car.

"Wow—look at how high it goes!"

Noah nodded as he stepped out. "It said it's a luxury apartment. Plenty of storage space for your clothes."

Esme laughed. "That's all I need."

When they stepped inside, the lobby passed their inspection test. Inside, it had a streaming waterfall of different colors with plenty of benches around to sit on. The elevator had a bunch of buttons to press, connecting to a screen that let you make phone calls and contact the landlord. The staff wore fancy suits and looked friendly.

"This place isn't so bad," Noah said, getting into the elevator. "I think we might have a winner here."

Esme grinned as the elevator ascended. "I don't want to celebrate too early, but I think you could be right."

After they stepped off the elevator, they followed it down the corridor to the luxury apartment. The door was already open with multiple couples checking it out. A woman in a black suit with a clipboard stood near the door, smiling at them.

"Hello. Here to view the apartment?" she asked.

"We are," Noah said, shaking her hand.

As Esme stepped inside, her jaw dropped. The apartment matched the pictures perfectly. Everything was spacious and inviting with plenty of space in the living room to have guests over. The bedroom even had a walk-in closet, the bathroom had a jacuzzi, and a small cupboard opened for a private washer and dryer.

"This place is perfect!" Esme squealed. "Do you have an application?"

The landlord laughed, handing her the sheet. "Of course—here you are. I'm sure some of those other couples will want to put their names in, so you'd better hurry. This apartment is going to go fast."

As Esme took a pen from Noah, she heard a loud sawing sound outside. The rest of the couples stopped what they were doing and murmured. Esme walked toward the window, looking down before she noticed a construction site. The sounds of drilling, hammering, and power tools echoed in the distance, shaking the entire apartment every few minutes.

"What's that noise?" Noah asked, placing his hands over his ears.

"Oh, that's nothing to worry about!" the landlord bellowed. "It's just a little construction."

"Doesn't sound little to me," Esme said, trying to block her ears. "How much longer will it go on for?"

"About two years. But they're building an amusement park, so that's something to look forward to!"

Esme glanced at Noah, fear written on her face. Two years? Esme could barely take two more minutes. She handed back the application. To her surprise, the other couples did, too.

"Sorry," Esme yelled, "but it's too noisy for me."

"Wait!" the landlord cried, following them out the door. "You can always buy earmuffs. It's still a great apartment!"

Esme didn't look back as she followed Noah to the elevator. Once they were away from the apartment, the noise started to decrease. The other couples left the building as she looked outside and sighed.

"What if I never find a place, Noah? That's at the top of my father's checklist!"

"You will—I promise," he said, placing a hand on her shoulder. "You just need to have faith."

Esme shook her head. "No, I'm sick of having faith. I had faith my mom would beat her sickness and she didn't. I tried to have faith when my father abandoned me here, and besides your help, Toronto's been a disaster! Faith hasn't gotten me anywhere..."

Noah sighed. "I'm sorry, Esme. Why don't I take you out for some chocolate milkshakes? I know a great diner close to here. The milkshakes there are delicious."

Esme turned around, nodding. "All right—if you say so."

Noah smiled, pressing the button to the main floor. "This is one thing that won't disappoint you—I promise. And hey, I went through about ten apartments before finding mine. It's a process."

Esme sighed. "Oh, I don't know if I can wait *that* long..."

Once they left the apartment, Noah drove her to Lucky's Diner—a small, red and black restaurant a few blocks away. He opened the door for her with a chime, ordering two chocolate milkshakes for them.

As she waited in the booth, he brought them over to her. "Here you go—you get the first sip."

Esme sipped the milkshake and her eyes widened. "That's actually good."

Noah grinned. "I told you. And look, I know you probably don't want to see any more apartments, but I found another listing."

"Can I see it?"

"There aren't any pictures, but it says it's spacious with a giant closet."

Esme groaned. "No pictures? That doesn't sound good."

Noah nodded. "I know, I know—but I actually have a good feeling about this one. What do you say?"

Esme sipped her milkshake again. "All right—but this is the last one. If it doesn't work out, I'll have to crash on your couch."

Noah beamed. "It'd be an honor to host a princess. I'm no court jester, but I'll try my best to entertain."

As Noah shimmied in his seat to show off his dancing skills, Esme laughed, and suddenly, her worries of finding an apartment went out the window.

CHAPTER 9

After Noah paid for the milkshakes, he plugged in the last apartment's address in his GPS and drove off. Esme looked out the window, hoping and praying that this place would be the one. She didn't know what else to do—and she had grown tired of disappointment.

"Oh, Sunnyview Apartments," Noah said, looking up at the street sign. "I've heard good things about this place. Now I remember why it looks so familiar—Jill and I looked at an apartment here before finding the one I'm in now."

"And was it nice?" Esme asked.

Noah smiled, pulling into the parking lot. "Oh, yeah—much better than the old places. You'll see."

Esme took a deep breath as she stepped out of the car, her suitcase of money in tow. "You know, I really respect your people for apartment and house hunting. It's a lot of work."

Noah laughed, walking toward the front doors. "You got that right. What I wouldn't give for my father to let me stay in a castle."

After he opened the door for her, they walked into the lobby. It didn't have a waterfall like the last place, but it did look and smell clean. People who lived there passed by and smiled politely at them—some with their young children in strollers, others elderly.

"Friendly people and a nice, clean lobby," Noah whispered. "We're off to a good start. The listing said the apartment's on the second floor, so it's not too high."

After they got into the elevator—more spacious than the first apartment building they had looked at—they rode it to the second floor. They noticed a well-dressed man standing at the end of the hallway, checking his watch.

When he heard their footsteps, he looked up and smiled. "Hello. Are you here for the apartment showing?"

Esme nodded. "We are. And before we go in, I need to ask... does it have cockroaches?"

"Absolutely not," the man exclaimed. "I'm deathly afraid of them."

Esme sighed in relief. "Oh, that's good to hear."

Noah nodded. "Yeah, you wouldn't believe the places we've been to before this one."

"Really?" the man asked, raising his eyebrows. "Well, I hope this one is more to your liking. I *do* need to warn you about something, though."

Esme's heart pounded in fear. What was it this time? A leaky roof? Violent neighbors?

"What is it?" Noah asked, cautiously.

The landlord sighed. "Actually, why don't I just show you? It's probably better if you see it for yourselves. Then you can decide if you want the apartment or not."

The landlord unlocked the door, gesturing for Esme and Noah to enter first. As they stepped through the doorway, Esme glanced around, gasping. The apartment was average-sized with a single bedroom, open-concept kitchen, and a cozy living room...except the walls were painted a bright, hot pink.

Someone had picked out pink furniture to match. Esme ran her hands along the pink couch, pink leg rest, and fuzzy pink rug. She glanced into the kitchen and noticed the countertops, stove, and fridge had gotten painted over with magenta. When she poked her head inside the bedroom, the sheets were pink with the curtains, carpet, and walk-in closet.

"Wow," Noah muttered, glancing around. "All I can say is... wow."

"I know, I know," the landlord scowled. "It's too pink, isn't it?"

Noah snorted. "Looks like Barbie threw up all over this apartment."

The landlord sighed. "Yeah, my last tenant was a big fan of the color pink. Without my permission, she painted multiple coats of it across the room before she moved out. She left all her furniture here, too, saying it went better with the walls."

Noah turned to him. "You haven't tried to paint over it?"

The landlord sneered. "I did—many times! But the color is too bright. Nothing works! Everyone who's seen this apartment has passed on it."

Esme touched the wall behind them, mesmerized by the color. "I love it!"

The landlord turned to her, frowning. "You do?"

"Are you kidding?" Esme asked, turning around. She fluffed her gown. "Look at what I'm wearing!"

"Well...yes, I saw that," the landlord said, glancing at her gown. "But wearing it is one thing. Very few people would want to live in an apartment so bright and pink—"

"You should see my room back home," Esme said, falling onto the couch. "In fact, I think there isn't enough pink."

The landlord perked up. "Does that mean you want to lease it?"

"That's right," Esme said, opening her suitcase, "and I've got enough money for first and last month's rent."

The landlord's eyes widened. "You aren't messing around, are you? I can't believe someone actually wants this place. I've been trying to rent it for five months. Wait here—I'll be back with the rental agreement."

As he rushed off down the hallway, Esme rose to her feet. "Check out the bathroom. I've got my own tub!"

Esme dragged Noah by his arm into the bathroom, his eyes widening at how pink it was in there. Everything from the fuzzy pink toilet seat to the shower curtain to the bathmat had been painted over. Even the tub—which looked big enough for two and faced the window overlooking Toronto—had been painted pink.

"She really went overboard with that paint, didn't she?" Noah muttered.

Esme got into the tub, stretching out. "I used to have a jacuzzi at the castle. It's not the same thing, but it feels like home. Oh—and the best part is the walk-in closet!"

Noah laughed as Esme rose to her feet, rushing into her bedroom. She opened the pink closet doors, revealing a walk-in closet with plenty of room for shoes, gowns, and slippers. There was even a nook for jewelry.

"Can you believe how perfect this place is?" Esme squealed, turning back to look at Noah. "It's like it was built for me!"

Noah smiled. "See? And you wanted to give up. I told you better things were coming."

Esme flung herself into Noah's arms, surprising him. She hugged him tight as her gown engulfed him. "You were right, Noah. Thanks for never giving up."

He hugged her back. "You're welcome, Esme. I'm just happy you found somewhere to live."

When they heard a throat clear, they pulled back. The landlord stood there with the contract in his hands. "Sorry to interrupt..."

"That's okay," Esme said, pulling out a pink pen from her pocket. "Is this where I sign?"

The landlord nodded, noticing the pink pen. "Yep, right on the dotted line. You remind me of my last tenant..."

Esme laughed, signing her name. "Don't worry—I won't make any changes to the apartment without your permission."

"That's a relief," he muttered, taking the contract back. He held out his hand for her to shake. "My name's Antonio. You ever need anything, knock on my door for help. I live on the first floor in apartment ten."

Esme smiled. "Thank you—you don't know what it means to finally have a place."

"No, thank *you*. This was my last apartment to rent out, and I feared I'd never find a tenant. Will you two be living together, or...?"

"Oh, no," Noah said, glancing at Esme. "I live over in Creek-side Apartments. I just came along to help Esme."

"Here's first and last month's rent," Esme said, handing him the bundle of money. "I'm only supposed to be in Toronto for a month, but...maybe longer. I don't know yet."

"You can stay as long as you like," the landlord said, counting the dollars, "as long as you can afford it, of course. I always value tenants who pay their rent on time. Well, the apartment's yours. Feel free to throw out any furniture you don't like. Oh, and here's your key."

After Esme took the key and thanked him, Noah turned to her. "I'm going to get your things from the backseat."

Esme pocketed the key. "Do you need my help?"

He smiled, shaking his head. "Nah—stay here and enjoy your apartment."

As he walked away, the landlord turned to Esme. "Are you sure you two aren't a couple?"

Esme blinked. "No—we just met today."

The landlord looked surprised. "Oh, I wouldn't have guessed that. The way he looks at you…"

Esme leaned in. "Yes?"

The landlord laughed. "It's probably not my place. Forget I said anything."

"Come on," Esme said. "I won't get upset."

"Oh, all right. Well, I used to work as a professional match-maker before I became a landlord. I ran a business downtown and could spot chemistry from a mile away."

Esme glanced at the door, making sure Noah hadn't returned yet. "So, what are you saying?"

"Let me put it this way—the way he looks at you isn't the way you look at someone you just met. There's an affection there…a spark. If I could see it, I'm sure others will, too."

Esme thought about what he said for a few seconds, the apartment turning silent. Did Noah have feelings for her? She certainly had feelings for him. But her mission was too impor-tant—she wasn't sure she could give time to a relationship right now. And she still hoped to make it back to Fairhaven one day, her true home, and prove to her father that she was a better person.

"I should get going," the landlord said, looking awkward. "Welcome to Sunnyview Apartments. All utilities are included, even cable. And boy, am I glad you came around."

After the landlord left, Esme took a seat on the couch, enjoying the silence. A smile spread across her face. She was in a place that was all hers. Her father, Lady Nyssa, or Senator Remus couldn't control her anymore.

But then she felt a pang of anxiety. Could she be independent? Could she survive on her own?

Her thoughts were interrupted by the door opening. Noah walked in, lugging several suitcases and shopping bags with him. He placed them on the pink rug, doubling over to catch his breath.

"Next time...pack lighter, please," he muttered, taking in a big gulp of air.

Esme rose to her feet, looking through her things. "Did you bring everything at once?"

Noah grinned. "Yep—I live by the motto of one trip or die. Plus, now that I've carried all that, I don't have to go to the gym today. Oh, I just need your safe. Be right back!"

He hurried downstairs, then returned with her safe. He set it down on the couch, huffing and panting.

Esme smiled. "Well, thanks. I should put these clothes away —and change into something that helps me blend in. Wait here."

Noah nodded, sitting down on the couch to turn on the television as Esme pulled her shopping bags into her walk-in closet. She put away clothes she wasn't going to wear, including her pink gown.

"Goodbye, gown," she whispered, caressing the soft fabric. "I'll see you again soon."

She cut the tag off the pantsuit Noah had bought her, pairing it with a simple pair of black flats. Once she had combed her hair and fixed her pink lipstick, she walked out into the living room, standing in front of the television.

"So?" she asked. "How do I look? I've never been in clothes like these before."

Noah turned off the TV, his eyes widening. "You look amazing! But you're beautiful no matter what you wear."

Noah looked embarrassed, blushing as though he hadn't meant to say it. Esme giggled. "Thank you. And now, I can finally check off the biggest thing on my list."

Esme ran into her walk-in closet, removing the checklist from her gown pocket. She walked back into the living room where she scratched off 'find your own place' at the top of the list. When she held it up, Noah rose to his feet with a smile.

"You did it, Esme! I knew you could."

She blushed, putting the checklist in the pocket of her pantsuit. "Yeah, but you helped. If it weren't for a kind stranger running me over—"

"I'm still sorry about that," Noah interjected. "Please, let me make sure you're okay. I'll check you over for bruises."

Esme nodded, sitting down and letting Noah check her out. "All right. But I'm not sorry about it. We probably wouldn't have met, and who knows where I would've been then?" Esme's eyes twinkled. "So, thank you, Noah. And I want you to have this."

When she reached into her suitcase of money, pulling out a wad of bills to hand to Noah, he shook his head. "I can't take that."

Esme frowned. "Why not? I'm only paying you back for the day out and all the clothes you bought me."

Noah took the money out of her hands, tucking it back into the suitcase. "Esme, I think you need it more than I do. Keep it —and use it wisely. Besides, I had fun, so it was worth the dent in my wallet."

Esme smiled. "Thank you—and I had fun too. I guess I should put the money in the safe now."

Noah helped her put the money away, then checked Esme over. When she was fine, healing quickly as her people did, Noah tucked the safe beneath the bed. "Happy to report you're doing better. And it'll be fine here. No one would think to look under the bed."

"Good—I'll need it. And if it's not too much trouble, I could use your help with something else."

Noah shrugged. "Of course—name it."

"Laundry," Esme said, peering in at the bedroom. "The bed is cute and all, but I can't sleep there until I wash those sheets. My gown could use a good washing, too, and I never learned how."

Noah laughed. "Of course—let's get all the stuff you want to wash. I spotted a laundry room down the hall. I guess servants did your laundry back home?"

Esme had flashbacks of her fairy godmother magically removing stains and dirt from her clothes. "Yeah, something like that."

Noah ripped the sheets off the bed while Esme grabbed her dirty gown. She locked the door to her apartment—with Noah teaching her how to use a key because not everyone was as trust-worthy as him—before they walked down the hallway. He opened the door to the laundry room, walking over to a giant washer and dryer.

"Whoa, what are those things?" Esme asked. "They look like robots!"

Noah laughed. "They'll wash your clothes for you. Here— put a dollar in the coin slot."

After Esme did, the washer lid opened. Noah stuffed the bedsheets inside. She put another coin in the washer next to it, shoving her gown and dirty clothes in.

"You want to wash the bedsheets in hot water to kill any bacteria," Noah said, grabbing a bottle of detergent. "This is the soap for your clothes and sheets. For your clothes, you don't normally mix colors."

Esme frowned. "Why not?"

Noah laughed. "Because everything will turn that shade! Believe me, when I first started doing laundry as a teenager, I washed a red hat with a shirt and turned it pink. I learned my lesson. Since you're mixing colors, I recommend cold water."

After Noah clicked the ON buttons to start the two washers, Esme stepped back as they began making noise. "Wow, you're really good at this."

Noah shrugged. "Not really—I've just been doing it a lot longer than you. And now, we wait."

"For how long?"

"Usually an hour."

Esme gawked. "An hour?"

Noah laughed. "You really have a lot to learn. Why don't we head back to your apartment to pass the time? You've got a lot of free channels."

Esme nodded, opening the door. As she and Noah walked into the hallway, they nearly smacked into an older woman. She had gray hair, wrinkles, and a yellow sundress. She was carrying a big punch bowl and swerved out of their way so it wouldn't fall.

"Oh, my!" she cried, glancing back at them. "I almost spilled my punch bowl."

"We're so sorry," Noah said, looking the woman over. "Are you all right?"

She nodded, her thick glasses falling to the bridge of her nose. "I think so. It was probably my fault—I'm a total klutz. My name is Gina Lorenzo."

"Esme Fairhaven," she said, holding out her hand. "This is my friend, Noah Crawford. I just moved into that apartment down the hall."

Gina's eyes widened. "The one with the pink walls? I'm surprised that one was finally rented out. Anyway, you'll love it here—the tenants are real friendly."

"That's good to hear," Esme said, glancing at the punch bowl. "Are you heading somewhere with that?"

"Oh, how silly of me! We're throwing a welcoming party on the roof and I was asked to bring the punch. There've been a lot of new renters over the past few months, so we wanted to welcome them all. I've lived here my entire life."

Esme nodded. "Oh, that sounds nice. Well, have a good time."

As Esme walked away, Gina turned around. "Wait! I'm such a scatter-brain. I meant to ask if you wanted to come, too."

Esme turned to Noah. "Do you want to?"

Noah glanced at the woman. "Will there be food?"

Gina nodded. "Of course—it's a barbeque."

Noah grinned. "Then I'm there. Lead the way. And do you need me to carry that for you?"

"Oh, no, no—I'm fine, but thank you." Gina began walking toward the staircase. "Follow me—we'll have to take the stairs to the roof. So, are you two newlyweds?"

Esme blushed. "Oh, we aren't—"

But Gina wasn't listening. "I was in love once—before my husband died. Another woman in the building recently lost her husband, too. Life goes by so fast. Make sure to appreciate each other while you still can, all right?"

Noah just nodded. "We will."

Esme was out of breath when they reached the top floor, stopping in front of a door that read ROOF ACCESS. Noah opened it since Gina had her hands full, and she nodded at him to thank him and carried the punch bowl onto the roof. Esme and Noah walked out a second later and noticed dozens of renters had gathered.

Several buffet-style tables were set up with all kinds of food —from pizza to hot dogs to apple pie. Gina placed the punch bowl down, spilling some on her dress before she walked away to mingle with the others. Esme walked toward the edge of the roof, looking down.

"Has it sunk in yet?" Noah asked, walking toward her. "That this is your new home?"

Esme laughed. "Not really. Give me a few days and it might."

"Well, it looks like a nice place. I wouldn't mind living here myself."

As Noah trailed off, Esme heard a clatter on the street. She went to the far edge of the roof and noticed a group of people coming out of the closest storm drain. The guards her father promised to send to check on her had arrived—and she hoped she would impress them with what she'd accomplished so far.

CHAPTER 10

Noah followed Esme to the edge of the roof, noticing the men in armored suits. "Whatcha doing over here? Oh, who are those guys? They look like knights. Are they...coming out of the storm drain? That's weird."

Once the knights had helped each other out of the storm drain, they looked around. People walking by stared at them strangely—just as they had done to Esme. One guard looked up, noticing her on the roof, and beckoned to the other guards. They began walking toward the building.

"Oh, it's nothing to worry about," Esme said, turning to Noah. "How do you think I look? Confident? Independent? Unafraid?"

He frowned. "I guess so. Why—what's going on? Do you know those guys?"

Esme knew she wasn't allowed to tell any human where she was from, and she didn't want to get caught explaining it as the guards approached. "As I said, everything's fine. Why don't we enjoy the party?"

Noah looked like he had more to ask, but Esme walked away, heading toward the buffet table. She grabbed a slice of greasy pepperoni pizza, then placed it on a plate. She sat down at a small table that had been set up and used a knife and a fork to cut into the cheesy bread.

When she placed a bite in her mouth, her eyes widened. "Wow...this is really good!"

Noah laughed, sitting beside her with his own piece of pizza. "We have the Italians to thank for it. Pizza is probably my favorite meal ever."

"I can see why. It's very tasty," Esme said, glancing around. "Everyone else is eating it with their hands. Should I?"

Noah nodded. "It's probably best—you'll get the full experience that way."

She put down her fork and knife, grabbing the pizza with her hands. When she took a bite, she closed her eyes, savoring the taste. "Definitely better."

Noah laughed when a drop of the sauce landed on Esme's blazer. He reached over, grabbing a napkin to wipe it off. "As fun as it is eating with our hands, sometimes, we make a mess."

"Oops," Esme said, taking the napkin from him. "Thanks for cleaning me up."

He shrugged, taking another bite of his pizza. "No problem. I bet this food is different from what you had back home, huh?"

Esme continued to rub out the pizza stain. "Very. We didn't eat with our hands, for starters. We had many different forks, spoons, and knives to learn about."

Noah shook his head. "I don't know if I could live with all those rules."

Esme chuckled, remembering all the trouble she had caused. "Oh, I didn't always follow the rules. I got on my father's nerves a lot. It's how I ended up banished, actually."

"Well, no one's going to banish you here," Noah said with a smile. "So, eat as messy as you want."

Esme smiled back. "Maybe I will."

Once they had finished their pizza, Esme glanced toward the staircase to the building, wondering where the guards had gone. Noah rose to his feet and grabbed their dirty paper plates, taking them to the trash.

Esme knew the guards would arrive any second, so she stood up, trying to mingle and look like a regular person. She walked over to Gina who was standing with a middle-aged woman. She wore an old, faded pair of blue jeans, a plain t-shirt, and had bags under her eyes.

"...thanks for coming anyway, Tanya," Gina was saying. "I know these days must not be easy, but we've all missed seeing you around."

Tanya nodded, sadly. "Thank you, Gina. I figured I should start getting out again. No use in moping around my apartment all day. That won't help me..."

"Sorry to interrupt," Esme said, walking over to them. "I just wanted to thank you, Gina, for organizing this party. And thanks for inviting Noah and me."

Gina smiled, moving forward to embrace her. "Oh, it was my pleasure, dear—"

Her wedge heel got caught on the cement, and she went falling forward. Esme caught her before she could fall. "Are you all right?"

Gina nodded after Esme helped her back up on her feet. "Oh, yes—I'm so sorry. I can be very clumsy at times. Thank goodness I didn't have the punch bowl in my hands!"

The other woman clutched her heart. "Glad you're okay, Gina. You scared me there for a second."

Esme noticed Gina's trembling hands. "You're shaking. Are you sure you're fine?"

Gina placed a hand over the other one, trying to stop the shaking. "Yes—I told you, I'm just clumsy. Now, enough about me. Esme Fairhaven, I'd like you to meet Tanya Brewer."

Esme shook her hand, curtseying. "A pleasure to meet you."

"Oh, wow—a curtsy," Tanya said with a laugh. "How cute. Did you just move in? I don't remember seeing you here before."

Esme nodded. "Yeah, I moved in less than an hour ago. I'm renting that completely pink apartment."

Tanya's eyes widened. "I can't believe it finally got rented out. Antonio must've given it to you for cheap, too—he was really desperate for someone to move in. Anyway, welcome to the building. I live next door to you."

"And I live across the hall," Gina said, placing her hands behind her back so no one would notice their trembling. "We're here if you need anything."

Tanya nodded. "Yes—me, too. I work a lot, though, and have three kids, so I might not always be available."

Esme smiled, gesturing over her shoulder at Noah who was cleaning up the mess people had made. "That's all right. I just moved to Toronto and met a new friend—Noah Crawford. He's helped me out a lot."

"I met him earlier," Gina said, looking over at him. "He's quite handsome. Don't you think so, Tanya?"

Tanya looked at him, sighing. "Yes, very much so...but I thought my husband was the most handsome man in the world. He still is in my eyes."

"Your husband?" Esme asked. "Is he here?"

Gina hesitated. "Um, no, dear. I forgot to tell you—"

"It's all right," Tanya interjected. "She didn't know. My husband died a short while ago. Stage-four cancer. It's been hard on me, but especially my three children. He was every-thing to them."

Esme realized this was the woman Gina had spoken of earlier. Suddenly, it made sense.

Gina gave Tanya a side hug. "And they lost their home when

he fell ill and had to move into this building. I knew her husband before he passed—he was a truly kind person."

Tanya nodded, trying not to cry. "He hated that we had to move into this apartment building, but we had no choice. He lost his job and couldn't pay the bills anymore. He wanted to live to see his children grow up, but...life had other plans."

Gina sighed. "So much has been taken from you, dear Tanya."

"Oh, I'm so sorry," Esme said, feeling sad for her. "If you need anything, you know where I live now."

Tanya smiled, though it didn't quite reach her eyes. "Thank you, Esme. That means a lot—"

Their conversation was interrupted by the smashing of plates. Everyone turned around, noticing a ten-year-old boy shattering plates on the ground. He had a devious smirk on his face as he watched their broken pieces scatter everywhere.

"Hey, stop that!" Noah cried, moving toward him. "Those aren't yours to break, kid."

The boy looked up at him, scoffing. "Don't tell me what to do—and don't call me kid. You're not my dad!"

"Excuse me," Tanya muttered to Esme and Gina, rushing toward Noah and the boy. "That's enough, Dylan! You're causing a scene. Now, clean this mess up."

The boy named Dylan stepped on a broken piece, shattering it even more. "I won't. You can't make me!"

"Fine," Tanya huffed. "Then just go back to the apartment. You're grounded."

Dylan knocked over a bunch of red cups before he nodded. "Fine by me. I didn't even want to come to this stupid party, anyway."

He took off, disappearing into the stairwell. As his footsteps faded in the distance, Tanya walked toward Noah, and it looked like she was apologizing to him. Noah nodded and reassured her before helping Tanya clean up the mess. Esme and Gina watched from afar, the party-goers returning to their conversations.

Gina sighed. "Poor Tanya. It can't be easy raising three kids by herself—especially when one is a little troublemaker like Dylan. She told me he only started acting out after his father died. Isn't that so sad?"

Esme nodded, a lump forming in her throat. She felt like she could relate to Dylan. She knew the feeling of losing a parent—the intense grief and anger that followed.

"You said she has three kids," Esme continued, drawing her eyes away from Tanya and Noah. "Where are the others?"

Gina nodded, pointing across the roof. Two kids—a blond-haired boy and a red-haired girl—sat quietly at one of the back tables. The girl looked like she was drawing a picture while the boy was pressing buttons on his calculator. He looked deep in thought as he solved different math equations in a small booklet.

"Oh, they're so quiet that you didn't even notice them. They're nothing like Dylan," Gina said with a chuckle. "And thank goodness for that. Lindsey's six, and she's super creative —into writing, drawing, and painting. Tanya's other son, Vincent, just turned eight. He's a bloody math genius. I don't know how he does it, but I'm telling you—he's going to change the world when he's older. He'll probably invent something fascinating."

A second later, Tanya and Noah walked over, the broken plates disposed of. Tanya glanced over her shoulder, making sure her other two kids were still there. They hadn't moved the entire party except to eat their pizza or sip their sodas.

Tanya turned back to Gina, sighing. "Oh, I'm so sorry for what Dylan did to your plates. I know you worked hard on this welcoming party—"

"Tanya, don't worry about it," Gina interrupted. "Boys will be boys, right? He has been through a lot as well."

"I guess so. I wish he'd be more like my other son," Tanya said, looking over her shoulder again. "Esme, would you like to meet my other children?"

Esme nodded. "I'd like that. Are you okay, Noah?"

"I'm fine," Noah said as they walked over to the two kids. "Dylan didn't hurt me. The kid's probably just having a bad day."

"And he lost his dad," Esme added. "I know how hard that is."

Noah nodded, patting her shoulder to reassure her. It was a nice gesture—and Esme realized she liked him touching her. She almost wished he wouldn't stop when he lowered his hand.

When Lindsey and Vincent saw them approaching, they put down the pencils, rising to their feet. They rushed toward Tanya and hugged her legs. She laughed, ruffling their hair.

"Are you having a good time?" she asked.

Vincent nodded first. "I'm memorizing Einstein's theory of relativity. I want to practice a few more equations before school starts up again."

"Wow," Noah mumbled. "Smart kid."

"And I drew us a picture," Lindsey said, holding it up. "Look—it's us!"

Tanya took the picture, looking down at it with a sigh. Esme glanced at it over her shoulder and noticed it was of three children and two parents in a big house. She realized Lindsey had drawn her father in the picture.

"This is very good, Lind," Tanya said as she smiled, though it looked more like a painful grimace. "I'll put it up on the fridge when we get home. Speaking of which, we'd better get back."

"Can't we stay a little while longer, Mom?" Vincent begged.

Tanya shook her head. "I'm sorry, but I have to get up early for my shift at Fresh N Hot. I've been late before, and my boss made it clear I'd get fired next time. I'm leaving you in charge again tomorrow, okay, Vincent?"

Vincent nodded. "Okay, Mom. I'll do my best."

"I can come over tomorrow morning and check on your kids," Esme said. "I'm not doing much, anyway."

Tanya's eyes lit up. "Would you? That would be amazing. Thank you so much, Esme. Gina usually does it when I can't, but the more, the merrier."

"It's no problem," Esme said with a smile. "Just so I know, what's Fresh N Hot?"

"Oh, it's a silly name for a fast-food restaurant a few blocks away," Tanya said, rolling her eyes. "It's the biggest chain in Toronto. The pay sucks, the food's greasy, and the customers can be rude and demanding, but hey, it's a paycheck."

"How long have you worked there?"

"Not long—ever since my husband was diagnosed and we had to move here. I mostly work eight-hour days, though I try my best to be there for the kids. It'll be more difficult in the fall when I have to get them to school..."

Esme thought for a moment, remembering the checklist. Maybe getting a job would impress her father.

Tanya held her hands out, gesturing for Vincent and Lindsey to take them. "Well, we should be going now. See you all tomorrow."

After Vincent and Lindsey picked up their things, they followed their mother back into the building, taking the staircase down to their apartment. Once it was quiet, Gina nodded and looked around.

"The sun is starting to set, so we should be wrapping things up. I like to get to bed nice and early—sleep is important when you reach my age," Gina said, her hands still trembling. "I'll take care of what little is left. Thanks for coming—and for cleaning up."

Noah nodded. "It was the least I could do."

"I look forward to seeing you around the building, Esme. As for you, Noah, you're welcome back any time," Gina said with a wink. "Goodnight."

As Gina walked toward the party-goers to send them home, collecting the uneaten food and insisting she could do it all when someone else offered to help, Esme moved toward the edge of the building again. She looked for the guards but didn't see them anywhere.

"Are you okay?" Noah asked. "You seem nervous."

Esme turned around, faking a smile. "I'm fine. Come on—let's get back inside."

Noah walked toward the door, holding it open for her. "We can't forget about your laundry. It has to be moved to the dryer now which should take another hour."

Esme nodded, following Noah down the stairs. The party-goers followed and returned home. When Esme made it to her floor, she walked toward the laundry room, finding her clothes had finished washing. Noah showed her how to use the dryer and the importance of dryer sheets. After they turned it on, they walked back to Esme's apartment.

"I've learned a lot today," Esme said, stopping in front of her door. "Thank you, Noah."

He smiled a lopsided grin. "What did I say before? No need to keep thanking me—I had a good time. What do you say we watch some TV to kill the time before your drying is done?"

Esme nodded, excited to spend more time with Noah as she unlocked the door. "Sounds good to me. Oh, I must've forgotten to lock the door..."

Noah frowned. "Why do you say that?"

"It's already unlocked," Esme said, turning the handle. "Strange."

"I'll say," Noah muttered. "I remember you did lock it. Does anyone else have a key to your apartment?"

"Well, Antonio probably. But that's it."

"Stand behind me," Noah said, moving forward, "just in case there's an intruder."

As they entered the apartment slowly, all the lights were off. Esme spotted a few shadows moving in the dark. "There's someone in here!"

She fumbled for the light switch, turning it on. It illuminated the guards she had seen before on the street—all six of them. They looked between her and Noah in confusion.

"Who are you?" Noah demanded. "What are you doing in here? This is a private apartment. I have no choice but to call the police—"

"No—it's okay," Esme said, placing her hand on Noah's arm to stop him as he reached for his cell phone. "I know them."

Noah frowned. "You do? How?"

"Can you wait in the hallway for a minute?" Esme asked, turning to him. "I need to talk to them alone."

He hesitated, glancing back at the guards. "But—"

"Please, Noah. I promise—I'm not in any danger."

He didn't look convinced, but when he looked into Esme's eyes, he sighed and put his phone away. He stepped out into the hallway and shut the door behind him. Esme turned to the guards, looking angry.

"What are you doing here?" she demanded.

"Your father promised you he'd send guards to check on you. It's almost been a full day, and he was concerned," one of the guards said. "You appear to have done well for yourself so far. Are these your new living arrangements?"

"Yeah, that's right. It beats living on the street."

Thank goodness I found a place before they arrived, Esme thought. *Just in the nick of time.*

"What took you so long to find me?" Esme asked. "I saw you on the street a while ago."

The guard to her left nodded. "We wanted to get you alone to not scare the humans. We were watching you, too."

"And how'd you know this apartment was mine?"

"As you know, magic doesn't work on Earth, so we had to use a special compulsion potion on your landlord. Antonio, I believe his name was. It loosened his tongue enough to show us your room and loan us a key."

Esme frowned. "But I thought magic didn't work on Earth."

"Pure magic doesn't—like spells from a fairy godmother," one of the guards said. "But these potions are different—more like natural remedies. Antonio inhaled it quickly and told us everything we needed to know."

"Don't do anything like that again," Esme growled. "These humans aren't yours to use."

"You're one to talk," another guard spat. "Who's that human you're with? Your father made it clear this was your journey alone, yet we saw you talking with him."

"I *did* find this apartment on my own. I sold my tiara to pay for it," Esme snapped, and the guards looked surprised. "His name is Noah, and I didn't plan on making friends. I just happened to run into a good man on my first day here."

"I see. You haven't told him about magic, have you?"

Esme shook her head. "Of course not! I know the risks. If these humans found out about magic, there could be mass panic. That's what my father has always told me. I've done a lot of bad things, but I haven't disobeyed that rule."

"Good," the other guard said. "We should be going now. You still have a long list of things to do, but at least your father will be pleased to know you completed an important task—securing a home."

Esme had done a lot more than that. She kept it to herself, wanting to tell her father in person.

"Wait," Esme said, blocking them from the door. "Has anything strange happened while I've been gone?"

The guard blinked. "Such as?"

"Anything with Senator Remus or his daughter. And especially that evil fairy godmother of theirs."

"Nothing, Princess," the other guard replied, "though, we've barely seen them since the party."

"They're planning something," Esme mumbled to herself. "I just know it."

"What is that?"

"Nothing," Esme said, opening the door. "When you get home, tell Father I'm going to make it. He'll see—you'll *all* see."

As the guards bowed, leaving the apartment, Esme hoped she was right.

CHAPTER 11

Esme could hear the loud boots of the guards echoing down the hallway as Noah poked his head back inside the apartment. Once he saw them leave, he entered, locking the door behind him.

"What was that all about?" he asked. "Are you all right?"

Esme nodded, sighing. "I'm fine. If you promise not to tell anyone, I'll tell you who they were."

Noah sat on the couch, patting the seat next to him. "I promise. Now, can you tell me what's going on? I'm a little worried."

"Those were my old guards," Esme said as she sat down next to him. "The ones from my kingdom."

Noah's eyes widened. "They came out all this way?"

Esme nodded. "My father told me his guards would check on me. I didn't think it would be this soon, but they were impressed I've come this far—like getting my own apartment and money."

"I am, too," Noah said with a smile. "But you never told me where your kingdom was. Is it far away?"

Esme shifted anxiously. "Far enough. Technically, I wasn't

supposed to get help from anyone else—I was supposed to be completely independent. So, if the guards or my father ask, can you lie and say you haven't helped me?"

"I'll do whatever you need me to, Esme. You have my word on that," Noah said, nodding firmly. "But to be honest, I haven't helped you *that* much. Sure, maybe I drove you around, but selling the tiara was your idea. And you were the one who chose this apartment—not me."

A smile broke out on Esme's face. "Yeah, maybe you're right—but you were still by my side, encouraging me. Beyond that, my father doesn't need to know."

"Hey, he abandoned you here to fend for yourself," Noah said, flipping through the channels on TV. "As far as I'm concerned, he doesn't get to tell you how to survive."

"Oh, you don't know my father. He's a total control freak."

"I know the feeling," Noah said, glancing at Esme. "You're not alone."

Esme smiled at that. She rose to her feet, walking across the room to look out the window. She pushed open the pink curtains and saw the guards on the street lowering themselves into the storm drain. With the darkening sky, there were fewer cars on the road, and no one noticed them slipping away down there.

"What are you looking at outside?" Noah asked, walking up behind her.

Esme shut the curtains so he wouldn't see the guards vanishing below the storm drain. "Oh, uh—nothing. Just looking at how dark it is outside. Of course, in my kingdom, it's always dark, so I've gotten used to it."

Noah checked his watch. "It *has* gotten pretty late—which reminds me, we need to do one more thing before the night ends."

When she saw him pulling on his light jacket, she frowned. "What is it?"

"Groceries, silly," he said, walking toward the fridge. "There's probably nothing in here."

When he opened the fridge, he spotted a carton of milk and three slices of cheese. He sniffed the milk, pulling it away from his nose with a look of disgust. He held up the cheese and Esme noticed the spots of mold.

"Okay, correction—there's nothing *good* in here," Noah said, throwing the cheese in the garbage. Then he poured the milk down the drain before throwing out the carton. "We need to get you some food."

Esme nodded. "Right—I'll get my money."

After Esme walked into her bedroom, pulling out her safe from underneath her bed, she took out a few hundred dollars. When she walked back into the kitchen, Noah was going through her cupboards.

"What are you looking for?" she asked.

"Pots and pans," he replied, pulling out a giant pink wok. "The woman who lived here left all her kitchen supplies which is good. You just need food."

Esme opened the door. "Know of any good grocery stores around here?"

"Well, most of them are probably closed by now," Noah said, leaving the apartment as Esme locked the door behind them, "but there's a convenience store a few blocks away. Should be enough to stock your fridge for now."

Esme nodded, following Noah down the hallway. As they passed Tanya's apartment, they could hear her arguing with someone—and it sounded like Dylan. Then they heard the slamming of doors and screaming.

Esme sighed, continuing to walk down the hallway. "I feel

bad for Tanya. Not only did she lose her husband, but she has to parent a difficult child."

"Yeah, he's definitely got some issues. I hope her son gets the help he needs," Noah said, stopping by the laundry room to listen in. "I think your sheets and gown are still in the dryer. By the time we get back, it should be done."

Esme nodded, getting into the elevator with Noah. The apartment building was quiet at night and all the party-goers had returned home. When they reached the lobby, they took a right toward the doors, walking out into the parking lot to reach Noah's car.

"So, tell me, Esme," he said, starting the engine, "if you were back in your kingdom, what would you be doing now?"

Esme thought for a moment as he pulled out of the parking lot. "Hmm—that's a good question. I guess it depends. If Father was throwing a party, I'd have to attend. I hate those formal functions..."

"Yeah, I've been to a few parties my boss invited me to. Charity fundraisers, mostly. I only go for the finger foods."

Esme smiled. "Exactly—I'm so glad someone else gets it."

He took a left at the intersection. "Let's pretend there isn't a party. What else?"

"Well, I might hang out with Alva—my best friend. We've known each other since we were kids, and we got into all kinds of trouble together. I might spend time in my room, combing my hair and trying on outfits. Or maybe in the library."

"Oh? What kind of authors do you like?"

Esme blushed. "I'm sure you wouldn't know of them. Anyway, I haven't gone to the library in a long time. It was what my mother and I did when she was alive."

"I see," Noah said, softly. "Again, I'm sorry."

Esme nodded. "Thank you. But why do you ask?"

He shrugged, stealing a glance at her. "I'm just curious

about you—that's all. It's not every day I get to meet a princess."

Esme laughed. "I guess not. Despite my title, I'm just a regular person."

"Yes—I see that. It blows my mind that your father would send you away. You don't seem like a troublemaker to me."

Esme didn't want to go over all the things she had done, so she just took the compliment. "I wish my father thought the same way you do, Noah."

Noah slowed down, pulling into a small parking lot. "Yeah, but then we wouldn't have met."

Esme smiled as he parked his car. She looked up, noticing the small building next to the parking lot. It had bright lights on inside with a neon sign above the doors that read QUICK STOP SHOP. Noah opened his door, gesturing for Esme to follow.

"These kinds of stores are open twenty-four-seven," he told her. "So, if you ever need something in a pinch, this is the place to get it."

The door opened with the jingle of a bell, and the man standing behind the cash register nodded at them to welcome them inside. Noah grabbed a small basket, taking Esme down an aisle of bread, eggs, and milk.

"All right—let's start with the basics," Noah said, putting eggs, milk, and bread into the basket. "You'll also need butter, water, and maybe some frozen dinners. You aren't a vegetarian, are you?"

Esme shook her head. "No—I pretty much like everything. It's great that we're buying all this, but I don't know how to cook anything."

"Right. I guess your servants would do that for you," Noah said, picking up a book off the shelf. Esme glanced over his shoulder and noticed it read COOKING FOR BEGINNERS. "This will help—trust me."

Once they had a little for breakfasts, lunches, and dinners, Noah took Esme down the snack aisle. He pointed out his favorite snacks—All Dressed Chips, a Canadian classic—and let Esme pick out things she thought looked interesting. The gummy worms quickly became her favorite.

"You should also pick up some house supplies. You never know when you'll need them," Noah said, leading her down an aisle without food. "Let's go with the first aid kit, toilet paper, shampoo, and flashlights. Can't forget the toothpaste, toothbrush, and batteries, either."

"Wow, this is a lot of stuff," Esme said, looking inside the basket. "Are you sure I need it all?"

Noah laughed. "You've never been shopping for household things, have you?"

Esme shrugged. "Not really. The servants handled everything. Most of the time I didn't even pick out my own outfits—my godmother did."

"Seems pretty strict," Noah said, leading her toward the cash register. "But don't worry—I've kept myself alive for twenty-five years, and I intend to get you everything you need that'll keep you alive, too."

Esme nodded, trusting Noah as he put the basket down on the checkout counter. The man began scanning the items and sorting them into paper bags.

"Did you find everything you were looking for today, ma'am?"

Esme just shrugged. "I guess so. I've never shopped for myself before. What do I owe you?"

The man checked the cash register. "Two hundred and fifty."

Esme's eyes widened, grabbing the money out of her pocket to hand to the man. "Wow, groceries sure cost a lot."

Noah nodded as the man put the money in the register.

"They really do. It isn't cheap to live—which is why lots of people are struggling and have to rely on our organization."

Esme briefly thought back to the man selling his wedding ring and Tanya with her kids. Was this what the surface world had forced them to do? Pawn their most expensive things just to afford groceries and rent? That thought made Esme sick.

"Those poor people," Esme murmured, taking the change from the man's hands. "You do good work, Noah."

He smiled, carrying Esme's bags for her. "I try. Thanks for ringing up our order."

The man nodded before Noah walked toward the door, opening it with the chime of the bell. Esme followed him toward his car in the dark, having a strange sensation that someone was watching her. There was no one when she glanced around.

"You all right?" Noah called out as he put the groceries in the trunk.

Esme nodded. "Yeah—just paranoid at night, I guess. The streets are so quiet."

"It's a lot better than all that traffic noise in the day. You'll get used to it," Noah said, pulling out his receipt. "Oh, crap—the guy forgot to charge us for the milk. It must not have scanned. I'll pay for it and be right back."

Esme nodded, leaning against the car to wait for Noah. After he had vanished inside the store, she heard a rustling in the leaves. She spun around just as Duke Cullen appeared with a grin.

She gasped, taking a step back. "Cullen...is that you? What are you doing here?"

"I told you I'd make you regret rejecting me," he said, cornering her next to the car. "I've been watching you, Esme. Who's that human you were with?"

Esme ignored that question. "How did you get to Earth? Father made it clear no one was allowed to come here."

Cullen scoffed. "You think the precious King knows everything that's going on? Of course not. I'm not the only one who can get up to the surface, you know."

Esme crossed her arms. "What are you talking about? Who else is here?"

Cullen shook his head. "Answer my questions first. Who's that man you were with? Your boyfriend? You know your father would never approve of you being with a human. I'd be a better match—and you know it."

The fear Esme felt around him quickly changed to anger. "I don't know what you're doing here, or what you want, but you need to leave. Go back to Fairhaven—now."

He laughed. "What I want is simple, Esme. I'm going to ruin you for rejecting me."

Esme rolled her eyes. "Oh, really? And just how are you going to do that?"

He gestured at the car and her change of outfit. "You seem to be doing well for yourself, but it won't last. I'm going to ensure you never step foot in Fairhaven again. If I can't be king, I won't let you ever be queen."

Esme studied his face, realizing he was serious. A lump formed in her throat. Did Cullen mean what he said? Could he really destroy her life?

The doors to the convenience store opened and Noah stepped out, carrying the milk in a bag. He had a new receipt for it that he was slipping into his pocket. When he looked up, noticing Cullen, he frowned and rushed to Esme's side.

"What's going on?" he demanded. "Who's this?"

"Someone who won't take no for an answer," Esme said, glaring at Cullen. "We're leaving now. Don't follow us."

"This human fool doesn't know what you really are, does

he?" Cullen asked, glancing at Noah. "What secrets Fairhaven is hiding?"

"Shut up, Cullen," Esme said through gritted teeth. "Leave us alone."

Noah stepped in front of Esme, blocking her from Cullen. "I don't know what's going on here, but I don't like you. So, step away from her."

Cullen laughed, glancing at Esme over his shoulder. "Wow—such devotion. Your father was once tightly wrapped around your finger like that. Since you blew it with him, I guess you needed to find a new victim to—"

Noah lunged forward, punching Cullen in the face. Cullen cried out in pain and fell to his knees while clutching his cheek. Esme gasped in surprise, watching as Noah towered over the man. The imprint of his fist was still on Cullen's face.

Cullen glared up at him. "How dare you!"

"Hey, I told you to back off," Noah said, rolling up his sleeves. "Only creeps corner women in the dark."

"Calm down, you brute. We know each other," Cullen said, glancing at Esme. "Though, not as well as I'd like to."

Noah growled. "What the hell is that supposed to mean?"

Esme tugged on his arm. "Come on, Noah—let's just get home."

"Yeah, Noah," Cullen taunted, staggering to his feet. "Take Her Royal Highness home."

Esme got in the car quickly, looking out the window to make sure Noah was following. It looked like he wanted to punch Cullen again but thought twice about it and just sneered at him. He rushed toward the driver's seat, getting in before pulling away with a screech of the tires.

Cullen chased after their car. "I meant what I said, Esme. You and your new boyfriend will pay!"

"Who the hell was that guy?" Noah asked, watching him fade in the rear-view mirror. "He looks like an asshole."

Esme snorted. "It's because he is one. You just punched a duke, you know."

Noah's face fell. "Aw, crap…"

"Don't worry. If he tells my father, I'll explain the whole story. Lots of people at the castle know how handsy Duke Cullen is. He was the one I told you about who was trying to coerce me into marrying him."

Noah nodded. "Right—well, he's clearly a piece of work. I only regret not punching him again."

Esme glanced out her window, but Cullen had long faded. "Good—he's gone. I hope it stays that way."

"He said he'd make us both pay. Do you know what he was talking about?"

Esme shook her head. "I don't, but Cullen's made threats like that before. He's probably just trying to scare us."

"Maybe. If you see him next time, get help. I don't trust him," Noah muttered. "But he said something strange. Something about Fairhaven having secrets. What did he mean?"

Esme fidgeted with her hands. "Like I said, Cullen's only trying to get under my skin. He's all talk. He didn't even fight back when you punched him."

Noah nodded. "Cowards like him just like to run their mouths and cause trouble. Let's hope I put him in his place."

Esme said nothing, hoping that, too.

When they arrived back at her apartment, Noah helped Esme carry her groceries into the elevator. When they arrived on her floor, the dryers had stopped, and Noah grabbed Esme's clean sheets and clothes for her. She let him into the apartment, putting the food away first before helping Noah make the bed.

"It's not a luxury bed in a castle, but it'll do the trick," Noah said with a smile, smoothing out the wrinkles in her pillow-cases. "So, how do you like everything so far?"

Esme beamed. "Noah, I've got everything I need—a place to sleep and food to eat. Thank you for your help."

"Of course," Noah said, trying to hide his smile. He pulled out a business card from his pocket and left it on the night-stand. "Here's my business card—I always keep some in my pocket. It has my number on it. I know you don't have a phone, but I'm sure one of your neighbors would lend you theirs. Call me if you need anything. I'll give you my address, too."

After he wrote down his apartment building and number, Esme took it. "Noah, I don't know what to say. You've helped me so much—and you've barely known me for twenty-four hours."

"Some people you meet make you feel like you've known them forever. That's how it feels with you," Noah said, working up the courage to look at her. "This might sound weird, but... I'm glad I hit you with my car. We wouldn't have met if I hadn't."

Esme laughed. "Me, too—although my back is still pretty sore. I might take a hot bath after you leave. Thank goodness for painkillers."

"I hope you feel better," Noah said, walking toward the door. "I have work tomorrow, but I'll come over in the morning and check on you. If that's okay, of course."

Esme smiled. "Noah, you're welcome here anytime. I'll see you then."

"Goodnight, Esme."

He paused, looking like he had more to say before he turned and started walking down the hallway. Esme watched him get into the elevator and vanish before shutting the door. Within minutes, she felt herself missing him—even though she had met him only that morning.

"I need to be more independent," Esme chastised herself. "No more thinking of Noah."

When she tried not to think about him, suddenly, he overwhelmed all of her thoughts. She sighed, stripping out of her pantsuit before getting into a hot bubble bath. As she relaxed in the warm water, she looked out the window and noticed the moon in the sky.

"In your face, Senator Remus," she muttered to herself. "I made it—my first day is ending. Maybe Earth won't be so bad at all."

CHAPTER 12

After her bath, Esme felt like she was on top of the world. She had never been alone before—not in her own place. Instead of catering to her father's whims, she got to do whatever she wanted. She eventually decided on eating ice cream and watching late-night television.

"Mmm," she murmured, looking at the ice cream container. It read ROCKY ROAD. "This is seriously good. I need to ask Noah to find more of this for me..."

She let herself grow tired naturally instead of having to go to bed at the time her father told her. When her eyes became heavy, she turned off the television, then entered her bedroom. After she brushed her teeth and changed into her pajamas, she glanced outside.

"The stars are bright tonight," she muttered. "I never got to see them from Fairhaven. Well, goodnight, human world—see you tomorrow."

She turned off the light, climbed under the covers, and fell fast asleep as soon as her head hit the pillow.

When she woke up, she heard birds chirping outside and sunlight peeking through her pink curtains. She sat up in bed, stretched and yawned, and put on her slippers. She had no alarm clock—no servants yelling at her to get downstairs for breakfast.

Esme smiled, realizing it felt good.

She got dressed, then turned on the small radio the old tenant had left in the kitchen. It took a second for Esme to figure out how to use it, but when she did, pop music flooded the apartment. Everything was new and exciting to her.

She opened the fridge, peering in. "Now, what do I want to eat? Oh, I know…"

She reached for the cookbook she kept on the counter and flipped to a random page under the BREAKFAST section. She landed on an omelette that looked good in the picture and read the instructions carefully.

"Okay—eggs, cheese, and peppers," Esme muttered, opening the fridge door again. "Doesn't sound too hard."

But ten minutes later, she had already burned three of the omelets she had tried to make. The smoke wafted through the apartment. She picked up a towel, trying to push the smoke out the window so it wouldn't set off the fire alarms.

"Okay, maybe I should stick to easy meals," she muttered. "Let's try this thing called cereal."

It took less time to make the cereal as she grabbed a box of Cheerios on top of the fridge, then added milk into the bowl. As she dug her spoon into it and brought it up to her mouth, she nodded.

"Much better," she said to herself. "I'm sticking with cereal from now on."

After she put her empty bowl in the sink, she could hear yelling coming from the apartment next door. She recognized the voices as Tanya and Dylan—just like last night. She couldn't make out what they were saying, but it sounded serious.

The knock on her door startled her. She walked toward it,

looking through the peephole. When she saw Noah's face patiently waiting on the other side, a giant smile spread across her face. She tried to force it away as she opened the door.

"Hey, Esme," Noah said, holding something behind his back. "How did you sleep?"

"Like a baby," Esme said with a grin.

Noah laughed. "Glad to hear it. I take it you like living in your own apartment?"

Esme nodded, gesturing around. "It's a place just for me. It feels...special."

"It is. You've taken a big step, and I'm proud of you," he said, moving his hand around. "And I brought you a housewarming present."

When Esme looked down, she realized Noah was holding a big bouquet of fresh roses. She took them immediately, inhaling their sweet fragrance.

"It's not much," Noah said, looking nervous, "but I wanted to get you something nice. Something to mark the occasion."

"They're lovely, Noah. Thank you," she said, smiling at him. "Would you like to come in? I need to put these in water."

Noah nodded, entering the apartment and gently closing the door behind him. Esme approached a pink vase that sat on the coffee table and put the roses inside. Then she walked to the sink, filling it halfway with water.

"There—that looks nice," Esme said, placing it on the kitchen counter. "Makes me feel like I'm back at home. We had a huge garden behind the castle. When I was allowed, I spent a lot of time there."

"Sounds amazing," Noah said, thrusting his hands into his pockets. "Glad I could help you remember a nice memory—"

Noah quieted when the yelling started again next door. Esme sighed, leaning on the counter. "Not again..."

"Unfortunately, you don't get to pick your neighbors," Noah

said, glancing at the wall. "They didn't keep you up too much, did they?"

Esme shook her head. "No, they were fine last night. Everything was fine, in fact."

Noah sighed in relief. "Good—I was a little worried about you, especially after we ran into that guy. What was his name again?"

"Duke Cullen."

"Ah—right. He didn't show up?"

Esme shook her head. "No—no one did. I think I'm safe here. The guards know where I am, anyway, so they might come back to check on me."

"I will, too. You know, just to make sure everything's okay," Noah said, checking his watch. "Well, I have to leave for work now. Will you be okay on your own?"

Esme laughed. "Noah, I'm not a child. I'll find something to do with myself."

"Right. Sorry," Noah said, laughing nervously. "Just checking."

She placed a hand on his arm. "Everything's fine, Noah. No need to worry."

She felt his tension beginning to ease. "All right—though I probably will, anyway. Can't help it."

Esme laughed, stepping back. "Whatever you say. Tell me, Noah...is your job difficult?"

"Not to me," he said, shrugging. "The paperwork sucks sometimes, but it's all for charity. Why do you ask?"

"Well, I think getting a job with a humanitarian organization would be good for me. Father wants me to help others. Is there any way we could work together?"

Noah's eyes lit up. "There might be. I can talk to my boss—Giselle McMillan. She's the one who started the non-profit. I might be able to get you a job interview, but no promises."

"That's all right—I know you'll try your best," Esme said, leading Noah to the door. "Thanks for coming over. I feel much better with you around."

He nodded, glancing at his feet. "Me, too. Anyway, I'll check on you again later. Have a good day, Esme."

She watched him walk away again, noticing the ripple of his muscles. She hadn't taken a proper look to admire him, but he was in good shape. She briefly wondered what he would feel like against her skin—

No—those thoughts are inappropriate, Esme told herself. *Noah's been a good friend and nothing more. You have a mission to do here, so focus.*

The screaming next door interrupted her thoughts, making her jump.

She removed the checklist from her pocket and looked it over. "Do something unselfish for someone else, Father wrote. Here goes nothing..."

Esme put the list back in her pocket, leaving her apartment. After she locked it behind her, she walked to the apartment next to her, knocking loudly on Tanya's door. She hoped they'd hear her over all the yelling.

When the door opened, Tanya stood there in a bright yellow waitress outfit. The words FRESH N HOT were written in black and gold ink. Her hair was in a messy ponytail, and she looked exhausted. Esme looked in and noticed Dylan throwing things around again, mostly his own toys this time.

"Oh—hello, Esme," Tanya said, trying to smooth down her hair. "Are you here to watch the kids?"

Esme nodded. "I am, but I heard screaming earlier—"

"That's just Dylan being his usual self. Look, I'm late for work," Tanya said, picking up her keys off the table. "There's plenty of food in the fridge, so feel free to help yourself. They've already eaten breakfast, but they'll need lunch around noon.

Oh, and don't feed them sugar—it gets them too hyped up. Emergency numbers are on the fridge..."

As Tanya kept talking, Esme's head felt like it would start spinning.

"...and my work address is on the fridge, too, along with the phone number. Call me if something goes wrong," Tanya said, rushing out the door. "Good luck, Esme—and thanks again. I should be back around dinnertime!"

After she had rushed down the hallway, Esme gulped, entering the apartment. It was only her now—and three children. She almost felt like she was going into battle.

She didn't know where Lindsey and Vincent were in the small apartment, but Dylan was still in the kitchen, throwing toys around. Esme ran toward him and reached for his hands.

"Stop! Stop destroying your toys."

Dylan looked her in the eye and dropped another toy. "Make me."

Esme noticed his bleeding hands from where a toy had cut him. "You're injured."

He pulled back. "So what?"

"Does your mom have a first aid kit?"

He shrugged, reaching for another plate. "I don't know. Why do you care?"

"Because I'm going to help patch you up," she said, grabbing his arm before he could drop another toy. "My fairy godmother gave me an ointment that should help. Come with me."

"Your fairy godmother?" Dylan asked as she dragged him out of the apartment. "You should know I grew out of those fairytales. I also know Santa Claus doesn't exist."

Esme had no idea what he was talking about as she led him back to her apartment. "Just have a seat on the couch and don't touch anything, okay? Please."

He sighed but finally listened, sitting on the couch. She rushed into her bedroom and found her pink suitcase that her fairy godmother had given her. As she searched through it for the potion, she heard something else shatter.

"Dylan," she muttered.

When she rushed back into the living room—with the magical ointment in hand—she gasped. Dylan had knocked over the vase Esme used to keep Noah's flowers inside. The water dribbled down the counter, rose petals scattering everywhere.

"I told you not to touch anything!" Esme cried, picking up the vase. "Now I need to find something else to put these in."

She grabbed a mug as a last resort and filled it with water before thrusting the roses inside. They hung over the rim, turning limp as Esme sighed. Dylan stood there with his arms crossed.

"Aren't you going to say sorry?" Esme asked.

Dylan shrugged. "Why should I? I'm not."

And Father thinks I'm a difficult child, Esme thought.

Esme kneeled beside him. "You *should* be sorry, Dylan, because that hurt my feelings. And you need to be mindful of other people's feelings in life."

He shrugged again. "If you say so."

Esme sighed, taking his hands. "You're still bleeding. This is why you're supposed to avoid breaking glass, you know. Here—hold still..."

When Esme applied the ointment, Dylan flinched. "That stings!"

Esme nodded, rising to her feet. "Only for a second. How does it feel now?"

"Better," Dylan said, looking down at his hands. The blood and scratches had disappeared. "Hey, where did it go? How did you do that?"

"Would you believe me if I said this was a magical ointment?"

Dylan looked up at her with a frown. "No."

"Then I guess you'll just have to take my word for it. I'm keeping this on me in case you try something else again," Esme said, reaching for the broom. "Go back to your apartment, Dylan. I'll be there after cleaning this up—but *you're* going to clean up the mess in your kitchen."

He scoffed. "No, I'm not. And you can't make me!"

As he stormed off, Esme sighed and swept the glass into the garbage. She locked her door behind her before returning to the apartment. As she turned the doorhandle, she realized Dylan had locked it.

She pounded on the door. "Dylan, let me in!"

"No!" he cried on the other side. "Go away!"

Dealing with children is harder than I imagined, Esme thought.

"Come on, Dylan. Is this any way to treat someone who healed your wounds?"

The door opened a second later and Esme thought she had gotten through to him. But Vincent and Lindsey had opened the door, looking up at her in pity.

"Sorry about my brother," Vincent said. "He can be mean sometimes."

"Are you okay?" Lindsey asked.

Esme nodded, pushing into the apartment. "I am—thank you. Where did Dylan go?"

"He's in his room," Vincent said, pointing down the hall. "Me and him used to share, but Mom separated us."

Esme sighed. "I'm sorry you have to deal with Dylan's tantrums. It must be hard on you."

Lindsey shrugged. "He wasn't like that before Dad died. He misses him a lot. We miss Dad, too."

"I know—and I'm very sorry he's gone," Esme replied. "Well, I'm going to go talk to Dylan. You two can get back to whatever you were doing before."

Vincent nodded. "Okay. Come on, Lind—we have to finish our puzzle."

After they went to their room, Esme walked down the hallway, finding Dylan's room. It had a poster with a skull on it that read KEEP OUT. She pushed open the door, finding Dylan lying in bed. It looked like he was clutching something.

"Dylan?" Esme asked, gently. "Can I talk to you?"

"How did you get in here?" he asked, trying to hide whatever was in his hands. "I told you to go away!"

"Things can't always go away because we don't like them," Esme said, sitting on the bed. "Death and grief are some of them. You miss your father, don't you?"

Dylan shifted, and Esme noticed he was holding a picture frame of him. "What do you think?"

"I lost my mother, too. She died less than a year ago."

Esme expected Dylan to say something snarky, but he didn't. The room turned silent so Esme decided to continue.

"I miss her, too. Sometimes, it feels like I can't breathe without her. In fact, the only reason I'm in Toronto is that my father kicked me out of our home. I was banished. And you know what? It was my own fault. I was irresponsible and lashing out, something I still struggle with. I became so consumed by my grief that I became a monster—causing trouble and lashing out at people."

Dylan still didn't say anything. She hoped he was listening and that she was getting through to him as she rose to her feet.

"I probably should've treated my father better while I still had the chance," Esme muttered. "My point is simple. Your father may be gone, Dylan, but your mother isn't. And the more you act out, the more you hurt her—the only parent you have left. She won't be around forever, either, you know."

Dylan burrowed his head into his pillow. "I just miss him…"

"I know," Esme said, patting his shoulder. "I know."

Esme walked toward the door, intending to leave him alone when Dylan sat up in bed. "I'll clean up the mess."

Esme turned around, shocked. "You will?"

He nodded. "And…I'm sorry for breaking your vase."

"Thank you, Dylan," Esme finally said.

Dylan rose to his feet, putting the picture frame back on his nightstand. Esme watched from the hallway as he grabbed the dustpan and began cleaning up the broken toys. When he threw them out, he went to watch television on the couch without making a sound.

"Wow," Esme muttered to herself. "I think we just had a breakthrough…"

With Dylan entertained, Esme walked into the bedroom that Vincent and Lindsey shared. They were sitting on the floor, putting a giant puzzle together.

"Is everything all right in here?" Esme asked.

Lindsey looked up, nodding. "We're fine. What happened with Dylan?"

"He's watching TV, actually," Esme said, then an idea hit her. "Would it be okay if he joined you?"

Vincent shrugged. "Sure, but he doesn't like to hang out with us."

"It's worth a shot. Wait here."

Esme walked into the living room, finding Dylan still watching cartoons on the television. To her surprise, he hadn't moved an inch.

"Dylan?" she asked, carefully. "Your sister and brother are doing a puzzle. They'd really like you to join them."

Dylan hesitated, then turned off the TV with the remote. "Well...okay. But I'm not good at puzzles."

Esme laughed. "Me, either—but we can still have fun."

After they walked into the bedroom together, Vincent and Lindsey welcomed Dylan. Esme helped them find the rest of the pieces of the puzzle. They backed away from it, realizing it made a horse.

"Look at that," Esme said, proudly. "The power of teamwork. I had a good time with you all."

"I guess I had a good time putting it together, too," Dylan said, awkwardly.

Lindsey smiled. "Yeah—me, three. Can we have lunch now? Mom usually makes us peanut butter and jelly sandwiches."

Esme frowned. "I've never heard of such a thing."

Vincent rose to his feet. "We can show you. Come on!"

As Esme joined the kids in the kitchen, they taught her how to make a peanut butter and jelly sandwich. As they sat down to eat their lunch, Esme heard a knock on the door and got up to answer it.

Gina stood there, looking in. "Hello, Esme. I came over to help, but...it looks like you have it all under control."

Esme glanced over her shoulder, watching Dylan chat with Lindsey and Vincent. For once, it hadn't turned into another screaming match. "Yeah, it wasn't as bad as I thought."

"How on Earth did you get Dylan to behave?" Gina whispered.

"I talked to him honestly," Esme said, shrugged. "I think that helped."

"Well, good for you—"

When Gina dropped her purse, Esme bent down to pick it up. "Are you all right? This fell out of your hands."

Gina nodded, trying to stop herself from trembling as she

took the purse. "Yes—thank you, dear. I don't know what happened."

"Your hands are shaking again, Gina. Is there something wrong?"

Gina looked nervous as she pushed into the apartment. "Oh, don't be silly, Esme—I'm fine. Hello, kids!"

Dylan kept his distance but Lindsey and Vincent rushed into her arms, hugging Gina like they would a grandmother. Esme knew something was up with the woman—and just like she had with Dylan, she was determined to get to the bottom of it.

CHAPTER 13

Esme closed the door, watching Gina play with the kids over her shoulder. She was a natural with them—making them laugh and relax. Dylan still shied away from her, taking a seat on the couch.

Esme sat next to him. "Are you doing okay?"

"I just hate laughter," he muttered. "I haven't laughed since..."

Esme nodded. "I understand. I couldn't for a while, either."

She briefly thought back to Noah making her laugh, realizing it was genuine. He seemed like the only one who could take her mind off things. She wondered if maybe she could become like Noah to Dylan—the one person he trusted.

"Is what you said before true?" Dylan asked, looking up at her. "That you were banished from your home?"

Esme nodded. "That's right—and I can't go back until I change."

Dylan said nothing for a few seconds, just sitting there. "Would my mom ever kick me out?"

"Of course not," Esme said, placing a hand on his shoulder.

"It doesn't matter how much you fight. Your mother loves you unconditionally—I can see it."

Dylan said nothing again, but Esme could tell he was thinking it over. Was it possible she was getting through to him? When he turned silent, she started to think about how much she wished her father could've been more forgiving over the years.

"Mom never talks about Dad anymore," Dylan said quietly.

"She probably just doesn't want to upset you. Do you want to talk to her about him?"

Dylan shrugged. "Maybe—I don't know. It could be nice."

"What would you kids like as a snack?" Gina asked, poking her head into the living room.

"Scrambled eggs!" Vincent cried.

"With cheese and crackers!" Lindsey added.

"Is that all right with you, Dylan?" Gina asked.

But Dylan didn't respond to her—he glanced at Esme. "It's fine."

Esme nodded, rising to her feet. "Okay, then—let's get started."

"Do you want to cook the eggs?" Gina asked.

Esme shivered, having flashbacks of the omelet. "You'd better do it. I can handle the cheese and crackers."

Esme and Dylan followed Gina into the kitchen where Vincent and Lindsey were sitting at the table. Dylan took a seat beside them, saying nothing as Gina cracked the eggs and put them in a pan. Esme opened the fridge and grabbed the cheese before getting a knife and cutting it on a plate.

Once it was finished, she got crackers from the cupboard and brought them to the table. She found juice boxes she gave to the kids who dug into the cheese and crackers immediately. As Vincent and Lindsey chatted, Dylan didn't talk, but Esme was just glad he was eating.

She walked toward Gina who was already looking at her. "What?"

"Dylan never talks to me," Gina said, scrambling the eggs in the pan. "You've managed to get through to him, Esme. This is fantastic."

Esme smiled, starting to feel as though she was making a difference. "Well, you're good with Vincent and Lindsey—they adore you. I'm still a little awkward with kids. There weren't many where I come from, so I tend to treat them like little adults. Maybe that's why Dylan's been open with me—I haven't tried to baby him."

Gina shrugged. "Maybe. I hope you keep it up. God knows that boy needs someone..."

Esme nodded. "I won't give up on him. But tell me—did you ever have children?"

Gina sighed, turning back to the pan. "No, but I worked as an elementary school teacher when I was younger, so I learned how to handle them. My husband and I couldn't have children."

"Oh, I'm sorry," Esme said, softly. "I didn't know."

"That's all right, dear. At least we had each other for as long as we did," she replied, turning off the stove. "Can you get us some plates?"

Esme looked down and noticed Gina's hands were shaking —again. Esme nodded, reaching for several plates before putting them down on the table.

"Here—why don't I plate the eggs?" Esme asked.

Gina hesitated. "Are you sure? I could do it."

"No, that's all right," Esme said, grabbing the pan off the stove. She was afraid Gina would drop the food if she touched it again. "I don't mind. Besides, someone should sit with the kids and make sure they're behaving."

Gina nodded, walking toward the dining room table. Vincent and Lindsey immediately started talking to her while

Dylan kept his distance. Esme scooped the eggs evenly onto the three plates, then carried them toward the table.

"You should be a waitress," Gina said with a chuckle. "Only they have the power of carrying more than one plate at a time."

Esme thought about it as she put the plates down. Working a service job was exactly what her father wanted, and it wasn't a bad idea. After Esme sat down, they ate their meal while chit-chatting. Dylan didn't say much, but he wasn't breaking things anymore.

"What do you want to do now?" Gina asked after they finished eating.

"I'm watching TV," Dylan said, rising to his feet. "May I be excused?"

He was looking directly at Esme, so she nodded. "Of course—thank you for asking, Dylan."

"Wow, such manners," Gina muttered.

As he walked away, Vincent nodded. "I think I want to do that, too."

"Not me," Lindsey said. "I'm almost done with my drawing. It's a present for you, Esme."

"For me?" Esme asked, bewildered. "Well...thank you, Lindsey."

Lindsey giggled. "I hope you like it. I'll show it to you when it's ready!"

After she rushed into her room, Gina was still watching Dylan sitting calmly on the couch. "Seriously, Esme—I don't know how you did it, but that boy's been better behaved today than I've ever seen him."

"I think I relate to him. I lost my mother, too."

Gina frowned. "But my husband passed away not too long ago. Why doesn't he want to talk to me?"

Esme shook her head. "It's not the same as losing a parent.

And no offense, Gina, but I'm closer in age to Dylan than you are. Maybe he feels more comfortable."

Gina chuckled. "I know I'm not a spring chicken anymore—no need to dance around the subject. Those days are long gone…"

As Gina rose to her feet, she nearly fell again. Esme caught her and helped her to the chair in the living room. "Gina, I'm getting worried about you."

"Really, dear—"

"You keep denying it, but I used to lie to my father all the time. I can spot a liar—and I know you aren't telling me the full story," Esme said, making Gina hush. "Like I told Dylan, I'm always here to listen. The same goes for you, too."

It looked like Gina was going to open up before Lindsey rushed into the room. She carried a hand-drawn picture that she thrust at Esme. "Here it is! Do you like it?"

Esme took the drawing from her, looking down. It took her a minute to recognize the people who were kissing. They looked like stick figures, but she recognized the chestnut brown hair of one of them. "Is that…me?"

"And Noah," Lindsey said with a smile. "He has a crush on you."

"He does?" Esme asked, her head shooting up.

Lindsey nodded. "Are you two going to get married?"

Esme blushed. "Oh, uh…I don't know about that. But thanks for the wonderful picture—I love it."

"Isn't that adorable?" Gina asked with a big smile, glancing at the drawing. "Noah's very handsome. I for one am in support of you two getting married."

"And I could be in the wedding!" Lindsey cried. "I want to be the flower girl."

As Lindsey walked over to the couch, Esme shook her head at Gina. "Don't encourage her."

Gina just smiled. "What do you mean, dear?"

"Noah and I are just friends—nothing more. I don't want to promise the kids anything."

"Whatever you say," Gina said, still smirking as she sat down next to Lindsey.

Esme rolled her eyes, shoving the picture in her pocket. To pass the time, they watched television, played board games, and ate snacks. Hanging out with the kids was the most normal Esme had felt in a long time—and a part of her didn't want it to end.

Around dinnertime, Gina looked at her watch. "Tanya should be home any minute now. I wonder what's taking her so long. Anyway, I should get started on dinner—the kids voted for hamburger helper."

Esme nodded, walking toward the front door. She peered out the peephole and noticed Tanya had arrived—but hadn't knocked yet. She stood in the hallway with her back turned.

Esme opened the door, gently shutting it behind her when she heard Tanya crying. "Tanya? Are you all right?"

"Oh, Esme—it's you," she mumbled, drying her eyes. "I was just..."

"You don't need to explain. Sometimes, you just need a moment alone to let it out."

She nodded, turning around. "Good—I couldn't think of an excuse, anyway."

"Did you have a bad day?"

"Every day is bad when I wake up without my husband. He wasn't supposed to die so young."

Esme placed a hand on her shoulder. "I know. I wish I could do more for you."

Tanya gestured at the door. "You already have. How are the kids?"

"Fine. Gina came over and helped. Dylan and I got to talking, and he seems a little better."

Tanya raised her eyebrows. "Dylan talked to you?"

"That's right. He's hurting, too. Maybe you should talk to him about his father. He says you never do."

Tanya sighed. "I just don't want to make him sadder than he already is."

"You won't—trust me. It could be cathartic to get it out together."

The door opened behind them and Gina peered out. "I thought I heard voices. What are you two doing out here?"

"Tanya was just coming in," Esme said. "And I should get going."

"Are you sure you don't want to stay for dinner?" Tanya asked. "We'd love to have you."

"I was actually hoping to put in a job application at Fresh N Hot. Do you think they'd hire me?"

Tanya scoffed. "Of course—they'd hire anyone. But why would you want to work there? Believe me, customer service jobs suck."

Esme smiled. "That's what I'm counting on. See you two later, and tell the kids I said goodbye. And tell Dylan he can come talk to me whenever he wants—my door is always open."

Tanya nodded. "Thank you, Esme. Really."

Esme watched as Tanya entered the apartment, hugging her children. When she went to hug Dylan, this time, he didn't refuse. Esme smiled and began walking down the hallway. After she reached the lobby, she exited through the doors and found a familiar car pulling into the parking lot.

Noah. Just the thought of him could brighten her day.

"Hey, stranger," he joked, leaning out the window. "Going somewhere?"

Esme nodded. "I'm going to apply for a job at Fresh N Hot."

"How funny," Noah said, gesturing inside the car. "I brought us takeout from there. It's not glamorous food, but it gets the job done. Hop in."

Esme got into the passenger seat, smelling the greasy French fries. "Well, if I'm going to work there, I may as well try the food."

"Well, I was still hoping you would work with me. And I can't imagine why anyone would want to work at that restaurant...unless it's something for your checklist, right?"

"Right. I only plan to work one shift to satisfy my father," Esme said with a smile. "I know I agreed to work with you, but I'd like to do this first. A little test run to see how I do on my own. So, how was your day at work?"

He shrugged. "Oh, it went fine. More boring paperwork. And to be honest...my mind wandered back to you a lot. I couldn't really concentrate."

"Me, too," Esme blurted out before she could stop herself.

Noah cleared his throat. "How'd it go watching Tanya's kids today? Couldn't have been easy."

"It went well—Vincent and Lindsey are very sweet. Lindsey even drew a picture of us."

"Oh, yeah? Can I see it?"

Esme blushed. "Oh, I left it in the apartment. Anyway, I got through to Dylan. He and I had some nice conversations, and I got him to clean up his mess."

Noah looked shocked. "I can't believe it. Here I thought that boy was a lost cause..."

"No one is," Esme said, firmly. "Do you think there's something you can do for him?"

"Like what?"

Esme thought for a moment. "Well, he needs help dealing with his grief and anger. You work for a humanitarian organization. See where I'm going with this?"

Noah laughed. "Well, we have grief counselling. I can talk to my boss about what they offer for children. Speaking of which, I got you an interview."

Esme's eyes widened. "You did? When?"

"Tomorrow at noon. I talked you up a lot—my boss is super excited to meet you. I think you could have a real shot at working there."

She grinned. "I'm so excited."

"Me, too," Noah said with a smile. "Anyway, let's dig in. I'm starving!"

When Esme reached into the bag, she pulled out the two wrapped burgers, large sodas, and fries. She gave half the meal to Noah while she opened her burger and bit into it.

"Oh my gosh," she muttered, pulling back. "This has got to be the greasiest, most unhealthy thing I've ever eaten in my life...and I love it!"

Noah laughed. "That's takeout for you. So bad, it's good."

After they ate their dinner—chit-chatting about their days—Noah drove Esme to the closest Fresh N Hot, the same location Tanya worked at. The line-up was around the corner for dinner with loud, impatient customers.

"Now, are you sure you want to work here?" Noah asked. "It won't be easy."

Esme took a deep breath. "I have no choice—I need to do this for my checklist."

Noah nodded. "All right—I'll wait for you."

"You will?" she asked, wide-eyed. "Don't you want to get home?"

Noah scratched the back of his head. "I just want to make sure you're okay. Trust me—it's fine."

Esme nodded as Noah took a seat in one of the booths. She pushed through the line-up, getting to the cash register. "Can I talk to the manager, please?"

The cashier—who was dressed in a bright yellow uniform —sighed. "Yeah, all right. Cindy? A woman wants to talk to you."

A dark-haired woman in full uniform walked over from the backroom, looking busy and frantic. "How may I help you? Was there a problem with your order?"

Esme shook her head. "No—I'd like to work here. Do you think you could hire me on the spot?"

Cindy's eyes widened. "Are you kidding? We're already short-staffed—we'd love to have someone else. Ever worked in a fast-food restaurant before?"

Esme shook her head. "No, never—"

"That's all right—you look like a fast learner," Cindy said, reaching underneath the counter. She pulled out a yellow uniform. "Put this on and get back here. Hurry!"

Esme nodded, taking the uniform as she pushed through the crowds. The bathroom was smelly and dirty as she walked in, but she plugged her nose and entered a stall. After she had her uniform on, she walked toward Noah who was still sitting down and handed him her old clothes.

"Can you hold onto these for me?" she asked.

He nodded, taking the clothes while looking her over. "I will. Have you, uh, looked at yourself?"

Esme glanced down at her outfit. "It's horrible, isn't it? Way too bright and yellow."

Noah tried to stifle a giggle. "I was just thinking about how you reminded me of a bumblebee."

She pretended to roll her eyes. "Laughing at my misery, are you? You're a mean, mean man, Noah Crawford."

Noah chuckled again as Esme walked toward the manager. Before she could say anything, the manager grabbed her, pulling her toward the back of the restaurant.

"We need someone to work the drive-thru," she said,

putting a headset on Esme. "Just listen carefully and punch the orders into the screen. Shouldn't be too hard."

Esme glanced at the screen, nodding. "Okay. But what if I need help—"

"No time to talk!" Cindy cried, rushing toward the fryer. "I have a dozen orders I need to cook. Tell every customer 'Welcome to Fresh N Hot' and that you'd love to take their order. Remember—the customer is always right and big smiles!"

Esme sighed, talking into the headset. "Welcome to Fresh N Hot. Can I take your order, please?"

"One strawberry milkshake," a voice said through the screen, giggling. It sounded like a teenage boy with a bunch of laughing friends in the background.

It took Esme some time to find the button on the screen. Once she pushed it, she nodded. "Anything else?"

"That's it," the boy said, still laughing.

Esme frowned, wondering what was so funny. "All right—drive up to the window."

Cindy rushed toward her, holding the milkshake with a straw. "Good job. Now, get their money first and then give it to them. It costs a dollar fifty."

Esme nodded, holding the milkshake as she opened the window. She had been right about them—they were teenage boys, about sixteen or seventeen. They had big smiles on their faces as the scruffy-haired boy in front drove up. She wondered why they had only ordered one milkshake.

She leaned out the window. "Hello, there. Your total is—"

The boy honked, making all his friends laugh. Esme got startled and jumped, causing the milkshake to splatter down her uniform. The boys laughed even harder when they noticed the mess.

"Got you!" the driver cried.

"You've just been pranked!" another kid in the back yelled.

And then the driver put his foot on the gas, speeding away. Esme watched them go as the milkshake dribbled down her chest. "You boys are jerks!"

Cindy rushed over, gasping. She picked up several nearby napkins and tried to wipe the mess off Esme's uniform. "Are you all right?"

Esme nodded, putting the milkshake down. "Yeah, I think so. Are you going to call the police on those boys?"

Cindy frowned. "Why would I do that?"

"For one, they made you make something without paying for it. Secondly, they scared me and drove off."

Cindy sighed. "You must be *really* new at this customer service thing, huh? Unfortunately, we have to put up with rude customers in this line of work."

"It isn't right," Esme said, firmly.

"No, it isn't—but we have no choice," Cindy said, throwing the napkins out. "Just throw that milkshake in the garbage. We aren't allowed to give it away. Hurry—another customer's waiting."

Esme threw out the milkshake, sighing at the loss of food. She was beginning to have more respect for people who worked in customer service. As she adjusted her headset again, she glanced at the monitor.

"Welcome to Fresh N Hot. Can I take your order?"

"Yes, I'd like a cheeseburger combo meal," the voice said on the other end. "With extra ketchup."

Esme nodded, punching it in faster that time. "I'm getting good at this. All right—pull up."

When the driver pulled up to the window, Esme gasped. It was the last person she wanted to see—Jill, Noah's ex-fiancée.

CHAPTER 14

When Jill pulled up to the window, Esme's mouth was still open in shock. She couldn't believe she had run into Jill here—of all places. There was something about the woman that she didn't like. She seemed nice enough, but her lingering gaze on Noah back at the coffee shop made Esme uncomfortable.

I can't tell Noah I saw her here, Esme thought. *I don't want him thinking of her any more than he already has. Just keep calm and maybe she won't recognize you.*

"Excuse me?" Jill asked, peering into the restaurant through the window. "What was my total?"

Esme snapped back to reality as she glanced at the screen. "Uh, right—it came to nine dollars and twenty cents."

Jill nodded, reaching into the purse she kept in the passenger seat. Esme didn't see her fiancé with her in the car and wondered why. After Jill handed the money over, she looked at Esme with narrowed, confused eyes.

"Do I know you from somewhere?" she asked. "You look familiar, but I can't put my finger on it."

Esme looked away, putting the money into the cash register. She hoped the uniform hat would hide her facial features and ignored her question. "Your food will be ready in just a moment—"

"Here it is!" Cindy yelled, bringing over the food in a paper bag. "Nice work this time, Esme. Sorry about those boys before."

As Cindy scurried away to work on more orders, Jill's eyes widened. "Ah, right, your name is Esme—I *do* know you! You were with Noah at the coffee shop."

Esme sighed, handing the food over. "Yes, that was me. Nice to see you again, Jill."

Jill took the food and placed it in the passenger seat, though she didn't drive away. "You, too, Esme. I didn't know you were working here."

Esme shrugged. "It's only a temporary gig."

Jill looked at the uniform. "And I see you changed your outfit. No more pink gowns?"

"Noah bought me new clothes. He said I needed to fit in better in Toronto."

The expression on Jill's face changed when she brought up Noah. She looked uncomfortable, her hands gripping the steering wheel almost painfully. "That was nice of him—he's always been really generous, even before he worked at a humanitarian organization. And Noah seemed really happy with you. That's good."

Esme nodded. "He's a good man. I like being around him."

"Of course, you do," Jill said with a sad nod. "Noah's the best. Kind, caring, thoughtful. More men should be like him."

Esme leaned on the window. "If you don't mind me asking... if he's all those things, why did you leave him?"

Jill sighed. "I keep asking myself that these days. And to be honest, I don't know why. I thought I still loved Jerry."

"Well, do you?"

Jill nodded, looking up at Esme again. "Of course, I do—I've loved him since high school. But my feelings for Noah aren't as done as I thought they were when I got back together with Jerry. Seeing him at the coffee shop reminded me that I still love him—even now."

"Does Noah know any of this?"

Jill shook her head. "No, I haven't worked up the courage to tell him. And now he's dating you, so maybe the opportunity to get back with him is gone forever."

Right, Esme thought. *The fake romance.*

"Where *is* Jerry?" Esme asked, wanting to change the subject fast. "I don't see him in the car."

"Oh, he had to work late. It's kind of a relief. I've been spending a lot more time by myself—just thinking. Mostly wondering if I'm making the right decision, especially with my wedding day approaching. It suddenly sunk in that I'll never be single again..."

Esme didn't know what to say. She looked over her shoulder, noticing Noah sitting in a booth by himself. It looked like he had ordered a coffee and was reading the newspaper. She didn't want to encourage Jill to get back with Noah—she just couldn't.

So, she made a choice—her last effort to keep Jill away from him.

"I think you should marry Jerry. He clearly loves you, and you two look good together," Esme lied, trying to convince her as hard as she could. "Noah's already moved on, and you don't want to throw away what you have with Jerry."

Jill sighed. "Maybe you're right. Thanks for the advice, Esme. Will I see you and Noah at the wedding?"

Esme faked a smile. "Of course—we wouldn't miss your big day. I wish you and Jerry the best."

"Thank you. And please—take care of Noah. He's a special

man, and he's already had his heart broken by me. I couldn't bear to see him get hurt again."

Esme nodded. "You have my word, Jill. Take care."

A car honked behind them in the drive-thru, and a man shoved his head out his window. "What's the hold-up? We're starving back here!"

"I'd better go before there's an angry mob behind me," Jill said with a roll of her eyes. "Thanks again for being honest with me, Esme."

As Jill sped away, Esme sighed, knowing she had been anything *but* honest.

The rest of Esme's shift seemed to pass quickly after that. Cindy made her leave the drive-thru when the front of the restaurant became busier, and she hated working the cash register. Customers were rude and impatient.

"I ordered fries with no salt!" one woman yelled, throwing the fries on the counter. They sprayed everywhere and fell onto the floor. "I want you to make them again."

Esme checked her receipt. "You never told me—"

"Just make them again!" the woman shrieked.

Esme sighed, following Cindy to the fryer. While she was coaching her on how to use it, Esme burned her hand, needing to run it under cold water and wrap it in a bandage. She had never felt so stressed in her life with people yelling at her and Cindy trying to train her on the spot.

Even after she got the customer her new French fries, the woman didn't thank Esme at all. The next person in line wasn't any better. He was a middle-aged man who squinted as he looked up at the food board.

"Now, what comes on the cheeseburger?" he asked.

Esme read through the ingredients. "Cheese, ketchup, pickles—"

"I don't want any cheese on it."

Esme nodded, turning to the cash register. "Okay, so you want a hamburger—"

"No," the man said, firmly. "I want a cheeseburger without the cheese."

Esme sighed, punching it into the register. "All right, one cheeseburger without the cheese coming up…"

The next customer was an elderly woman who took forever to decide. The next one had a child who wouldn't stop screaming. And the next woman had a baby who threw up everywhere—and Cindy made Esme clean it up.

The line continued to grow around the corner, even as it got later in the evening. When Esme noticed how dark it had gotten outside, she took a break. She walked over to Noah who was still sitting in the same booth.

"There you are," Noah said, looking up from his newspaper. "Everything all right?"

Esme nodded, grabbing her clothes where they sat beside him. "I'm fine—I got what I needed by working here. I think I have more respect for service workers now. That was *not* easy—especially when I burned my hand."

When she held up her bandaged hand, Noah reached for it. "Ouch. Will you be okay?"

Esme's butterflies returned as she gently removed her hand from his. "Yeah, I think so. I don't know how Tanya can work here every day and not lose her mind."

Noah chuckled. "I told you it wouldn't be fun. Tanya's a brave, brave woman. Anyway, get changed and I'll drive you home."

Esme nodded, noticing the drawing Lindsey had made sitting next to Noah. "Did you...did you see that?"

"I did. Sorry, but it fell out of your pocket, and I got bored," Noah said, picking it up. "Is this the drawing Lindsey did? You said you left it in the apartment."

Esme blushed. "In truth, I didn't know how you'd react. She seems to think we'd make a cute couple. Even asked me if we were getting married."

"Huh," Noah said, still looking down at it. "It's...a very nice drawing."

He didn't say anything else, and Esme feared if she kept looking at him, her cheeks would burn even hotter. "Well, I should get changed and tell Cindy I'm quitting. Wait here."

Noah nodded as Esme rushed into the bathroom and removed her uniform, bringing it over to Cindy at the fryer. The other employees scrambled behind Esme, trying to get all the orders down and cook the food in time.

"Well, I think my shift is over," Esme said, handing the unform to her. "Thank you for letting me work here, but I'm afraid I can't come back."

Cindy frowned, looking down at the uniform. "But...why not? You were my best employee!"

"Really?" Esme asked, wide-eyed.

Cindy nodded. "Oh, yes—most of my other employees would've been complaining or freaking out after all that. But you never backed down once!"

Must've been my royal training, Esme thought.

"That's very kind of you to say, but I really can't take the pressure of the job. And I only needed to work a few hours to prove myself to my father."

Cindy sighed, taking the uniform back. "I see. Well, that's too bad. If you ever need a job again, Fresh N Hot would be lucky to have you. I can see you having a bright future here—or anywhere you set your mind to, really."

Esme smiled. "You don't know how badly I needed to hear that. Thank you. Say, do you know my friend, Tanya?"

Cindy nodded. "Oh, yes—she never stops talking about her three kids. She's sometimes late to work, too. Drives me nuts..."

"Be gentle with her," Esme said. "Her husband passed away and she has a son who can be hard to handle sometimes. Instead of paying me for my shift here, just have more patience with Tanya."

Cindy sighed. "I didn't know any of that about her. I guess I can try to be more lenient."

Esme nodded, thanking her again as she returned to Noah. He had already risen to his feet and thrown out his coffee. "Ready to go?"

Esme nodded. "You bet—and I never want to step foot in a fast-food place again. Too many bad memories."

Noah chuckled, leading her out the door. "I was a pizza delivery driver as a teen. I didn't work the frontlines like you, but I know the stress of a customer service job—believe me."

"People can be real jerks sometimes," Esme said, rubbing the hand she had burned. "I'm going to take a very long bath when I get home..."

"Why don't I take you out for some ice cream first?" Noah asked as they walked toward his car. "You deserve a treat. And I want you to be in a good mood for your interview tomorrow."

Esme smiled as she opened the passenger door. "I'd like that. But first things first..."

She pulled out the checklist, crossing off *help a friend* and *work at a customer service job.*

Noah smiled. "Nice work—the list is getting smaller by the day. Too bad it didn't have easier things. You know, like eating ice cream."

"I'd have that checked off in no time!" Esme said, making Noah chuckle.

After Esme got into the car, Noah drove her a few blocks down to a late-night ice cream shop. It had a giant sculpture of a spoon on the front lawn as Noah and Esme walked through the chiming door.

"Why would they keep an ice cream shop open this late?" Esme asked. "Not that I'm complaining, of course."

"In case all those drunk people coming from the bars want a treat," Noah said with a chuckle. "Maybe I speak from experience."

Esme laughed as she walked up to the employee, pointing at the Rocky Road ice cream. "I love Rocky Road. Your biggest scoop on a cone, please."

Noah looked at her, his eyes twinkling. "I'll take chocolate on a cone, thanks."

The employee smiled, putting on his gloves. "Coming right up."

After the employee handed them their ice cream cones, Noah paid. Esme reached into her pocket and pulled out a hundred-dollar bill. "Here—your tip."

The employee shook his head. "I really can't accept—"

"Trust me," Esme said. "I understand what the customer service industry is like now, and let me just say, you're a total saint. Please, take it."

After some cajoling, the employee finally accepted it. Esme and Noah walked outside with their ice cream and took a seat at one of the outdoor tables. As they ate their cones, they had the perfect view of the stars.

"Wow," Esme murmured. "The stars are so bright tonight..."

"Beautiful, isn't it?" Noah asked, briefly glancing at her.

She nodded, licking her Rocky Road ice cream. "I wish we could see them back home. We...can't really see the sky."

Noah shook his head. "That's too bad. I have lots of fond memories as a kid, watching the stars with my parents."

"Sounds nice," Esme said before a silence spread. She cleared her throat. "Can I ask you a question?"

Noah looked away from the stars to focus on her. "Of course."

"If you could, would you ever get back with Jill?"

Noah was silent for a long time—much longer than Esme would've liked. "I...I don't know. That's a hard question. Why do you ask?"

Esme shrugged. "Just wondering. How do you feel now that she's getting married?"

He sighed. "Lots of confusing, conflicting emotions. I'm happy for her, but...I'm still angry she broke up with me so quickly. Even if she wanted me back, it would be tough when there's all that pain."

It wasn't the definite no Esme was searching for, but she'd have to take it.

They finished their ice cream, wiping the table with a napkin before throwing it out. Esme followed Noah through the dark to his car. Before they stepped inside, she reached for his arm.

"I don't know if I said it, but thank you for waiting for me tonight."

He shrugged. "It was more exciting than watching TV at home, believe it or not. And I got ice cream, too."

Esme laughed. "Not many people would wait for me or do the things you've done. So again, I thank you."

Noah nodded. "Don't worry about it. I've had a really good time with you. Maybe the best time of my life—"

Esme heard a rustling in the leaves in the parking lot. Something that sounded like glass broke before a thick, gray smoke began to spread around them. Noah looked around in concern.

"What *is* that?" he asked.

Esme looked down at it, beginning to cough. "A...fog potion. Quick—get into the car!"

When Noah started coughing violently, Esme had to help him into the car. She heard something ping off the trees before she realized it was a gun.

"Shooter!" Esme cried, crawling over Noah to get into the passenger seat. "Keep your head down!"

Noah managed to close and lock the doors, still coughing hard. Esme threw herself over him as the bullets pelted their car. Noah reached into his pocket and fumbled for something. A second later, he had it in his hands, and Esme realized it was a cell phone.

"I've got to call the police—"

Esme shook her head, placing her hand over his phone. "No, you can't. These are my people, Noah—I recognize that potion."

"So?" Noah asked. "Why can't I call the police?"

"Because they won't know what to do with my people. Just put your key in and drive out of here!" Esme cried. "Please!"

Noah nodded, starting the car. He pulled out of the parking lot with a screech and took off down the street.

"Now, circle back around," Esme said, "and hide your car in the trees. We might be able to see the shooter escaping."

Noah gawked at her. "Are you crazy? I don't want to go back there!"

"Please, Noah—just do it!"

Noah turned the car around down a back street. He circled back to the ice cream parlor and hid his car in the field. Esme and Noah kept their heads down, looking for the shooter.

"See anyone?" Noah whispered.

"No—wait! Look over there."

Esme pointed at a shadow figure walking down the street. They had a pistol in their hands—a unique model made only in Fairhaven. When they stepped beneath the light, heading toward the storm drain, that was when Esme recognized them.

"That's one of the guards," Esme whispered. "He's under General Orion's command, the one who watches over my father. He's the father of my best friend, Alva."

"You think she's in on it too? That she wanted you to get shot?"

"No—I don't. She's been my best friend forever. She couldn't."

But would she? Esme didn't know anything for certain anymore.

"Hold on a second," Noah said, watching the guard vanish into the storm drain. "Why would a guard want to kill you? Did your father send them?"

Esme shook her head, having a sinking suspicion that Senator Remus was involved somehow. "No—I'm certain this isn't my father's doing. As the royal family, we've made some enemies. I don't know why they want me dead, but I'm pretty sure they have a plan."

"You can stay with me if you don't feel safe. I'm really, really concerned about you, Esme. This is getting dangerous. I don't want anything to happen to you."

Esme's jaw set, determined. "Thanks for offering, Noah, but I won't let them drive me away from my home. They did that already with my kingdom."

"Can you tell your father what happened?"

She felt torn. "I don't know. I want to warn my father about all of this, but I'm not allowed to go home yet. Even if the guards come back to check on me...there's no telling how many of them are involved in this conspiracy. And they know where I live, too."

"Surely, your father has people who can absolutely be trusted."

Esme thought of Fairy godmother Odelia. "My godmother promised to watch over him. I would trust her with my life. And my father's." Feeling reassured, she turned back to Noah.

"Now, are you sure you're okay?"

He nodded, coughing again. "Yeah, I think the last of that stuff is out of my lungs. You said it was a potion?"

"Yes—specially made in my kingdom. The shooter most likely was watching us and wanted to knock me out to kill me without a fight, but I noticed it."

"Good thing," Noah said, his hands shaking. "Just give me a minute to calm down. It's not every day I'm attacked like this."

Esme placed a hand over Noah's, liking the way it felt. "I know. I'm really sorry."

"Don't apologize. Not your fault." He squeezed her hand. "Are *you* okay? You threw yourself on me when the shooting went off. I should've been the one protecting you—you're a princess, for crying out loud!"

Esme shook her head. "I couldn't let you get hurt over a feud in my kingdom. I don't want to lose you."

Noah couldn't stop himself from smiling. "Well, thank you. Does that duke, Cullen, have anything to do with this?"

Esme paused, thinking. "Murder doesn't seem like his style, but he *did* threaten us. It's too early to say. But if they were bold enough to try to assassinate me when I was with you, you might be in danger, too. Maybe we shouldn't hang out anymore —for your safety."

Noah shook his head, starting the engine again. "Don't worry about me, Princess—just keep yourself safe. I'm not going anywhere."

As he drove her home, Esme stole glances at him from the passenger seat, hoping his kindness wouldn't cost him more than she could bear.

CHAPTER 15

After Noah dropped Esme off at her apartment, they said goodnight before she changed into her pajamas. She watched him drive away from the window, hoping and praying that he wouldn't get hurt. It had been a close call already.

And Esme was sure she wouldn't forgive herself if she got Noah killed.

As soon as she pulled back the blankets to her bed, she heard a rustling at the door. Fearing it was the guard returning, she grabbed a knife from the kitchen, tip-toeing toward the noise. When she looked out the peephole, she sighed in relief.

It was Fairy Godmother Odelia! She'd never been so glad to see anybody in her life. But what was she doing on Earth?

She flung open the door, her eyes widening. "Fairy Godmother Odelia!"

"Oh, my dear Esme!" Fairy Godmother Odelia cried, throwing herself into her arms. "I was so worried about you. My goodness, how much you've changed."

Esme looked down at her pajamas. "Yeah, I guess I have. No more pink gowns for me—I've been trying to blend in better."

"I see. It suits you very well," Fairy Godmother Odelia said, pulling back. "And my, what a lovely apartment! Anyway, I just wanted to come to the surface and check on you. The guards gave me your address and your father let me go for one hour. I suppose everything is going well, then?"

"I ticked off a lot of things on the checklist already, but—"

"I knew you could do it," Fairy Godmother Odelia interrupted with a big grin. "You'll be home in no time and everything will be perfect again."

Esme rose to her feet, pacing. "It's not perfect. In fact, something is terribly wrong. I wasn't sure I'd be able to get a message back to warn my father."

Odelia's eyes widened with alarm. "What message?"

"An assassin came after me. They tried to knock me out with a potion before shooting at me...and they were wearing a guard uniform when I circled back to look."

Fairy Godmother Odelia gasped. "But the guards have taken an oath to never hurt any member of the royal family! They've sworn their loyalty. Alva's father and his guards would never do this to us."

"Maybe they've given their loyalty to someone else. Maybe they believe that person could rule Fairhaven better."

Fairy Godmother Odelia paused. "And I suppose you have someone in mind?"

"Senator Remus, his wife, Lady Nyssa, and Fairy Godmother Zamira. You were the one who told me how evil Zamira is, and we both know they want to bring magic to the surface. Senator Remus has been obvious in his hatred of my father's rules. They fight like dragons and phoenixes!"

"Well, it *has* been a while since I've seen Zamira or the Senator. I just assumed they were busy," she mused. "But Lady Nyssa's been constantly by your father's side since you left."

Esme raised an eyebrow. "Doing what?"

"Royal duties, mostly. Eating dinner with him, giving him advice. She hasn't left him for one moment."

Esme paused, thinking. Why was Lady Nyssa so desperate to get closer to him?

"No wonder she wanted me gone," Esme muttered. "With me out of the picture, she can suck up to him now. It must be related to her father's plan—I know it is. And I stand by what I said before—Nyssa was the one who gave me the alcohol."

Fairy Godmother Odelia tipped her head, considering. "She *is* her father's daughter, after all. Senator Remus is a sneaky, methodical man. Perhaps something *is* going on that we don't know about..."

"Whatever it is, keep watching them. You might be my father's only hope if the kingdom's at stake."

Fairy Godmother Odelia nodded, rising to her feet. "Alva's been watching her like a magical hawk, too. But back to the guard. Did you see what he looked like?"

Esme shook her head. "No—sorry. I was too far away. But I *am* certain he was wearing his guard's uniform, and he must've acquired the potion from a fairy godmother. They're the only ones with magic."

"Zamira is a very good potion master—better than me. Perhaps I should invite myself over to their mansion and snoop through her things."

"Just be careful," Esme said, placing a hand on her shoulder. "I don't want you to get hurt."

Fairy Godmother Odelia smiled. "I could say the same thing to you, dear. Only a few more weeks and then you can come back home."

When she said that, Esme thought she'd feel relieved—happy to be going back home. But now, it only made her sad. Going home meant giving up her apartment, new friends, and more importantly, Noah.

"I'll be counting down the days until you're back in the palace where you belong—and I'll be keeping a closer eye on the guards, too."

Esme nodded. "Good idea. If they want me dead, they'll probably want the same for my father. Why else would they want to kill a princess if not for a coup?"

"I just don't know, dear. Everything has gotten so complicated..."

"Tell me about it," Esme mumbled. "Have you seen Duke Cullen lately?"

She shook her head. "No—he's gone missing, too."

"And I know why. He's been to the surface to harass me. He's still angry I rejected his marriage proposal."

"That's ridiculous!" Fairy Godmother Odelia cried. "The King didn't give him permission to go to the surface."

"I know, I know—but I can handle him. It's the assassin I'm more worried about."

Fairy Godmother Odelia frowned. "Me, too. Well, I should get back home before my hour is up." She stroked Esme's hair. "I've missed you dearly. Alva, too, and even your father."

Esme felt a pang. "Does he regret sending me away?"

"I don't know about that," Fairy Godmother Odelia said, shifting uncomfortably. "He still insists time in the human realm will help you. I think it has. Alva's been petitioning to see you, too, but your father fears you two will get into trouble."

Esme rolled her eyes. "Of course, he does. Tell Alva I miss her and warn her about the guards."

"I will. Should I also tell your father?"

Esme hesitated. "I don't know. Someone could overhear, like a snooping guard and alert the culprits. They'd be even more dangerous if they knew we suspected what they were up to. And this situation...it's getting deadlier by the day. I don't want my father—or anyone else in either world—to get hurt."

She rubbed her temple. "Would he even believe it, coming from me?" she said, feeling sad. "No. Don't tell him. I know you'll keep him safe."

"I'll personally watch over the kingdom and ensure your father will be all right. I'll be your insider." Fairy Godmother Odelia smiled. "You speak like a wise general, Princess. You could take General Orion's place one day, you know. Especially if he or anyone else in the guard is a traitor."

Esme surprised herself with a laugh. "No, thanks. I had a taste of combat with the assassin, and I have to say, I didn't like it."

"Very well," Odelia said, glancing around. "Will you at least give me a tour before I leave?"

Esme nodded. "Certainly—follow me into the bedroom. I have my own bathtub and walk-in closet."

"Oh, my," Fairy Godmother Odelia said, impressed as she looked around her bedroom. "It's not a castle, but it looks cozy. And what is this?"

She walked to the nightstand, picking up the picture of Esme and Noah from the aquarium. Esme blushed and ran to take it out of her hands. She placed the picture against her body, trying to hide it.

"It's nothing," Esme muttered.

"Oh?" Fairy Godmother Odelia asked, turning around. "Is that a blush I see on your cheeks, dear?"

"What? No! You're just seeing things. Must be the stress of coming to Earth."

"You can't lie to your Fairy Godmother, dear. I know all your secrets," she said with a smile. "What's his name?"

"Noah," Esme said with a sigh, setting down the picture frame. "And he's been driving me around town. But you can't tell Father—I'm not supposed to have help."

"I see nothing wrong with making a friend. You two look

like you had a good time," Fairy Godmother Odelia said, glancing at the picture. "Do you care for him?"

"Yes," Esme said, without hesitation.

"Hmm. Well, I'll just give you this advice. Always listen to your heart."

Esme paused for a moment. What was her heart telling her about Noah? She wasn't sure yet.

Fairy Godmother Odelia walked toward the door, her blue gown trailing behind her. "Since there's no magic on the surface, I must walk back to the storm drain. But I will *always* be with you. Best of luck on your journey, Esme."

As she disappeared down the hallway, Esme closed the door, getting into bed as her mind filled with fear about the assassin—and what would happen if she couldn't protect Noah, her friends, and her kingdom.

ESME HAD NIGHTMARE AFTER NIGHTMARE, each one with Noah getting killed. Then Senator Remus, Duke Cullen, and Lady Nyssa's faces would appear. When she woke up the next morning, her pillow was damp with tears.

After she had showered, dressed, eaten cereal, and brushed her teeth, a knock sounded on the door. A big smile spread across her face when she looked through the peephole and saw Noah. She flung the door open, noticing him grinning before hugging him tight.

He smiled, hugging back. "Well, that was a warm welcome. What gives?"

Esme pulled back, shrugging. She didn't want to tell him about the nightmares and worry him. "Just happy to see you, that's all."

"The feeling is mutual. How'd you sleep?" he asked, then frowned. "You look tired. Still stressed about everything?"

Esme nodded, yawning. "Yeah, I guess I am. Who wouldn't be? But at least the bed was very soft."

"Silver linings. Did you have any more trouble last night? No one came around, did they?"

Just my Fairy Godmother, Esme wanted to say. It hurt to lie to him.

She faked a smile. "It was quiet. Was it the same where you live?"

"Yes—thank goodness. Are you ready for your job interview? My boss is really excited to meet you."

Esme nodded, grabbing her keys. "Lead the way."

"Oh, before I forget," Noah said, reaching into his pocket to pull out a business card. "This is for Dylan. I found a youth counselling service through my organization. One therapist even specializes in grief in children."

She grinned. "Thank you, Noah. I should check on him and give this to Tanya."

After Esme locked the door behind them, they went and knocked on Tanya's apartment. She answered the door a second later in her uniform and smiled.

"Esme! My boss just called me," Tanya began. "She said you worked there last night. Is that true?"

Esme nodded. "I just needed one shift. I...wanted to see what the fast-food industry was like."

"Well, she said you were a guardian angel during the busiest hour. And you'll never believe this, but she's offering me a raise!"

Esme grinned. "I'm so happy for you, Tanya. I hope the extra money will help."

Tanya nodded, stepping outside. "Oh, it will. And about Dylan...he's been doing much better since you talked with him yesterday. I don't know what you said, but he's been nicer to me. Nicer overall, actually."

"That's wonderful. Did you talk with him, too?"

"Yes—we had a heart-to-heart about his father. We shared our favorite memories. Vincent and Lindsey did, too. I wasn't sure about showing my children just how badly I've been struggling with my husband's death, but it brought us closer. Thank you for suggesting it, Esme."

"Glad I could help. And speaking of struggling, Noah found you this counselling service for Dylan. Maybe you and your other children could look into it as well."

Tanya took the card, nodding. "I'll call the number and go from there. Thank you both—you have no idea how much your support has meant. Is there some way I can repay you?"

Esme shook her head. "No—just take care of yourself. Do you have someone to look after your kids today?"

"Yeah, Gina's coming over in a few minutes. Thanks for watching them yesterday. I can pay you for babysitting—"

Esme held up her hand. "Tanya, that isn't necessary. Knowing that I helped Dylan is payment enough."

Tanya beamed from ear to ear. "Really, you two are incredible. I'm so happy you moved here."

After Tanya went into the apartment to get her kids breakfast, Esme began walking down the hallway. Noah was smiling at her for a few seconds before she noticed and frowned.

"What?" she asked. "Do I have something on my face?"

He laughed as he pressed the elevator button. "No—nothing like that. You've just made a difference in so many people's lives, and you've only been here a few days. You're amazing, Esme."

Esme blushed, getting into the elevator. "It's not a big deal. Besides, I'm only doing what the checklist is telling me."

Noah shook his head as they got off on the lobby floor. "I

think you've gone above and beyond that list, Esme. It's just a blueprint—you're the one with the good heart who's making it all happen. I believe you're a good person. It's too bad your father doesn't see all your wonderful qualities, too."

Esme thought about his words as they walked to his car. It was true—she *did* enjoy helping Tanya, Dylan, and anyone else she came across. Before, living in Fairhaven as a spoiled princess, she didn't care about anyone but herself. Her time on Earth had served her well. Maybe Noah was right.

"You're a good person, too, Noah," Esme finally said as they got to the car. "I mean that."

It was his turn to smile as he got inside.

He drove her to his work building downtown, pointing out more tourist spots along the way. Esme noticed the tall skyscraper with the words HUMAN CONNECTION and the symbol of two clasped hands. When he parked around the back, she followed him into the lobby.

"Wow," she muttered, looking around at the busy offices and phones ringing. "Big place."

Noah nodded. "And lots of projects are being worked on right now. We're helping people all over the world."

As they walked by a giant door, Esme peered in and noticed it connected to a homeless shelter with a food pantry. The man she had seen from the pawnshop was in there, getting food.

"And here's my office," Noah said, opening a glass door that read FUNDRAISER MANAGER. "I'm in charge of setting up fundraisers and making party lists. It's less glamorous than it sounds, but it does help people."

Esme glanced around the office. She noticed a desk, computer, printer, and several accolades on the wall. Noah had put up pictures of people they had helped and the events that had raised money for their outreach. She noticed many causes

—from fighting homelessness to raising money for cancer research and school programs.

A man knocked on the glass door, peering in. "Mr. Crawford? I need your help with that spreadsheet again."

Noah turned to Esme. "I'll be right back. Wait for me—I want to personally introduce you to my boss."

Esme nodded as Noah left, sitting in his chair. She spun in it a few times before she noticed a familiar picture frame on his desk. It was the same picture she had from the aquarium of the two of them. As she held it up with a grin, she couldn't help but wonder...

Did he feel the same way about her, too?

When she heard footsteps approaching, she put the picture down and rose to her feet. Noah entered a second later with a smile. "All finished. Are you ready for your job interview?"

Esme nodded, smoothing down her pantsuit. "I think so. How do I look?"

"Perfect—as always," he said with a twinkle in his eyes. "Follow me."

Esme walked with Noah down the hallway, politely saying hello to the other employees. They stopped at a glass door that read GISELLE McMILLAN, CEO. Esme could see a red-headed woman in her mid-fifties sitting behind her desk on a phone call.

When Noah knocked on the door, Giselle looked up and noticed Esme. She grinned and hung up the phone before walking across the room. She opened the door, gesturing for them to come inside.

"I take it this is the Esme I've heard so much about?" Giselle asked.

Noah nodded. "Yes—and I think she'd be a real asset to your team, Ms. McMillan."

"I hope so. I don't give interviews to just anyone, you know. Come on in, Esme. Noah, you can wait outside."

Noah looked a little disappointed he couldn't come in but nodded, sitting in a nearby chair in the lobby. Esme entered and shut the door behind her as Giselle took a seat at her desk. She had many pictures of herself at different functions on the walls. Esme noticed Giselle had expensive taste—her pantsuit was designer, and her gold watch glimmered in the light.

"Come sit," Giselle said. "I don't bite."

Esme nodded, sitting down. "Thank you. Noah tells me you've done good work with your non-profit."

She shrugged. "I like to give back. I started small and built this organization from the ground up. But enough about me—let's talk about you. Noah says you have a lot of experience with parties?"

Especially in crashing them.

Esme nodded. "More than I can count."

Giselle grinned. "Perfect! I'll need you to use that skill. Right now, I'm planning a charity auction. Would you be willing to work long hours?"

Esme shrugged, remembering magical auctions from back home. She assumed this one would be a lot simpler. "If it helps people, why not?"

"Excellent, excellent. And what would you say your best asset is?"

Esme had never been asked that before. She was expected to be loyal and proper all the time—she didn't have the opportunity to be anything else. Esme took a second before responding.

"My best asset is that I believe everyone has potential. Everyone can help and be a better person."

"A very good answer. Now, do you have any questions for me?"

"Sure. What kind of work would I be doing here?"

Giselle pointed at the row of offices. "Mostly what you see the other employees doing. I'm very busy, so they do most of the legwork. We're talking setting up fundraisers, charity balls, traveling. That sort of thing. Answering phone calls and ordering supplies, too."

Esme sighed in relief. None of it sounded too hard. "I'd love to do that. Sounds exciting."

Giselle looked at her. "You know, I like what I've heard in here. I want to offer you the job of fundraiser manager. I want you to start right away."

Esme grinned. "That sounds wonderful! But...isn't that Noah's job?"

Giselle sighed, rising to her feet. "You're right—it is. And your first responsibility as my new employee is to fire him."

CHAPTER 16

Esme blinked. "Pardon me?"

"You heard me," Giselle said, frowning. "Although it doesn't bring me any pleasure, I need Noah Crawford fired. I don't want to do it myself—I have a kind reputation to uphold, you know."

"But I don't understand," Esme said. "Noah's a good man and a hard worker—I've seen it myself. Why would you ever want to fire him? Did he do something wrong?"

Giselle sat down. "All right—I'll tell you. But you have to promise not to breathe a word of this to anyone. It could severely damage my organization's reputation. Do you understand?"

Esme nodded, fearing what it could be.

"Last night, I got a phone call from a man named Cullen," Giselle began, and Esme's stomach dropped. "He claimed an employee of mine—Noah Crawford—had assaulted him on the street. When I asked him to come in, he had the bruises to prove it."

Esme sat in silence for a few seconds, unable to believe it. Cullen had *really* been that petty as to contact Noah's work and get him fired? Was this all part of punishing her for rejecting him?

"But how do you know the assault *really* happened?" Esme asked, trying to cover for Noah. "Bruises don't mean anything. Do you have proof?"

"Well, not exactly," Giselle said, sitting up straighter. "He described Noah in great detail, through—blond hair, blue eyes, even the freckles on his face. It was a very good description. He's clearly seen Noah before."

Esme scoffed. "That doesn't mean anything. He could've seen Noah on the street before—"

"And why would this man lie?" Giselle asked. "What would he have to gain from it? It doesn't make any sense."

Esme couldn't tell her the truth, but she didn't want to give up. "Cullen could be a troublemaker—"

Giselle held up a hand to silence her. "Look, it doesn't matter. Cullen threatened to go to the police and report Noah if he wasn't disciplined harshly. And if word gets out that an employee of mine got into a fistfight on the street, it wouldn't look good for me—uh, my organization. We're trying to avoid scandals."

"How did Cullen even find out about Noah's job?"

"Apparently, a business card fell out of Noah's pocket after the alleged assault. Cullen had it—stained with his blood and dirt—that further corroborated his story."

In Esme's mind, it all began to make sense. Without that business card, Cullen wouldn't have known Noah's name or where he worked. Noah had given Esme one, too, and she knew he carried them around.

Esme cleared her throat. "This man didn't mention me, did he?"

Giselle frowned. "No, he didn't. Should he have?"

"No," Esme said, quickly. "Not at all."

Esme wondered what kind of game Cullen was playing. He was trying to ruin only Noah and not her? That didn't make much sense in her mind.

"Anyway, it leaves me with no choice," Giselle continued, sighing. "Noah has to be terminated from our organization. It wouldn't look very good if word got out that a humanitarian assaulted an innocent man on the street, would it?"

Cullen's not as innocent as you think, Esme wanted to say.

"Please—I know Noah. If he *did* do this, I'm sure it was for a good reason," Esme said, putting on the same puppy dog eyes she used to manipulate her father. "Don't fire him. He's been a loyal employee and deserves better."

Giselle sighed. "As I said before, I don't want to. I like Noah—I really do. But Cullen is demanding I take a stand or else he'll go to the police or media. I need you to do this as your first task, Esme. Prove yourself to me."

Esme stole a glance out the glass door, noticing Noah in the waiting area. He was pacing back and forth, looking nervous on Esme's behalf. He really wanted her to get that job. She knew at that moment that she couldn't do anything to hurt him—a man so pure and good-hearted.

Esme rose to her feet, making her decision. "If my job here hinges on firing Noah, then I'll be leaving. Noah's my friend—and I won't hurt him like this. You'll have to break the news yourself. Good day and thank you for your time, Ms. McMillan."

As Esme walked toward the glass door, Giselle rose to her feet. "Wait! I really *do* think you'd be an asset to our team. I'd like you to work for us."

Esme spun around. "Then keep Noah employed. That's my only request."

Giselle and Esme stared at each other for a few seconds, neither woman refusing to back down. Giselle might've been a savvy businesswoman who always got what she wanted, but Esme was a princess.

And princesses always won.

Giselle looked away first, sighing. "Fine—Noah can stay. But he must be demoted. He has to pay for what he did somehow, and Cullen won't be satisfied until he is."

Esme nodded, realizing it was better than nothing. "All right—I agree to those terms. Do you still want me to tell him?"

"Yes, please," Giselle said, taking a seat behind her desk to go through some paperwork. "And when you're finished, come and see me. We have to set up your office. And I'll need your help on your first project."

Esme nodded, opening the glass door to the office. When Noah noticed her, he rushed over immediately, looking nervous. "So? Did you get the job?"

Esme sighed. "I did, Noah."

"That's wonderful!" he cried, then his smile faded. "Why don't you look happy about it?"

Esme glanced around, realizing how busy and loud the row of offices was. "Can we talk in your office? I have to tell you something, and you're not going to like it."

Noah looked confused. "Yeah, sure. Follow me."

After Esme followed Noah to his office, she shut the door behind them. Noah looked even more worried as he took a seat behind his desk. Esme decided to stand, pacing in front of him.

"I don't know how to say this, so I'm just going to come right out with it," Esme said, working up the courage to look at Noah. "You're being demoted."

Noah's face fell. "What? Why? Oh my God, this is awful."

"One word—Cullen," Esme grumbled. "Your business card fell out of your pocket after you punched him. He found it and contacted your boss—"

Noah groaned. "Oh, I see where this is going. Giselle values her reputation above everything else. I guess I should just be happy I'm only getting demoted. I do understand the dangers of bad publicity. Doesn't make it hurt less, though."

"Yeah, I know. She actually *did* want to fire you," Esme said, sitting across from him. "I managed to convince her not to."

Noah raised an eyebrow. "You did? Giselle doesn't change her mind that often. How'd you manage that?"

"I told her I wouldn't work for her unless you were still here. She likes me and was desperate to have me here. I'm sorry I couldn't let you keep your old position—"

"Are you kidding?" Noah asked with a smile, but there was still pain written across his face. "Esme, you saved my skin. Thanks to you, I'll be able to keep working here. You're amazing."

Esme shrugged. "I know you would've done the same for me. I still feel bad about it, though—how I'm taking your job."

"Don't be," Noah said, firmly. "It was Giselle's decision after Cullen forced her into it. If anything, I blame him. And I know you'll do well here. I can't say I'm not disappointed by all this—I do love my job—but I understand."

Esme sighed. "I just hate Cullen for what he's done to you. If he thinks he has a chance with me now, he's got it all wrong. And this kind of stuff is more up his alley than sending assassins."

"Thank goodness for that, I guess," Noah muttered, glancing at the door. "Esme, we need to talk in private."

Esme frowned. "Isn't that what we're doing now?"

"People are always listening," Noah said, cryptically. "I have a quiet, private spot in mind. What I have to tell you is important."

"Well, okay," Esme muttered, growing more worried. "But it can't take long. Giselle wants me back in her office soon."

"Don't worry," Noah said, opening his door. "I'll talk fast."

Esme nodded, following him down the corridor. "Okay. Here I thought I was the one bringing news..."

Noah laughed, reaching the unisex bathroom. He made sure no one was looking before he opened the door and pulled Esme inside.

Noah locked the door, then turned to her. "Esme, I think I've known you long enough to realize you can be trusted. Am I right?"

Esme nodded. "Of course. You've kept my secret that I'm a princess, after all."

Noah smiled. "Right. Well, I think it's time I tell you why I'm really working here—and why being demoted will make my mission harder."

"Your mission?" Esme asked, frowning. "What's going on?"

"Do you remember when I said my dad was hard to please? And that he was a police detective?"

Esme nodded.

"Well, to finally measure up to him, I decided to become a private investigator. And he asked me to get a job here a year ago on a special mission. It's about Giselle McMillan, my boss—*our* boss now."

Esme gasped. "Is she a criminal?"

"Well, that's what my dad wants me to figure out. He's heard reports from old employees that Giselle's gotten so rich because she's been stealing from charity donations."

Esme thought for a moment, nodding. "Her watch *did* look pretty expensive. You'd think a leader of a humanitarian organization would want that money to go to helping people—not herself."

"Unfortunately, I think Giselle only cares about herself and her image," Noah said with a sigh. "I hope you aren't mad that I lied to you about why I'm here."

Esme shook her head. "I'm not mad. It's a noble thing

you're doing, Noah. If Giselle *is* stealing money—even from her own business—she needs to be stopped."

Noah sighed in relief. "Glad you see it my way. I was worried you'd be upset with me."

"And *I* was worried you'd be upset with me for taking your job."

Noah chuckled. "Then I guess we were both worried for no reason. But it's true what I told you before—I *do* enjoy working here and helping people. No one knows I'm undercover. Well, except for my dad and you now."

"I'll keep my mouth shut—I promise. But you said you've been here for a year. Has your investigation turned up anything?"

"Not yet, but I think I'm close. I managed to read some financial records last week, and there have been thousands of dollars unaccounted for in the last month alone. I'm sure a lot more money has gone missing within the last year."

"Hmm—suspicious," Esme muttered. "Why hasn't anyone else noticed it?"

"That's the thing—the records always go missing a few days later. No one has time to look into it before they vanish."

"And you think Giselle took that money?"

"Why not? She'd have the perfect cover. No one would suspect her, and if they did, she could just lie and cover it up."

Esme nodded. "Well, I hope you stop her. Best of luck."

As Esme tried to leave, Noah grabbed her arm. "There's a reason I'm telling you all this, Esme. I don't like keeping secrets from you, but there's something else."

"Oh?"

"With my demotion, I won't have the same freedom as before to snoop. And Giselle might be watching me more closely to make sure I don't misbehave again. I was hoping that since you have my job, you could also work undercover with me."

"You want me to spy? Oh, I don't know…"

"Please, Esme," Noah said, looking into her eyes. "I need your help. Not only to prove myself to my father but also to save this organization. If you won't do it for me, think about all the people that money could've helped. Of how many more will suffer because of her greed."

When he put it like that, Esme realized she couldn't refuse.

"All right," she said. "I'll keep my eyes peeled for anything strange. And I'll go snooping through her things when she's not looking."

"Thank you, Esme," Noah said, releasing her. "I know this is a big ask on your first day, but I really appreciate it."

Esme felt the butterflies fluttering in her stomach again. "Don't mention it."

"I'd better leave the bathroom first. People might think we're dating if they see us leave together, and believe me, rumors spread like wildfire in small offices like these," Noah said, rolling his eyes. "I'll meet you out there."

Noah opened the door, poking his head out to make sure the coast was clear. When he had left, Esme hung around for a few minutes, smoothing down her hair in the mirror.

"I can do this," she muttered to herself. "I can do this…"

As she left the bathroom, all she could think about was Noah's honesty. He had taken a real risk telling her about his undercover work. She wanted to tell him everything about her magical home, too, but couldn't. It made her feel like a liar—like their relationship was only one-sided.

Esme found Noah waiting outside Giselle's office. She nodded at him before knocking on the door, smoothing down her pantsuit. Giselle got up from her desk and opened it as her eyes flickered between Esme and Noah.

"You're back," Giselle said. "How did it go?"

"I told him," Esme said, gesturing at Noah. "He understands."

Giselle sighed. "Noah, I'm so sorry. I hope you know I've come to see you like family—like my most trusted confidant. I hope there aren't any hard feelings between us that would jeopardize that now."

"Of course not," Noah said, faking a smile. "I get why you did it. And thank you for letting me keep my job here."

"That was all Esme, actually," Giselle said. "She convinced me."

Noah smiled at her. "I know. Anyway, I promise to be on my best behavior from now on."

Giselle nodded. "Good. The same goes for you, too, Esme. Each employee represents this organization—its ideals. People are watching, and we have to be shining examples of kindness and generosity."

Noah gave her the side-eye.

Esme stood up straighter. "I understand, Ms. McMillan. I won't let you down."

"That's what I like to hear," Giselle said with a grin. "Now, for your office..."

Giselle rushed into her office, picking a plaque up from her desk. When she brought it over to them, Esme looked down, realizing it had her name on it. It said ESME FAIRHAVEN, FUNDRAISER MANAGER.

"I had this custom-made in our printing room while you spoke with Noah," Giselle said, handing it over. "Just slide it into the slot where Noah's name used to be. As for you, Noah, you'll be given a cubicle. Unfortunately, your demotion means you won't have an office anymore."

"I understand," Noah said, nodding. "I don't mind."

"Good. Now, let's get this over with—we have much to discuss."

Esme and Noah followed Giselle down the corridor, stopping at Esme's new office. Giselle ripped the nametag that belonged to Noah out of there—handing it to him for his new desk—before she placed Esme's nametag on the door. It shimmered bronze in the light.

"Collect your things from the office, Noah, and I'll show you to your new cubicle. And be quick about it."

After Giselle's high heels clicked away to the office area, Noah turned to Esme and lowered his voice. "While Giselle is showing me to the cubicle, this is your chance to snoop around her office. There're no cameras in there—she values her privacy. Once I'm finished gathering my stuff, run off and look through her desk. I've never been able to get in there."

"And if I find something incriminating?"

Noah handed over his phone, opening the camera feature. "See this button? Press it to take a picture of whatever you find. Good luck, Esme."

Esme nodded, waiting as Noah entered his office. He collected his things—including the picture of them, which he tried to hide from Esme—and put them in a box. As he left the office, he winked at her, following the path to the cubicles. Giselle waited for him there, lecturing him as he set up his new workspace.

After Esme glanced around to make sure no one was looking, she tiptoed toward Giselle's office and opened the door. She knew she didn't have much time, so she rushed to the desk, opening all the drawers. She found normal things in there—from makeup to pens to paper—but the last drawer made her eyebrows raise.

It had a bunch of receipts—with Giselle's signature on them. She had bought more expensive things than the watch, like a new car, a new iPhone, and custom-made jewelry. Esme quickly snapped a picture of the receipts before she rushed to the door. As she opened it, she came face-to-face with Giselle.

Giselle frowned. "Esme—you're in my office. Can I help you with something?"

Esme had to think of a lie quickly. "I was just waiting for you. You said you had an event I needed to plan?"

She feared Giselle wouldn't buy it, but then she smiled and entered the office. "I like a dedicated employee. In many ways, you remind me of myself, Esme. Take a seat."

When Esme did, she hoped Giselle wouldn't notice she had been searching through her desk. If she did, she didn't mention it, taking a seat in her leather chair.

"I need you to finalize a fundraiser at the local art gallery. I've already gotten approval to host it there, wrote out a guest list, and yadda yadda yadda. People can browse the paintings and eat while they donate to a great cause," Giselle said, handing Esme a notepad and a pen. "Write down everything I tell you. We need caterers ASAP, decorations, a safe to hold the generous donations..."

As Giselle rambled on, Esme tried her best to get it all down.

"...and don't forget to double check the RSVPs from the guest list. Some of my favorite people in town are coming. Celebrities, mostly, and the mayor," Giselle said with a grin. "Speaking of which, I have an important announcement to make at the fundraiser. Make sure all the guests know about it in advance— it'll be a good incentive to show up. And donate, of course."

Esme nodded. "Got it. Anything else?"

"Yes—one thing. After you send off the guest list, I want you and Noah to meet me outside," Giselle said, fluffing her hair. "We're going to the soup kitchen next door. I want journalists there, so invite them—quickly. We're going to be feeding the homeless."

Esme rose to her feet. "Consider it done."

Giselle smiled. "I think I like you already, Esme."

Spending years answering to my demanding father has finally come in handy, Esme thought.

As Esme left her office, Noah was hanging around outside. He pulled her away from the crowd and lowered his voice. "So? What happened?"

"I'm planning a fundraiser at the art gallery where she has a big announcement. No idea what it is—she says it's a surprise. And we're supposed to go next door to the soup kitchen. I need to call some local journalists and get them over there."

Noah rolled his eyes. "See what I mean? It's all about her image. Did you find anything in her office?"

Esme nodded, handing over his phone. "Yes—and I think it's going to help your investigation."

CHAPTER 17

Noah looked at the pictures Esme had taken on his phone, zooming in on a few of them. "Receipts—and they show big purchases! Nice work, Esme."

She smiled. "Just trying to help."

"Oh, you did—believe me," Noah said, thrusting the phone back in his pocket. He looked over his shoulder to make sure no one was listening and lowered his voice. "This is a good start, but we need something more. Do you think you can keep looking?"

Esme nodded. "I'll try my best. Thanks for including me in this, Noah."

It was his turn to smile. "I figured you deserved to know."

"Giselle seems to think highly of you. She was really upset to have to demote you. Has she ever confided in you about stealing money?"

He shook his head. "No—but if you were doing shady things, would you really tell someone?"

"Good point. Too bad she hasn't let something slip."

"Yeah, I know. Anyway, I have some paperwork to do, but

don't hesitate to come get me for anything, okay? I'll try to help if you have any questions about the job."

"Thanks, Noah. I'll let you know."

"And you should probably keep this," Noah said, handing his phone back. "Just in case. I'll go get another phone after work today and send you a text so you know it's from me."

"Wow—thank you," Esme said, putting it in her pocket. "I'll take good care of it."

Noah nodded, walking back to his cubicle as Esme entered her office. It felt strange to call it that—*her* office. She never had anything like that back home. She closed the glass door, sitting behind the desk in the comfy chair. Everything still smelled like Noah's comforting cologne of sandalwood and cinnamon...

"Snap out of it," Esme muttered to herself. "You have a job to do."

She cracked her knuckles, looking down at the computer. It took her a few minutes to figure out how it worked before she opened a spreadsheet and the calendar on the computer. It had a list of names of the big celebrities in town—or so the internet claimed when she looked them up.

She found as many as she could—like Mayor Bryce Haggarty as Giselle requested—and put them in the spreadsheet. Then she found their contact information and forwarded them the fundraiser invitation. Some personal assistants emailed her back right away, RSVPing to the fundraiser already. After hiring a caterer and a band, she sat back in pride.

"First task complete," she said to herself, smiling. "Not bad, Esme. Not bad at all..."

The next task was the journalists. She looked up all the journalist agencies in Toronto, then emailed them about Giselle's upcoming visit to the soup kitchen. They responded even quicker and told Esme they'd be there soon.

The knock on the door startled Esme, and she looked up to

see Giselle standing there. She had put on makeup, combed her hair, and looked much more glamorous than before. "Is everything ready?"

Esme nodded. "The fundraiser is set up, and the journalists are on their way to the soup kitchen."

"Excellent!" Giselle cried, beaming from ear to ear. "I knew you were the right person for the job, Esme. I think you're going to have a bright future here."

But your future still remains to be seen, Esme thought, *especially if you're skimming donation money.*

"Anyway, let's go find Noah. I want him with us, too," Giselle said, checking her reflection in her handheld mirror. "If word ever does get out about what he did, he needs a strong reputation to get out of it. The journalists will photograph him at the soup kitchen, and that'll look good on his resume."

"Well, then I'm glad he's coming."

Giselle put her handheld mirror down, looking at her with a smirk. "You are? Is there something going on between you two?"

Esme blushed. "No—we're just friends."

"Ah, I see," Giselle said, studying her. "But you want to be more?"

Esme shrugged. "Oh, I...uh—"

"It's all right. I won't tell him," Giselle said, winking. "But just so you know, if you two start dating, I expect your loyalty to me—my non-profit—to come first. We have a lot of work to do —an image to protect."

Esme couldn't believe the things that came out of Giselle's mouth. She sounded so self-centered, so demanding. She knew if her father would've met her, he would think Esme was a saint. She bit her lip to hold back her real opinion.

"I understand," Esme said. "Nothing's going on between us, anyway."

"I think he's still hung up on his ex. He moped around after she dumped him. It really bummed me out, you know. I think her name was Jazz or something."

"Jill, actually."

Giselle's eyebrows raised. "Oh, so he told you about her? You two must be close, then."

Esme shrugged, feeling uncomfortable. "We've talked a little, sure. He helped me settle into Toronto when I first got here, so I owe him a lot."

Giselle glanced over her shoulder, watching Noah working at his desk. "Well, he looks much better since you got into town. And he's taking his demotion well. Must be your effect on him. It's a good thing, too—him whining about his ex all the time was getting on my nerves."

Giselle's ignorance aside, Esme wondered—was it true? Had Esme changed Noah's life for the better?

Esme cleared her throat. "Anyway, can we get going now? The journalists will be next door soon, waiting for us. Wouldn't want to be late."

"Don't think I don't see you changing the subject," Giselle said with a smirk. "But yes, we should get going. Punctuality is important. But there are some things you need to know first— some rules I have."

Esme gulped. She knew the rules would probably be obnoxious and ridiculous—just like her boss.

"First off, don't get in the way of my spotlight. The cameras need to be on me at all times," Giselle began. "Secondly, I need you to wear a big smile. Pretend like you're having the time of your life."

The rules were absurd, but Esme faked a smile. "Got it. Anything else?"

"One last thing," Giselle said, eyeing Esme from head to toe.

"Your outfit's fine—it doesn't upstage me. But you're wearing makeup, yes?"

Esme frowned. "A little bit. Why?"

"I need you to remove it. There are makeup wipes on my desk and a bathroom down the hall," Giselle said, pointing toward the door. "No offense, but I need to stand out. I can't have you looking better than me. Understand?"

"Perfectly," Esme said through gritted teeth.

"Great," Giselle said with a smile. "When you're ready, get Noah and meet me next door. I think I hear journalists pulling up right now. I'll go talk to them while you finish."

Esme watched in disbelief as Giselle put on a big smile, leaving her office. The journalists had arrived and were already snapping their pictures when Giselle stepped outside. Giselle began talking to them in a sweet, soft voice as Esme walked into her office.

She quickly grabbed the makeup wipes, unable to snoop as employees walked down the hallway to see what was going on. She heard them gossiping about Noah's demotion before rushing to the bathroom. She peered into the mirror, looking at her makeup.

"So much for looking my best," Esme muttered, rubbing off her blush and lipstick.

After she threw the makeup wipes out, she walked over to Noah's desk. He looked up at her. "Is it time?"

Esme nodded. "Yeah—her Royal Highness is talking to the journalists right now. I swear, she's even more of a princess than I am."

Noah laughed, rising to his feet. "Tell me about it. Say...did you do something? You look different."

"Oh, I'm not wearing any makeup. Giselle made me wipe it off. Something about me upstaging her."

"Well, you look good even without makeup," Noah said,

grabbing his keys before he began walking to the doors. "Are you coming?"

Esme stood in shock for a few seconds that he had complimented her before nodding. "Right behind you."

When they stepped outside, the cameras began flashing again. Giselle turned around and looked a little jealous that they were getting some of the spotlight. Esme waved, putting on a big smile as Noah did the same.

"Ah, there you two are. You can't blame them for not being as punctual as I am," Giselle joked to the crowd. Esme felt anger bubbling inside of her, but she pushed it away. "Ready?"

Noah nodded. "Always ready to help out."

Giselle walked toward the door to the soup kitchen, turning back to look at the journalists following her. "Volunteering at the soup kitchen is very important to me. If I could, I'd come here every day, but work keeps me busy. We had the soup kitchen put in next door a few years ago…"

As she rambled on to the journalists, Esme turned toward Noah. "She sure does talk a lot."

Noah snorted. "I know. At least the journalists aren't asking me about Cullen. If they knew, I doubt they'd be able to resist."

"We'll see how long he'll keep his mouth shut," Esme whispered back. "I wonder what else he's planning—and if I'm his next target. He obviously went after you to hurt me."

"Don't worry," Noah whispered. "I won't let him get to you. If I have to be your human shield, so be it."

Esme smiled at him only to see a camera flash in her face a second later. When her eyes stopped seeing bright lights, she finally looked to notice a journalist snapping more pictures of them. Noah held up his hand to stop them.

"What are you doing?" he asked.

"I saw you two smiling at each other. Are you two dating?" the journalist asked, lowering her camera. "Because that would be adorable. I can see the headlines now—two humanitarians saving the world and falling in love. Sounds like a Hallmark movie, doesn't it?"

The other journalists nodded, swarming around them. Giselle crossed her arms as her smile faded.

"They aren't dating," Giselle muttered as she moved toward them. "Just friends. Now, come on—let's get inside."

Esme didn't miss the glare Giselle gave her as she entered the soup kitchen. It had many tables set up for the needy, along with televisions and a giant buffet in the back. A chef was handing out cups of soup, turkey sandwiches, and bottled water to the people who needed it most.

"Hello, Ms. McMillan," the chef said. "We're pleased to report that we've fed over two hundred people already today."

Giselle smiled. "That's wonderful. We'd like to help feed even more. Is it okay if the three of us pitch in?"

"Absolutely," the chef said, picking up three hairnets and aprons. "Here you go—please, put these on. Then I can get back to the kitchen while you hand out the bowls of food—"

"Esme?" a man in the crowd asked. "Is that you?"

Esme spun around, noticing the man from the pawnshop. He had set aside his bowl to approach her. "Yes, that's me. I remember you, Edgar. How are you doing?"

"Much better because of you. Because of both of you," he said, glancing at Noah. "Thanks for helping me out and telling me about this place. It's been a godsend."

When the journalists noticed, they began snapping pictures of the three of them talking. Giselle had just put on her hairnet and looked furious.

"It was our pleasure," Noah said.

Esme nodded. "We're just glad you didn't have to sell your wife's ring."

"In love *and* helping people," one of the journalists

murmured before Esme and Noah had a chance to correct them. "How sweet. It'll be front-page news tomorrow!"

As the journalists nodded in agreement, Giselle cleared her throat. "Esme, Noah? Care to help me?"

"Of course," Esme said, turning to Edgar. "Take care of yourself."

Esme and Noah walked toward Giselle who angrily handed them their hairnets and aprons. She didn't chastise them there, but Esme and Noah glanced at each other, knowing it would come as soon as they finished at the soup kitchen. While the chef delivered the food to the front, Esme, Noah, and Giselle handed it out to the line of hungry people as the journalists snapped pictures.

Giselle did the least amount of work, faking a smile every time the cameras flashed. Esme rolled her eyes and focused on feeding the people. As Esme handed out another bowl of soup, she looked up, noticing a familiar face in the window.

Cullen. He was just standing there, looking in at them. Esme glanced at Noah, making sure he was looking at her before her eyes flitted to the window. Noah followed their path and noticed Cullen. He grew tense as Cullen smirked, then turned and vanished down the street.

Esme didn't know what he was planning, but she sighed in relief that he hadn't made a scene—for now. But she was still on edge, just waiting for Remus' moment to strike. And Giselle's anger was like a ticking time bomb.

Both of them were bound to explode sooner or later.

They continued handing out bowls of food for another hour until Giselle smiled at the journalists. "Well, that's all we have time for today. Thanks for coming."

One of the journalists handed Esme a card. "If you two ever get married, we'd love to know about it. The public goes wild for cute love stories like yours."

Before Esme could deny their relationship, the journalists left. Giselle's smile faded immediately as she removed her hairnet and apron. "In my office—both of you."

She stormed off ahead as Esme removed her apron. "Think we're in trouble?"

Noah sighed. "Giselle looks pissed, so I'd say so. I think we stole too much of her limelight."

"I really had no intention of that," Esme said, leaving the soup kitchen with Noah behind her.

Noah shrugged. "I know. I guess we just look good together."

Esme hid a blush as they stepped back into the humanitarian building. They walked toward Giselle's office, finding her pacing behind her desk. Esme closed the door after she and Noah entered.

"Here I thought I could count on your loyalty, Esme," Giselle spat. "And you go and upstage me like that!"

Esme shook her head. "We didn't mean to—"

"But you did," Giselle interrupted. "The story was meant to be about me giving back to the community. If I knew you were going to outshine me, I wouldn't have invited those journalists!"

"Respectfully, I think this organization should be about helping as many people as we can," Noah spoke up. "We need to keep our egos out of it."

Giselle looked flustered. "Well, yes...of course I want to help people. But our reputation is important, too. I thought you understood that."

"We do," Esme said. "And we're sorry if we upset you."

"Because it's your first day, I'll let it slide. But I expect less attention on you both in the future. Good thing I still have that fundraiser tomorrow to get the media back on my side," Giselle muttered. "Anyway, I'm giving you both the rest of the day off. Go home and think about what you did."

"Well, okay," Esme muttered. "See you tomorrow for the fundraiser, Ms. McMillan."

She only huffed as they left. Noah glanced at Esme as they walked to her office. "Well, at least we didn't get fired."

Esme nodded, pulling out her checklist. "Yeah, good thing. And now I can check off volunteering at a soup kitchen and getting a job."

Noah smiled. "I'm happy for you. Wait here—I'll get my things and drive you home."

After Esme grabbed her jacket, Noah walked her to his car. When they got inside, Esme wasn't sad to see the humanitarian organization fade behind them. As much as she liked helping people, she couldn't stand Giselle—especially after she had demoted Noah.

"I'm still going to make it up to you," Esme said, breaking the silence. "For getting you demoted."

Noah shook his head. "Really, Esme, you don't have to—"

"I want to," Esme said, firmly. "And you know I don't take no for an answer."

Noah laughed. "All right—just don't break the bank. I don't know about you, but I could use some music after a stressful day..."

Esme nodded as Noah turned on the radio inside the car. He flipped through the stations, searching for good music. He came across a talk show that made him pause.

"...and police are investigating a strange murder on Dundas Street," one of the radio hosts said. "No details yet, though our sources say the victim died under mysterious circumstances. Detective Dan Crawford is on the scene..."

"Crawford?" Esme asked, frowning.

"That's my dad," Noah replied. "Do you think that strange murder has something to do with your assassins?"

Esme shrugged. "Maybe. I don't know."

"Let's find out," Noah said, putting his foot on the gas. "My dad will let us through."

It took them ten minutes to reach Dundas Street, but when they did, they noticed a swarm of people standing on a sidewalk. Police officers had the area blocked off with yellow crime scene tape. Noah parked on the side of the street, getting out and walking toward the scene as Esme followed.

"No one's allowed beyond the tape, sir," the police officer said. "Please, step back."

Noah looked over his shoulder and noticed his father. "Detective Dan Crawford's my dad. I'm sure he won't mind us being here."

The police officer didn't look convinced. "I'm afraid this is a crime scene, and we can't allow anyone—"

"Dad!" Noah cried, waving his arms. "Dad, it's me!"

"Noah?" the man with the black hair and moustache asked, rising to his feet. "Let my son through, officer."

The police officer nodded, letting Noah and Esme through. Esme immediately noticed the dead woman lying on the ground. She looked middle-aged with her shopping bags around her as if she had just come from the store. But the strange part was that she didn't have any bruises, gunshot holes, or knife wounds.

"Dad, what happened?" Noah asked.

"People walking by found this woman not too long ago," Detective Crawford said, pointing at her. "The woman looks young and healthy, so we suspect murder. A few eyewitnesses say they heard a scream. No suspect was found here, though. It's like they just vanished."

"But...how did she die?" Esme asked. "I don't see any injuries."

"A good observation *and* question. We'll know more at the autopsy," Detective Crawford said, frowning. "Who are you again?"

"Oh, right. Dad, this is Esme Fairhaven."

Esme waved. "Nice to meet you, Mr. Crawford."

"Huh," Detective Crawford muttered. "I've heard about you. My son talks about you non-stop."

"Dad, please," Noah said, trying to hide a blush. "What can you tell us?"

"Well, it happened in broad daylight. A pretty brazen killer, if it *is* murder..."

As the detective rambled on, Esme noticed magical dust on the ground. It was either from a potion bottle or a recently-cast spell...

Which meant magic was slowly beginning to work on Earth.

Esme wondered if it had been used on the woman to kill her. Magic didn't usually leave a trace—Esme proved that when she spiked the punch. As she pondered everything, she looked a few feet over, noticing the unbalanced storm drain.

She hid her gasp. Someone from Fairhaven had come up through there recently—and Esme felt sure they had killed that poor woman. The only question that remained was why...and did it have something to do with Senator Remus and Fairy Godmother Zamira?

CHAPTER 18

"Esme?" Noah asked. "Are you okay?"

Esme's head shot up from the storm drain, noticing Noah and his father staring at her. She faked a smile. "Yeah, I'm fine. Just thinking."

Just worrying, more like, Esme thought. *I hope Fairy Godmother Odelia is okay. I wouldn't want her to get hurt snooping around for me...*

"All this death can be distressing to some people," Detective Crawford said. "If you need to step away to catch your breath—"

"No," Esme said, firmly. "I mean...I'd like to stay. I find it all interesting."

"If you say so," Detective Crawford said with a shrug. "We're almost ready to leave for the autopsy. We're just waiting for the coroner to get here first."

"Can we go, too?" Esme asked. "To the autopsy?"

"If you think you can handle it. But whatever we find, just don't go blabbing about it to the media. This is still a police investigation."

"We promise. And while we wait, I figured I should tell you," Noah said. "I told Esme about my undercover work at Human Connection. She knows I'm looking for evidence against Giselle."

Detective Crawford's eyebrows raised. "You did *what*? You know it's supposed to be a secret, right?"

"I know, I know," Noah grumbled. "But I got demoted this morning. I asked Esme to step in for me since she took my job."

Detective Crawford glanced at Esme. "And you're sure she can be trusted?"

Noah nodded. "With my life."

Esme smiled, grateful Noah had that much confidence in her. "I'll do my best, Detective. You have my word. I like working for Human Connection—I believe in their mission. And if my boss is stealing money, she needs to be stopped."

"And Esme's already found some incriminating evidence," Noah added. "Like receipts in my boss's office. She's been buying some awfully expensive things."

"Hmm. Maybe you'll be valuable," Detective Crawford said, grabbing a business card from his pocket. He handed it to Esme. "Here—take this. It has my phone number. If you need anything, let me know."

Esme nodded, pocketing the business card. "Thanks, Detective."

"Good. Now, back to my son," Detective Crawford said, turning to Noah. "You got demoted? For what?"

Noah looked uncomfortable as he glanced away from his father. "For...punching a man."

"Punching someone?" Detective Crawford asked. "Noah, I am *so* disappointed in you. I taught you to use your words, not your fists! And now you might've jeopardized your undercover work..."

Noah didn't say anything, and Esme noticed the look on his

face. He was hurt—ashamed. She knew Noah had a hard time impressing his father, and she couldn't just stand there and let him berate his son.

"Wait a second," Esme said, and Detective Crawford paused. "Noah didn't tell you the full story. A man was harassing me, and your son came to my rescue. Who knows what he would've done to me if Noah wasn't there?"

Noah nodded. "And then the jerk went to my boss. Something about a business card that fell out of my pocket."

"I know the guy who came after me. He's a vengeful, cruel man," Esme continued. "Your son did the right thing, Detective. You raised a truly caring, compassionate human."

Detective Crawford looked taken aback. "Well...I don't know what to say. I'm glad you saved your friend, but I'm still upset you were demoted, Noah."

Before Esme had a chance to intervene, the coroner—a man in a white doctor's coat, carrying a medical kit—arrived. Detective Crawford excused himself to go talk with him.

When they were alone, Esme placed a hand on Noah's shoulder. "I'm sorry for what your dad said to you. You were right—he *is* harsh."

Noah sighed, watching his father from across the crime scene. "Story of my life. No matter what I do, I just can't win with him. He's impossible to impress."

"Well, if it's any consolation, you've impressed me. I'm glad I met you, Noah."

Noah smiled as he glanced back at her. "It's a big consolation, Esme. Thank you."

A few seconds later, Detective Crawford walked over. "The coroner's taking the body on a stretcher now. We're supposed to meet him at the autopsy. You two coming?"

Noah nodded. "We'll get in my car and meet you there."

After Detective Crawford walked over to his unmarked

police car, Esme joined Noah in his sedan. She waited until they were inside and had started following his father and the ambulance before speaking up.

"Noah, I need to tell you something," Esme began. "I think one of my own people is behind this murder. Several of them, actually."

Noah stole a glance at her, his eyes widening. "What are you talking about?"

"The storm drain, Noah—it had been moved. My people… use storm drains a lot to travel. It's why you saw me coming out of one on my first day here. The guards, too."

"Well, it doesn't mean your people did it," Noah said, his hands tightening on the steering wheel. "Maybe…a construction worker moved it or something."

Esme shook her head. "No, I don't think so. And I saw these particles on the body. My people…have special potions they use, like the time that guard threw that smoke at us. I think they might've killed that woman with a potion."

Noah frowned. "All right—let's say your people did this. Why?"

"I don't know why they killed this woman. Maybe she was just in the wrong place. Enemies sent that assassin after me—and I'm sure it's the same leader," Esme muttered. "It's all for power. There are some people—like Senator Remus, who I mentioned before—that don't agree with the way my father runs things. I think they're attempting a coup."

"What don't they like about your father?"

Esme sighed. "Where do I start? They think he's a weak leader, for one. They really hate some of his policies."

Like the fact that he wouldn't allow them to work on a way to make magic compatible with the surface. Her father would never support ruling over or enslaving the humans, unlike Senator Remus.

"Politics. It sucks." Noah shook his head. "And you suspect this senator guy?"

Esme nodded. "Yes—and his daughter, Lady Nyssa, who's been sucking up to my father since I left. She conspired to get me banished from my kingdom. Her mother, Dr. Breya, is a bright scientist who's...running some new experiments."

Like making magic compatible on Earth, Esme thought. *But how? And would more people die?*

"Some of the guards may be in on it, too," Esme added, leaving out Fairy Godmother Zamira. She wasn't sure how to explain her involvement. "Maybe even Alva's father. Since he commands the guards, after all."

"So, how are we supposed to prove it?" Noah asked.

"I'm not sure we can. Your people don't even know about mine," Esme said. "And Senator Remus isn't easy to catch. Believe me."

"Well, if this is the first in a string of murders, we can't let them get away with it!"

Esme nodded. "I agree. Don't worry, Noah—I'll find a way to stop them."

"*We* will. I want to help you," Noah corrected. "And I guess you want me to keep this from my father?"

"For now, please," Esme said, "just until we get more evidence. My people can be dangerous, and...I'm not sure your police department could stop them. Trust me on that."

The rest of the drive was quiet with Esme silently worrying about what Senator Remus and Fairy Godmother Zamira were going to do next. Everything Esme loved—from Noah to her friends to her real home, was in danger, weighing on her. When they arrived at the coroner's office, Esme followed Noah inside, meeting his father down the long corridor.

"The coroner should be finished in an hour," he said. "We can wait here until he's done."

Esme nodded, taking a seat next to Noah. A few minutes passed in awkward silence before his father spoke up.

"Are you still coming to the cottage tomorrow for dinner?" Detective Crawford asked. "We're getting the whole family together. I know you're busy these days, but your mother and I would like to see you. I even asked Veronica to come, too."

Veronica? Esme's eyebrows rose, wondering who she was in Noah's life.

"I am. Hey, Esme—you should come, too," Noah said. "It's okay if she does, right, Dad?"

Detective Crawford shrugged. "Sure—why not? Your mother loves having guests."

"So, can you make it?" Noah asked as he turned to Esme.

"I guess so," Esme replied. "I don't think I have anything planned."

Noah grinned. "Great—it means a lot that you're coming. You can meet Ronnie, too."

"Who's she?" Esme asked.

"Oh, Veronica—I call her Ronnie. She's been my best friend since high school. I'm sure you two will get along great."

Esme faked a smile, but deep down inside, she worried that another woman had already laid claim to Noah's heart. And here she thought Jill was her biggest competitor if she stayed on Earth to be with Noah—unless she would return home after all.

That decision was still undecided in her heart.

"The entire family's already heard about you—thanks to Noah," Detective Crawford said with a hearty laugh. "So, I'm sure they're all eager to meet you."

Noah blushed, looking down. Esme thought it was adorable.

An hour later, a secretary walked down the hallway, stopping in front of Detective Crawford. "You can go ahead in now. The coroner said he's finished with his autopsy."

"Thank you. Now, lots of people can get queasy during an autopsy," Detective Crawford said to Esme and Noah as he rose to his feet. "I've seen it a million times, so it doesn't bother me. But feel free to step out at any time if you feel sick. Ready?"

Esme and Noah nodded as Detective Crawford opened the door, letting them inside. The coroner stood over the dead woman's body which was covered by a sheet. The coroner had made several incisions, taking everything, from the woman's fingerprints to blood.

"Ah, Detective Crawford," the coroner said, noticing him. "I think you'll find this woman's death as bizarre as I do."

Detective Crawford pulled out his notepad. "Why? What have you learned?"

"Well, for starters, she has this odd glitter substance on her body," the coroner said, showing off the bits of sparkles under the light. Detective Crawford leaned in to look. "I didn't know what it was, so I sent it to the lab. After numerous scans, they can't figure it out, either. I've never seen anything like it before."

Potions, Esme thought. *You'll never understand it.*

"Uh-huh. Strange," Detective Crawford said, writing it down. "Anything else?"

"Yes—perhaps the oddest thing of all. This woman had her major organs removed. The heart, brain, and lungs, which killed her instantly."

"She looks pretty good on the outside," Noah said. "But this...it's awful. All her organs, gone. It's almost evil."

The coroner nodded. "It really is. And another strange part —she has no sagging skin where the organs used to be. No discoloration or incision marks, either."

"Wait a moment," Detective Crawford said. "How could her organs be gone if no one cut them out? They couldn't have just magically disappeared from her body!"

The coroner shrugged. "A very good question. I'm afraid I

have no answers. I assume the loss of those organs was cause of death, but it's all very confusing."

"It makes no sense," Detective Crawford muttered. "The bystanders found the woman seconds after her scream. It would've been impossible for the killer to remove her major organs that quickly without someone seeing it. And without leaving a wound. What kind of monster is responsible for this? I'm really worried for the streets of Toronto."

"At times like these, I'm glad I'm not a detective," the coroner said, covering the woman's face. "Good luck solving this one."

"Thanks," Detective Crawford grumbled. "I'm going to need it."

A witch must've done this, Esme thought, *with some kind of spell.* Esme thought for a moment, wishing her Fairy Godmother Odelia was there so she could ask her which one. Then it hit her—the library!

She had been to her castle's library many times, reading books on fairy godmothers and their spells. One truly wicked one was *Aufer intra praecordia*—which from Latin, translated to 'remove the insides.' It was a dark, dangerous spell, used only in wartime.

There was no doubt in Esme's mind anymore. This woman's murder was magical—and evil.

"Well, thank you for the autopsy," Detective Crawford said as he put his notepad away. "As for you two, Noah and Esme, I'll see you tomorrow evening."

As Noah left with Esme, he glanced at her. "You look like you've seen a ghost. Did that autopsy make you feel nauseous?"

Esme shook her head. "No—it gave me an idea. My people *are* behind this, Noah. They have ways of...removing organs that your people can't comprehend. We're advanced in some ways."

"I see," Noah muttered, walking toward his car outside. "I

guess I should've known something was up after the potion and guards. My dad doesn't know what kind of investigation he's getting into. I'm worried for him."

"I am too. And for you," Esme said, getting into the car. "And it won't stop here. Senator Remus is planning something big—I just know it. I wish I knew what."

"Yeah—me, too," Noah muttered as he started the car's engine. "Just be careful, okay, Esme?"

She laughed. "I could tell you the same thing. Make sure all your organs stay in your body, all right? I don't want to lose you."

Noah patted his chest. "I'll try."

On the ride home, Esme glanced out the window, feeling guilty. It was her people who had killed that innocent woman. It was her people who were plotting to bring magic to Earth, doing all kinds of evil tests to make it happen.

And worst of all, she couldn't even get word to her father to warn him. He didn't want to see her—not for another month. She wasn't sure things could wait that long. She needed to see her father now before something else went horribly wrong.

When Noah pulled into the parking lot of her apartment building, he pulled his key out and turned to her. "I think I'll walk you up to your apartment—just to make sure you get in safe."

Esme stepped out, thinking Noah was being sweet. But he couldn't protect her—not from this—yet he still wanted to. "You don't have to do that."

"I know," Noah said, slamming his door shut. "I want to."

Esme followed Noah up to her apartment. "Well, thanks for walking me up. After today, I think I need a long bath—"

She froze when she looked down at the doorhandle, realizing someone had kicked it open.

"Esme?" Noah asked, frowning. "You okay? Shit, your door."

"I think someone's in my apartment," Esme whispered. "They didn't have a key, so they had to break in."

Noah looked startled. "What? Let me call the police—"

"No," Esme said, standing up straighter. "I'm getting to the bottom of this myself."

Esme kicked the door open, finding the apartment dark. She glanced around, noticing a shadowy figure standing in the kitchen, perfectly still. She watched as the face came into the light and she noticed the gun in their hands.

It was the same guard from the ice cream parking lot. They had found her—at long last.

"Finally, you're home," the guard grumbled. "I've been waiting here forever."

Noah stood in front of Esme. "Look, I don't know what's going on, but we can talk about this. Just put the gun down."

"I can't do that. I have my orders," the guard snarled. "Now, get out of the way, human."

Esme watched as Noah refused to back down. "I won't."

The guard laughed. "You think I won't shoot you? Because I will. A quick death might be kinder for you than what's coming."

"And what is coming?"

The guard smiled. "Humans in chains, exactly where they belong. You'll all see soon enough. If you get in the way, well... we won't be too happy."

For a moment, the image of Noah and all her friends chained up flashed across Esme's mind. She couldn't let that happen. Not in a million years.

Esme noticed a chair to her right. If she could reach it, she could kick it into the guard and dislodge his gun. She slowly crept to it as she made conversation. "Who's your boss?"

"I can't tell you that," the guard replied. "I promised I wouldn't betray them."

"Is it Senator Remus?" Esme asked, slinking closer to the chair.

The guard didn't seem to notice what she was planning as he laughed again. "You think it's just Senator Remus? Oh, Princess—lots of people don't like your father. They hate that he won't allow magic on the surface, that he's too traditional and old-fashioned. He won't listen to any other opinion and it bothers them. It goes deeper than you know. It might even be someone he trusts."

Someone he trusts? Esme wondered. *That's a lot of people. Like Alva's father, for one, and maybe even her.*

"But enough talk," the guard continued. "Once I kill you and fulfil my duty, it won't be your problem anymore."

"What will killing me do?" Esme asked.

"It'll be the beginning of wiping your pathetic family from Fairhaven," the guard snarled. "Goodbye, Princess."

"No, wait!" Noah cried.

Esme flung the chair at the guard, causing him to groan and drop the gun. Noah immediately lunged onto him as the guard recovered, both of them struggling to get it. Esme wanted to do something as she watched them wrestle.

"Noah, be careful!" she cried, looking around for a weapon.

When a gunshot rang out a second later, it was too late. Esme feared the worst as Noah and the guard went still. When Noah stood up, looking down at the guard's gunshot wound, Esme sighed in relief.

He was all right.

"Are you hurt?" Esme asked, rushing toward him.

Noah shook his head. "No...but he is. The gun went off, and..."

Esme checked the guard's pulse. "He's dead. My assassin is dead."

"Oh my god," Noah muttered. "What have I done?"

"It was self defense," Esme said, rising to her feet.

Noah sat down. "Maybe. But I still killed a man."

Esme sighed. "You didn't kill a man, Noah. My people... aren't exactly human."

"What?" Noah asked, looking up. "Then...what are you?"

"I can't tell you more, but don't worry. You won't get in trouble for this, either. Your Earth laws wouldn't even apply here."

Noah ran a hand through his blond hair. "Well, what are we supposed to do with him? With...his body?"

"We'll have to wait until dark and drag him to the storm drain," Esme said, still staring at the body. "My people down there can deal with him. And maybe my father will see it as a warning—that he can't trust everyone around him. I have to tell him about this, my banishment be damned."

"Yeah, okay," Noah muttered, still in a daze. "But I think I deserve answers. Who are you really, Esme? What are your people? Why do you live in the storm drains? What's up with the missing organs and potions and all these guards?"

Esme didn't know where to begin. "Noah, it's not that simple to explain—"

The knock on the door startled them both. Noah immediately grabbed the guard, dragging his body to the bathroom. "We have to hide him. Put some paper towels down to cover the blood—say you spilled some wine. See who's at the door."

Esme nodded, looking out the peephole. It was only Tanya. Once she had laid the paper towels over the blood, it seeped through bright red. She opened the door, faking a smile. "Hey, Tanya. Everything all right?"

"I was just coming to ask you that," she said, looking over Esme's shoulder into the apartment. "We heard a loud noise next door. Sounded like a boom. Wow, is that...blood on your floor?"

"Oh, no, no, no. Just spilled wine," Esme lied. "I'm trying to clean it up. And the boom...well, Noah and I were just..."

"Popping popcorn," Noah said, walking out of the bathroom. "It got a little out of control, but it's nothing to worry about."

"Oh, okay. Glad you're all right," Tanya said with a shrug. "Anyway, I came over to tell you Dylan agreed to grief counselling. He's meeting with a counselor the day after tomorrow."

Esme nodded along, hoping to get Tanya out of her apartment as soon as possible. The body was still in her bathroom. "That's great. Now, I really need to get back to—"

"But only if you go with him. He asked for you specifically."

Esme paused, torn between helping her own people and Dylan. "Well, I am pretty busy these days...but I can try."

Tanya smiled. "Great—I'll come get you when it's time. I hope you can come. Trust me, it would mean the world to Dylan. Thanks for all you've done, Esme."

Esme faked a smile as she closed the door, then turned to Noah. "Thank goodness it wasn't the police."

Noah nodded. "Tell me about it. With all this assassin business, I think I should stay overnight with you. Just to make sure you're safe."

"All right," Esme said, walking closer to him. "I just hope you don't blame yourself for what happened."

"I don't—I blame that assassin for coming after you. I'm just glad you're safe. He nearly killed you."

"He nearly killed you, too. You didn't have to stand in front of the gun for me."

"Didn't I?" Noah asked, cryptically. "But back to the woman's murder. Whoever killed her wasn't human, either, right? None of your people are?"

Esme nodded. "That's right. I wish I could tell you everything, Noah—I really do. But my father wants it to be kept a secret."

Noah sighed, sitting on the couch. "All right—I respect that. But tell me...will that assassin be the last?"

Esme glanced out the window. "I don't know, Noah. I just don't know."

CHAPTER 19

For the rest of the night, the tone was somber.

Noah and Esme didn't talk much. She threw in an oven pizza for dinner, then ate it quietly at the dining room table with Noah. She kept staring at him, waiting for Noah to say something, but he didn't.

And it was driving Esme crazy.

"Okay, we have to talk about this," Esme said, setting down her pizza. "Are you all right? That was probably a dumb question. I know you killed someone and just found out about a plot to overthrow my father and enslave humans."

Noah glanced at the bathroom where they had hidden the guard's body. "Yeah, it's a lot to take in. No, I'm really not okay. I know you said he wasn't human, but...I still feel awful."

Esme placed a hand on Noah's arm. "I know it's hard, but focus on the good. You saved me from that assassin, Noah. If you weren't here—like the night Cullen came after me—who knows what would've happened?"

He sighed. "Yeah, you have a point."

"Are you done eating?"

Noah nodded. "Yes—thank you. It was delicious."

Esme took the plates to the sink, then she checked the time on the stove. "I think it's gotten dark enough. We need to move the body to the storm drain—and not get caught."

Noah rose to his feet. "Okay, good idea. Maybe we should alert the authorities? Let them know what this guard said?"

"And who would believe all this? Plus, you might get arrested for murder. I can't let that happen."

Noah took a deep breath. "Okay, I see your point. Can you imagine if my dad found out? Or Giselle? If she thinks me punching Cullen was bad, I know she wouldn't approve of this."

"No one will know," Esme promised, walking over to him. "It's not a human problem, anyway. It's between my people."

Noah raked his hand through his hair. "Look, I'm not trying to pry, but you didn't answer my questions before. Who are you? And what's so different about your people?"

Esme hesitated, wishing she could tell him everything. But then she remembered her father's rules and wondered just how dangerous it might be.

"Noah, if I could tell you, I would in a heartbeat," she said, softly. "But my father doesn't want me to. For now, I have to keep everything a secret. Maybe I can tell you the truth one day, but until then, I'm sorry."

Noah was growing more frustrated. "Esme, come on—I deserve some answers. A woman's organs were removed without an instrument. And I just killed someone, for Christ's sake!"

"Please," she whispered. "It's been a long day. I don't want to fight."

Noah took a deep breath. "All right, all right. I'm sorry I yelled at you. I just don't like being kept in the dark."

"Neither would I, but you have to trust me." She reached for his hand. "Please."

Noah looked disappointed but nodded. "All right—if you

think it's best. Wait here. I'll drag the body out so you don't have to. It's dark enough now, I think."

"Are you sure? I could do it. I know how upset you are—"

Noah shook his head. "Really, I'll be fine. But thanks, Esme."

"Okay. How will we avoid getting caught?"

"You'll have to go ahead and be my lookout," Noah said. "Then I'll drag the body behind you. The storm drain isn't far from here. And I guess if someone sees us, we'll just have to pull a *Weekend at Bernie's.*"

"A weekend at what?" Esme asked, confused.

"Right," Noah said. "I need to teach you some more about movies. I'll be back."

Esme waited in the living room as Noah took a deep breath, entering the bathroom. When he didn't come out a minute later, Esme grew worried.

"Noah? Are you okay?" she called out.

"Esme, you'd better see this," he muttered. "I can't believe it!"

Esme rushed into the bathroom, finding Noah alone. Besides the blood on the floor, the body was gone. Esme looked around in confusion.

"Where did the guard's body go?"

Noah nodded, glancing at her. "That's a good question—I was wondering it myself. We haven't left the apartment or let anyone in. Are you sure he was dead?"

"Positive. I checked his pulse, and there was no heartbeat. My people aren't human, but they aren't invincible, either. A gunshot wound to the chest is fatal for both of us."

Noah bent down, glancing at the blood on the floor. "Not to sound too much like my father, but there's blood spatter here. Let's see where it goes..."

Noah and Esme followed it to the window, noticing it was

open an inch. It led directly to the fire escape. When Esme looked out, she saw no one outside.

"So, do dead bodies come back to life and walk away where you come from?" Noah asked, breaking the silence.

Esme shook her head. "No—never. Not unless…"

When Esme trailed off, Noah frowned. "Unless what?"

Esme's mind immediately went to Fairy Godmother Zamira. If she was capable of killing people with her magic, she could easily make someone come back to life. But how? It took Esme a second before an idea popped into her head.

"I told you before that my people are good with potions," she began. "Maybe…maybe she gave the assassin something so that if he died and failed his mission, he'd get a second chance to return to her."

"Some potions your people have," Noah muttered. "We don't have anything like that in Toronto. I'm starting to wish we did, though."

Esme shook her head. "Trust me, Noah—this stuff is evil. It isn't legal in my kingdom for a reason. We have no right to play with life and death."

"And let me guess. The same person who's behind this is responsible for that woman's murder?"

Esme nodded. "And she's very smart—believe me. A force to be reckoned with."

Noah pointed at the window. "Should we go looking for him?"

"No—it's too dangerous. Let's hope he doesn't come back. His next death could be more permanent," Esme muttered. "And the woman who's behind this—Zamira, who's working with Senator Remus—must have a plan. The assassin included."

"I'm a little afraid to find out what it is. Will you be all right?"

Esme shook her head. "Not if they succeed, no. And I'm pretty sure my father's in trouble, too. Even if I go back, it'll be hard to prove—and he never believes me."

As Esme sat onto the couch, feeling defeated, Noah took a seat beside her. "At least I didn't kill anyone, right?"

"Believe me," Esme muttered, "you would've been doing my kingdom a favor if you had. Zamira and Senator Remus, too. I don't know if there's a non-violent end to all this. The only question is who's going to die next—my family and I, or them? That's just as bad as enslaving the human race."

"Sounds like a war is coming," Noah said, making Esme nod. "Whatever happens, I'll be on your side. Even if I don't know much about your people."

Esme smiled. "Thanks, Noah. Now, I think we should clean that blood in the bathroom—just in case someone sees it."

After Esme fetched a mop from the closet, she and Noah got to work scrubbing the bathroom. Esme glanced out the window again—looking for any sign of the guard—but he had vanished. She wondered if he had gone back to Fairhaven or on to something else for Senator Remus and Fairy Godmother Zamira.

"All done," Noah said, putting the mop back in the closet. "Hey, there are some pillows and blankets in here. I can sleep on the couch tonight. Mind if I use them?"

Esme shrugged. "Go right ahead. And thanks for staying with me. I feel much better when you're around."

Noah smiled. "Yeah, I feel the same."

Once Esme had led Noah to the couch, she helped him set up his blankets and pillow. After he had brushed his teeth with a spare toothbrush and got under the covers, Esme turned off the light, glancing at him one last time.

"Goodnight, Noah."

"Goodnight, Esme. See you tomorrow."

She had so much she wanted to tell him, but it wouldn't fall off her tongue. Instead, she waited for Noah to fall asleep and then got ready to head out.

There was something important she had to do.

ESME KNEW the way to the sewer drain, tiptoeing through the dark. Noah hadn't even noticed she was gone. She removed the lid and slid down the ladder. A guard waited for her as she headed back down to Fairhaven, putting his sword up to stop her.

Was this guard a traitor too, Esme wondered?

"Halt," the guard said. "You've been banished from Fairhaven. Head back to the surface—or face imprisonment."

"Listen, something bad is going on up there. A woman's organs were removed, I've been threatened multiple times, and apparently, humans are going to be enslaved soon—"

Lady Nyssa came around the corner, smiling. "Ah, if it isn't Esme. So nice to see you."

Esme's eyes narrowed. "You. Where's my father? I need to speak to him."

"He's busy—and he doesn't want to see you, remember? You were banished for that terrible prank you pulled."

"That you encouraged me to do. Don't think I've forgotten about that," Esme sneered. "I know there's a plot going on. Is Senator Remus involved? Why enslave all the humans? I need to warn my father before—"

Lady Nyssa pulled a potion out of her pocket, then flung it at Esme. It exploded in a spray of silver light that clamped her lips together. Esme pulled at her lips, trying to talk, but she couldn't. Then Lady Nyssa threw another potion—blue in color this time—that forced Esme up the ladder, then sent her exploding through the storm drain and back up onto the surface. She landed with a thud on the street.

"And there's something worse for you if you come back," Lady Nyssa called out. "Wouldn't want anything to happen to your precious father, now, would you? So, stay out!"

The storm drain sealed itself with magic, unable to be opened no matter how much Esme pulled. She groaned before her lips broke apart. She could talk again, but it wouldn't do her much good. Not with Lady Nyssa in the way.

Disappointed, she headed back to her apartment, worried about her father's safety. If she couldn't warn him, then what?

She shuddered to think of the possibilities.

AFTER SHE FELL ASLEEP, forcing herself to get some shuteye, the radio woke Esme up the next morning.

She rolled over, about to turn it off when she heard something interesting from the host. "...and our first caller will win tickets from our prize package. Two seats at the Blue Jays game and two tickets to Toronto's Wonderland! The Blue Jays game was sold-out yesterday, so if you missed out, this might be your last chance to snag some seats..."

Esme sat up in bed. The Blue Jays *and* Wonderland tickets? It would be the perfect way to cheer Noah up. And, in the meantime, it would kill some time before she could try again to reach her father—maybe without Lady Nyssa in the way. She reached for the phone on her nightstand, dialing the radio's number. It rang and rang in her ear before she heard the radio ding.

"Congratulations, caller one!" the radio host said, making Esme sigh. It wasn't her number—she was still on hold. "What's your name?"

"Chelsea," the name on the other end said with a giggle.

"I'm so excited to win the tickets! I'm going to take my sister with me—"

"Oh, I'm afraid you haven't won them yet," the radio host said. "We forgot to mention that the first caller only wins if you can answer our trivia question correctly. Are you ready?"

"Uh—sure," Chelsea said, sounding nervous.

"What's the tallest building in Toronto?"

Chelsea's hesitated. "Oh, that's easy. It's...uh..."

"I know what it is—thanks to Noah!" Esme cried, staying on the line. "Come on, come on...get it wrong!"

"I'm sorry, but you're out of time," the radio host said. "Too bad, Chelsea—but thanks for calling. Will our next caller get the answer right? Let's see! Hello, caller. What's your name?"

It took Esme a moment to realize they were talking to her. "Uh, Esme. Sorry—I'm just shocked I made it through."

"Well, good morning, Esme. Tell me—who would you take if you won the tickets?"

"My good friend, Noah. He's been down lately and I want to cheer him up."

Esme stole a glance at her door, making sure Noah hadn't woken up yet. She could still hear his light snoring coming from the living room sofa. It was a miracle he hadn't heard her slip away last night for Fairhaven.

"Well, that sounds nice. He's lucky to have a friend like you," the radio host said. "Now, do you know what the tallest building in Toronto is? We really want to give these tickets away."

Esme nodded. "I do—it's the CN Tower. Noah was the one who taught me that when I first arrived in Toronto."

Esme heard celebration music playing on the radio before the host spoke again. "Well done, Esme! You'll get a text with our address on it soon. Come down to our radio station as soon as you can to pick up your tickets. We hope you and Noah have a good time!"

"Thank you!" Esme cried before she hung up.

As she rose to her feet, she grinned. What were the odds that she won the tickets? After the terrible past few days, she couldn't wait to tell Noah.

After she dressed and brushed her teeth, she tip-toed into the living room. She was about to gently nudge Noah's shoulder before she realized he had slept shirtless. She hadn't notice before, but he had tight, muscular abs.

When he moved in his sleep, she figured she'd better stop ogling him before he woke up. She touched his shoulder. "Noah? Wake up."

He jolted awake, looking up at her. "Is everything all right? Did the assassin come back?"

Esme shook her head. "No—everything's fine. We have to get ready for work. Want some breakfast?"

"Oh, sure," he said, sitting up and rubbing his eyes. "I'll get ready."

Esme nodded, flipping through the cookbook in the kitchen. She came across a breakfast sandwich that looked good. She cooked two eggs in the microwave, turning them into patties before placing them on toasted English muffins. Then she added melted cheese, microwaved bacon, and a side of fruit.

"That smells good," Noah said, walking into the kitchen.

Esme smiled. "Thanks. Turns out I'm getting better at this cooking thing."

As he sat down, he dug into his sandwich. "Today's the fundraiser at the art gallery. I wonder what Giselle's up to."

Esme laughed. "Knowing her, it'll be over the top. Before work, can you drive me somewhere?"

"Sure. Where do you need to go?"

"The radio station. I have the address—it's not too far from here."

He frowned. "Why do you need to go there?"

"It's a surprise," Esme said with a grin. "And I'm good at keeping secrets, so don't think you can break me."

"All right—I won't pry. I need to get a new phone, too."

As they continued eating, still worried about everything going on, Esme heard a knock on the door. She looked through the peephole—worried it might be the assassin again—but it was only Tanya and Gina. They had big smiles on their faces and looked like they were holding something.

Esme frowned, opening the door. "Hey, ladies. What's going on—"

"Have you seen this?" Gina asked with a grin, shoving a newspaper in Esme's face.

Esme took it, looking down at the headline. It read IN LOVE AND DOING GOOD. Under the headline sat a picture of Esme and Noah. It was when they were outside the soup kitchen, whispering to each other.

Esme had to admit—they *did* look really close. And they made a cute couple.

"You said you were only friends," Gina said with a wink. "When did that change?"

Esme shook her head. "It hasn't. Those journalists are wrong."

"Oh?" Gina asked, poking her head inside and noticing Noah. "Then why did he stay the night?"

"He wanted to watch over me," Esme said, trying to hide a blush. "Friends can do that."

Gina didn't look like she believed her, still smirking.

"Well, whether the story is true or fake, everyone will be talking about you two now," Tanya said. "I think it's nice you're working together and helping people. You've certainly helped us."

"What's going on?" Noah asked, walking up behind Esme.

"See for yourself," Esme said, handing him the newspaper.

Noah read the headline and sighed. "How much trouble do you think we'll be in with Giselle again?"

"A lot," Esme said, but knew there were worse worries. Like those thugs after them and her father's fate. For now, though, this was still a problem as she turned back to Tanya and Gina. "How many people will have seen this already?"

"Oh, just everyone in Toronto who reads a newspaper," Gina said, grinning. "Only a million people."

Esme rolled her eyes. "Great—and Giselle's probably one of them. Thanks for the warning at least."

Tanya nodded. "You're welcome. And don't forget about Dylan's therapy tomorrow. When I told him you were coming, he was excited to go."

"That's great," Esme said with a smile. "I hope he gets the help he needs."

"Tanya's heading to work, but I'll be with the kids all day," Gina said. "And if you two have any exciting news—like maybe that you're officially dating—don't hesitate to call me."

Esme shook her head with a laugh. "Whatever you say, Gina."

After the women left, Esme did the dishes and grabbed her keys. She locked the apartment behind her before she and Noah walked toward his car in the parking lot. Noah glanced at her as he started the engine.

"I'll buy my phone first and then take you to the radio station. It won't take long."

"Can't wait," Esme said, trying to hide her smile.

When they arrived at BestBuy, Noah chose the latest iPhone

and charged it to his credit card. As he waited to pay at the front desk, Esme bounced on the balls of her feet.

Noah looked at her with a chuckle. "What's gotten into you?"

"Nothing," Esme replied. "Ready to go?"

"Yeah, I've got my new phone," he said, picking up the bag. "Here—give me your phone. I'll put my number in it and take yours. When you have to leave for Fairhaven, we can stay in touch."

"That would be nice, but I'm not sure Fairhaven has cell phone reception," Esme said, his thoughtfulness tugging at her heart. "We're old-fashioned, remember?"

Noah punched the number in, but he wasn't laughing. "That's too bad. I was hoping we could stay in contact."

"Yeah, me, too," Esme said quietly. "I wish we could."

Noah didn't say anything, looking upset as he took Esme to his car. He put his new phone in his pocket and drove to the radio station. When they reached the front doors, a burly security guard stopped them.

"This is private property," he said. "You can't get by without a pass."

"My name is Esme. I won the giveaway package, remember?"

Noah frowned. "What giveaway package?"

"I remember," the guard said, opening the door for them. "And congratulations."

When they entered the radio station, it was like nothing Esme had ever seen before. It had tons of television screens, computers, and cups of coffee. A small recording booth with two radio hosts sat inside. She recognized the man's voice immediately—he was the one she had spoken to on air.

"And we'll be right back after this commercial break," he said, then rose to his feet. When he walked out of the booth, he noticed Esme with a smile. "Ah, are you the one who won the tickets?"

Esme smiled back. "That's me. Thanks for running the contest."

"My pleasure." The man reached into a nearby drawer. He pulled out four tickets—two to the Blue Jay's game, and two to Toronto's Wonderland. "Here you are, Esme. Enjoy them."

"Thanks," she said, pocketing the tickets.

"Wait a second," Noah interrupted. "You won tickets to the baseball game *and* Wonderland?"

"I did—and I wanted to surprise you. I only called because of you."

"This is the Noah you talked about?" the radio host asked. "Nice to meet you. Esme must care a lot about you."

Esme blushed while Noah looked dumbfounded. "I just… can't believe it. Thank you, Esme. I couldn't get tickets to the game. They were sold-out. It was too bad—I wanted to take you."

"Things have a way of working out," Esme said with a smile. "Come on—we need to get to work."

"Wait," the radio host said. "You two look familiar. Have we met before?"

Esme shook her head. "No, I don't think so. I'm new to town—"

"Now I remember!" the radio host said, picking up a nearby newspaper. It had their picture as the headline. "You two were in the paper together. Now I'm glad you won the tickets—you deserve it for all the good work you're doing. And when you get married, remember to invite me to the wedding, all right?"

Esme laughed nervously. "Oh, we're not—"

"We're back on in one minute," a man with a clipboard said as he rushed into the studio.

"Sorry—gotta run," the radio host said as he entered the booth again. "Enjoy the tickets, lovebirds!"

Esme walked out of the studio with Noah behind her. "I guess we'll have to get used to people thinking we're dating."

Noah laughed. "Probably. But seriously—thanks again, Esme. I know we're going to have the best time. I can't wait for you to see your first baseball game and explore Wonderland with me."

Esme smiled, following Noah to the car. His happiness was enough to make her forget about assassins and how angry Giselle was going to be when she saw the newspaper.

Among everything else going wrong.

CHAPTER 20

When Esme and Noah arrived at the Human Connection building, all their co-workers were staring at them in wide-eyed silence. They had newspapers sitting on their desks.

"This can't be good," Esme muttered.

Noah shook his head. "Not one bit."

They passed through the sea of staring eyes, intending to head to their desks when Giselle poked her head out of her office. "In my office. Now!"

She slammed the door shut, walking back over to her desk. Esme gulped and looked at Noah. "What happens if we both get fired?"

Noah sighed. "I don't know. We need to keep these jobs— it's the only way to find more evidence. Just follow my lead."

Esme nodded, following Noah to Giselle's office. They opened the door and shut it behind them before taking a seat in front of her desk. She was still sitting there, clicking her pen in annoyance as she glared at them.

"So, tell me," she said, sitting forward, "how are you two feeling this morning?"

Esme and Noah glanced at each other, confused.

"Well?" Giselle asked.

"Uh, we're fine," Esme said, blinking. "How are you?"

Giselle reached into her desk drawer, pulling out a newspaper. It had Esme and Noah's faces on it. "How wonderful—because I'm doing terrible! Imagine my surprise when I saw this sitting on my front step this morning. I thought I told you both not to upstage me—"

"And we didn't mean to," Esme said. "It wasn't our fault the journalists took an interest in us."

Giselle scoffed. "Oh, no? You two were attached at the hip yesterday. Don't think I didn't notice. No wonder they thought something was going on!"

"Look, Ms. McMillan, we told you already—we're not dating," Noah said, gesturing at the newspaper. "They got it wrong. And quite frankly, I find it a little disturbing that they think a woman and a man can't be friends."

"I don't care what you think," Giselle spat. "I only care what the public thinks. And right now, all they can talk about is you—not me! First, you put my organization in jeopardy by punching some man on the street—"

"Again—sorry," Noah said quietly.

Giselle glared at him. "Then you get all the attention of the journalists. They even wrote about how you helped some man named Edgar Little keep his wife's ring. Is that true?"

Esme nodded. "It is—but that was before I was even working here!"

"Uh-huh—how convenient. If you ask me, I think it was a setup that he was there at the soup kitchen. I think you wanted all the spotlight on yourselves!"

Esme protested. "What? Of course not!"

Noah nodded. "Esme's right—that's insane."

"Well, excuse me for not knowing what to believe," Giselle muttered, rising to her feet. "This is my organization—I'm the face running it. And I won't have you two going behind my back and stealing my spotlight."

Esme gulped. "Does that mean you're going to fire us?"

Both she and Noah held their breath, waiting for Giselle's answer.

"I wish," Giselle muttered. "If I had my way, I'd demand you both get out of here right now. I feel sick just looking at your guilty faces!"

"But?" Esme asked.

Giselle turned back to them. "*But* the public loves you. We've gotten dozens of calls from people, asking if you're coming to my fundraiser at the art gallery today. Can you believe that? They want *you* at a fundraiser *I* set up!"

Esme raised her hand. "I invited all the guests. Technically, I'm the one who—"

When Esme saw Giselle's glare, the words died in her throat.

"Anyway, if I fire you two, I'll be known as the bitch who fired the lovebirds just looking to do good—according to this damn newspaper," Giselle said, throwing it in the trash. "So, no —you aren't fired. For now."

"And we're still going with you to the fundraiser?" Noah asked.

"Yes—unfortunately," Giselle grumbled. "But make no mistake. If you two do anything to overshadow me again, there *will* be a price to pay. Understand?"

"Perfectly," Esme said as Noah nodded. "What do you want us to do at the fundraiser?"

"Make yourselves scarce. Seriously, I want you to sit in the shadows and not talk to anyone."

"But what if the journalists talk to us?" Noah asked. "You said people want us there."

"Tell them their story was wrong and then excuse yourselves promptly," Giselle said through gritted teeth. "And besides, once I make my announcement, they'll be more focused on me, anyway."

"What *is* your announcement?" Esme asked.

Giselle shook her head. "No way—I'm not trusting you with it. But believe me, *everyone* will be talking about it."

Noah and Esme glanced at each other, wondering what it could be.

Giselle checked her watch. "We need to be at the fundraiser in twenty minutes. I have to prepare, so get out of my sight."

Esme rose to her feet. "Of course. Again, we're sorry."

As she turned, Giselle held up a hand. "Wait a moment—I need you to do something else for me. Tomorrow, we're holding a charity auction at City Hall. Some very generous celebrities in Toronto have donated things to be bid on."

"How nice," Noah said with a shrug. "What does that have to do with us?"

Giselle rolled her eyes. "Must I spell out everything for you? I want you both there at the auction."

Esme frowned. "Really? You aren't worried we're going to steal your spotlight again?"

Giselle smirked. "Of course, not...because I have a plan. You're both going to bid moderate amounts on various items."

"But...we don't have the money for that," Noah said. "We aren't rich."

Giselle rolled her eyes. "I know that, you fool. Instead, I'm going to swoop in and outbid you. Then, when I give the most money to charity, the spotlight will be on me again. I'm hoping to make it on that 'most charitable celebrity' list."

"Right," Noah muttered. "We'll be there, then."

"You'd better—your jobs are on the line if you don't. And for Heaven's sake, don't get in a bidding war with me. Let me win and don't make a scene."

After Esme and Noah nodded, they left the office, closing the door behind them. Everyone was still whispering about them as they walked back to Esme's office and entered the small room.

"Well, at least they're not gossiping about my demotion anymore," Noah muttered, watching the people through the window.

"Small mercies," Esme said with a smile. "But I just can't believe Giselle. Every day, she gets worse!"

Noah nodded. "Yeah, I know—but don't worry. I think we're close to catching her."

"I hope so," Esme said, glancing at Giselle down the hall.

Twenty minutes later—after Giselle had applied more makeup and changed into a black party dress—she walked by Esme's office. She gestured outside, motioning for them to walk with her. Esme and Noah left the office and rushed to catch up.

"Remember—big smiles," Giselle said, glaring at Esme, "and keep the hell out of my way."

Esme and Noah followed Giselle outside, noticing a black limousine waiting on the curb. Giselle got in first, then Noah let Esme get in before he hopped in behind them. Giselle motioned at the driver, and he sped off into the busy Toronto traffic.

"So, Giselle," Esme began, watching as she applied more blush, "bought anything nice lately?"

Giselle put her blush down, motioning at the dress. "Only this for the fundraiser. I have to look nice, after all. Why do you ask?"

Esme shrugged, thinking back to the receipts. "Just wondering."

"I usually reinvest all my money in building our organization," Giselle continued. "There are so many people in need, and it warms my heart to help them. I believe very strongly that giving is better than receiving."

Esme and Noah resisted the urge to roll their eyes.

When they arrived at the art gallery, Giselle pushed Esme's hand out of the way so she could get out of the limo first. There were dozens of journalists there, snapping pictures and shouting questions. Giselle waved and followed the red carpet inside without a second glance back.

"Ready?" Noah asked. "It's going to seem a little overwhelming."

Esme took a deep breath. "I'm ready. I just hope we can avoid the spotlight."

When Noah and Esme stepped out, the cameras immediately started flashing.

"Are you two getting married?" one journalist asked.

"How did you meet?" another asked.

"Or not," Noah muttered, grabbing Esme's hand. "Follow me."

Esme pushed the butterflies away and held onto Noah, making the journalists flash their cameras even more. When they had made it into the art gallery, it was much quieter inside, with waiters serving appetizers and people browsing the paintings. Giselle stood with a large group of people, chatting and laughing. She glared at Esme and Noah when she noticed them before turning back to her conversation.

"How much do you want to bet we'll be in the papers again tomorrow?" Esme asked.

"All the money in this art gallery," Noah said with a chuckle.

Esme looked down, realizing their hands were still connected. Noah followed her eyes until he noticed as well. He promptly pulled away, thrusting his hands into his pockets.

"Come on," he said, blushing slightly. "Let's try to fade into the background."

Noah found them both seats in the corner, snagging some appetizers for the two of them. They watched as Giselle continued to mingle and promote herself. When she began talking to a balding, sweaty man in a tux, Esme pointed at him.

"Who's that?" she asked.

"Oh, it's Mayor Haggarty," Noah said as he looked over. "He's running for mayor again. The election's coming up soon."

"Giselle told me to invite him. I wonder why it was so important..."

Giselle tapped her fork against her champagne glass, making everyone hush. "Thank you for coming. Because of your generous donations, we've collected over a hundred thousand dollars for my organization!"

Everyone clapped and cheered, even Esme and Noah.

"Your money will help many needy people around the city. And tomorrow, you're free to join us at the charity auction at City Hall. You'll be able to take home a prize for your generosity," Giselle said, winking. "Now, I'm sure you're all wondering what my big announcement is?"

Everyone in the crowd nodded. Noah and Esme glanced at each other, realizing this was the big moment.

"I'm pleased to announce that I'm running for mayor," Giselle said with a grin. "And I hope I can count on your support."

When people started clapping, Esme leaned in to whisper in Noah's ear. "Really? She thinks she'd make a good mayor?"

Noah shrugged. "Why not? Most politicians are corrupt. She'd fit right in."

Esme giggled. "Good point."

Mayor Haggarty shook Giselle's hand. "It will be an honor

to run against you, Ms. McMillan. May the best man—or woman—win."

Giselle smiled, shaking her head. "Oh, you won't be running, Mayor Haggarty. I have a feeling you're going to drop out of the race."

Mayor Haggarty frowned. "Why would I do that? The people of Toronto elected me as their mayor last time, and they still trust in me. Not to sound cocky, of course, but I think I have a very good chance of getting re-elected."

"Not when I show everyone this," Giselle said, pulling pictures out of her purse. "Tell me, Mayor...who's in these photos?"

As people swarmed the pictures, he glanced at them, looking nervous. "Well...that's me, of course."

"Right—I figured that. And who is this red-haired woman you're kissing? It doesn't look like your wife to me."

A middle-aged, blonde-haired woman in a green dress walked over with a glass of champagne. She looked at the pictures, gasping. "You bastard! How long have you been having an affair?"

Mayor Haggarty looked more nervous as sweat formed near his hairline. "Marjorie...I can explain!"

His wife slapped him across the face, making everyone gasp. "These pictures explain it all. You'll be hearing from a divorce lawyer very soon."

As his wife stormed out of the art gallery, Giselle giggled. "Don't worry—I'll be forwarding these pictures to every news-paper in town. I imagine it'll hurt your approval rating in the polls. After all, if you can't even stay faithful to your wife, how can the public expect loyalty from you?"

"No—please," Mayor Haggarty cried. "Don't show the public. I beg of you!"

"Too late," Giselle said with a shrug. "I already have my

private investigator on it. I made dozens of copies, of course. All is fair in love, war, and politics."

"You are a terrible woman," Mayor Haggarty snarled.

"He's right about that," Noah whispered to Esme as Mayor Haggarty rushed out of the art gallery, chasing after his wife.

Giselle put the pictures back in her purse, turning to the people in the art gallery. "When it comes time to vote, I hope you'll think of me—Giselle McMillan. I've done a lot to help people with my organization, and I'd love to do the same as mayor."

As people murmured in approval, the door to the art gallery slammed open. Everyone gasped and looked in the direction of the person who entered. When Esme looked, her jaw fell open.

It was Senator Remus. What was he doing on Earth, Esme wondered? How did he get there? And was he involved with that thug in her apartment?

He had to have been. It was all just a little too coincidental. But would anyone in Fairhaven believe her, especially with Lady Nyssa stopping her from getting to her father?

"I heard there was a big announcement happening at the art gallery," he began. "I hope I'm not too late."

Giselle shook her head. "Of course not, Mr....?"

"My name is Remus," he said with a smile. "Just Remus."

"Well, Remus, I just announced I'm running for mayor. I hope I can count on your vote. Something tells me Toronto's current mayor won't have a chance in hell anymore."

Senator Remus shook his head. "I'm afraid I can't vote for you. I'm running for mayor myself."

Everyone began murmuring in confusion.

"Really?" Giselle asked, looking amused. "No one even knows who you are, Remus. And as they say—politics is a popularity contest."

"Oh, don't worry. I plan to launch an aggressive campaign,"

Remus said, still smiling. It didn't seem like he had noticed Esme yet. "And I intend to win."

"Is that so?" Giselle asked, crossing her arms. "Do you know I am? I built one of the biggest humanitarian organizations in the world. You don't want to run against me—I'm ruthless."

"So am I," Remus said, refusing to back down. "You'll all see soon enough. In the meantime, here's a little gift."

Remus reached into his pocket, pulling out wads of dollar bills. He began to hand them out to the people at the art gallery. They eagerly took what was offered, grinning while Giselle looked horrified. Esme realized Remus didn't have a job or money, so it must be counterfeit—made from magic. Maybe there was even a spell in it to make people vote for him.

She wouldn't put anything past a man like Remus—even enslaving everyone on Earth.

"Have a pleasant day," Remus said, turning around and leaving the art gallery.

As the people began murmuring about how generous and mysterious he was, Giselle looked flabbergasted. "Well...don't mind that rude interruption. Let's get back to the art, shall we?"

When she popped another bottle of champagne, Noah scoffed. "Looks like Giselle met her match. I wonder who that guy was..."

Esme's eyes were still on the door. "Noah, that's Senator Remus. You know, the man I told you about who hates my father? I think he's the one responsible for murdering people and sending the assassin after me."

Noah's eyes widened. "Are you sure?"

Esme nodded, rushing toward the door. "Positive—and we need to stop him."

Noah followed her, immediately blinded by the bright lights of the journalists outside. Esme and Noah pushed them aside and followed Senator Remus. He was heading toward a storm drain in the distance, reaching down to lift it.

"Senator Remus, stop!" Esme cried.

He paused, spinning around with a grin. "Princess Esme—look at you. You've come a long way from that helpless, spoiled brat I knew before."

"I told you before—I'm capable of more than you think. I know you conspired with your daughter and Zamira to get me out of Fairhaven."

He crossed his arms, chuckling. "You can't prove that."

"I can't prove you killed that woman or sent the assassin after me yet, either, but I will soon," Esme said, firmly. "I know Zamira gave that assassin a potion to come back to life if he died. Trying to kill me, were you?"

Senator Remus shrugged. "If I were, it didn't appear to have worked. A certain guard told me you have this human fool watching over you."

"*This* human fool stopped your assassin," Noah said. "And we'll stop whatever you have planned next."

Senator Remus laughed. "Oh, I doubt that. Maybe you've survived on Earth, Esme, but that doesn't mean you can stop me. I'm more powerful than you could ever imagine."

"What are you doing here on Earth? How did you get past my father? You know you're not allowed here."

Senator Remus rolled his eyes. "A most foolish rule. Don't worry—I plan to change things real soon when I become mayor. This world will bow before me, so enjoy your time here while it lasts, Princess."

"Where's Zamira and your wife? What's your daughter's *real* reason for sucking up to my father? For getting me kicked out of Fairhaven? To enslave humanity like that loose-lipped thug said? Should've told him not to brag."

"Questions, questions! They bore me. The plan is coming

together nicely, and you'll find out soon—along with everyone on Earth. You really must work on your patience, Esme."

And then he lifted the storm drain, lowering himself down. When he vanished, Esme clenched her fists. "So much for answers."

"I was right before—that guy *is* an asshole," Noah muttered.

They heard high heels clicking behind them. They spun around, noticing Giselle standing there with her arms crossed. "Well? Who was he?"

"What?" Esme asked.

"Don't play coy," Giselle snarled. "You were talking to that man—Remus, he said his name was. How do you know him?"

"From a long time ago," Esme said. "He hates my family—my father in particular. Trust me—I wish I didn't know him. We're definitely not friends."

"Do you have anything on him? Some juicy dirt I could sell to the tabloids?"

Esme had a lot on him, but she didn't know how to prove it —or how to admit he had a fairy godmother capable of evil magic.

"Sorry, I have nothing," Esme finally said.

"A pity," Giselle muttered. "Well, that little money stunt won't get him elected. No one will vote for a nobody."

Esme glanced at Noah, worried Remus might have more tricks up his sleeve than Giselle knew possible.

"Anyway, I think the art gallery was still a success. You did well in not drawing too much attention to yourself," Giselle continued. "Take the day off—you deserve it. You need to be well-rested for the charity auction tomorrow afternoon. Don't come into the office—we'll meet directly at City Hall."

As Giselle turned on her heel and walked inside the art gallery, Esme glanced at Noah. "What do you want to do now?"

"Let's head back to your apartment," Noah said, checking

his watch. "We have that dinner at the cottage with my family tonight."

"Right. Maybe it'll distract me for a little while. If anything can," Esme muttered, walking with Noah to catch a taxi. "I'm worried about Remus, Noah. Really, really worried."

"I know," he said, taking her hand. "But we'll get to the bottom of it—the bottom of everything—together."

Esme admired his optimism, but as she glanced at the storm drain Remus had vanished into, she had her doubts.

CHAPTER 21

After Noah drove Esme back to her apartment, they passed the time by watching movies on her couch. He found *Weekend at Bernie's* for rent on the television and put it on. Two hours later, Esme began to understand Noah's references.

"Oh, I see what you meant about the guard," Esme said. "Kind of a silly movie."

Noah laughed. "Oh, for sure—but silly movies are just what you need sometimes."

Esme nodded. "True—it helped distract me from worrying about Senator Remus and Giselle."

"Glad I could help," Noah said with a grin. "I still have more movies to show you. Star Wars, Star Trek, the Marvel cinematic universe."

"Do we have time to watch them all right now?"

Noah checked his watch, shaking his head. "It would take us weeks to watch all of those—and that's only the beginning."

"Wow," Esme muttered. "Your people have been busy."

Noah laughed. "We like our entertainment. I'll wait here

while you get ready, then we can drive to my apartment so I can change."

"What should I wear?" Esme asked, rising to her feet.

"Something dressy, but not too formal. It's a dinner at a cottage—not a royal ball."

"Right," Esme said, walking into her bedroom closet. "I think I have just the thing…"

Esme searched through her old clothes, finding a pink dress that went to her knees. It was made for negotiations instead of ballroom parties. Once she had it on, she paired it with white heels, a diamond necklace, and some light makeup. She walked out into the living room after she had combed her hair.

"So?" she asked, twirling to show off the full outfit. "What do you think?"

Noah's eyes twinkled. "You look incredible, Esme. Really."

Esme blushed. "Thank you. Should we get going now?"

Noah nodded, leading Esme into the hallway as she locked the door. She followed him to his car before they got in and sped off. He drove them to a tall apartment building a few miles away, one that had a doorman letting people in.

Noah showed his I.D., walking past the doorman. Esme whistled. "Too bad there weren't any apartments for rent here."

"Yeah, it would've been awesome to live next to you. It's a good place," Noah said, pressing the button on the elevator. "Not too pricey, either."

When the elevator arrived, they both got in, riding it to the sixth floor. Noah led Esme down a long hallway—which smelled heavenly of cinnamon and lavender—to a red door. Noah fumbled for his keys, thrusting them into the lock.

"I've never seen your apartment before," Esme said. "I'm excited."

Noah laughed as he unlocked the door. "It's nothing special."

"Nonsense," Esme said, stepping inside. "You live here. That makes it special."

Noah blushed, turning on the light switch. "Well, here it is—my humble abode. What do you think?"

Esme took a moment to look around. It was more spacious than her apartment with two bedrooms, a large seating area, and a kitchen with an island. Noah had cozy furniture, and Esme wanted nothing more than to sit down and relax with him for a while.

"It's very nice," Esme said, turning to face him. "Feels like I'm right at home."

Noah grinned. "I've stayed at your apartment long enough, so it should only be fair that I open my home to you, too. If you ever need a place to stay, my door's always open."

Esme smiled. "Thanks, Noah. I'll keep that in mind."

She noticed a corkboard set up on the wall and walked over to it. It had Giselle's picture and name with several pieces of evidence—pictures Noah had snapped of Giselle.

"That's my investigation board," Noah said, walking over. "Which reminds me—can I borrow your phone?"

Esme nodded, handing it over. He walked over to a printer, turning it on before he pressed a button on Esme's phone. It began printing something off on different sheets of paper. He walked back over to the corkboard, hanging up the receipts Esme had snapped pictures of at the office.

"I wanted to add the new evidence," Noah said, handing Esme's phone back. "Thanks again."

Esme shrugged as she slid her phone into her purse. "Anything I can do to help."

"Oh, believe me—you've helped a lot. Wait here—I'll change into something nicer. I shouldn't be long."

Esme nodded, sitting down on the comfortable sofa as Noah vanished into his bedroom. She looked around the apartment, realizing this was the place Noah was supposed to have his happily ever after with Jill. The place they were supposed to get married and live in and have children.

Esme was glad it hadn't worked out.

She looked toward the kitchen, noticing something poking out of the trash can. When she walked over, she realized it was a picture frame. It had a picture of Jill and Noah in it, smiling at the camera. It looked like they had taken it at a waterpark. They both looked happy—and in love.

"Found that, did you?"

Esme spun around, startled to see Noah. "Sorry—I didn't mean to go snooping through your trash. It's just...I saw it and couldn't help myself."

Noah nodded, looking down at the garbage can. "It's all right. Did you know I kept that picture until a few days ago? I guess I was holding out hope that Jill might come back to me."

"What made you throw it away?"

Noah finally looked up at her. "You. You showed me I deserve to be with someone who appreciates me. Someone who doesn't see me as an option, but as a priority."

Esme smiled. "I just want the best for you, Noah."

"I know—thank you. I used to think the best was Jill," he mumbled, looking away. "But now I know better."

Something tugged at Esme's heart. She wanted so much to be the happy ending Noah was looking for—and deserved—but she still planned to return to Fairhaven one day. After all, this entire adventure had been to prove herself to her father enough to return.

What was she going to do?

When everything turned quiet, Esme took a better look at him. He had dressed in a floral blue shirt, black slacks, and brown loafers. He paired with it a watch, combed back his blond hair, and looked very handsome.

"Anyway, that picture frame is going to stay in the garbage. It's where it belongs," Noah said, reaching for his keys on the table. "Ready to head out to my parents' cottage?"

Esme locked her arm with Noah's, throwing the picture back in the trash. "Absolutely."

After they made it downstairs, Noah began driving them toward the outskirts of Toronto. The skyscrapers and apartment buildings became smaller behind them until it was replaced by large fields of corn, rivers, and farmhouses. Esme looked out her window, fascinated by it all.

"Does your kingdom have land like this?" Noah asked, sneaking a peek at her.

She shook her head. "No—it's always dark in my kingdom. Lots of swamps, too."

"I don't know if I could live there, then. I like sunshine and fresh air."

Esme laughed, turning back to look at him. "You'd get used to it. I've never known any different—until now."

Noah smiled. "Well, I'm glad I helped you see some new things."

"You did. And as hard as it was leaving my only home...I'm glad it happened. I wouldn't have met you or gotten to explore this beautiful new place. I do regret putting everyone in danger, thanks to all the drama back home following me. But you've been a bright spot through the darkness."

Noah beamed from ear to ear after that.

Half an hour later, they arrived at a large cottage with a wrap-around porch. It sat next to a sparkling lake and a giant deck for fishing and lounging. When they pulled into the driveway of gravel, several other cars were already parked. Esme recognized Detective Crawford's sedan.

"Here it is," Noah said, turning off the engine. "My childhood cottage. My parents and I would come up here to hang out with family when I was a kid."

"Sounds like fun," Esme said with a smile. "Anything I should know about your family? I want them to like me."

Noah laughed. "Don't worry—they're nice people. You've already met my father, so he'll be a familiar face. I'll introduce you to everyone."

Esme smiled as she opened her door. "Thanks, Noah. If your family's as kind as you are, I'm sure I'll like them, too."

When Noah stepped out, they heard the front door fling open. An older woman with graying hair and an apron poked her head out. When she saw Noah and Esme approaching, she grinned.

"I thought I heard tires," she said. "So glad you could make it, Noah. It's nice to have the family together."

"Hey, Mom," he said, kissing her cheek. "This is Esme Fairhaven. I mentioned her on the phone."

"Hello, Esme," his mother said, smiling at her. "You're even more beautiful than he described."

Esme grinned. "Oh, thank you. It's nice to meet you. And thanks for letting me come over for dinner, too."

"Oh, of course! Any friend of Noah's is welcome here," she said, stepping aside. "Come on in and make yourself at home. You can call me Teresa."

Esme nodded, stepping inside and taking off her jacket. As Noah hung up their coats, Esme looked around, realizing how spacious the cottage was. It had a large kitchen with a deck out back, two separate living rooms, and tons of fireplaces. A spiral staircase led to an upstairs with dozens of rooms.

"Dinner should be ready in ten minutes," Teresa said, adjusting her apron. "Go ahead and meet everyone else. The last I saw of them, they were out on the deck, enjoying the fresh air."

As Teresa vanished into the kitchen, Noah turned to Esme. "Yeah, come on—I'm eager for you to meet Ronnie."

Esme smiled and followed him, though she was nervous about meeting another woman in Noah's life. He opened the back door, stepping out onto the deck. Esme noticed several people sitting there while looking up at the clouds as the sky darkened.

"Noah, there you are!" Detective Crawford cried, glancing at him. He had a beer in his hand and looked relaxed. "And you brought Esme. Hello again."

Esme waved. "Hello, Detective Crawford."

"Oh, no need for that here. Just call me Dan," he said with a smile, gesturing at an elderly woman next to him. "This is my mother, Louise."

Louise smiled at Esme, bowing her head. She had hair as white as snow, sparkling green eyes like Noah, and wore an old-fashioned dress. "Nice to meet you. We've all heard a lot about you."

"Hello, Grandma," Noah said, kissing her cheek. "Glad to see you again."

Louise patted her hip. "Not even a sprained hip could stop me."

Noah grinned. "Glad to hear it, Grandma. And you should know I got Grandpa's watch back—the same one I sold to buy a ring for Jill."

His grandmother's eyes lit up. "You did? How? Where?"

Noah laughed, gesturing at Esme. "It was all Esme, actually —she bought it back for me. We were lucky we found it at the pawnshop."

"Oh, I'm so happy you got it back," his grandmother said, turning to Esme. "Thank you, dear. It belongs with Noah."

Esme smiled. "Glad I could help. I didn't know it was such a cherished family heirloom."

Noah nodded. "We've had it in our family for decades. Now, where's Ronnie?"

"Right here," a feminine voice said behind them. "Think fast!"

A woman came running up to Noah, throwing herself into his arms. He laughed and caught her as he spun her around. Esme stood off to the side, watching them, awkwardly. Under the moonlight, the woman was beautiful—curly, black hair, ocean-blue eyes, and a red bikini that showed off her curves.

This was the kind of woman Noah deserved—someone from his own world who was beautiful and compatible with him. Even thought it felt like a kick to the gut to admit.

Esme suddenly felt self-conscious.

"Sorry to get you wet," the woman said, stepping back from Noah. "I just went for a dip in the lake. Can't go up to the cottage without going for a swim."

"Agreed," Noah said, pointing at Esme. "Veronica, meet Esme Fairhaven. Esme, meet Veronica Hutton. Veronica and I go way back—elementary school, in fact. She even has her own room here."

"Call me Ronnie," she said, shaking Esme's hand. She pulled back and began drying her hair with a towel. "Everyone else does."

Esme faked a smile. "Nice to meet you, Ronnie. Noah told me about you."

Veronica grinned. "Noah told me about you, too. A *lot* about you."

Noah blushed. "Ronnie—"

"Dinner's bubbling!" Teresa said, poking her head outside. "I made stew. I hope that's all right with you, Esme."

Esme nodded. "It's fine, Teresa. Thank you."

As everyone rose to their feet, Ronnie turned to Esme. "I

need to get changed. Esme, do you think you could help me pick out something to wear?"

Esme shrugged. "Sure, no problem."

"I'll meet you in the dining room," Noah said. "See you girls soon."

As Louise, Noah, and his father followed his mother into the dining room, Esme walked with Veronica up the staircase. She didn't say anything to her until she escorted her into a bedroom and closed the door.

"I wanted to talk to you alone," Veronica said. "Are you and Noah dating?"

Esme shook her head. "No—we're just friends. Why?"

"Because I know he likes you," Veronica said with a grin. "The way he looks at you...I've never seen him look at anyone like that before."

"Not even Jill?"

"Ah, so you know about that heartbreaker?" Veronica asked, crossing her arms. "And no, not even Jill. He just seems so... relaxed around you. Like he's right at home."

Esme played with the hem of her dress. "Oh, I'm sure that's not true. We're just friends—"

"Uh-huh. Keep telling yourself that," Veronica said, pulling on a black dress. "I don't know much about men, but I know they don't gush about women for hours unless they like them."

"For hours?" Esme asked, her head shooting up.

Veronica laughed. "That's what it felt like on the phone, at least. He called me the night you two met and told me all about you. I'm happy he found someone else."

"Are you?" Esme asked, growing bolder. "Because you two looked close. Really, really close."

Veronica laughed so hard it threw Esme off. "You think...oh my gosh, no! Noah's not my type...if you know what I mean."

"Then why did you throw yourself in his arms?"

Veronica shook her head. "That's just how we've been with each other since we were kids. It's not romantic at all—I assure you. And even if I *was* straight, it would be wrong. I think of Noah like...a little brother. When my parents died in high school, his parents took me in."

"Oh," Esme said, feeling silly. "Sorry—I didn't mean to pry."

Veronica laughed. "Hey, it's all right. I'd probably be jealous if the roles were reversed, too. But there's nothing to worry about—he's all yours."

"I told you—we're just friends."

"Sure, whatever you say. I think you two would look cute together."

Esme laughed. "You remind me of a friend back home—Alva. She was always meddling in my love life and causing trouble. And Noah wouldn't be her type, either, if you know what I mean."

"Really?" Veronica asked with a twinkle in her eyes. "I'd like to meet her, then. Maybe I could take her out to dinner."

"She...lives really far away. But I'll tell her about you. Maybe you two could meet up one day."

Deep down, Esme knew it wasn't true—that their people couldn't mix. It was just another reminder that she would never be normal and fit in.

"I'd like that. Now, let's get back downstairs—I'm starving."

Esme followed Veronica downstairs, entering the dining room behind her. The aroma of stew filled Esme's nostrils and made her mouth water. Everyone was sitting at the table, waiting for them.

Noah patted the vacant seat next to him. "Saved you a spot."

Esme ignored Veronica's wink, sitting next to him. "Thanks."

As Veronica sat next to Louise, Noah's mother smiled. "We

were waiting for you before digging in. I don't know about you, but I'm hungry. Let's eat!"

As they reached for their spoons and ate their meal, the table filled with mindless chatter. Topics of sports, the weather, and work around the cottage became popular. Noah leaned in toward Esme.

"You all right?" he whispered. "You two were gone for a while."

Esme nodded, swallowing a piece of potato. "We're fine. I like Veronica—even if she came on a little strong."

"That's just her way," Noah said with a grin. "But I'm glad you two are becoming friends."

"So, Esme," Teresa began, biting into her stew, "Noah tells me you're working at Human Connection now?"

Esme nodded. "That's right—and I *do* enjoy my job, even if my boss is a little self-centered."

"More than a little," Noah muttered.

"I trust she'll get what she deserves soon enough," Detective Crawford said, looking up from his bowl of stew. "Anyway, I wanted to tell you that there was another murder. A woman was found burned to death—but strangely, no accelerant was found. How can you die in a fire when there was no fire in the first place?"

Esme and Noah glanced at each other, knowing Senator Remus and Fairy Godmother Zamira were up to their old tricks again.

"Oh, Dan—let's not talk about that stuff at the table," Teresa said with a shiver. "It makes me uncomfortable."

"Sorry, dear. Let's change the subject. I'm excited to see if the Blue Jays win their game this week. I've got a bet with the other detectives at work."

"Speaking of Blue Jays, Esme got us tickets," Noah said,

glancing at her. "Which is probably the best gift I've ever gotten."

"Really?" Veronica asked, smirking. "How cute."

Esme blushed. "Noah's been so kind to me—I only wanted to repay the favor. So, you've all lived in Toronto for a long time. What's your favorite thing about it?"

Esme changed the subject quickly, listening to Noah's family tell tales of Toronto. When dinner had finished, everyone went to sit in the living room, but Esme insisted on helping Teresa clear the table.

"Really, you don't have to help me," Teresa said. "You're our guest, after all. And I worked as a cleaner for twenty-five years, so this comes naturally."

"It's no problem," Esme said, putting away old dishes. "I don't mind helping."

"You're too kind," Teresa said, plunging the dishes into the soak with soap. "Do you think you'll be staying in Toronto long?"

"I don't know," Esme said, glancing at Noah through the open door. "I'd like to, but...I miss my home, too."

"I see. A tough decision," Teresa muttered, turning to Esme. "Can I be honest with you?"

Esme shrugged. "Sure."

"I don't know if you're aware, but my son speaks highly of you. The only person he spoke of like that was Jill—and it didn't work out."

Esme nodded. "I heard."

"Well, I don't want to see him get hurt. So, please—be careful with him. I don't know if you care for him like he does for you, but I can't stand to watch him get his heart broken again."

"Trust me, Teresa—hurting Noah would kill me. I'd never do that to him."

On purpose, at least. Leaving would hurt him too. Esme hated the thought, trying to push it out of her mind for now.

Teresa smiled. "Good. Noah's been through a lot. He deserves a happily ever after—and he seems very happy with you."

After Esme had finished drying the dishes with Teresa, she walked into the living room. Noah stood up right away. "It's getting late, but before we go, I think we should do one last thing."

"Oh? What is it?"

"We should go for a swim in the lake first. Like Ronnie said, it wouldn't be right to go to a cottage without it."

Esme glanced down at her dress. "That sounds nice, but I didn't bring a change of clothes."

"I have a bathing suit you can borrow," Veronica chimed in, smirking. "You two will have a great time—the water is nice and warm."

Esme nodded. "All right. Give me a minute to change."

Noah waited, standing by the door. As Veronica led Esme upstairs to her room, she glanced around at Noah and his family, realizing there was no other place she'd rather be.

CHAPTER 22

Esme stood in Veronica's room, her eyes widening at the number of bathing suits she had in her dresser drawer. "And here I thought *I* had a lot of clothes..."

Veronica laughed. "I'm a swimming instructor. I like to have a lot of bathing suits to choose from."

"Ah—then that explains why you were in the water when I got here."

Veronica nodded. "Yeah—I love to swim. It's really peaceful. And if you think I have a lot of bathing suits here, you should see how many I keep at home. The same old clothes get boring after a while."

"You sound like a woman after my own heart," Esme said, chuckling. "I don't have any bathing suits, though."

"Well, that needs to change," Veronica said, pulling out a sleek, black bathing suit. "This one would look great on you."

As Esme held it up, she frowned at how small it was. "Isn't it a little revealing?"

"So?" Veronica asked. "You have a nice body—you should show it off. And I'm sure Noah wants you to show it off, too."

Esme blushed, clearing her throat. "All right—I'll wear it. Where should I change?"

Veronica walked toward the door. "I'll wait in the hallway. Holler if you need me."

After Veronica shut the door, Esme changed out of her dress, sliding the bathing suit on. As she looked at herself in Veronica's mirror, she grinned.

"Veronica was right," Esme said to herself, twirling around. "I *do* look good in this..."

A knock sounded on the door, and Veronica's voice came through a moment later. "Everything okay in there?"

"Yes—you can come in now!" Esme shouted back, moving out of the way of the door.

When Veronica entered the room and noticed Esme, she gasped. "Oh my god—you look amazing! You're in great shape, too. Do you work out?"

Esme's mind flitted back to the castle—how much walking and running she did. They didn't exercise per se, but there was a lot of movement at parties and events.

Esme shrugged. "A little bit. Thanks again for letting me borrow this."

"Of course—and you can keep it. It's yours now."

"Really?" Esme asked, looking down. "Because I can take it home and wash it—"

Veronica shook her head. "Really—it's my gift to you. I just want you to promise me one thing."

"What?"

"If you can't be with Noah, break his heart gently," Veronica whispered. "Please. It would destroy me to see him hurt again."

Teresa had told Esme the same thing. She smiled, grateful that Noah had so many people who cared about him.

"It's not my intention to hurt him," Esme said. "Honestly.

When I arrived in Toronto, I didn't expect to meet him or become his friend. I love being with him. But..."

"Let me guess," Veronica said, leaning against the doorframe. "It has something to do with your home? Noah mentioned you come from a faraway place. That you're only visiting."

Esme sighed, playing with the picture frames Veronica had on her dresser. "I have...certain responsibilities to my home. I'll have to go back eventually. And unfortunately, there's no way for me and Noah to stay in contact. My father forbids outside communication."

Veronica sighed. "That's rough. What are you going to do?"

"I don't know," Esme said, softly. "The whole reason I came to Toronto was to prove to my father that I could be independent. But the more I do that...the closer I get to having to go home. And a part of me doesn't want that. I feel like my brain and my heart are in a constant battle..."

"I feel for you," Veronica said, placing a hand on Esme's shoulder. "Having to choose between your home and a person you're falling for is a hard decision. I don't know what I'd do."

"And the final hour is getting closer. I have to make a decision soon," Esme said, turning from the dresser. "But that's not tonight. I think I should enjoy my time with Noah—however long we have left."

Veronica smiled. "That's the spirit. Go get him. And Esme?"

Esme paused in the doorway, looking over her shoulder. "Yes?"

"I hope you make the right choice—a choice you can live with."

"Me, too," Esme muttered, turning toward the staircase.

When she had made it downstairs, Noah was still standing near the door, chatting with his mother. His father and grandmother were watching television in the living room. Esme heard her name pop up in Noah's conversation, so she hid behind the wall to listen in.

"...and I do like her, Mom," Noah was saying. "It's just... things are complicated."

"Aren't they always when it comes to love?" she heard Teresa ask.

"I guess. Esme wasn't born here—she comes from another place. And one day, she might have to return to her people."

"Will you be able to let her go?"

Noah was quiet for a moment. "I don't know. But if she chooses to go back, I'll have no choice. I'm not going to force her to do anything she doesn't want to do. It has to be up to her."

Esme poked her head around the corner, seeing Noah in his swim trunks. He had changed out of his formal clothes while she was upstairs. He looked good, Esme had to admit, now that she had a clear view of his toned biceps and abs. Teresa hugged Noah.

"Follow your heart," Esme heard her whisper. "It'll never lead you astray."

"Thanks, Mom. You always have the best advice."

Teresa pulled back, smiling. "I'm just looking out for you. I'm protective of my baby, especially after..."

"Jill. You can say her name—she's not an evil spirit."

Teresa laughed. "Well, she feels like one in my books. Be careful with your precious heart, Noah—and do what feels right. I'm rooting for you. Always."

After Teresa walked by, joining Noah's father and grandmother in the living room, Esme snuck around the corner. "Boo!"

Noah spun around, clutching his chest with a laugh. "Oh, Esme—you scared me."

"Sorry," Esme said with a giggle. "But you should've seen your face."

"Very funny," he said, then stopped laughing when he noticed her bathing suit. "My God, you look…"

"Like Veronica?" Esme asked. "This is her bathing suit."

"Incredible," Noah finished. "I wish there was a word better than that, but I can't think of one."

"Showstopping? Scintillating? Utterly radiant?"

Noah laughed. "Yeah—all of the above. Ready to get in the lake?"

"You bet. I've never been in a lake before. Back home, the swamp was too dirty to swim in."

"Then you're in for a nice surprise," Noah said with a smile, opening the door.

She followed him outside, taking the gravel path to the deck in front of the lake. Noah walked to the edge, dipping a foot in the water. The moonlight bounced off it like a spotlight.

"Not too cold," he said, stepping in. "Are you coming?"

Esme nodded, wading into the water slowly. She plunged deeper into the lake and swam over to Noah. They floated there for a few seconds in silence as they stared up at the stars.

"It's beautiful," Esme whispered. "The cottage, the lake… everything."

Noah nodded. "It's why I wanted to take you out here. I thought you deserved a break."

"Thank you," Esme said with a smile. "It's just what I needed. And there's something I always wanted to try in a lake. Something I saw on TV."

"What?" Noah asked, raising his eyebrows.

"Splash fight!" Esme cried, throwing some water on Noah.

He laughed as the water hit him in the face. "Oh, you're going to pay for that!"

With uncontrollable giggles, Noah and Esme took turns splashing each other until they were both soaked from head to toe. When Esme tried to splash him again, he grabbed her hands, pulling her closer to him.

"Got you," he said, his lips inches away from hers. "Can't splash me now, can you?"

Esme laughed. "Well played. You know, you could get in a lot of trouble for grabbing a princess like that. They might even throw you in the dungeons. But don't worry—I'd rescue you."

"My hero," he whispered. "Though, in the fairytales here, it's usually a brave, handsome knight who saves the beautiful princess."

"Why can't we both save each other?"

Noah didn't say anything—he just continued to stare into her eyes. She found herself mesmerized in his grasp, unable to pull away. And the next thing she knew, they were both leaning in, their lips touching underneath the moonlight.

A million things ran through Esme's mind as she kissed him, wrapping her arms around his neck. He had his hands tied tightly around her like he never wanted to let go. Why did it feel so right kissing him? And what would her life be like if she chose to stay?

But then it always came back to Fairhaven, her true home. Her friends and family she'd have to give up if she stayed in Toronto. And what it meant for Senator Remus, Fairy Godmother Zamira, and his conniving daughter. Not to mention her responsibilities as a princess and what would happen if she left it all behind, abandoning her kind while Remus was still out there.

And those fears won over her feelings for Noah.

Esme pulled away, breathlessly. "I'm sorry, Noah. I can't do this."

As she swam back to the docks, he frowned. "What? What do you mean?"

"I think we should stay friends," she said, pulling herself up onto the docks. "I'm probably only going to hurt you if we go any further."

He looked confused as he swam over to her. "I just thought...I thought you felt the same way."

"I *do* care about you," she said, softly. "How could I not, after all this time together? But that's not the problem."

He sighed, sitting next to her. "Your kingdom is."

She nodded. "That's right. And it wouldn't be fair to keep stringing you along, knowing I'm going back to Fairhaven soon. As much as I care about you...those are my people. My destiny, my birthright. With everything going on with Remus and those guards, I think I'm needed now more than ever."

"Right," Noah muttered, looking down. "I get it."

Esme felt awful as she looked at him. She hadn't meant to hurt him, but she already had. There was no going back.

"I'm sorry, Noah. Really—"

"Hey, don't worry," he said, faking a smile as he looked up at her. "You have nothing to apologize for."

Esme forced herself to look away, nodding. "Glad you understand. I guess we should probably get changed and head home."

As she rose to her feet, his voice stopped her. "Before we leave, can I ask you something?"

She turned back. "Anything."

He rose to his feet, coming face to face with her again. "Did that kiss mean as much to you as it did to me?"

"It meant everything," she said, softly. "And if things were different, that would be enough."

He nodded, staying silent. Esme feared she had ruined things between them forever as they walked quietly toward the cottage. She glanced up, noticing Veronica watching them from the window. She quickly closed the curtains when she realized Esme had seen her.

When they entered the house, Veronica rushed down the staircase. "Back so soon?"

"Yes," Esme said. "We need to get home now—we have a lot to do tomorrow. If you'll excuse me, I need to change."

She kept her head down, avoiding Veronica's stare as she went upstairs to put her dress back on. She knew how badly Veronica wanted Esme and Noah to get together, but Esme didn't know if that could happen—ever. When she tip-toed down the stairs a few minutes later, she heard Veronica and Noah talking. She paused again to listen in.

"What happened?" Veronica asked.

"I don't want to talk about it," Noah muttered, walking into the bathroom. "I need to change."

While she waited for Noah to put his clothes back on, Esme walked into the living room where Teresa, Dan, and Louise were sitting. "Thank you for having me. The food was delicious and the cottage is beautiful. This place is like a paradise."

"It was our pleasure," Teresa said, rising to her feet. "You're welcome back anytime."

"And we hope to see you again soon, dear," Louise said sweetly, reminding Esme of Fairy Godmother Odelia.

When Teresa hugged Esme, she realized how good it felt. Her father hadn't hugged her—not in a long time. Veronica watched from the doorway curiously, wondering what had happened in the lake.

Noah walked into the room, dressed in his formal clothes again. "Ready to leave?"

Esme faked a smile. "I am. Goodnight, everyone."

As they waved goodbye, Veronica continued to watch them. Esme and Noah got into his car and started the engine. Esme watched the cottage fade behind them in the rear-view mirror, wishing she could stay there with Noah forever.

Noah cleared his throat, driving along the backroads. "I hope I didn't make things awkward between us. If we can't be together...then I hope we can stay friends. Somehow."

Esme nodded. "I'd like that. And no—you didn't make anything awkward. I'm still glad you're in my life, Noah."

She finally saw him smile again. "Yeah, I feel the same."

The drive back to Esme's apartment was quiet. They didn't bring up the kiss again when they talked, and Esme hoped she hadn't hurt Noah too much. After he pulled into her parking lot, he got out, walking her into the building.

"I had a good time at the cottage with you," he said, pressing the button to the elevator. "Probably the best time I've had in a while."

"Me, too," Esme said as she stepped inside. "I wish I could live in that cottage."

"Yeah, but I bet a castle is much better," Noah said, a hint of sadness in his voice about them having to inevitably part.

"I do like the castle, yes. But it doesn't have everything."

It doesn't have you, Esme wanted to say.

As Noah walked Esme to her apartment, he turned to her. "Well, I should get home now. I'll see you tomorrow?"

Esme nodded. "Bright and early. Dylan has his first therapy session tomorrow, and I was hoping you could drive us. Is that okay?"

"Of course—whatever you need," Noah said. "I'm sure it'll be more fun than the charity auction."

Esme forced a laughed. "Don't remind me. There's only so much of that woman I can take."

Noah thrust his hands into his pocket, looking awkward. "Well, goodnight, and thanks for coming—"

"Wait," Esme said, noticing something over his shoulder. "What happened to Gina's apartment?"

Noah frowned, turning around to notice what Esme was staring at. The door to Gina's apartment was half open. Esme wasted no time pushing it open and stepping inside, glancing around.

"Gina?" she called out. "Are you here? Is everything okay?"

Noah trailed in behind Esme, noticing the apartment didn't look too out of shape. "Well, it doesn't look like a robbery—"

"Gina!" Esme cried, noticing Gina laying on the floor.

She rushed to her side, finding Gina's head bleeding. It looked like she had fallen and hurt herself, then tried to crawl toward the door. Esme pressed an ear against Gina's chest, listening.

"She's still breathing," Esme said.

"Call 9-1-1," Noah ordered as Esme pulled out her cell phone. "I'll go tell Tanya what happened!"

Noah rushed across the hall. Esme could hear Noah explaining everything to Tanya and her kids as the 9-1-1 operator picked up. "Hello, 9-1-1. What is your emergency?"

"My friend hit her head and she's bleeding a lot," Esme said. "We're in the Sunnyview Apartments."

"I have an ambulance on its way. Please, stay on the line..."

Tanya walked in a second later, gasping. "Oh my God—Gina!"

Her children tried to look into the apartment, but Noah stopped them from seeing Gina like that. Tanya and Esme hovered above her for what felt like forever until the ambulance arrived. The paramedics lifted Gina onto a stretcher, dragging her into the elevator and down the stairs. Esme briefly told the paramedics how shaky Gina had been lately but that no one knew why.

"We have to go with her," Esme said, watching as they took her away. "I don't want her to wake up alone."

Noah nodded. "I can drive you. Tanya, do you need a lift?"

She shook her head, on the verge of tears. "No—I have my own car parked outside. I'll take my kids, too. I'm sure they'll want to know what's happening—they love Gina. Oh, I hope she'll be all right..."

Once the ambulance had driven off, Noah and Esme got into their car while Tanya took her children. They followed the ambulance, arriving a few minutes later at the Toronto General Hospital. They rushed through the front doors and sat in the waiting room to hear the results.

When a doctor came out with Gina's chart, all their heads shot up. "Gina is doing much better. We think she'll make a full recovery."

Everyone sighed in relief.

"What happened?" Esme asked.

"She claims she collapsed, hitting her head. She made it to the door and opened it, but before she could call out for anyone, she fell unconscious. We managed to stop the bleeding."

"Can we see her?" Tanya asked, rising to her feet.

"She's only asking for Esme right now," the doctor replied. "She says she has something to tell her."

Esme frowned, wondering what it could be. "I'm Esme, doctor. Lead the way."

"We'll wait right here for you," Noah said, sitting back down with the kids. "Take your time."

When Tanya and her children nodded, Esme took a deep breath, following the doctor into the hospital room. Gina was lying in the bed with a bandage wrapped around her head. Her eyes were open, and she looked much better than before.

"I'll give you two some privacy," the doctor said as he left the room, closing the door behind him.

"Oh, Gina," Esme cried, taking her hand. "I'm glad you're okay. How are you feeling?"

"My head is sore, but I'll be all right. Thank you for finding me. If you hadn't...maybe I wouldn't still be here."

"Well, I'm glad you are. It was a smart move leaving the door open an inch. Why did you only want to see me? The others are worried, too."

Gina sighed. "Because you know something's wrong with me. You've known all along."

Esme thought back to her shaking hands. "What's going on?"

Gina sighed, looking out the window at the darkness. "I have Parkinson's disease. I was diagnosed shortly after my husband died. I've been taking medication for it, but trembling hands, clumsiness, and falling unconscious are common side effects."

Esme sighed, sitting next to her. "Why didn't you tell anyone?"

"Tanya's kids. It's always been about them," she said, tears welling in her eyes. "I love babysitting them. They've been my lifeline since I ended up all alone. I didn't want Tanya to think I couldn't take care of her kids."

"She'd never think that," Esme said, wiping away a tear. "To go through losing your husband and suffering from a disease... well, I think you're the strongest person I've ever met. And you're never alone. Not while we're here."

"Really?"

Esme nodded. "Of course. Is there any way I can help?"

"Well, my doctor recommended physiotherapy. It could help my condition. It's covered with my health insurance, but I haven't gone. I...don't want to face it alone."

Esme tightened her grip on Gina's hand. "I can go with you. You aren't alone, Gina—ever."

She smiled. "Thank you, Esme. Truly."

Esme rose to her feet. "Of course—anytime. Now, I think I should bring Tanya, Noah, and the kids in here before they collapse with worry."

Gina laughed. "Good idea. I'm so glad I have you and the others, Esme. Without you...I wouldn't have had the strength to go on anymore. Thank you."

Esme only smiled as she left the room.

CHAPTER 23

When Esme walked back into the waiting room, she took a minute to watch Noah with the kids. He was gentle and patient, bouncing Lindsey on his knee while he chatted with Vincent about science. He also made sure to include Dylan in the conversation so he wasn't left out.

He'd make a great father one day, Esme realized.

She felt a pang of sadness that she couldn't have children with Noah—that he'd eventually move on after she left and have children with someone else. Esme closed her eyes for a moment, trying hard to forget that mental picture of him and his new wife. Or what his children would look like with someone else.

Could she even have kids with Noah? Their species had never intertwined like this before.

Tanya sat beside her children, nervously shaking her leg. Her head shot up when she noticed Esme. "So? Is everything all right?"

Esme smiled, pushing those intrusive thoughts about Noah aside. "Yes, Gina's fine. She wants to see all of you now."

"Good," Noah said, removing Lindsey from his lap so he could stand up. "We were worried out here. What took you so long?"

Esme led the five of them toward Gina's room. "I think she should tell you herself."

When they entered Gina's room, she was still lying in the hospital bed. When she saw the children, her eyes lit up. She held out her arms and beckoned for them to come toward her. Tanya and Noah smiled behind Esme, relieved to see her awake.

"Gina!" Lindsey and Vincent cried, rushing into her arms.

"Hello, kids," she said, giving them a big hug. "I'm so glad to see you again."

"You aren't going to die, are you?" Lindsey asked, looking at her with big, worried eyes.

"Of course not," Gina replied. "But I do have something to say. I...have a disease."

Tanya frowned. "What kind of disease?"

Gina looked down. "Parkinson's, unfortunately. It does run in my family. I've been struggling with it since last year—right after my husband died."

"What's Parkinson's?" Dylan asked, hanging by the door with his hands in his pockets.

Vincent raised his hand. "Oh, I know! I heard about it on TV. It's a brain disorder, right?"

Gina nodded. "That's right—well done, Vincent. It gets worse over time and can involve shaking, difficulty with balance, and stiffness. You can even pass out from it."

"Which explains why we found you on the floor," Noah said, sighing. "I'm so sorry you're going through this, Gina."

"Me, too," Tanya added. "If I knew you were sick, I wouldn't have asked you to babysit so much—"

"Nonsense," Gina said, shaking her head. "I love babysitting. It's all I have now that Al's gone and I'm retired. I live for these little munchkins."

When she squeezed Lindsey and Vincent's cheeks, they giggled.

"That's why Gina didn't want to tell anyone," Esme said, turning to Tanya. "She didn't want you to think she wasn't capable."

Tanya shook her head. "Oh, Gina—I think you're capable of anything you set your mind to. Of course I'll let you babysit and see the kids whenever you want."

"See?" Esme asked, walking toward Gina. "You had nothing to worry about."

Gina sighed in relief, hugging them all tight. "I'm glad. Sorry I worried you all, but thanks for being here for me. It means the world."

Lindsey tugged on Gina's hospital gown. "Is there a cure?"

Gina turned silent for a moment, then shook her head. "No, not yet. I can only take medication to deal with it."

"In the future, is there anything we can do to help your condition?" Noah asked. "Something that could make it better?"

Gina smiled, glancing at Esme. "There's physiotherapy I've been offered by my doctor. I never went because I was scared to go alone, but Esme graciously agreed to accompany me. I could use some moral support. When I get home, I'll set up an appointment."

"That was nice of her," Tanya said, nodding at Esme. "I'd offer, too, but work keeps me busy."

Gina nodded. "That's all right, Tanya. I understand. I'm just grateful you're going to let me be around the kids."

"I can drive the two of you to your appointments," Noah said. "Whatever you need."

Gina grinned. "That would be great. Thank you, Noah."

"What if you pass out again?" Vincent asked. "Like, when you're babysitting us? Can we help?"

"In that case, the best thing to do would be to call 9-1-1," Gina said. "But the hospital is giving me new medication that should prevent that in the future."

"And...I could help you watch my siblings," Dylan piped up. "You know, if you're having trouble making food or something."

Gina smiled. "Thank you, Dylan. That's very kind of you."

Dylan cautiously moved toward the bed. "I'm glad you're going to be okay. Really."

"We all are," Tanya said, ruffling Dylan's hair. "So, when are you getting out of this place?"

"The doctor said I can leave tonight. Someone just needs to check on me every now and then."

"I can do it," Esme said. "I know Tanya's really busy."

Tanya nodded. "Yeah—thanks, Esme. I'll stop by when I can."

"Tanya, can you sign me out at the front desk?" Gina asked, kicking her legs over the side of the bed. "And Noah, I'll need your help getting out to the car."

"No problem," Noah said, holding out his hand. "I'll take you and Esme home."

Tanya nodded, walking toward the door. "I'll sign you out and be right back."

As she left, Noah helped Gina out of bed. Esme stood back with Dylan as Lindsey and Vincent gave Gina words of encouragement.

"I never used to like Gina," Dylan whispered to Esme. "I thought she was bossy."

Esme laughed. "Well, she used to be a teacher—I guess old habits die hard. What changed your mind?"

"I saw how happy she makes Vincent and Lindsey," Dylan

whispered. "And...she was always nice to me, even when I wasn't nice to her."

Esme nodded. "She cares about you, too, Dylan. We all do. I know you're going through a tough time now, but never forget that."

Esme swore she saw a hint of a smile on Dylan's face. "Thanks."

Tanya returned to the room as Gina pulled her clothes back on, holding up a white bag. "Sign-out is complete. And the front desk gave me your medication, too—much stronger than your old stuff."

"Great," Gina said as Noah helped get her coat on. "Thank you—all of you—for your support. It means the world to have you with me. With my husband gone...you're all I have now."

"We're glad to have you, too," Esme said, smiling. "I know you want to do everything by yourself, but we're here for you. Don't be afraid to ask for help."

Gina nodded, sadly. "Yes—that's a skill I most desperately need to learn. I'm always afraid of being a burden."

"You—a burden?" Tanya asked, leaving the hospital together. "Never. You've done a lot for us. Let us repay the favor."

Gina smiled the whole way home as Noah drove them. Tanya followed in the car behind them with Vincent, Dylan, and Lindsey. When they arrived back at the apartments, it was pitch-black outside. Noah helped guide Gina into the elevator and up to her apartment.

"Home sweet home," Gina said, unlocking the door with her trembling hands. "I think I'm just going to get into bed. Can you help me, Noah?"

He nodded, leading Gina into the bedroom. She put on her pajamas as he turned around before he helped her get under the covers. When she looked cozy and comfortable, the six of them stood in the doorway.

"Sweet dreams, Gina," Tanya said. "Remember—we're always right across the hall."

"I hope you feel better!" Lindsey cried. "I'll draw you a picture so you never forget we love you."

Gina beamed. "Thank you, Lindsey. I appreciate all of you. Goodnight, everyone."

After Esme turned off the light, they left Gina's apartment, locking the door behind them. Tanya gestured at her apartment. "Well, I should get the kids to bed. It's way past their bedtime."

Esme nodded. "Sounds good. And I'll be over tomorrow morning to get Dylan for his therapy appointment. After I check on Gina, of course."

"Thank you," Tanya said, turning to Dylan. "Are you still going?"

Dylan nodded, looking at Esme. "Yeah, I think so. As long as you go with me."

Esme bent down to his level. "I'll tell you what I told Gina—you're both special to me. Of course I'll go with you. Now, get some rest for tomorrow, okay?"

Dylan nodded, entering his apartment with Lindsey and Vincent. Tanya said goodbye before she closed the door and vanished inside. When it was only Noah and Esme left out in the hallway, everything turned quiet.

"Well," Noah said, clearing his throat, "I should get home, too. So...goodnight. Again."

Esme leaned in and, to Noah's surprise, kissed him on the cheek. She pulled away, looking up into his eyes. "Goodnight, Noah. Thanks for coming. You've been a big help."

"Me?" Noah asked, grinning. "Esme, you're the one who's

been incredible. Look at all the good you've done—with Gina, with Tanya, with Dylan. With me."

Esme smiled. "I've made great friends here, haven't I?"

"I'd say it's more like family. And sometimes, the family you make is better than the one you were given. This city needs people like you, Esme. The world does. Remember that."

As Noah walked off down the hallway and disappeared inside the elevator, Esme entered her apartment and considered his words. He didn't want her to go back to Fairhaven—that much was clear. She didn't want to, either.

Was it possible she could stay? Was it possible her father would let her?

As she went to bed that night, she dreamed of what could be.

~

WHEN HER ALARM clock went off the next morning, Esme wasted no time.

She quickly ate some cereal, brushed her teeth, and got dressed. She locked her apartment behind her before she rushed over to Gina's. Using the key Gina had given her, she unlocked it, entering the foyer.

"Gina?" she called out. "I'm just checking on you. I hope you aren't sleeping."

"In here!" Gina yelled from the bedroom.

When Esme entered, she found Gina sitting up in bed, reading a book. Esme smiled. "You look much better this morning."

Gina nodded, putting her book aside. "Thank you. I feel much better, too—maybe it's because I know I have you looking out for me."

"Well, I'm glad. What would you like for breakfast?"

"Just some toast and tea, please. My usual."

Esme nodded, entering Gina's kitchen to make her breakfast. When it was ready, she brought it to Gina in bed on a platter, making chit-chat while she ate. When she finished, Esme washed the dishes and checked her watch.

"I need to take Dylan to his appointment now, and I'm sure Tanya has to go to work. Will you be okay watching over Vincent and Lindsey today?"

Gina laughed. "Are you kidding? Those two are easy—they barely make any noise. I have cable and board games they can play. And Dylan's been a lot nicer to me lately—surprisingly."

Esme nodded. "I know—I'm proud of how far he's come. And before I go, I'll give you my number. If you have any trouble —with the kids or anything else—call me, okay?"

Gina nodded as Esme scribbled her number down. When Esme left the apartment and crossed the hall, Tanya flung the door open with her work uniform on. "So? How's Gina doing this morning?"

"Happy to report that she's much better. She'll be able to watch the kids."

"What a relief," Tanya said, grabbing her keys. She turned to Dylan who was waiting behind her and kissed him on the cheek. "Good luck at therapy, sweetie. I hope it helps."

He nodded. "Thanks, Mom."

"Vincent, Lindsey?" Tanya called out. "It's time to see Gina. Mommy has to go to work."

"Yay!" they cried in unison, grabbing their things before rushing across the hallway.

Tanya laughed. "I'm glad they have Gina. My parents died a long time ago—my husband's, too. We don't have any other family."

Esme placed a hand on Tanya's shoulder. "Of course, you do. You have us."

If Esme had to leave, at least Noah and the others would still be there. Esme had brought them all together. That was something at least.

Tanya smiled wider. "The day you came to Toronto was a very lucky day for all of us. Thank you, Esme—I can't say it enough."

Esme thought about her words for a second, knowing she was going to miss them when she went back home.

As Tanya walked off down the hallway, Esme heard Vincent and Lindsey talking to Gina in her apartment. They sounded excited which made her smile. When she felt a buzz in her pocket, she pulled it out.

Hey, Esme, Noah's text read. *I'm waiting downstairs whenever you and Dylan are ready.*

"There's our ride," Esme said, putting her phone back in her pocket. "Ready, Dylan?"

He nodded, grabbing his jacket. "I'm ready. What do you think will happen today?"

"Well, I've never been to therapy before," Esme said, reaching the elevator, "but don't worry. The therapist won't do anything you're not comfortable with."

Dylan sighed in relief and rode the elevator downstairs. They walked out of the lobby, finding Noah waiting as promised by his car. He smiled when he saw the two of them.

"Hey, Esme. Hey, buddy. Are you doing okay this morning?"

Dylan nodded, getting into the backseat. "Just nervous."

"I know. New things can be scary, but they can also be good for you," Noah said, poking his head inside the car. "I went to therapy after my fiancée left me."

Esme's eyebrows raised in surprise. Noah hadn't told her that. She knew he had been hurt after Jill left him, but she didn't realize how much.

"Did it help?" Dylan asked.

Noah nodded. "Definitely. Sometimes, talking it out helps you deal with those pent-up emotions. So don't be worried—therapy is a good thing."

When Esme got into the car, she smiled at Noah. "Thank you for calming him down."

Noah shrugged as he started the car. "Just speaking the truth."

"Are you still in therapy?" Esme asked as Noah pulled out of the parking lot.

"No," he said, watching the road. "Not anymore. Not since I met you."

Esme smiled, hoping that was a good thing.

When they arrived at the doctor's office, Dylan trailed behind Esme and Noah, looking nervous. Esme walked up to the front desk where a secretary was on a phone call. When he put it down, Esme reached for Dylan and gently pulled him forward.

"Hello—we're here for Dylan's appointment," she said.

The secretary nodded, rising to his feet. "Right this way—the therapist's ready for you. You and your husband can wait for your son in the lobby."

Esme blushed, unable to believe how many times people thought they were together.

"Oh, we aren't his parents," Noah said, "or married. His mother is a good friend of ours who made the appointment, and she asked us to take him today. She was working and couldn't come."

"I see. Well, you can wait here—"

"No," Dylan said, firmly. "Esme has to come with me or I'm not going."

"Is that okay?" Esme asked the secretary.

"It's not usually how we do things," the secretary said,

glancing at Dylan, "but I'm sure it'll be fine. After all, therapy is about making sure you're comfortable."

Dylan sighed in relief.

"Right this way," the secretary said, walking off down the corridor. "You're seeing Dr. Wells today. She's a very nice woman—don't you worry."

When they reached the door at the end of the hallway, the secretary knocked on it. A dark-haired woman answered it a moment later. She wore casual clothes, had a clipboard in hand, and smiled down at them.

"Your client is here to see you, Dr. Wells," the secretary said. "Please don't hesitate to let me know if you need anything— drinks, a snack. I'll be right over there."

After he walked off, Dr. Wells bent down next to Dylan and held out her hand. "Nice to meet you, Dylan. I'm Dr. Lorraine Wells."

"Hi," Dylan said, shyly.

"I'll wait for you in the lobby," Noah whispered. "Good luck."

After he walked off, Dr. Wells turned to Esme. "Hello. What's your name?"

"Esme Fairhaven, Dylan's new neighbor. He wants me to sit in on his therapy session today."

"No problem," Dr. Wells said, gesturing inside the office. "Come on in."

When they entered, the office was cozy. It had leather chairs set up, ones that could recline. It also had a giant window that overlooked the city and a computer and a desk in the corner.

"So, Dylan," Dr. Wells said, sitting down, "how have you been feeling lately?"

Dylan shrugged as he plopped down into the chair. He played with the upholstery, still looking uneasy. "Okay. Better with Esme."

"I see," Dr. Wells said, glancing at Esme as she took a seat. "I take it Esme's special to you?"

"She gets me. I can't really talk to Mom too much—she's always working."

"Yes—that can be difficult. How does Esme understand you?"

Dylan didn't speak, so Esme sat forward. "Like Dylan, I lost a parent, too—my mother. Things...have been hard without her."

"Were you close with her?"

Esme swallowed a lump in her throat. "Yeah, I was."

"How about you, Dylan?"

Dylan finally looked up, holding back tears. "My dad was my favorite person. I miss him a lot."

"Losing someone we love is the hardest thing to experience in life," Dr. Wells said, writing down a few notes. "And sometimes, that pain can become unbearable. That's when we turn to therapy—and it's a good thing you're both here."

"What can you do for us, Doc?" Esme asked.

Dr. Wells smiled. "I'm glad you asked. Today, we'll just chat and go over some grief coping mechanisms. Feel free to speak up whenever you'd like..."

For the next forty-five minutes, Dr. Wells shared tips for grief—like writing in a journal, talking to someone who understood, and crying when needed. She even recommended going to the gravestone and talking to it. Dylan and Esme both shared things they missed about their parents, and Dr. Wells let them vent until the timer went off.

"Well, that concludes our session for today," Dr. Wells said, rising to her feet. "I hope it's begun to help you, Dylan. We still have a long way to go. I'll see you again soon, okay? Take care."

Dylan nodded, leaving the room with Esme. She glanced at

Dylan as she walked with him down the hallway. "So? How do you feel?"

"Good," Dylan said, looking up at her. "It wasn't so scary. Maybe next time I could go by myself."

Esme smiled. "You got it, Dylan. Whatever you need."

"Are we going home now?"

Esme glanced out the window, getting an idea. "Soon. I want to do something first—something Dr. Wells recommended."

CHAPTER 24

Dylan looked confused, following Esme back to the waiting room. Noah stood up when he saw them and put the magazine he was reading aside. He bent down beside Dylan, smiling at him.

"Hey, buddy. How'd it go in there?"

"Good," Dylan said with a shrug. "I think."

"Is it over?" Noah asked, rising to his feet. He reached for his car keys and pointed at the door. "Are we leaving?"

"The session's done, and I'd say we both learned a lot," Esme said, ruffling Dylan's hair, who smiled up at her. "But I want to take Dylan somewhere before we take him home."

"Oh, okay. Where?"

Esme glanced at Dylan. "Do you know where your father was buried?"

Dylan nodded. "Eaglewood Cemetery. I memorized the spot."

"Good job," Esme said, glancing at Noah. "Dr. Wells said going to the cemetery could help. Do you think you could drive us there?"

"Of course," Noah said, walking with them toward the doors. "Have you been to your father's grave before, Dylan?"

Dylan shook his head. "No, not since the funeral. Mom didn't want to go back there."

"It might help," Esme said, reaching the car. "You never know."

After they got in, Noah drove a few miles to the Eaglewood Cemetery. Crows squawked from the trees as they entered through the creaky gates. Rows upon rows of headstones decorated the fields, some with flowers and gifts in front of them. People dressed in black paid their respects to those they had lost.

"I don't like the cemetery," Noah said as they walked through the field. "It's too sad."

"I know," Esme said, placing a hand on Dylan's shoulder. "Everyone here has people who love and miss them. But it proves that love doesn't get any weaker in death."

Noah nodded. "Very true, Esme. Now, Dylan—do you know what plot your father's in?"

"I think it's this way," he said, rushing off ahead. "Follow me."

Noah and Esme let Dylan guide them through the gravestones, taking them to a secluded area near a few trees. A giant headstone sat there that read PHIL BREWER with his birth and death date. FOREVER MISSED with a few hearts were carved into the stone beneath his name.

"This is it," Dylan whispered. "This is where my dad lives now."

"This is where your dad was *buried*," Esme said, placing a hand on his shoulder. "Your dad lives in your heart—and he's always there."

"I wish he was really here," Dylan muttered, running his fingers along the stone. "I wish I could tell him I miss him..."

"You can. It's why I brought you here," Esme said, stepping back. "Noah and I will give you a few minutes. Take your time—tell your dad everything you've always wished you could say."

"Will he really hear me?" Dylan asked, looking over his shoulder at her.

Esme smiled. "Absolutely. Don't hold back—say how you feel."

She turned to Noah, walking toward a tree in the distance. They hid in the shade as Dylan sat crisscrossed and began talking to the stone. If Esme strained, she could hear what he was saying—telling his father about school, his mother, and meeting Esme.

"Are you sure this'll help?" Noah whispered. "What if it just makes things harder on Dylan?"

"Dr. Wells was the one who told us to do it. Dylan needs to know that his father isn't coming back, but it doesn't mean he's gone forever. No one is—not really."

At that moment, Esme wasn't sure who she was talking about—Dylan or herself. She had spent so many sleepless nights sobbing over her mother's death. She realized she needed to move on, too.

"You see a lot of yourself in Dylan, don't you?" Noah asked, quietly. "That's why you've helped him so much?"

Esme nodded as she continued to watch Dylan. "I see a child who's hurting. In many ways, we're more alike than Dylan knows. He might not be royalty, but to him, his father was his everything—and he feels sad and empty without him. I know the feeling."

"Did you ever go to your mother's grave?"

"No, but I wish I had," Esme muttered. "I didn't even go to the funeral—I couldn't. Her body's entombed in our castle. That's what happens to all the royals."

"Well, I didn't know your mother," Noah began, "but I

know this. She'd be very proud of how far you've come. And for how you've helped Dylan."

Esme found herself smiling. "Thanks—I hope so. I know she'd like you."

"If she's anything like you," Noah said with a grin, "then I'm sure I'd like her, too."

"Oh, she was much more of a handful than me. Opinionated, determined, strong."

Noah laughed. "Really?"

Esme wiped away a tear, still smiling. "Really. And she only got away with it because she was the queen. It helped me get away with things, too. I think my father even found it amusing."

"Then what changed? Why did your father kick you out?"

"My mother died," Esme said, softly. "And Father was never the same. He came down on me harder with more rules and restrictions. I think he was afraid of losing me, too."

Esme felt Noah link his hands with hers. "I'm sorry—for everything you've lost."

Esme said nothing for a few seconds. "I know. And coming to Toronto has really helped. I'm the happiest I've ever been since my mother died. I never thought I'd say that again..."

Noah shrugged. "Then stay."

Esme sighed. "Noah, you know it isn't that simple."

He reached for her hand again. "But it can be. I know you love your kingdom, but you just said this place makes you happy. And you deserve better than your controlling father. Won't you miss Dylan?"

"Of course, I will," she said, glancing at him again. "I'll miss you, too—and Gina, Tanya, the kids. Even Human Connection."

"Then please—I'm begging you," Noah said with desperate eyes. "Don't go. My family loved you, you know, and you have a home here. It wouldn't be right to turn your back on it."

"Oh, I don't know…"

"Maybe all of this happened for a reason," Noah continued. "Maybe you weren't ever meant to go back. Maybe you were meant to realize this is where you belong. Once you get your kingdom under control and there's no danger anymore, of course."

Esme didn't know what to say. How could she make a decision? Either way, her heart would break. She knew it.

Before she could respond, Dylan walked over. "I did it, Esme—I told my dad everything."

Esme wiggled out of Noah's grasp as she bent down beside Dylan, smiling. "You did? That's wonderful!"

Dylan nodded. "And you were right. It did feel good. I think I'm going to ask Mom to take me here—all of us. Vincent and Lindsey should talk to him, too."

"Well, I'm glad Dr. Wells gave us that advice. Now, what do you say we get some ice cream?"

Dylan's eyes lit up. "Can I get chocolate?"

Esme laughed, walking toward the path with him. "You can get whatever you'd like. Coming, Noah?"

"Yeah—right behind you," he said, though Esme knew he was still hoping she'd agree to stay.

After they got into Noah's sedan, he drove them to the closest ice cream parlor. Esme got her favorite—Rocky Road—while Noah got strawberry and bought chocolate ice cream for Dylan. They ate it outside, staring at the cemetery from across the street.

"Do you think the people come alive at night?" Dylan asked.

"Maybe," Esme said with a shrug. "Maybe they talk about their loved ones and how they can't wait to see them again one day."

"Or maybe they throw a dance party," Noah said, gently nudging Dylan's shoulder. "Like the Monster Mash."

When Dylan giggled, it warmed Esme's heart to see how far he had come. It was hard to believe he was the same child who would break things and throw tantrums.

After they finished their ice cream, Dylan looked at the cemetery one last time. "Bye, Dad. I'll come back soon and see you again."

"I'm sure your dad would be very happy you came to see him," Esme said, guiding him back to the car. "Now, let's get you home. It's been a long morning."

After they drove back to the apartment, Esme and Noah led Dylan up to Gina's apartment. They knocked on the door, then pushed it open to find Gina out of bed. She was sitting on the couch, watching cartoons with Vincent and Lindsey.

"You're back," Gina said, glancing up at them. "Hello, Dylan. How was therapy?"

"Good," he said, taking off his coat. "Then we went to Dad's grave and got ice cream."

"No fair!" Lindsey cried, pouting. "I want ice cream."

Vincent nodded. "Me, too."

Esme laughed. "One day, we'll go to the cemetery together and get ice cream as a treat. I promise, okay?"

The kids nodded, excited about the ice cream. Gina moved over on the couch to let Dylan take a seat. Once he had sat down, he looked as absorbed by the cartoons as Vincent and Lindsey. It was a big step up from before when he was always hiding in his room.

"We have a charity auction to get to," Noah said. "Will you be okay here alone, Gina?"

Gina laughed. "Of course! I've done it a million times before. I may have Parkinson's, but I'm not fragile."

"We know," Esme said with a smile. "Still, don't hesitate to call me if you need anything. We'll see you later tonight."

"Have fun at the auction!" Gina called out as they reached the door.

"Yeah, right," Noah whispered to Esme as they left. "When Giselle's involved, nothing's ever fun."

Esme giggled. "True. What kind of drama do you think she's going to cause today?"

"God only knows," Noah said, pressing the elevator button. "We should probably get all dressed up for the auction, huh?"

"Sure. I've got some spare dresses at home—"

"Actually, I was thinking we could buy some new threads." Noah smiled. "We'll charge it to Giselle's company. It's the least she can do for us."

Esme nodded, linking arms with Noah before they went on a shopping spree. After dressing up in something formal but not too expensive, they headed to City Hall, driving quietly. Noah didn't pester Esme again about staying—something she was grateful for. It hurt too much to think about the choice she'd have to make soon.

When they arrived in the parking lot, hundreds of other cars had already shown up, including Giselle's limousine. They found a vacant spot and pushed through the crowd to make it into City Hall. Other than the auction, it seemed very busy with politicians holding important meetings.

"This way," Noah said, pointing at a sign on the wall that read AUCTION. "I think it's in here."

Esme and Noah took a left, entering a large room with a stage and dozens of seats. There were platters of food and drinks on a buffet table. Next to it sat different bidding paddles —each one for the taking. A woman helped them register their numbers and allowed them to take the corresponding paddles.

"Here you go," Noah said, handing a board to Esme. "I think you're supposed to bid on stuff using this thing. I don't know for sure—I've never been to an auction before."

"Too bad we can't actually bid on anything," Esme said, following Noah to find a seat. "Everything's probably too expensive, anyway."

"Ah, there you two are!" a voice cried behind them.

As they sat down, Giselle rushed over, beaming. Esme noticed how glamorous she looked—a new dress, polished nails, makeup, and an expensive watch. Her purse and shoes looked expensive, too.

Esme glanced at Noah, wondering if he was thinking the same thing. How could Giselle afford it all?

"Are you ready for the auction?" Giselle asked, leaning in. "Do you remember the plan?"

Esme nodded. "We remember."

Giselle stepped back, grinning. "Glad to see you're on the ball. After the auction, everyone will know how generous I am."

Esme rolled her eyes. "How wonderful."

"And one more thing," Giselle said, ignoring her comment. "Don't get in my way. I mean that."

Esme and Noah didn't understand what she was talking about, but they nodded, anyway.

As Giselle rushed off to find her seat, Noah shook his head. "Sometimes, I really hate working for that woman."

Esme snorted. "You and me both."

"I wish you could run the non-profit, Esme. I think you'd be good at it. And then maybe...you'd have to stay in Toronto."

Esme sighed. "Noah, we've been over this—"

"I know, I know. Just think about it. Ronnie called me last night, too—she said she loved you. She hopes you stay in Toronto. I bet Gina, Tanya, and the kids do, too."

If Noah was trying to make her feel guilty about leaving, it was working, Esme realized. She said nothing, silently waiting for the auction to begin. A man in a blue suit walked onto the stage as people took their seats.

"Hello, everyone. My name is Mr. Henriksen," the man said, moving toward the podium. "I'll be your auctioneer this afternoon. Mayor Haggarty was supposed to be here, but...he was unavailable."

Everyone in the audience glanced at Giselle who was smirking.

"He means Mayor Haggarty's disgraced now," Noah whispered. "Giselle made sure of that."

"Anyway, let's get started, shall we? The funds from everything auctioned today will be going to charity. We thank you for your contributions," Mr. Henriksen said as an employee brought out a vase. "Here is an eighteenth-century vase. Do I hear one thousand as the starting bid?"

After Esme raised her paddle, the auctioneer nodded. "I hear one thousand. Do I hear two thousand?"

This time, Giselle raised her paddle. She glanced back at Esme to make sure she didn't attempt to bid again. A few other rich celebrities in the crowd raised their paddles, but Giselle made sure to outbid them every time.

"Sold!" the auctioneer cried, "to Giselle McMillan for fifteen thousand dollars."

"All that for a vase?" Noah whispered. "Doesn't seem worth it."

"I doubt she wants it—or even cares about charity," Esme whispered as the employees wrapped up the vase. "It's all about her image, remember?"

Noah scoffed. "How could I forget?"

For the next hour, the auction went on and on. Esme and Noah quickly grew bored of the repetition. Whenever the auctioneer would bring out a new item, they would raise their paddles to bid, then Giselle would swoop in and bid even more. It never seemed like it would end.

"This classic painting is sold to Giselle McMillan for thirty thousand," the auctioneer said, grinning. "Before we bid on our last item, I'd like to take an intermission. I'm sure everyone could use a snack and a chance to stretch their legs. But trust me, you don't want to miss our final item. It's the most expensive of all!"

People began murmuring in excitement as they stood up. Some went to the bathroom. Others ate more food. Esme and Noah stayed where they were, checking the time on their phones.

"Is this auction ever going to end?" Esme groaned.

"That's just what I was thinking," Noah said with a laugh. Then it faded when he glanced around. "Hey, where'd Giselle go?"

Esme looked around the auction room for her, but she didn't find her anywhere. She shrugged. "Beats me. Maybe she went outside for some fresh air?"

"Yeah, maybe. I still can't believe she had money to bid on all of those things."

"Well," Esme whispered, "if she's skimming from her organization, she could have more money than we know about."

"True," Noah said with a nod. "I hope we can bust her soon. The longer it takes to find evidence, the more money she gets to steal. That really pisses me off..."

A few minutes later, the people in the crowd returned—including Giselle. Esme frowned, realizing she had come from the backstage area and was fiddling with her purse. She took her seat as the auctioneer walked onto the stage again.

"Welcome back, everyone," he said with a grin. "Glad you're all still here. Now, for our final item..."

Esme fanned herself with the paddle as an employee climbed onto the stage. He whispered something in Mr. Henriksen's ear, making him gasp. The people in the crowd began to murmur in confusion.

"Did I zone out and miss something?" Esme asked.

Noah shook his head. "No, you didn't. I don't know what's going on."

"Folks, this has never happened before," the auctioneer said. "I'm very sorry to report that our last item—our most expensive bracelet—has gone missing."

"Missing?" someone in the crowd asked.

"How is that possible?" another person shouted.

"We aren't sure yet," the auctioneer said, "but we plan to investigate. It was there before the break, and now, my employees tell me it's just gone."

"It couldn't have vanished by itself," a person in the crowd said. "Someone must've stolen it!"

"Please, everyone—calm down," Mr. Henriksen said as people began murmuring in fear. "I'm sure it'll turn up soon. Give us a few minutes to search…"

The crowd rose to their feet, panicking about a potential thief on the loose. In the pandemonium, Esme saw Giselle sneak out the back door, clutching her purse a little tighter. Esme rose to her feet and kept her eyes glued on Giselle's back.

"I think I know where that bracelet is," Esme muttered. "Come on."

"What are you talking about?" Noah asked.

"Just hurry!"

They pushed through the crowd, making their way toward the back door. When Esme stepped outside, she saw Giselle hustling toward her limousine, fiddling with her purse again. As she opened the door to the back, Esme ran over.

"Stop!" she cried.

Giselle jumped, turning around. "Oh, Esme—you scared me. What are you doing out here?"

Esme crossed her arms. "I could ask you the same thing.

Don't you want to stay to bid on the final item when they find it?"

Giselle laughed. "No—I've already spent enough money today. As much as I love giving to charity, I can't bankrupt myself."

"Of course not," Esme said, eyeing the purse. "You had to make sure you still had money left...which is why you stole the bracelet."

Giselle gasped. "Me? You've got to be joking!"

"Then open your purse. We'll find out if you've taken it or not."

Giselle's sneered. "I'm not doing anything like that! I know my rights. I didn't steal any bracelet—and you're walking on thin ice here, Esme."

"Oh, please. I saw you coming out of the backstage area where the items were kept. Then, when the crowd started panicking, you rushed out the door. Pair that with the receipts we've found and how you told us to not interfere tonight, and I think it all adds up."

Noah nodded. "Esme has a point."

"Receipts?" Giselle asked, blinking innocently. "What receipts?"

"Don't play dumb," Esme said, shaking her head. "Hand over the purse—now. Don't make us hold you down."

CHAPTER 25

When Giselle refused to hand over the purse, Noah towered over her, trying to look intimidating. Esme thought she was going to hold her ground until she sighed. She turned her pockets inside out, then took off her shoes.

"See?" she asked. "There's no bracelet on me—anywhere."

"What about your purse?" Esme asked. "I saw you clutching it earlier—a little harder than usual. And you raced out of the auction pretty fast when the bracelet went missing."

"So? That proves nothing. I'm telling you, there's nothing in my purse—"

"Hand it over," Noah demanded. "Now."

Giselle scoffed, handing it to Esme. "Fine—whatever. See for yourself."

Noah watched as Esme opened the pockets to the purse, unzipping the compartments. She found a wallet, more receipts, makeup, and a cell phone, but no stolen bracelet. They both glanced at each other in confusion.

"This can't be possible," Esme muttered. "I know she stole that bracelet."

Giselle scoffed. "I didn't take anything. And you two are *so* fired for this. Now, can I have my purse back?"

Esme felt her heart pounding. She couldn't believe she had gotten it wrong—she was so sure.

"Fine," she said with a huff.

Esme was about to hand it over when she heard something jingle inside the purse. She shook it once more, and it jingled again. Giselle looked nervous as Esme held it up to her ear.

"You're wasting my time now," Giselle said, tapping her heel nervously. "I have places to go, so please, hand over my damn purse—"

"I think there's a secret compartment in here," Esme said, opening one of the smaller pockets. "Got it!"

Esme felt the inner lining of the purse, then ripped it open. The small bracelet fell out and onto the ground. Noah bent down, picking it up as it glistened in the sunlight. Giselle said nothing as her throat bobbed.

"That's the bracelet, all right," Noah said, holding it in his hands. "Shiny."

"Giselle tried to hide it in this secret compartment. She even ripped off the zipper so no one would think to look there," Esme said, glancing at her. "Pretty smart—but not smart enough."

Giselle sneered. "Have I ever mentioned how much I hate you both?"

"Why would you steal the bracelet, Giselle?" Noah demanded. "You already have money."

"No—I don't," Giselle huffed. "You see, I was going bankrupt keeping up with my lifestyle. The clothes, the makeup, the jewelry. It's how I was able to bid on so many things. I knew I'd be getting my money back by selling that bracelet. People would kill for it on the black market. It's unique—one of a kind. And the maker died which upped the price even more."

"How'd you find out about the bracelet?" Esme asked. "It was a surprise."

"I know the auctioneer. We got to talking and he mentioned it," Giselle said. "I knew I had to take it. No one would ever suspect me—Giselle McMillan, worldwide humanitarian—except for you. How'd you know?"

"We've been watching you, Giselle," Noah said. "That's the reason I applied to your organization a year ago. As much fun as it was helping people, I was there to stop you. We'd heard rumors from former employees that you were skimming money from donations."

Giselle gasped. "Those traitors! Are you some kind of cop?"

"A P.I., actually. My father is Detective Dan Crawford. He's the one who asked me to do this undercover mission."

"I've heard his name before. Too bad I didn't connect the dots sooner," Giselle said angrily. "I should've fired you both a long time ago. You were always getting in my way."

"We're not here to talk about us. Is it true?" Esme asked. "Were you really taking from the needy?"

"I'll admit, I've...dipped into some funds," Giselle muttered, "but it's not like I stole everything. My organization *did* help people, you know!"

"True," Noah said with a nod, "but it's clear helping yourself was a bigger priority. It's why you loved the spotlight. It was all about your image, wasn't it?"

"Don't you dare judge me," Giselle spat. "I grew up poor—I had nothing. I built my organization from nothing and helped lots of people. I thought it was only fair to help myself in the process!"

Esme shook her head. "It's more than that, Giselle. You were in a position of power—of authority—and you abused it. We've seen your receipts. You tried to live like some glamorous celebrity. You should've known better."

Giselle sneered. "Don't give me that self-righteous crap. You two aren't holier-than-thou."

"Maybe not," Noah said with a shrug, "but we've never stolen from an auction or charity donations. It's low—even for you. And you're going to answer for what you've done here."

Giselle laughed. "Oh, really? With what proof?"

"The receipts we mentioned," Esme said. "You've got a bunch more in your purse. We're going to hand them over to Detective Crawford."

"And? You can't prove I stole from the donations. And if you say the employees will testify against me in court, I could claim they're disgruntled. You forget I've built a reputation—one that commands respect. No one would believe you."

"What about the bracelet?" Esme asked, pointing at it in Noah's hands. "We caught you with it."

"I could just as easily say *I* caught *you* with it. I could say you both got a job at my organization to set me up and steal it from under me. Don't try to beat me at this game—I know what I'm doing."

Esme glanced at Noah, gulping. Was it true that they had nothing on Giselle?

Noah scowled. "I was really hoping you'd be the bigger person, Giselle. But I see that's impossible."

"*Me* be the bigger person? You've got some nerve!" Giselle cried. "You're the one who got a job at my non-profit to spy on me. That won't look very good when I rush inside to tell the security guards you stole the bracelet."

Giselle darted around them, intending to rush inside when Noah reached into his pocket. He pulled out his cell phone. "I think you'll want to hear this."

Giselle spun around, agitated. "Hear what—"

"I'll admit, I've...dipped into some funds," Giselle said from the voice note. Noah sped up to her next admittance of guilt. "You can't prove I stole from the donations."

Esme turned to Noah, grinning. "You got it recorded?"

Noah nodded. "I had a feeling Giselle might try to twist things around—she's done it before—so I came prepared. And now, I'm going to send this to Esme and my father to back it up."

After Noah hit send, Esme got a ding on her phone. She had the entire voice note—complete with Giselle's confession.

"You...you traitor!" Giselle cried. "You used to be my favorite employee, Noah. I even came to see you like a son. How could you do this?"

Noah shook his head. "Don't try to guilt-trip me, Giselle. It's over for you."

Giselle scoffed. "I'll say I was coerced into a confession. A confession doesn't hold up in court if the jury thinks it was forced!"

Noah began texting his father. "Believe whatever you want, Giselle, but you'll have to face the truth sometime. We caught you—your little operation's over. I just texted my dad and told him we busted you, so he'll be here any minute."

Giselle said nothing as she glanced between Esme and Noah. Esme thought she would give up and accept her fate, but then she sprinted toward the limousine. She lunged into the backseat, glancing at the chauffeur.

"Quick—drive me home!" she cried. "These two are trying to kill me!"

The chauffeur nodded, thrusting his key into the ignition before Noah got into the passenger seat. "What she doesn't want you to know is that she stole from the auction—and she's also been stealing from her non-profit's donations, too. The police are on the way to arrest her. Take her home and you'll be accessory to a crime."

The chauffeur looked nervous, glancing at Noah and then at Giselle. Esme leaned into the driver's side window. "Noah's right—Giselle's a criminal. It isn't worth it."

The chauffeur sighed, removing his key. "I'll let the police tell me what to do when they get here. Until then, I'm staying put."

Giselle sneered. "What on Earth do I pay you people for? There's no loyalty anymore."

"People are plenty loyal," Esme said, looking at Giselle in the backseat. "You know, when you're not a lying thief."

Giselle crossed her arms. "I regret the day I ever met you, Esme. You should've stayed wherever you came from."

Noah got out of the limo, chuckling. "Come on, Giselle—I thought all was fair in love, war, and politics?"

Giselle didn't find that very humorous.

They waited in silence for the police to arrive, and a few minutes later, they heard sirens approaching. Detective Crawford arrived in his unmarked police car first before the other cop cars pulled up to the scene. He stepped out, walking toward Noah and Esme.

"I'm impressed, son," he said, smirking. "Taping Giselle's confession was very police-like."

Noah shrugged. "What can I say? I learned from the best."

Detective Crawford sighed. "Look, I know I've been hard on you growing up, and I'm sorry for that. Being a cop, you see things...and, well, it changes you. But despite that, you turned out to be the best son a father could ask for."

Noah looked shocked. "Thanks, Dad. That means a lot."

He nodded, turning to Esme. "And you, Ms. Fairhaven—thank you. Noah texted and told me you were the one who suspected Ms. McMillan had stolen the bracelet."

"I was only following the evidence, Detective," Esme said with a shrug. "It wasn't anything special."

"Oh, I beg to differ. You could've had a career in law enforcement. You've been one hell of a friend to my son, too—and I'm grateful."

Esme smiled, glancing at Noah. He was already grinning at her.

Detective Crawford walked up to the limousine window, looking in at Giselle. "Tell me, Ms. McMillan—do you think orange is a good color on you? Where you're going next, you'll be wearing it a lot. Step out of the vehicle, please."

Giselle got out of the limousine, slamming the door behind her with a scowl. She glared at Noah and Esme as Detective Crawford tightened handcuffs around her wrists. A crowd formed nearby, pointing and murmuring. "My lawyers will get me out of this. You'll see!"

"Not this time," Detective Crawford said, nudging her toward a nearby police officer. "Take her to the station and book her."

"How many years will she get?" Esme asked, watching as the cop sped off with Giselle inside.

"Not sure yet—that'll be up to a judge. But believe me, they won't look too kindly on her stealing from the poor," Detective Crawford muttered. "She'll be charged with theft, fraud, and embezzlement—to say the least."

"That's good," Esme said with a nod. "But what about her non-profit?"

Detective Crawford smiled. "Ah—I have a little surprise. She made provisions in case she was somehow incapacitated. We found legal documents designating who would inherit Human Connection if she were unable to continue as president."

"You mean, like if she died?"

"If she was unable to run the organization."

"Why would she do that?"

"She must have known there was a risk she might be caught, and in spite of her embezzling funds, it seems she cared enough about the work of Human Connection that she wanted the work to go on."

"Who did she name to take her place?" Noah asked.

"The non-profit will be given to the board of trustees—they can decide what to do with it," Detective Crawford explained. "Turns out Giselle was doing other criminal stuff that'll add to her sentence. Harassing employees, stealing their money too. Awful woman. Anyway, I think we should get the bracelet back to the auction, huh?"

Esme and Noah nodded, following Detective Crawford back into City Hall. People were still murmuring and looking around for the bracelet. The auctioneer looked horrified, standing near the podium.

"If I may have everyone's attention?" Detective Crawford asked, walking onto the stage while flashing his badge. "We found the rare bracelet. It was stolen by Giselle McMillan, CEO of Human Connection."

People began murmuring in the audience.

"Without my son, Noah, and his friend, Esme, we wouldn't have known it was her," Detective Crawford said. "Or that Ms. McMillan has been stealing from charity donations. We owe everything to them."

"It's all Esme," Noah said, modestly. "You should be thanking her."

Esme shook her head. "Oh, no you don't. It was both of us."

Noah smiled as the crowd began cheering. Some of the journalists began snapping pictures, blinding them with light.

"Thank you for finding this," Mr. Henriksen said. "I never would've suspected Giselle McMillan. She was our most generous buyer."

"That's what she was counting on," Noah said with a nod. "Good luck with your auction."

"Yes, best of luck," Detective Crawford said. "Unfortunately, I'll have to hold onto the bracelet. It's part of a criminal investigation so it won't be auctioned off today. I'll get it back to you as soon as I can, though, Mr. Henriksen."

Mr. Henriksen nodded, shaking Detective Crawford's hand. The crowd began murmuring again.

"Perfect," Noah said. "Come on, Esme. Let's get going."

Detective Crawford followed them out. "Be careful out there, you two. We've had more strange murders—like a woman completely cased in ice. When we thawed her out, her body fell apart."

"Jesus," Noah muttered. "That sounds terrible. And you have no suspects? No evidence?"

"None at all. Trust me—it's bugging the hell out of me," Detective Crawford muttered. "Everyone at the precinct is stumped and scared, fearing some ruthless serial killer's on the loose. Let me know if you see anything weird, all right?"

Noah nodded. "We will."

Esme felt a knot tightening in her stomach. She wished more than anything that she could stop Senator Remus—and find out what he was planning with all those strange murders.

"I'm going to head to the station and get started on Giselle's processing in the meantime," Detective Crawford said. "And Esme, I hope we can eat dinner at the cottage again soon. We had a great time."

They quickly gave their statements to Detective Crawford. He promised he'd be in touch if he had more questions. After he walked away, Esme smiled, beginning to feel like part of the family.

"Well, I think we should celebrate," Noah said, walking to his car. "Maybe a fancy dinner?"

Esme smiled, getting into the passenger seat. "I'd love that. Let's invite Gina, Tanya, and the kids, too."

When they pulled up to her apartment, they took the elevator to her floor, unlocking the door to Gina's place. When they entered, Dylan and the kids ran up to them.

"Is it true?" Dylan asked.

"Did you stop that mean lady from stealing from the poor?" Vincent asked.

Esme laughed. "Yes—yes, it's all true."

"Wow," Lindsey said, looking at her with wide eyes. "That's so cool."

"Thank you," Esme said, checking the time on her phone. "It's almost dinner—your mom will be home soon. Why don't we go out to eat?"

Gina smiled. "That sounds lovely."

As the kids cheered, Esme looked around, realizing she had finally found a place to belong. Even if she left for Fairhaven, following the original plan, everything she had done here had been a triumph.

CHAPTER 26

For the rest of the evening, Esme and Noah stayed at Gina's apartment, hanging out with her and the kids. They watched movies, finished puzzles together, and talked about all sorts of things. Esme enjoyed telling them things about her kingdom—things she was allowed to talk about.

"Wait," Lindsey said, wide-eyed. "You're a real-life princess? You live in a castle and everything?"

Esme nodded, smiling. "That's right. It's why I own those pink gowns."

"What about a tiara?"

"Esme had one. I saw it myself," Noah said. "She had to sell it to afford her apartment, but I'm sure she'll be able to get it back one day."

"When you do, can I see it?" Lindsey asked.

Esme laughed. "Of course."

"Do you have butlers?" Vincent asked. "And maids?"

"What about servants?" Dylan asked.

"All of the above, actually. They look after my castle and me and my father."

"That's so cool," Vincent said, and Dylan and Lindsey nodded. "Why would you want to leave that place and come here?"

"I know why," Dylan said. "Her dad banished her."

Lindsey gasped. "Oh, no!"

"Really?" Vincent asked, turning to Esme. "What did you do?"

"Some things I shouldn't have," Esme said with a sigh. "But as much as I miss my kingdom, I've enjoyed getting to know you. All of you."

Gina smiled. "We feel the same way, Esme. Whether you're a real-life princess or not—"

"She is!" Lindsey cried. "She wouldn't lie to us!"

Gina just laughed. "What I was trying to say is that it doesn't matter if you're a princess or a common citizen like us. You're one of us now—part of the family."

That was all Esme wanted—to feel like she belonged somewhere after her mother had died. She couldn't believe she had found it in a city so large and unfamiliar.

"I want to be a princess, too!" Lindsey cried. "Can you make me one, Esme? Pretty please?"

Esme laughed, rising to her feet. She used the television remote like a magic wand and swept it over the kids. "I hereby make you all princesses and princes—in this world *and* in Fairhaven."

The kids cheered, and it didn't take long for Lindsey to draw paper crowns of pink, red, and black. Esme helped her cut them out with scissors, then placed them all on their heads. Gina, Noah, and Esme laughed as they watched the kids strut around in them.

"Poor Tanya. She won't be able to get them to bed tonight—they'll be too hyper," Gina said, chuckling. "Thank you, Esme. You've done a lot for us."

"Agreed," Noah said quietly.

"And we don't want you to go back home. Please stay," Vincent said. "Pretty please?"

"With a cherry on top?" Lindsy asked. "So you can teach me how to be a princess?"

"And finish more puzzles with me," Vincent added.

"I just like having her around," Dylan said, shrugging.

Noah turned to Esme. "The kids are pretty clear. I don't want to pressure you, and I know things are messed up for you back home, but…I agree with them. What do you say?"

Before Esme could respond, a knock sounded on the door. A face poked inside the apartment. "Hello? Is anyone home?"

"Mommy!" Dylan, Vincent, and Lindsey cried out.

When Tanya appeared in her uniform, the kids went running toward her. She opened her arms and held them close. "Hello, kids. Did you have a good day today?"

"We did—Esme and Noah played with us," Lindsey said. "She told us she used to be a princess!"

Tanya laughed. "Is that right? How nice. How did your therapy go, Dylan?"

He shrugged. "It went fine. I'm going to go by myself next time. It wasn't so scary—plus, I like Dr. Wells."

"I'm so glad," Tanya said, turning to Esme. "Thank you for taking him and helping him through this."

"It was our pleasure," Esme said, and Noah nodded. "We took him to the cemetery, too, since Dr. Wells suggested it."

"You did?" Tanya looked a bit upset. "Without my permission?"

"It's okay, Mom. I got to talk to Dad," Dylan piped up. "Maybe we can all go together next time? There's an ice cream shop that Esme and Noah took me to."

Tanya nodded. "Yes, maybe we should. I'll admit—I've

stayed away from that cemetery because it was too hard. But maybe it's exactly what we need to do."

"Whatever it is, you have our support," Gina said. "Always."

"Thank you. Now, we need to talk about what I heard at work," Tanya said, grinning at Esme. "Something about you stopping a thieving CEO? You don't hear a rumor like that every day."

A knocking in the hallway caught their attention. When Esme looked out, she saw Antonio, her landlord. He was knocking on Tanya's door.

"Come on, Tanya!" he yelled. "Open up. We need to talk."

Tanya walked out into the hallway, frowning. "Is there a problem?"

"You bet there is," he said, turning around. He smiled when he noticed Esme. "Oh, Esme—I heard the news. Congratulations."

Esme nodded. "Thank you."

He turned to Tanya. "Now, Tanya—I need last month's rent."

Tanya sighed. "I told you, you'll have it soon—"

"That's what you've been telling me for the past month!" he cried. "I'd really hate to kick you out, Tanya, but you're leaving me no choice."

"No—you can't!" Tanya cried, on the verge of tears. "Please, Antonio—think of my children."

He sighed. "I'm sorry, but unless you can pay what you owe right now, I'll have to ask you to pack your bags."

"Have a little compassion," Noah said, leaning out the door. "She's a single mother who works at Fresh N Hot for crying out loud. She's doing her best!"

"I'm not heartless. I understand that money is tight," Antonio said, shrugging. "But I have a property to run. And if

I'm not getting rent, it puts a strain on me, and I have my own butt to worry about. Now, do you have the money or not?"

"I don't," Tanya said, shaking her head. "But...maybe I could sell something. Like my husband's old Blue Jays jersey..."

"You can't do that," Esme said. "You should keep everything you have of your husband's."

Antonio shrugged. "I don't care what you sell. I'm giving you until midnight tonight, and if you're still short, then I'm giving you three days to get your stuff out so I can show the apartment to new renters."

"What's going on?" Dylan asked, walking into the hallway. "Do we have to move out, Mom?"

Tanya didn't say anything—she only put her head into her hands and cried. Esme knew she couldn't let them get evicted.

"Wait here," Esme said to Antonio. "I'll be right back."

As the others gave her looks of confusion, Esme walked into her apartment, dragging her safe out from under the bed. She took out a big wad of money and locked the apartment door behind her. She walked up to Antonio, handing it over.

"I'd like to pay on her behalf. Here—last month's rent and then some," she said. "Tanya will be covered for a few months now. Call me if she's late again and I'll continue to help."

Antonio's eyes widened at the stack of cash. "How generous of you. But if Tanya is late for her rent again—"

"She won't be," Esme said. "I swear it."

Antonio nodded. "All right—I hope so. Now, if you'll excuse me, I need to go put that money into the bank."

After he walked off, Tanya turned to Esme, drying her tears. "You...you saved us."

Esme shrugged. "It was nothing, really. I had money to spare—"

Esme was unprepared as Tanya flung herself into her arms,

hugging her tight. "Thank you, Esme. You don't know how much you've helped me."

"You're welcome," Esme said, patting her back. "Come on—let's head to a nice restaurant."

After they had put on fancy things to wear, Esme and Noah left in his car while Tanya drove Gina and her kids. They chose a classy restaurant—The Grill House, an upscale steakhouse—and walked up to the host.

"We need a table for seven," Esme said, looking around the crowded restaurant. It was loud with most of the tables gone. "Do you have any room?"

"I'm sorry, but the wait will be an hour," the host said, making them groan. When he looked up, he frowned. "Do I know you from somewhere?"

Esme shook her head. "No—I don't think we've ever met."

"Wait a minute," he said, pulling out his phone. He went to the Toronto news website. The headline read HUMAN CONNECTION CEO GISELLE MCMILLAN ARRESTED FOR FRAUD AFTER BEING CAUGHT BY EMPLOYEES. "This is you, isn't it? You stopped her?"

Esme glanced at the photo on his phone that the journalists had taken of her. "Yeah, that's me—"

"Oh, it's such an honor," he said, shaking her hand. "Human Connection helped my sister find a place to live. Granted, that was when the old boss was stealing money, but still. I'm so glad you stopped her."

Esme nodded. "Me, too. This way, we can help more people without her greedy fingers dipping into the funds."

He grinned wider. "That's what I like to hear. Come on—I think we can find a table for your party."

"Wow," Noah whispered as they followed the host to the back of the restaurant. "I guess you're a celebrity now."

Esme laughed. "Hardly. But if it gets us a table, then I'll gladly pretend."

"And here we are," the host said, gesturing at two tables in the back. The waiters had pushed them together so everyone would have a seat. "Here are your menus. The waiter will be by soon to take your order, and I hope you enjoy dining with us."

As Esme and the others took a seat, a waiter brought over a pitcher of water with glasses for everyone. Esme poured a cup for her table, then raised her glass into the air. Noah, Gina, and Tanya did the same.

"I'd like to make a toast," Esme began, "to you all. When I first got to Toronto, I didn't know how I was going to survive. I had nothing—no place to live, no friends, no money. And now I have everything—thanks to you all."

"We're glad we have you, too," Tanya said, and everyone nodded.

Esme smiled. "I didn't know any of you a month ago, and now I can't imagine living without you. So, here's to you—to finding where you belong."

"Hear! Hear!" Noah cried, clinking his glass with Esme's.

After skimming the menu for five minutes, everyone had decided what they wanted except for Tanya. The waiter took everyone else's order and hung around for hers.

"Just get the steak dinner," Noah persuaded. "It looks delicious."

"Oh, I don't know," Tanya said, sighing. "It's expensive."

"No need to worry about that," Esme said, placing her hand over hers. "It's my treat. Take whatever money you have and spend it on your kids."

"Then I'll take the steak dinner," Tanya said, handing the menu to the waiter. "And thank you, Esme. I swear—I'll make it all up to you."

Esme shook her head. "You already have—with your friendship. I don't need anything else."

Tanya smiled.

When the food arrived, everyone dug in. The kids ordered off the children's menu—getting the small cheeseburgers—while everyone else opted for the large steak dinner. The waiters brought crayons and paper so the kids could color.

"Look what I drew!" Lindsey cried, holding the paper up.

When Esme saw the drawing, she smiled. It was all of them, holding hands with big smiles on their faces. It had everyone she loved in the picture.

"I want you to have it, Esme," Lindsey said. "In case you ever go back home and be a princess again and forget about me."

"Impossible," Esme said, grinning. "But I'll take it. Thank you, Lindsey."

After dinner, they ate dessert—chocolate cake, Esme's new favorite—before the waiter brought their check, and she slipped him a few bills to cover their meal. They stood out in the parking lot a few minutes later, each taking home leftovers from the big meal.

"Oh—I'm stuffed," Gina said, patting her stomach. "Thanks for the grub, Esme."

"My pleasure. And I'll be there tomorrow morning to take you to physiotherapy."

Gina grinned. "Thanks. Let's hope I haven't gained ten pounds when they weigh me tomorrow."

After they said goodbye, Esme got into Noah's car. He turned on the radio and searched for a station before it landed on the news. They caught the tail end of what the announcer was saying.

"...which leaves a man calling himself Remus as the last running candidate for mayor," the announcer said. "If no one opposes him, he'll have a sure victory. Giselle's arrest and Mayor Haggarty's scandal worked out in his favor, and he's been building his popularity by making appearances around town..."

"Great," Esme muttered, turning off the radio. "We took out all his competitors."

"Hey, maybe someone else will challenge him," Noah said. "And the murders must fit in somehow, too," Noah added. "I really hope we can stop him."

"Me, too," Esme muttered.

AFTER NOAH DROPPED Esme off at her apartment, she went to bed, thinking about what Remus was going to do. Was it his plan all along to become mayor? Would he have taken out Giselle and Mayor Haggarty if they hadn't dropped out already?

Esme shuddered, hoping she hadn't helped his plan.

The next morning, after she had dressed, eaten, and brushed her teeth, she got a text from Noah. *I'm waiting downstairs*, it read. *You and Gina can meet me as soon as you're ready.*

Esme walked across the hallway and knocked on Gina's door. When she opened it, Gina was already dressed, waiting on the couch.

"Hey, Gina. Ready for your physiotherapy?"

"Oh, you bet," she said, rising to her feet. She held up her shaking hands. "I know my bones could use it."

After they walked downstairs, they said hello to Noah and got into his car. He drove them to the doctor's office where it led into a giant room for physiotherapy patients. Once they had checked in, Gina went into the change rooms to put on her workout outfit while Noah and Esme waited for her.

"I had a good time last night," Noah whispered. "It's

starting to feel like Gina, Tanya, and the kids are part of my family now, too."

Esme nodded. "I know what you mean."

Noah reached for her hand. "And you, Esme...you're at the heart of it all. We wouldn't be so close without you. And whether it's as friends or something more...I just like having you in my life."

Esme smiled. "Me, too, Noah. More than you know."

When Gina came out of the change rooms, she had put on shorts and a t-shirt. Esme smiled to reassure her as she walked toward her trainer. For the next hour, they had her do all kinds of things—tai chi, posture exercises, yoga. Whenever Gina felt like quitting, Esme would stand up.

"You can do it, Gina!" Esme called out. "Don't give up now!"

And despite her trembling hands, it gave her the strength to keep going. Once the physiotherapy had finished, Gina was drenched in sweat, downing a water bottle. "They want me to come two or three times a week. They say it'll help."

"And did it?" Noah asked.

Gina looked down at her hands which had stopped trembling as bad. "I think so. Time will tell."

Esme smiled. "Well, I'll be here the next time and the next time after that. Whatever you need, Gina."

Noah checked his watch. "We'd better get you home. The baseball game is starting soon, and we have tickets to Wonderland, too."

Gina winked. "How exciting. Have fun, you two."

Esme rolled her eyes, though she was blushing. And when she left with Noah and Gina, she gave herself permission to have fun, knowing she needed it after the past week.

CHAPTER 27

After they dropped Gina off at home, Esme went into her apartment to change into something more casual for the game—a pair of shorts, sandals, and a t-shirt. While she tugged them on, she could hear Tanya and her kids through the wall.

But this time, they were laughing instead of shouting. It brought a smile to her face.

After she grabbed her sunglasses, tickets, and locked the door, she began walking down the hallway with Noah. He wouldn't stop gushing about baseball—or let Esme get a word in.

"...and Grayson West, he's my favorite player," Noah said, pressing the button to the elevator. "He scored three home runs last game!"

"Is that...good?" Esme asked, confused.

Noah laughed as they stepped into the elevator. "Yes, it's very good. I'd better teach you the rules of the game before we get there..."

Noah went over the basics as they walked to the car, answering any questions Esme had. She didn't completely understand baseball—or why it was so popular among the humans—but she let Noah explain it, admiring the passion in his eyes. He was still talking as they got into the car and drove off.

"...and a home run means everyone who is on base, including the batter, gets to score. So, whoever gets the most runs, wins. And the team that wins in the World Series gets the Commissioner's Trophy."

Esme nodded. "I see. Very interesting."

Noah laughed. "Sorry—I can get a little carried away when it comes to baseball. Did I bore you to death?"

"Of course not. Nothing about you bores me, Noah. We had sports back home, too—though...they were much different from yours."

"Oh? How so?"

It had magic for starters, Esme thought.

"It was just different—trust me," Esme said. "And we didn't play them very often. I didn't, at least. My father said it wasn't proper behavior for a princess."

Noah shook his head. "That's too bad. Although we aren't playing baseball, I hope you'll enjoy watching a game. Maybe it's just what you need."

Esme smiled. "I'm looking forward to it."

At a red light, Noah looked down at his shirt and groaned. "Oh, no—I forgot my jersey at home! It says Grayson West's name on it and everything."

Esme checked her watch. "There's still time before the game starts. You can drive to your apartment and grab it."

When the light turned green, Noah put his foot down hard on the gas. "Sounds good. I was in a rush this morning to get to you and Gina, so I completely forgot. How else will Grayson West know how much I respect him if I don't wear his jersey?"

Esme laughed. "I'm sure he won't even be able to see you in the stands. Isn't he supposed to be looking at the game?"

"Yeah, but you never know. They have this big screen—called a Jumbotron—at the stadium that shows off the crowd. I have to look my best for him."

Esme just shook her head, amused at Noah's hero worship. He took a left at the next intersection and drove to his apartment building. When he parked, he unbuckled his seatbelt and turned to her.

"Want to come upstairs? It beats waiting in the car—it can get pretty hot."

Esme shrugged, opening her door. "Why not? Your apartment's cozy. I don't mind waiting in there."

"I was thinking of moving, actually," Noah said, using his card to unlock the lobby door. "I only moved into that apartment when I thought I was going to marry Jill. Boy, did that backfire."

Esme followed Noah to his elevator. "You shouldn't move out just because of her. You like your apartment, don't you?"

"I guess so," he said, pressing the elevator button. "But it's too big for one person. And it has too many memories. I was... actually thinking of moving closer to you."

"Really?" Esme asked as she and Noah stepped into the elevator.

"Well, why not? We spend a lot of time together. And you *are* my boss now, so I'd be able to get to you faster if you needed me."

As the elevator ascended, Esme smiled. "I'd like that."

When the elevator dinged, Esme stepped out. Noah began following her before he sighed. "You know, when Jill left me...I thought I had nothing left. I fell into this giant black hole."

"I'm sorry. That must've been hard."

He nodded. "Yeah, but then you came along. And I

thought to myself, maybe I don't have to be miserable anymore. Maybe there are still good things left in the world."

Esme smiled. "There are *always* good things left, Noah. And I feel the same way about you. When I first got to Toronto, I thought I'd be alone and afraid."

"But?"

"*But* then I met you and the others. So, I guess we both got the second chance we were looking for."

Noah grinned. "Aren't we lucky?"

"Very," Esme said with a smile. "Now, come on—we don't want to be late to see your precious Grayson West."

Noah just laughed, following the winding corridors to his apartment. Esme trailed behind him and felt excited that he could be moving closer to her. But when he stopped dead in his tracks, she nearly bumped into him, wondering why he had blocked her path.

"Noah, are you okay?" she asked.

Noah didn't say anything. Esme finally darted around him, looking at his face. His eyes were wide in shock. When Esme turned around, she noticed Jill standing in front of his apartment. She was pacing back and forth before she knocked on the door.

"Noah?" she called out. "Are you in there? I need to speak with you."

"Jill?" Noah asked in disbelief.

Jill turned around. "Oh, Noah—there you are. And hello, Esme."

Esme faked a smile. "Nice to see you, Jill."

It was a lie, but Jill didn't need to know that. In reality, Esme was worried about why Jill had come to his apartment—and what it meant for her and Noah.

"You, too, Esme. And congrats on catching Giselle McMillan, by the way. I met her at a gala once. You know, I always had a bad feeling about that woman."

I could say the same about you, Esme thought.

"Yeah, me, too. I'm looking forward to getting the non-profit back on track," Esme said, and Jill nodded. "Anyway, are you ready for your wedding tomorrow?"

Jill hesitated, glancing back at Noah. "Actually...that was what I needed to talk to Noah about. In private."

"Is the wedding called off?" Noah asked.

Jill shook her head. "No, it's still on. Well, it depends. This is urgent, Noah. Can we go inside and talk?"

"Of course," Noah said, turning to Esme. "Wait for me out here, okay? We won't be long."

Esme nodded, though the bad feeling she had began to make her stomach twist. Jill took one last look at Esme as Noah unlocked the door. Once they had both walked into the apartment, he closed it, shutting her out. Esme could only hear muffled voices when she pressed her ear against the door.

"Not good enough," Esme muttered. "I need to hear what they're saying—and I have an idea."

Esme rushed to the elevator, taking it down to the lobby. She ran around the side of the building—hoping their conversation wasn't over yet—and looked up. She noticed a fire escape that connected the apartments.

"Jackpot," she muttered with a grin. "Time to find out what's going on."

She climbed up the fire escape, passing many windows on her way to the fourth floor. She tried not to look down and lose her appetite. When she found Noah's apartment, she hid beneath the window, grateful he had left it open a crack.

She heard Noah's voice immediately. "...are you kidding me, Jill? A day before the wedding?"

"I know, I know!" Jill cried, and Esme heard her rise to her feet. "But what else was I supposed to do? I have to know your answer before I marry him."

What answer? Esme worked up the courage to look inside the window, seeing them both standing up in the living room. The situation looked tense as Noah ran a hand through his hair.

"My answer? Here's my answer, Jill," Noah said, turning to her. "When you left me for Jerry, you broke my heart. Do you have any idea what it's like to feel second place?"

Jill nodded, tears welling in her eyes. "I know I hurt you, and I'm sorry. It's just...when I ran into Jerry, all those old emotions came back. It was the same when I saw you. I still love you, Noah. I always have."

"Well, you have terrible timing," Noah muttered.

"I know. And now, you've moved on with Esme..."

Noah sighed. "Actually, we're not dating. That was a lie. I just didn't want to seem like a miserable loser when I showed up at your wedding."

"I see. Then it makes it easier on you," Jill said, stepping closer to him. "If you still love me, Noah...I'll call off the wedding and come back to you."

"But what about Jerry?"

"He'll be hurt, but I know he'll accept it. The heart wants what it wants, as they say."

Noah scoffed. "Why now? Why couldn't you have realized you loved me more before you left me, instead of getting engaged and planning a wedding?"

"Because I was confused. I thought Jerry was the one I wanted, but the closer the wedding gets...the more I don't know. And if there's even a small chance we could get together again, I have to know before I say my vows. What do you say, Noah?"

Esme was hoping he would say no—that he had moved on.

But he turned silent for a moment. Esme's heart pounded, wondering what his answer would be.

"I...don't know," Noah muttered. "I need time to think—about us, about all of it. You sure know how to drop a bomb on someone."

Jill nodded. "All right—I'll give you some space. Let me know your answer by midnight tonight. If it's a yes, I'll tell Jerry the wedding's off."

"What if it's a no?"

Jill hesitated, looking sad. "Then I'll accept that and marry Jerry. I'll let you move on and never bother you again."

Yes, please, Esme thought.

"Does Jerry even know you're here? That you're having second thoughts before the wedding?"

Jill shook her head. "No—and I'd appreciate it if you wouldn't tell him."

Noah turned to her, a little more upset. "It's natural for people who are getting married to have cold feet before the big day. How do you know if you really love me or if you're just having anxiety?"

Esme hid her gasp as Jill leaned forward, kissing Noah. He hesitated before he kissed her back. Esme wanted to intervene—to stop it from happening—but she couldn't. She hid beneath the window, realizing how much it hurt to see Noah with someone else.

They continued kissing for a few seconds before Jill stepped away. "That's how I know—those butterflies, Noah. They've always been there when I'm around you."

"And when you're with Jerry? Are they there, too?"

Jill sighed, nodding. "Yeah, but with him...it's different. It feels *too* comfortable. With you, it feels new—exciting. God, why does love have to be so confusing?"

"If I knew, I'd be the richest man alive," Noah muttered. "At midnight, you'll have my answer. I promise."

Jill nodded, picking up her purse. "I'll be waiting for your text. And whatever happens, Noah...I'll always love you. You're the kind of man a woman doesn't get over."

As she left the apartment, shutting the door behind her, Noah sat down on the couch, sighing. Esme knew he was in pain when he put his head in his hands. Not wanting to get caught, she climbed down the fire escape, walking toward the building as Jill left in her car. She watched her drive away before she slipped in through the building as other people were coming out.

She rode the elevator back up to Noah's apartment, then rushed to his door and knocked. "Noah? Are you in there?"

"Yeah," he called out, sadly. "You can come in now, Esme."

Esme opened the door, shutting it behind her. Noah was still sitting on the couch and looked conflicted.

"What's wrong?" Esme asked, pretending not to know anything.

"Jill...wants to get back with me. I have until midnight to decide. If I say yes, she'll call off the wedding tomorrow."

"What did you tell her?"

Noah finally looked up at Esme. "That I don't know. God, she really knows how to mess with my head."

"Maybe that's all she's trying to do," Esme said, sitting next to Noah. "First, she breaks up with you to be with Jerry. Now, she comes crawling back right before her wedding. It seems like she wants to have her cake and eat it, too. Don't you think so?"

Noah sneered. "Yeah, you're probably right. She really knows how to play me."

"I thought you were over her. You threw out her pictures—"

"I know!" Noah cried, rising to his feet. "I think...a part of me is holding onto her because I don't want to be lonely.

Because I know you're going to leave. Most likely, anyway. You were right—your kingdom really needs you. Sounds pathetic, doesn't it?"

Esme shook her head. "It's not pathetic."

He turned to her. "Tell me what to do, Esme. I need advice."

As much as Esme wanted to tell him to say no, she knew she couldn't decide for him. "I'm sorry, Noah—but this is something you need to do alone."

"Yeah, I figured that," he mumbled. "I'll get my jersey. Maybe a day of fun will do me some good—even help me think."

As Noah went into his bedroom to find his jersey, Esme waited in the living room, wondering what he would choose. Did he still love Jill? Would he fall for her manipulation?

When Noah walked out of his room, he had on a blue jersey with the name GRAYSON WEST and the number 46 on the back. "So, what do you think?"

"You look handsome," Esme said with a smile. "It suits you."

Noah blushed. "Thanks. Come on—let's get to the game before we're late."

Esme left the apartment building with Noah, getting into his car. The ride was silent as he drove to the Rogers Center. She had no doubt he was considering Jill's words—and what he would say at midnight. Esme hoped and prayed he would do the right thing.

When they arrived at the Rogers Center, Noah paid for parking. Esme stepped out and noticed the thousands of people who had arrived—all wearing blue jerseys. She followed Noah into the stadium, feeling a little underdressed as he handed their tickets to the usher.

"Nice seats," the usher said. "You're in the front row, right near the net. Enjoy."

Noah grinned as he walked into the open stadium with Esme. "Not bad. That radio station didn't skimp on the tickets, huh?"

Esme nodded. "I have you to thank for all this, actually. You told me the CN Tower was the largest building in Toronto—and that happened to be their trivia question."

"Glad some of my knowledge rubbed off on you," he joked, looking for their seats. "Ah, here we are—the perfect view. And the roof opens, too. A beautiful day for a game."

"Cool," Esme said, looking up into the sky. "We didn't have anything like that back home."

"There's a whole world out here, just waiting to be explored," Noah said, grinning. "I'll get us some food before the game starts. You ever had a hot dog before?"

Esme frowned. "A...hot dog?"

"I'll take that as a no," Noah said with a laugh. "Be right back."

As Noah left to buy them food from the concession stand, Esme noticed some of the players practicing and setting up. More spectators poured in behind Esme, and she noticed how large the stadium was. When she turned her attention back to the field, she saw a handsome, curly-haired player—and the name GRAYSON WEST stuck out on his jersey.

Esme had an idea flash across her mind, so she waved her arms in the air. "Mr. West? Can I speak to you?"

She wasn't sure he would want to talk to her, but when he looked over, a smirk spread across his face. He walked over while tossing his baseball around. "Well, hello, pretty lady. What can I do for you?"

Esme glanced at the ball. "My friend, Noah, is a huge fan of yours. He has your jersey and everything. He's been upset lately, and it would mean a lot to have an autograph. Maybe a signed baseball?"

Grayson grinned, signing the ball. "Anything for a beautiful woman. Here you go."

When he handed it over, Esme noticed he had signed his name and written his phone number down. She looked back up, gawking as he winked at her before heading back out to the field to practice. A minute later, Noah returned with two hot dogs, napkins, and two sodas.

"Got our food," he said, setting them down. "Hey, what's that?"

Esme handed the ball to Noah. "A present. I asked Grayson West to sign the ball for you."

His eyes lit up as he took it. "You're kidding! Thank you, Esme. But...why does it have his phone number on it?"

Esme laughed. "I think he was flirting with me. Can you believe that?"

Noah scoffed. "I forgot to tell you, but Grayson West's a big player. He's dated a bunch of movie stars. You...you aren't going to call him, are you?"

Esme shook her head. "Cocky baseball players aren't really my type."

Noah blushed, handing her a hot dog. "That's a relief. You deserve someone better, anyway."

As Esme bit into the hot dog, her eyes widened. "Wow—this is delicious!"

Noah laughed. "I knew you'd like it. It's classic baseball game food. I couldn't take you here and not have you try it."

As they finished their meal, chatting about baseball, the game started. After the first few innings, Esme found herself getting more into the game—even cheering for the Blue Jays like Noah.

"Come on, umpire—that ball was foul!" Noah cried, falling back down into his seat. "No fair."

Esme laughed. "You're really passionate about baseball, aren't you?"

"I guess a little," Noah said with a smile. "Especially when it comes to bad calls—"

Noah hushed when cheering erupted around them. Esme frowned, wondering what the people behind her were celebrating when she looked up, noticing the Jumbotron. It said KISS CAM—and it had Noah and Esme's faces on the screen in a giant heart.

"What's happening?" Esme whispered.

"I should've warned you—sometimes, this happens at games," Noah whispered back. "We're supposed to kiss. It's a tradition."

"Well, who am I to fight tradition?" Esme asked, leaning in.

The people cheered when she kissed him lightly on the lips. Noah blushed, pulling back as the Kiss Cam focused on two other people in the audience.

"Sorry about that," Noah said. "I should've warned you."

"It's all right," Esme said, shrugging. "Not like we haven't kissed before."

"Right," Noah said, reaching for his soda. "Anyway, did you see that swing from Kessel? He's always been a strong batter..."

As Noah talked about baseball to hide his nerves, Esme smiled, hoping he'd remember that kiss when it came time to make a decision about Jill.

CHAPTER 28

A few hours later when the Blue Jays had won the game, Esme had never seen Noah so happy.

He cheered loudly with the crowd as the players embraced each other on the field. Esme still didn't understand the hype around baseball, but she liked seeing Noah smiling again, especially after his conversation with Jill.

"Okay, that was the best game I've ever seen," Noah said, picking up his hot dog wrapper. "Grayson West was amazing—as usual. I think they'll go on to win the World Series. So, what'd you think about baseball?"

Esme smiled. "I know that if there's another game, I'd like to go with you to see it."

"Yeah—me, too," Noah said, returning the smile. "Come on —let's get out of here. There's a lot of people, so stay close to me. Don't want to get separated."

Esme looked down in surprise when Noah grabbed her hand, leading her out of the stadium. The sea of people was almost overwhelming—she hadn't seen that many back home.

After Noah pulled out of the parking lot, he got into traffic and headed toward Canada's Wonderland. Esme could see the giant rollercoaster stretching toward the sky as Noah paid for parking and found a spot.

"Well, it's no Disney World, but I've been to Canada's Wonderland a few times," Noah said, stepping out of the car. "It's pretty fun. You ready to head in?"

Esme smiled. "Of course—you promised me the full Toronto experience when I first got here, remember?"

Noah laughed, leading Esme toward the long ticket booth. "How could I forget? Don't worry—I'll make sure you have the time of your life."

"I hope so. We don't have any of these kinds of places back home, so I'll have to enjoy it while I'm here."

Noah glanced at her. "Really? No amusement parks?"

Esme shook her head. "No—but after this, I think I might run it by my father..."

There were hundreds of people crowding the entrance as Noah and Esme pushed through. Noah showed his two tickets to the woman in the booth who stamped their hands and let them pass. As they entered, Esme noticed sidewalks made out of white brick leading to many different rides and exhibits.

"So, where do you want to start first?" Noah asked, glancing around. "There's a lot to see."

Esme shrugged. "You've been here before. I'll let you choose."

Noah grinned, grabbing Esme's hand. "Come on—I have a ride in mind."

Noah wove through the crowd, pulling Esme toward a tall rollercoaster. The giant sign read LEVIATHAN and the track went through the entire park. Esme looked up at it, gulping.

"It's...very high."

Noah turned to her. "Are you afraid of heights? We don't have to go if you don't want to—"

Esme shook her head. "No—I can do it. I said I wanted the full experience, didn't I?"

Noah laughed. "I'll be next to you the whole time, so if you need to squeeze my hand, I'm here."

Esme nodded, taking a deep breath as the line moved forward. The man operating the ride gestured at them to get inside. After Esme and Noah sat down, he helped place the safety latch over Esme and himself. The other people did the same thing as the operator walked over to the switch.

"Please keep all your limbs inside the ride and wait until it's stopped before getting out," the man said. "And most of all, make sure to have fun. Is everyone ready?"

When people nodded, Esme reached for Noah's hand. Just having him close made her feel much better. The operator pulled the switch, and the rollercoaster began moving slowly on the track.

Esme shrugged. "This isn't so bad. Why'd I think it was going to be scary?"

Noah laughed. "Esme, it's barely even started. Trust me, when it kicks in—"

Before Noah could finish his sentence, the rollercoaster barreled forward, plunging down the track. Esme screamed the entire way, but when she looked at Noah, she could only laugh at how much fun she was having. The ride went around in circles—up and down and side to side—and Esme had the perfect view of the city.

"You okay?" Noah yelled through the wind and screaming of the riders.

"Never been better!" Esme called out, her hair blowing wildly in the breeze.

Noah smiled as the rollercoaster went around a few more times before returning to the ground. The operator pulled the switch, turning the ride off after it came to a complete stop. The people removed their safety latches and stepped out. Esme was a little wobbly as she stepped back onto the ground, but Noah helped her.

"That was fun," Esme said, clutching her stomach, "even if I did feel like I had to vomit a few times."

Noah laughed. "Yeah, all that spinning will do that to you. Follow me—there are a few more things I want to show you."

For the next hour, Esme and Noah explored the park. They went through the Medieval Fair, went on a few more rides, and took a dip in the splash park. When Noah checked his watch, he gestured toward the food court in the distance.

"Come on—we can grab dinner before heading home."

But Esme hadn't heard him. She was busy looking around, feeling as though someone was watching them.

"Esme?" Noah asked, nudging her. "You okay?"

She finally looked back at him. "Yes—sorry. I just got this eerie feeling like someone had their eyes on us..."

Noah laughed. "Well, we *are* at an amusement park. Thousands of people are here. Do you want to get some food?"

Esme nodded, pushing her feelings aside. "You're right. I'm starved—come on."

After Noah took her to the food court, they pushed through the crowd to find an empty table. Esme kept it for them as Noah went up to the booth to order two burgers, fries, and sodas. When he returned with it on a tray, Esme looked up and noticed the one person she didn't want to see...

Cullen—and he had a camera, snapping pictures of them.

When he realized she had noticed him, he slipped into the crowd, vanishing in the distance.

Noah frowned. "What are you looking at?"

Esme pointed toward the coward. "Cullen. He was here—taking pictures of us."

"That guy again? I thought he was gone—along with that assassin."

Esme nodded. "Me too. I wonder why he was taking pictures. Stay here—I'll try to find him and get some answers."

"No, I'm coming with you. Just in case."

After Esme nodded, the two of them chased Cullen through the crowd. But they lost him when he blended in with a big family. Sighing, they headed back.

"Gone," she said. "Damn it."

Noah shrugged as he sat down. "Honestly, I'm kinda glad he got away. I'm not about to let him ruin our day. And don't worry—it would be stupid to try anything in a crowd this big."

Esme sighed. "You're right. I need to stop being so paranoid..."

"Hey, I think you're entitled to be a little paranoid. An assassin *did* try to kill you."

"Point taken," Esme said, biting into her burger. "But I don't want to talk about that. What was your favorite ride?"

"I liked the rollercoaster. You looked so happy on the ride that it made me happy, too."

Esme blushed. "Yeah—that one was fun. We'll have to come back again one day."

After they chatted over dinner, they pushed through the crowd to reach the exit. Esme didn't see Cullen anywhere when she looked around—and she was glad for that. Once they had made it back to Noah's car, he drove her back to her apartment, the sun beginning to set.

"Well, I had a great day," Noah began, "despite...how it started."

Esme nodded. "Do you know what you'll do at midnight?"

Noah sighed. "Not yet—but I know the answer will come to me. I'm just going to go home and think about everything."

"A good idea. And Noah...I'll support you no matter what."

That was partly a lie—she didn't want to support Noah's relationship with Jill. But if it made him happy, Esme knew she couldn't stand in the way.

Noah smiled. "Thanks, Esme. Sweet dreams."

After Esme got out and went into the lobby, Noah waited until she was safely inside before driving off. Esme headed up to her floor—checking on Tanya, Gina, and the kids first who were perfectly fine—before entering her apartment.

She flung herself on the bed, glancing outside. "I hope you make the right choice, Noah…"

And then she got into bed, worrying a little more as the clock inched closer to midnight.

THE NEXT THING ESME KNEW, a loud knock on the door had woken her up.

Heavy rain splattered against the window as she slid out of bed, checking the time. The flashing red light said it was five minutes after midnight. Esme sighed, wondering what answer Noah had given and who was at her door. She grabbed a steak knife and approached the peephole.

She gasped when she looked through and noticed Noah. What was he doing there at that hour?

She set the knife down, opening the door. "Noah? Is every-thing okay?"

It was dark, but she could still make him out. He was soaking wet from the rain. He didn't look injured, but he was panting as though he had run upstairs from the parking lot.

"I'm fine," Noah said, leaning against the doorframe.

Esme gestured at the clock. "It's midnight. Did you text Jill already?"

Noah nodded. "I did."

Esme's heart pounded with anxiety. "Well? What did you tell her?"

"I texted her no," Noah said, and Esme exhaled in relief. "I told her I was done being her second choice. That if she really loved me, she wouldn't have left me in the first place."

Esme smiled. "I'm happy for you, Noah—you deserve better. How did she take it?"

"She was upset, but the wedding's still on. Good luck to Jerry," Noah grumbled. "But do you know why I really told her no, Esme?"

Esme shook her head.

"Maybe I would've said yes if I hadn't met you. Maybe I would've let her treat me like I'm replaceable," Noah said, stepping inside the apartment. "But you've made me realize something."

"What?"

Noah cupped Esme's face, pulling her close. "That I am completely in love with you, Princess Esme Penelope Alexandria of Fairhaven—and Jill could *never* compare."

Esme stood in shock for a few seconds, unable to believe it. *She* was the reason he told Jill no—it was because he loved her.

"I don't even care if it's too soon. I can't help it," Noah continued. "Your kindness, your generosity, your ignorance about baseball—which is adorable, by the way."

That made Esme laugh.

"I just love it all. Everything about you," Noah said. "And I need to know that you could feel the same way about me. That I'm not crazy."

Esme paused. She had two choices—to admit she did love him and risk never returning to Fairhaven, knowing her father forbade her from mixing with the humans. Or she could walk away for her kingdom's benefit but lose the man of her dreams.

She made her decision.

Esme shook her head. "Oh, Noah—you're not crazy. I love you, too."

When they kissed, it was passionate and intense, unable to get enough of each other. Esme led Noah into her bedroom, and many times that night, they both showed each other how they felt.

❧

WHEN ESME WOKE up the next morning, she was naked and alone in her bed.

She stretched out, reaching for Noah, but he had vanished. Had she dreamt last night, she wondered? Had she imagined everything?

After she pulled on her robe, she walked into the kitchen and found Noah cooking eggs and bacon on the stove. It looked like he had prepared a feast—from toast to fresh fruit to parfait. She watched the outline of his back muscles ripple as he flipped the eggs.

"Good morning," Esme said, walking over. She draped an arm over his shoulder.

He glanced at her, smiling. "It's a *very* good morning. How'd you sleep?"

"It was the best sleep I've ever had."

Noah laughed. "Me, too. I feel right at home here."

"Good, I'm glad. So, are you ready for the wedding today?"

"Sure. I don't care who Jill marries anymore," Noah said, picking up his fork. "Not when I have someone better."

Esme blushed, hiding her reddening cheeks behind a piece of toast.

After they ate breakfast and chatted, Esme went into her bedroom to get dressed. She chose a shorter pink gown for the wedding. When she had finished getting ready, she and Noah left her apartment, driving back to his place so he could change and get the wedding gift.

He walked out of his bedroom in the blue tux he had bought at the thrift shop. "So? Do I look wedding-ready?"

Esme grinned. "Oh, yeah. The groom's going to be upstaged."

"Good," Noah said, locking his arm with hers. "And so is the bride."

He took the invitation with him, driving to the address. When they arrived, they realized the wedding was being held at a small chapel with a giant orchard in the back. Wedding pillars had been set up outside with dozens of seats as guests fumbled to sit down.

"Do you recognize any of these people?" Esme whispered, taking her seat next to Noah.

He nodded, pointing at an elderly couple. "They're Jill's parents—and they really wanted us to get together. I'm sure they aren't too happy she's marrying Jerry."

"Her loss," Esme said with a shrug.

Jerry walked down the aisle in a black and white tux. He joined the priest and his Best Man at the altar, then grinned and bounced on his feet. He looked so excited to marry Jill—and it made Esme feel awful. He had no idea his bride-to-be was having second thoughts.

The wedding music started playing a second later, and everyone's heads turned. Jill—in a flowing, white gown— glided down the aisle with an older man by her side. It looked to be her grandfather. He kissed her cheek, giving her away to Jerry at the altar.

"You look beautiful," Jerry said to her.

But when Jill smiled, Esme realized it didn't reach her eyes. It was the same kind of smile Esme gave her father back home.

Jill briefly glanced at the audience, her eyes roaming over it for one person—Noah. When she spotted him, her throat bobbed before she forced herself to look away. As the priest began speaking, Esme knew one thing for sure...

Jill had been foolish to let a good man like Noah slip away. And although Esme didn't know what to do about Fairhaven, she knew she couldn't let him slip away from her, too.

CHAPTER 29

The wedding ceremony dragged on for another half hour, and Esme spent the whole time glancing at her watch. Noah seemed fidgety, too—like he couldn't wait to get out of there. Jill and Jerry stood at the altar, holding hands as the priest read from his long speech.

"Should anyone know of any reason that this couple should not be joined in matrimony," the priest began, "speak now—or forever hold your peace."

Jill briefly glanced at Noah—hoping he would speak up—but he didn't. Esme reached for his hand, squeezing it, and he smiled at her.

"Then I now pronounce you man and wife," the priest said with a smile. "You may now kiss the bride."

Jill looked a little hesitant to kiss him, but Jerry pulled her in and planted a big kiss on her lips. The crowd cheered and rose to their feet, throwing rice on the couple as they walked off down the aisle. The guests and wedding party began heading inside the chapel where Esme could smell the delicious aroma of food.

"I don't get it," Esme whispered, walking to the chapel with

Noah. "Jill didn't have to marry Jerry just because she couldn't be with you."

Noah shrugged. "I know Jill—she can't be alone. I don't think she's been single a day in her life."

"Sad," Esme said, shaking her head in disapproval. "There's nothing wrong with being single."

"Very true," Noah said, opening the chapel door for her. "It beats being with the wrong person."

When they entered the chapel, dozens of tables had been set up for the guests. There was a small band, an open bar, and servers walking around with trays of appetizers. A giant cake— four tiers high with a small bride and a groom at the top— shimmered with purple icing. Noah found their names at a table near the giant pile of wedding gifts.

"Ah—here we are," he said. "These are our seats. What do you say we get some grub first?"

"Sounds good to me. That cake is looking pretty good, too..."

Noah laughed. "We'll get a piece after the bride and groom cut it. I swear, the food is the best thing about weddings."

As they took a plate and loaded it up with appetizers, Jill and Jerry walked into the room from the change room. Jill had changed into a shorter white dress, one that was easier to move in. People clapped as they walked in and waved at the crowd. Jerry had a big grin on his face, but Jill didn't look quite as happy.

"Thank you all for coming," Jerry said to the crowd. "Please, help yourselves to the food and have a good time."

"Already there," Esme said, taking another appetizer.

Jerry and Jill walked over to Esme and Noah, stopping them from reaching their table. Jerry shook Noah's hand wildly as Jill watched them both. Esme could see it—the jealousy in her eyes.

"Thank you for coming, Noah," Jerry said. "I'm so glad you could be here."

"Hey—no problem," Noah said, gesturing at the table of gifts. "And I brought you a present, too. Hope you like it."

"I'm sure we will," Jill said with a nod. "I'm...happy you came, too, Noah. It's always good to see you."

"Yeah—you, too. Congratulations on your wedding. I wish you many years of happiness together."

Jerry grinned. "Thanks. Now, if you'll excuse us, we have more mingling to do..."

As Jerry dragged Jill away, her eyes lingered on Noah. Esme followed him toward a table where they chit-chatted over their meal. A few minutes later, Jerry and Jill sat down, and Jerry raised his glass.

"I'd like to make a toast," he began, glancing at Jill, "to the wonderful woman I just married. She's my love, my light, and my life—and I couldn't imagine being with anyone else. To Jill!"

As everyone toasted to her, Jill looked like she felt guilty. Esme just shook her head as she sipped her champagne.

When the band started playing a slow song, Jerry held out his hand to Jill. It didn't look like she wanted to take it, but people around them encouraged her, so she placed her hand in his. They walked to the dancefloor, then began swaying to the slow song as everyone watched.

"Why isn't anyone else dancing?" Esme asked.

"It's the couple's first dance," Noah whispered. "They get the dance floor to themselves. Another tradition."

It went on for a few more minutes before the song stopped. The crowd cheered for Jerry and Jill, then joined the dancefloor as the music picked up. Noah rose to his feet, holding out his hand toward Esme.

"Will you dance with me?" he asked.

Esme smiled, taking his hand. "You don't even have to ask."

When they stepped onto the dancefloor, shimmying to the beat, Jill watched over Jerry's shoulder. But Esme didn't care—not when she had Noah in her arms. When the music stopped, everyone clapped for the band.

"That was fun," Esme said. "You're a good dancer."

Noah laughed. "I was dragged to a lot of these functions as a kid. You pick up a few things. Didn't you have a lot of parties back home?"

Esme groaned. "Yes—but they weren't this fun. No dancing was allowed. Of course, me and my best friend liked to break that rule—much to my father's disappointment."

"That's my girl," Noah said with a grin.

"Attention, everyone!" a bridesmaid said, grabbing the microphone from the band. "We're doing the bouquet toss now. All the women who want to participate should form behind the bride."

Esme frowned, glancing at Noah. "What's a bouquet toss?"

"I'll explain later," Noah said, nudging her forward. "Go ahead."

When Esme joined the group behind Jill, she noticed all the women looked eager. Jill turned around, throwing the bouquet into the air. The women around Esme screamed and tried to grab it before it landed right in Esme's hands.

"Did I win?" Esme asked, frowning.

The crowd laughed, cheering for her. Jill looked furious when she turned around and noticed Esme holding it. When the crowd thinned out, returning to their tables to eat, Esme walked back to Noah with the bouquet. He had a giant grin on his face.

"Looks like you're the next to be married," he said. "How does it feel?"

Esme frowned. "Huh?"

"That's the tradition. The bride throws the bouquet, and whichever woman gets it is said to be married next."

"What a strange tradition," Esme said, smelling the flowers as she took a seat.

"Maybe not so strange after all," Noah mumbled, playing with a napkin nervously. "It could be us getting married."

Esme blinked. "What?"

"I mean, not now. That would be too soon," he said, working up the courage to look at her. "But one day—when we're ready."

Esme looked down. "Noah, you know I love you…"

"And I love you," Noah said, sighing. "But why do I get the feeling I don't like where this is going?"

"I've tried to push it from my mind because I've liked spending time with you, but my time here in Toronto is running out. My people need me—especially with Senator Remus on the loose. And my father won't let me come back and forth…"

"So, what does that mean for us?" Noah asked, growing angry. "You're just going to leave your life here? Your friends? Even me—after we made love?"

Esme sighed. "It's not that simple. I'm still trying to decide what's best—"

"What's best for you is right here, in this city. You've been so happy here," Noah said. "I can't believe it's not clear to you yet."

"It *is* clear to me. But you knew when I got here that I had another life back home. It isn't easy to be stuck between two worlds."

Noah rose to his feet, throwing his napkin down. "It would be easy for me. I'd choose you in a heartbeat."

By now, some of the people in the chapel began to stare and murmur. Jill looked over with a little smile.

Esme peered up at him. "Noah, it's not an easy decision to make. You would be just as conflicted as I am."

He shook his head. "No—I would *always* choose you."

As Noah strode out of the chapel, Esme rose to her feet. "Noah, wait!"

When she looked back at Jill, she was smiling wider. Esme left her plate behind and chased after Noah. When she stepped outside, she found him sitting in the driver's seat, the car turned on. She walked over to his window and peered in.

"I'll drive you home," he said softly. "So you're not stranded here."

"Thank you." Esme jumped in the passenger seat, an uncomfortable silence spreading between them. "I think we should talk about—"

"I need some time first. To think," Noah said, not even looking at her. "Please."

She nodded, saying nothing the entire ride. Noah said nothing either. When he dropped her off, she stepped out and headed inside the apartment building. He waited until she was inside safely—always the gentleman, even when angry—before driving off.

Esme sighed. She didn't want to see Tanya, Gina, or the kids —she just wanted to be alone. She removed her dress, then crawled into bed.

If things were over between her and Noah after that fight, then she'd have to go home, she decided. She couldn't live in a city knowing he was out there somewhere and not able to talk to him.

As much as Esme loved him, she was also angry with him. Noah knew better than anyone that she had to resolve the drama back home. Why couldn't he have a little more compassion? At least until things were fixed?

God, love was infuriating.

Esme managed to fall asleep, and when she woke up a few hours later, the sky was dark. She made some dinner—

microwave pasta—and ate it in silence, trying not to cry. Was it really over with Noah? Just like that, after everything they had been through?

After she washed the dishes, she heard a knock on the door. She rushed to open it with hopeful eyes. "Noah?"

But it wasn't Noah—it was Alva. She beamed at her. "Esme! How are you?"

"Alva?" Esme asked as she threw herself into her arms. "Oh my God! I missed you. How'd you even get here?"

"We have to be quiet. Your dad doesn't know, but I got your address from one of the guards and snuck out," Alva said, pulling back. "Whoa—you look awful. You okay?"

Esme didn't want to talk about Noah, so she just nodded. "I'm fine—just tired. Look, I need to ask you something really important and you have to be honest. Are you doing something you shouldn't be? Are you helping Senator Remus?"

Alva frowned. "What? No, of course not. Where did that even come from?"

"Just curious. There's been a lot of traitors lately."

"Well, you can trust me. Always. You know that."

Esme nodded, hoping she could. For now, she would give Alva the benefit of the doubt until she found more evidence otherwise. "Anyway, what are you doing here?"

"To tell you Odelia's in a coma," Alva said. "Nyssa found her unconscious in Senator Remus' mansion. She was brought to your castle and examined by the doctors."

A lump formed in Esme's throat. Fairy Godmother Odelia had told her she was going to snoop around Senator Remus's mansion—and Esme had even convinced her.

"She...oh my gosh. I can't believe this. Do they think she'll wake up soon?"

"No one knows. She's getting the best care, though. King Tedros insisted on it. The doctors think she was hit by some powerful spell that's keeping her unconscious. Anyway, I'm so sorry, Esme."

Esme said nothing, on the verge of tears. This had to be Remus' doing—she had been in his mansion, after all.

"I'm here for you," Alva said, breaking the silence. "For whatever you need."

Esme took a deep breath. "Okay, thanks. Poor Odelia."

"I know—I'm rooting for her to pull through. Now, in the meantime, I thought we could go out for a night on the town. You know, just like old times? You can catch me up on everything I missed."

"Oh, I don't know. After everything that's going on with Odelia, I'm not really in the mood for—"

"Maybe getting out is just what you need to clear your head," Alva interrupted. "A nice distraction. Plus, I really want to see the human world a little more. Just in case I can't sneak away again. Please?"

Esme relented, gesturing at her bedroom. "Fine. Let me change into something nicer. Come check out my apartment."

"It's gorgeous," Alva said, glancing around. "Your own private castle."

"Not quite, but it *is* cozy. Okay, I'm ready. Let's head out."

When Esme had changed into a blue dress, she followed Alva into the street. While she was happy to see Alva again and show her some of the sights, she was worried about her fairy godmother. She couldn't bear to lose her.

With everything weighing on Esme's mind, it was pitch black as they walked to the nearest nightclub. Esme knew a place like that was right up her friend's alley. As they entered, pushing through the noisy crowd, they could feel the bass beneath their feet.

"Humans know how to party," Alva shouted over the music. "I think I like Earth already. Wait here—I'll get us some drinks."

"Here," Esme said, handing over some paper bills. "You'll need this."

When Alva took the money and went to the bar, Esme grabbed a seat in one of the booths near the dancefloor. As she waited, she had that feeling again—like someone was watching her.

"Here you are," Alva said, bringing two brightly colored drinks to the table. "Now, tell me everything that's happened up here."

For the next hour, Esme and Alva drank fruity cocktails and talked about life on the surface. When they were both a little tipsy, Alva convinced Esme to join her on the dancefloor, reminiscent of all their parties back in Fairhaven. The drinks made Esme's mind slip away, losing herself in the music. Men tried to dance with them, but Esme and Alva refused, having too much fun on their own. When Esme saw a bright light out of the corner of her eye, she spun around...

And ran right into Cullen.

"Got you!" he cried, looking down at his camera. "Twice in one day. Nyssa will be pleased."

"What are you talking about?" Esme asked, frowning.

"And what's a rat like you doing in the human world?" Alva asked. "You should be in the darkness underground—where you belong."

Cullen laughed. "So should you. You'll both see soon enough."

Before they could ask him any more questions, Cullen ran out of the club, disappearing into the street. Esme had a bad feeling in the pit of her stomach.

"Can we go now?" Esme asked. "I'm feeling a little tipsy, and I'm worried about what Cullen might do. Not to mention my fairy godmother."

Alva nodded. "Yeah—all right. I should probably get back

home before someone realizes I'm gone. Sorry if I pushed you to go out, I just wanted you to have a good time. I missed spending time with you and causing trouble."

Esme forced a smile. "I did too."

"Aww. Anyway, what do you think Cullen's up to?"

"I have no idea," Esme said, pushing through with Alva toward the door, "but I know it isn't good."

When they stepped out into the dark street, it was empty. The music faded the further they walked away. As they came across a storm drain, Alva nodded down at it.

"Before I go," she began, "Nyssa's been getting closer and closer to your father. I've never trusted that bitch or her family—"

When the storm drain jolted, Esme and Alva's heads snapped down in surprise. Several guards poured out—and Esme stepped back, fearing they were assassins—until King Tedros exited the storm drain. He fluffed his cape, looking around the dark street as Lady Nyssa, General Orion, and Cullen trailed behind him with smirks.

And Esme knew she was really in trouble.

"Father?" Esme asked.

"Your Lordship," Alva said, curtseying. "I was just...uh—"

"I'll deal with you sneaking out later," King Tedros snarled. "But I'm here for my daughter. You haven't learned anything, have you?"

Esme frowned. "What are you talking about?"

"Although I don't approve of Cullen sneaking out, he had good intentions," King Tedros began. "He wanted to ensure you were doing well."

Esme scoffed. "I assure you, Father, his intentions were anything but good—"

"You will *not* interrupt me," her father snarled. "He showed me the pictures—you and Alva sneaking out, and you spending time with some man at an amusement park. I didn't send you here to have fun!"

"Father, you're taking it all out of context!" Esme cried. "Didn't anyone mention everything I've accomplished here?"

Her father nodded. "My guards mentioned you found a place of your own, yes. And while that's commendable, I see you're up to your old tricks. Your rendezvous with Alva proved that. Your behavior still isn't fitting of a princess—or my daughter."

"Father, we don't have time to discuss this. Did you know Remus has been here, running for mayor? I think he's planning something, and Nyssa and Cullen are in on it, too—"

"Silence! You will not slander Lady Nyssa. She's been nothing but faithful to me since you left."

Lady Nyssa smirked. "Thank you, Your Majesty. It's a shame Esme hasn't learned."

King Tedros nodded. "Yes, it is. I thought the human world would help her—but I guess not."

"Your Majesty, please," Alva began. "Taking Esme out was my fault. I'll take responsibility. Can't you see Lady Nyssa and Cullen are manipulating you?"

Esme sighed, grateful she still had a true friend.

"I think if they were manipulating me, I'd know about it," he hissed. "Alva, return to Fairhaven. You'll be confined to your mansion for leaving. And as for Esme...I'm banishing you permanently from Fairhaven. I see now that you'll never change your ways, and it was foolish of me to think you could."

Esme's jaw dropped. "What?"

"You can't do that!" Alva cried.

"Hush, daughter," General Orion said. "King Tedros has made his decision."

Esme didn't miss the glance General Orion gave Lady Nyssa and Cullen.

"I'm sorry, daughter, but this is the way it must be," King Tedros said, sadly. "Goodbye, Esme. Take care of yourself. Now, come, Alva—you must get home."

Alva gave Esme a sympathetic look before she climbed down the storm drain and vanished. As King Tedros followed with his guards, Lady Nyssa, General Orion, and Cullen followed, each sporting smirks. Cullen had promised to get revenge on her—and he had gotten it, along with Lady Nyssa.

"Say goodbye to your father forever, Esme," she heard Lady Nyssa's cruel, taunting voice say. "You'll never see him again."

When the street turned quiet and empty again, Esme felt so alone.

She had gotten into a fight with Noah—maybe even lost him for good—only to be stuck in Toronto forever. There was nothing else she could do except turn around and go back to her apartment, tears streaming down her face.

CHAPTER 30

Esme didn't get a wink of sleep.

She tossed and turned all night, thinking of her future. No Noah. No Fairhaven. No Alva. She still had Tanya, Gina, and the kids, but what if she lost them, too? She knew she couldn't bear that.

And how would she cope with seeing Noah at work? Being his boss? She briefly considered quitting and moving far, far away, but she didn't know where to go. Everything had been going so well, and suddenly, it had all turned upside down—in no small part due to Lady Nyssa and Cullen.

"Foolish," she muttered into her pillow. "I should've known what they were trying to do..."

She lifted her head when her alarm clock went off, assuming she would see dawn, but there was no orange glow when she looked out her window. Instead, a green haze spread around the town, coating every building and person in it.

"What on Earth?" she muttered, peering outside.

She watched in disbelief as people got out of their cars, walking in one direction. It looked like they were heading toward an abandoned warehouse in the distance. But why? What was going on?

Esme quickly dressed, then rushed next door and pounded on Tanya's apartment. "Tanya? Dylan? Are you in there?"

There was no reply, so Esme kicked the door down. None of them were in the apartment when she searched the rooms. She ran across to Gina's apartment, unlocking it with her key, and found it empty, too.

When she peered out the window, she saw them—following a large crowd of humans toward the abandoned warehouse.

"This isn't good," Esme muttered. "It's magic—it has to be. Senator Remus's wife finally managed to make it compatible with the human world."

Esme rushed toward the elevator and rode it down to the lobby, finding it eerily empty. When she walked out onto the street, she grabbed one man, forcing him to look at her. He had this glossy, thousand-yard-stare in his eyes, and no amount of shaking him could make him snap out of it.

"What's happened to you?" Esme demanded.

"Must...serve King Remus," the man muttered, ignoring her. "Must get to him..."

As he took off down the street, heading toward the warehouse, Esme shook her head. "*King* Remus? It's all starting to make sense now..."

Lady Nyssa's words wiggled around in her brain. *Say goodbye to your father forever, Esme...*

"Father!" Esme cried, pressing her hand to her mouth. "He's in danger—I just know he is!"

She headed toward the storm drain, pulling off the lid. Even though she had been banned from Fairhaven forever, she still lowered herself into it, feeling the cool breeze on her skin. Her eyes adjusted to the darkness quickly.

When she dropped to the bottom, everything still looked the same—the castle, the people, the markets. As she rushed by, people gossiped about her, wondering what she was doing back when she had been banished. She ran up to the castle and flung open the doors.

"Father?" she called out. "Father, are you here?"

She heard voices coming from the kitchen, so she sprinted toward it. She found the servants gone—something highly unusual. King Tedros sat at the table as Lady Nyssa brought him a cup of tea.

"Here you are, Your Majesty," Lady Nyssa said with a big smile. "Drink up and enjoy…"

"Thank you, dear," he said, lifting the cup to his mouth.

"Father, no!" Esme cried.

She ran toward him, slapping the tea out of his hand. It landed on the floor and caused the tile to sizzle and disintegrate. King Tedros looked down in shock as Lady Nyssa's gaze hardened on Esme.

"Esme—what are you doing here?" she demanded.

"Saving my father's life," Esme spat. "Lady Nyssa is trying to kill you, Father. Senator Remus is taking over the human world right now—he's got his magic controlling them. It's all part of their plan!"

"Impossible," King Tedros muttered. "Magic can't work on Earth."

"It does now," Esme replied. "Don't you remember Dr. Breya was trying to make it compatible? You have to believe me, Father. The world is in danger—we all are!"

King Tedros looked up at Lady Nyssa. "Is that true?"

Lady Nyssa frowned. "I don't know what she's talking about, Your Majesty. You must believe me!"

Esme scoffed. "We saw your tea—it was more like acid!

Another one of Zamira's evil potions, no doubt. Are you really going to keep playing the victim?"

King Tedros nodded. "Just admit it, Nyssa. Don't make things harder on yourself."

"I guess the charade is over," Lady Nyssa said, sighing. "A pity—I enjoyed my performance. But all good things must come to an end. Guards?"

The guards who served Senator Remus—including General Orion and Cullen—came out of the shadows. King Tedros rose to his feet and gasped when he noticed them holding up their weapons.

"What's going on?" King Tedros demanded.

"I'm sorry, Tedros, but our loyalty lies with Senator Remus," General Orion said. "Which is why we sent your servants away. We must kill you—it's what the Senator demands."

"But...we've been friends for ages! If you have problems with the way I rule this kingdom, why didn't you say so?"

"We tried. We wanted to take over the human world, but you refused," General Orion said. "You've left us no choice."

King Tedros scoffed. "We must protect the human world. It doesn't need to know about us—and it certainly can't handle our magic. I'm sorry if you disagree, but my decision remains."

Lady Nyssa shook her head. "You fool! Good thing my father sees the truth and will lead us to victory. As we speak, the humans are under his spell thanks to Fairy Godmother Zamira and my mother's experiments. Their world will be ours!"

"No," King Tedros muttered. "I can't believe you would do such a thing, Lady Nyssa. It's evil!"

"I tried to warn you, Father," Esme said. "She was the one who gave me the spiked punch. She and her father planned this all along—Cullen, too."

Cullen nodded. "I tried to become your husband and kill your father to inherit the throne, but you denied me. I took pleasure in taking those pictures to banish you from your home. And now, I'll take pleasure in killing you both."

Before General Orion and the guards could attack, a bolt of magic came their way, knocking some of them unconscious. Esme spun around, watching as Fairy Godmother Odelia, Alva, and several of their loyal guards approached.

"Fairy Godmother Odelia!" Esme cried. "I thought you were in a coma?"

"So did we," King Tedros muttered. "Thank you for rescuing us, but...how?"

Fairy Godmother Odelia laughed. "Did you think I wouldn't have a plan to save my family? Before I went snooping around Remus' house, I took a potion that would protect me from evil spells. When Zamira attacked me—intending to kill me—I pretended to fall into a coma instead."

"Why?" Esme asked.

"Oh, this is the best part," Alva said with a smile. "She told me everything. Go on, Fairy Godmother Odelia."

"Yes—as I was saying, I faked my coma. With me gone, I knew Senator Remus and his plans would grow bolder. I waited until the right moment for them to expose themselves, then attacked."

"Genius, Odelia," King Tedros said with a smile. "Thank you."

When Esme caught Lady Nyssa trying to slip away, she grabbed her. "I don't think so. Guards?"

The guards nodded, restraining General Orion, Lady Nyssa, and the evil guards that had turned against them.

Alva shook her head. "I can't believe you, Father. I'm disgusted that we're even related."

General Orion scoffed. "Spare me, daughter. We both know Senator Remus would be a better ruler. King Tedros is too soft on the humans. Remus could expand our reach—helped us build an empire on the backs of human slaves!"

"Whatever helps you sleep better at night, Father," Alva spat. "And just for the record, this is the last time you'll ever see me. You can spend the rest of your life in jail, knowing you failed to take the human world and Fairhaven."

"Oh, we aren't the only ones," Cullen said. "There are more guards on the surface—including Fairy Godmother Zamira and Dr. Breya. They'll ensure our plans succeed no matter what happens to us."

"Guards—get up to Earth," King Tedros said. "Protect the humans and stop Remus. His magic must be stopped. In the meantime, we shall wait here."

Esme shook her head. "No, Father. I'm going back up there."

"What?" King Tedros asked, wide-eyed. "You can't do that!"

Alva crossed her arms. "You were adamant she was banished just last night."

"That was before I realized Earth was overrun by Senator Remus and his goons. I can't let you go up there—no matter our problems. It's too dangerous now."

"Father, the man I love is under Remus' spell," Esme said, making everyone's eyes widen in surprise. "I have to save him—and some of my friends, too. I refuse to sit by and do nothing."

King Tedros sighed. "Very well. But if you don't make it back, Esme...I'm sorry for everything."

She hugged him. "Me, too, Father. Stay safe—all of you."

As Esme ran back to the storm drain, she could hear Lady Nyssa's voice the whole way. "You'll never save them, Esme. It's too late!"

But Esme blocked her out, climbing back up to Toronto. She pushed the storm drain's lid aside, pulling herself up to the street level. She followed the group of people and searched their faces.

"Noah?" she cried. "Noah, where are you?"

She didn't see him anywhere—or Tanya, Gina, and the kids. Not even Veronica and Noah's family.

"Damn," Esme grumbled. "Only one thing left to do."

She blended in with the crowd, hiding from the guards on patrol on Senator Remus. When she reached the abandoned warehouse where the mist was coming from, she noticed Senator Remus on the roof, addressing the people like he was their leader. They crowded the street and looked up at him with doting eyes.

"Hello, humans," he began. "I'm sure you're all wondering why I've brought you here, so let me explain..."

Esme couldn't take his boring speeches so she pushed through the crowd, sneaking in through the backdoor of the abandoned warehouse. She noticed Remus and the others had set up a lab—complete with magical cauldrons and spells, all trying to crack the secret of making magic work on Earth.

And they had.

"Princess Esme," a scratchy voice said. "You shouldn't have come here."

When Esme turned around, she came face to face with Fairy Godmother Zamira and her wand. Dr. Breya stood off to the side, mixing new potions.

"You actually did it," Esme muttered. "You made magic compatible on Earth. How?"

"Wasn't hard, but it did take some tests," Fairy Godmother Zamira said with a smile. "Those dead bodies you found were just experiments before we cracked the secret."

"Why did you send that assassin after me?"

"To get you out of the way. It's why Lady Nyssa had you banished in the first place," Fairy Godmother Zamira said with a shriek of laughter. "I gave the assassin a potion that would revive him in the event of his death. When he returned to Fairhaven, I killed him myself for failing me."

"You're evil," Esme spat. "All of you! Don't you see this is wrong?"

"Spare us your lectures," Fairy Godmother Zamira hissed. "Life is all about predators and prey. Even the humans know the strong command the weak. It's the way it's meant to be—so why shouldn't we reign over this puny world?"

Esme shook her head. "I've gotten to know some of the humans, and they're good people. They deserve better than this. Stop what you're doing and go back to Fairhaven to face your punishment."

Fairy Godmother Zamira laughed. "Never, Princess. You're the one who's going to face punishment. Listen to my voice closely...you're under my spell. Go up to the roof and wait for what I tell. Abracadabra!"

When Fairy Godmother Zamira cast her spell, Esme was unable to think. She felt herself climbing the staircase to the roof and couldn't stop. Senator Remus stood on the other side of the building, still giving his speech to the crowd. Fairy Godmother Zamira walked up behind Esme as she teetered on the edge.

It was a long drop to the ground. Had she come this far only to die?

"You're more trouble than you're worth, Princess," Fairy Godmother Zamira spat. "We'll all be better off with you dead. So, listen to me closely. You're going to jump on my command—"

"Not today," a familiar voice said behind them. "Off the edge with you, I say. Abracadabra!"

With a flash of light, Fairy Godmother Zamira fell off the side of the building, landing below with a splat. Esme winced and looked away. When she turned around, Fairy Godmother Odelia was standing there with her magical wand.

"Fairy Godmother Odelia?" Esme cried. "You saved me—again!"

"That's what I'm here for, dear," Fairy Godmother Odelia said with a smile. "Now, for Senator Remus…"

With Senator Remus still distracted by his speech, Fairy Godmother Odelia cast a spell under her breath. Remus staggered back, falling onto the roof. Several of their guards climbed the staircase and put handcuffs on him.

"No!" Senator Remus cried. "We were so close—I almost had everything! This can't be happening!"

"Oh, but it is," Esme said with a smirk. "And you won't last a week in prison."

Senator Remus scowled at her as the guards dragged him away. Fairy Godmother Odelia turned to Esme. "Come on—we need to destroy that mind control spell and save the humans."

They rushed down the stairs, finding Dr. Breya still stirring the cauldron. Fairy Godmother Odelia had their guards grab her. She and Esme shattered the potions they had created, and with a spray of silver, the green mist began to vanish.

"I think it's working," Fairy Godmother Odelia said, glancing outside. "Look—the green mist is gone!"

When Esme looked outside, she realized she was right. The humans looked around at each other in confusion. Esme rushed outside, finally noticing Noah among them. He ran over to Esme when he saw her.

"Esme?" he asked. "What—"

Esme pulled him in for a kiss before explaining. "Magic, Noah. That was the secret I kept from you. I have a Fairy Godmother named Odelia."

Odelia waved. "Hello, young man."

"Uh, hi," Noah said, glancing back at Esme. "I still don't understand."

"It was Senator Remus. He got his fairy godmother to use a magic spell to control all the humans. They wanted you as slaves—and Earth as their empire."

"My God," Noah muttered. "Did you save us?"

Esme nodded. "I helped, yes. And Noah...I'm sorry about before."

"Me, too. I didn't mean to walk out on you, it's just—"

"I know," she said, softly. "And I'm going to stay in Toronto. My father banished me here, anyway."

King Tedros and Alva pushed through the crowd, making their way toward Esme. Alva hugged Esme immediately while Noah glared at her father. People stood behind them, still confused.

"You have some nerve kicking Esme out of her home, you know," Noah said, getting in the king's face. "She's the kindest woman I've ever met in my life. It's why I love her."

King Tedros shook his head. "Now, listen, human—"

"No—you listen," Noah spat. "You don't deserve her. You spent your whole life controlling her! Well, guess what? She's too good for your little magical kingdom. And others will agree, too. Just give me a minute to prove it to you."

As Noah rushed into the crowd, King Tedros glanced at Esme. She winced, hoping Noah hadn't ruined things further. Noah returned a second later with people he had gathered. Tanya, Gina, the kids, and Edgar Little were among them.

"Esme's helped all these people," Noah said. "She helped Tanya and her kids overcome loss. She helped Gina with her illness. She even helped this total stranger! Not to mention my family adores her, and she helped catch a CEO stealing from the poor. Would she be able to do all that if she was *really* as bad you claim?"

"Is that true?" King Tedros asked, looking around at everyone.

They all nodded.

"It's true," Tanya said as her kids hid behind her. "Esme's been a wonderful friend."

"She helped me when I really needed it," Edgar said. "When no one else would."

"And we can't imagine life without her," Gina added.

"See? You were wrong about your daughter," Noah spat. "It sickens me that you don't see it."

Esme thought King Tedros would get mad, but he said, "I know I've been tough on her since her mother died. It's just been so hard."

"I understand," Tanya said with a sad nod. "Truly."

"But your desire to save your friends proves you've changed," King Tedros said. "And so did their testimony. If I'm being honest, this has shown me I need to change, too. I need to be more willing to listen to my detractors—as well as my daughter."

Esme nodded. "Agreed. Maybe we all learned something important from all this."

"It seems that way. Anyhow, I'm letting you return to Fairhaven, Esme—and I'm proud of how far you've come."

"About time," Noah muttered, turning to Esme. "So...I guess this is goodbye."

Esme laughed. "No, silly. I'm staying in Toronto. I mean, I'll still go back to Fairhaven once in a while, but I've made a home here. Why should I choose one home or the other now that I have my father's blessing? I can have the best of both worlds."

Noah's eyes widened. "Really?"

"Of course! How could I leave my friends and the man I love?"

Noah beamed. "Esme...I love you. Thank you for being in my life."

As they embraced, Fairy Godmother Odelia turned to King Tedros. "Well, isn't that sweet? Perhaps there will be a royal wedding soon."

King Tedros nodded. "Indeed. We shall see."

A guard rushed over, completely out of breath. "Everything is back to normal on Earth, Your Majesty. We destroyed the potions and magic isn't compatible on Earth any longer. These humans won't have any recollection of what happened here, either, so our secret is still safe."

King Tedros sighed in relief. "That's good to hear. Thank you."

"See?" Noah whispered in Esme's ear. "Everything worked out—just like I promised."

Esme pulled back, smiling. "You were right. Thank you, Noah."

"Yes—thank you for looking after my daughter," King Tedros said, shaking Noah's hand. "You two may come in and out of Fairhaven whenever you please. Your friends, too."

Alva grinned. "Good—now we don't have to be apart again."

"As long as they promise to keep all this a secret, of course," King Tedros added.

Noah and the others nodded. "Of course. No one would believe us, anyway."

As the people began walking home, Esme watched them with a smile. "We did it, Noah. I finally found my happily ever after..."

"And we have the rest of our lives together," he said, kissing her forehead. "I think this calls for a celebration."

Esme nodded. "Father, Alva, Fairy Godmother Odelia—come with us. We know of this great little Italian restaurant."

King Tedros shrugged. "Why not? I'm not needed back urgently. I trust my guards have everything under control. Lead the way, daughter."

"But first things first," Esme said. "I'm getting my tiara back. That thing is mine!"

Everyone laughed as the humans returned home. As they walked to the restaurant, Esme reached for Noah's hand. She had found her prince, saved the world, and got her modern fairytale.

At the end of the day, what more could a princess ask for?

ALSO BY DANA GRICKEN

The Maidens of Fairhaven

Modern Fairytale

Enchantingly Yours

Spellbound Heart

The Soulless War Trilogy

The Dark Queen

The Dark Evolution

The Dark Cage

The Dragonwitch Chronicles Trilogy

The Girl Who Walked Through Fire

The Girl with the Invincible Blood

The Girl and The Silver Mark

The Hearts Companion

Ten Years: A Poetry Collection

Reverie: A Poetry Collection

Short Stories and Novellas

Whispers in the Woods: A Short Story Collection

Little Things: A horror novella

Drifting Darkly: A sci-fi novella

About the Author

Dana Gricken is an author from Ottawa, Ontario, Canada. The Dragonwitch Chronicles was her first series. Since then, she's published THE DARK QUEEN, THE DARK EVOLUTION, and THE DARK CAGE—the full trilogy in the Soulless War series. You can find those books at online retailers in both e-book and paperback forms.

In January 2020, she signed with Jessica Reino of the Metamorphosis Literary Agency. Please stay tuned for announcements on new books! In the meantime, if you've read and enjoyed her work, please don't hesitate to reach out to Dana on Twitter and Instagram—both @DanaGricken.

In her spare time, she enjoys watching Star Trek with her cats, reading, and playing video games. She hopes her books bring joy to people and wants to write over a hundred novels in her lifetime.